TO THE
HERMITAGE

TO THE ERMITAGE
MALCOLM BRADBURY

THE OVERLOOK PRESS
WOODSTOCK & NEW YORK

First published in the United States in 2001 by
The Overlook Press, Peter Mayer Publishers, Inc.
Woodstock & New York

Woodstock:
One Overlook Drive
Woodstock, NY 12498
www.overlookpress.com
[for individual orders, bulk and special sales]

New York:
386 West Broadway
New York, NY 10012

Library of Congress Cataloging-in-Publication Data

Bradbury, Malcolm.
To the Hermitage / Malcolm Bradbury.
p. cm.
1. Diderot, Denis, 1713-1784—Fiction. 2. Diderot, Denis, 1713-1784—
Appreciation—Fiction. 3. Russia—History—1689-1801—Fiction.
4. French—Russia—Fiction. 5. Novelists—Fiction. I. Title
PR6052.R246 T6 2001   823'.914—dc21   00-050147

Manufactured in the United States of America
ISBN 1-58567-131-2
1 3 5 7 9 8 6 4 2

TO REMEMBER

JOHN BLACKWELL

How did they meet? By chance, like everyone else. What were their names? What's that got to do with you? Where had they come from? The last place back down the road. Where were they going? How can anyone ever really know where they're going? What were they saying? The Master wasn't saying a word. And Jacques was saying that his old captain used to reckon that everything that happens to us on this earth, good and bad, was already written, or else was still being written, in the great Book of Destiny above.

MASTER
Now there's a weighty thought for you.

JACQUES
My captain also used to say that every bullet has its billet.

MASTER
And your captain was dead right.

Denis Diderot, Jacques the Fatalist

When, at my tomb, the weeping goddess Minerva
Points out with her tragic finger the engraved words
'Here lies a wise man' –
Don't laugh. Don't argue. Don't say she's wrong.
Don't spoil my name for Posterity with the words
        'Here lies a fool.'
Just keep it all to yourself.

    Denis Diderot, *My Portrait and My Horoscope*

Ah, how happy all the people will be, when all the Kings are
philosophes, or all the philosophes are Kings!

                    Anon, *Le Philosophe (1743)*

PREFACE

This is (I suppose) a story. It draws a great deal on history; but as history is the lies the present tells in order to make sense of the past I have improved it where necessary. I have altered the places where facts, data, info, seem dull or inaccurate. I have quietly corrected errors in the calendar, adjusted flaws in world geography, now and then budged the border of a country, or changed the constitution of a nation. A wee postmodern Haussman, I have elegantly replanned some of the world's greatest cities, moving buildings to better sites, redesigning architecture, opening fresh views and fine urban prospects, redirecting the traffic. I've put statues in more splendid locations, usefully reorganized art galleries, cleaned, transferred or rehung famous paintings, staged entire new plays and operas. I have revised or edited some of our great books, and republished them. I have altered monuments, defaced icons, changed the street signs, occupied the railway station. In all this I have behaved just as history does itself, when it plots the world's advancing story in the great Book of Destiny above.

I have also taken the chance to introduce people who never met in life, but certainly should have. I have changed their lives and careers, allowed them fresh qualities, novel opportunities, new loves. To my chief character – Denis Diderot, the most pleasing of all the philosophers, though alas now generally remembered only as a Parisian district or a Metro stop – I have been particularly kind. Diderot suspected himself that it was his fate to be a transient figure, a toy of Posterity: that strange form of collective memory that remembers and forgets, buries and retrieves, celebrates and defaces, constructs and deconstructs. He knew history was the future's complaint against the present; but that past, present and future eternally interfere and interface with each other. In this book I have been Posterity's spin-doctor. I have reshaped his life, adjusted his fame; I have granted him (as he would have liked) some pleasant extra months of existence, extended some of his ideas, developed some of his plots and mystifications. In fact I have amended and reorganized his entire website in the big Book of Destiny above.

I have been just as bold with our so-called contemporary reality. There really is a Boris Yeltsin. And there really is a Diderot Project: a splendid set of international conferences (organized by Professors Bo Goranzon and Magnus Florin of the Royal University of Stockholm) which over the years has encouraged some of our most splendid dons, writers, philosophers, scientists, actors and craftspersons to extend Diderot's educational and intellectual heritage, and for that purpose brought them comfortably together in some of the great cities of the world. I too have taken part in these congresses. In October 1993, when, as so often, Russian history trembled, I took a voyage with them over the Baltic. So this story began.

As all you practised readers of stories know, this means there can be no possible resemblance between the real pilgrims, our real hosts in Petersburg, or the real Diderot Project itself and the imaginary people and plans you find depicted here. This is, as I mentioned, a story. But I dedicate it to those real people (Bo Goranzon, Jon Cook, Stephen Toulmin, etc.), many of whom are my friends. I hope they remain so. My debts continue. This story was greatly encouraged by my splendid late editor John Blackwell who had much help to give me, if from another perspective, having once lived as a spy in a submarine under the Baltic. Another friend, Martin Hollis, late Professor of Philosophy at the University of East Anglia, contributed greatly. A believer in the cunning of reason, he often led me, wandering and peripatetic, up the Enlightenment Trail, aiming for the pub at the top, The Triumph of Reason. I fear we never reached it.

Many fine books helped me (see the coda), but one above all: P.N. Furbank's wonderful portrait of my deceptive hero in *Diderot: A Critical Biography* (1992). It was Furbank who recalled the difficulty of pinning down not just Diderot but his splendid writings. 'Diderot's stories present enormously complicated textual problems, since the manuscript copies all display all degrees of accuracy or carelessness, and Diderot continued to tinker with his texts . . . until the end of his life; moreover, new manuscripts have continued to turn up in quite recent years,' he notes in his edition of Diderot's *This Is Not a Story, And Other Stories* (OUP, 1993). So they do; that explains why I crossed the Baltic in the first place. And that explains how I came to write this . . . well, shall we call it a story?

M. B.

INTRODUCTION

HE'S AN AGEING SAGE NOW: warm and generous, famous and friendly, witty and wise. His journey across the huge mass of Europe has been a long and hard one, starting off in the southern spring, and ending in the chill of northern winter. He's certainly not a natural traveller: 'Travel is a fine thing if you're without any friends,' he once wrote somewhere, 'but what would anyone say about the owner of a splendid mansion who spent all his time wandering off alone through the attics and cellars, instead of sitting down comfortably by the hearth with his dear family and his friends?'

He's old, but he's done it; and the sheer fact of his arrival in Petersburg, his sudden appearance at the great Court of the North, is itself prodigious, one of the little wonders of the world. It so happens he arrives just in time for the great imperial wedding; the pug-nosed archduke Paul is marrying his sweet German princess. Royalty and a great corps of European ambassadors have all gathered in town. Within days – once the Orthodox pomp has been gone through, the fireworks exploded, the caviar digested, the champagne and vodka settled – they are all writing their duty letters home. The French ambassador, Monsieur Durand de Distroff, is soon alerting Versailles to announce the Philosopher's arrival and promising to make contact at once.

'I shall of course remind him, Your Serene Highness,' he advises his slothful and silk-stockinged sun-monarch, 'what is to be expected of him as a loyal Frenchman who has now acquired the most unrivalled access to a foreign court.'

The Swedish ambassador ferries the news down the Baltic to Stockholm: Our Cunning Beautiful Russian Despot has succeeded in dressing herself up in the false clothes of liberalism yet again. In

Petersburg, Sir Robert Gunning gets word back to the court at Whitehall: terrific wedding, lovely food and nibbles, bit of trouble out in the hinterland with the Don Cossacks, British presence gratefully appreciated as per usual (after all, the British have managed to provide the Empress with one of her favourite lovers), some French intellectual hanging round promoting daft Gallic thoughts. And with the greatest speed the news is shipped to Potsdam – where King Frederick the Philosopher King, feeling rudely neglected (don't all philosophers, like all countries, really belong to him?), puts down his flute and bursts into a right royal fury. *Voilà la trahison des clercs.*

In the shining corridors of the Hermitage, simply everyone is asking to meet him. It's only the Empress herself who's detained. But weddings are like that: great and demanding occasions, even if it's the marriage of an obnoxious son she once thought to dispose of in much the way she had his supposed father, the last tzar. For weddings, at least this one, are state events, demanding so much attention to this, so much protocol about that. There must be balls, parties, fireworks, cannon-shots, church blessings, state recep-tions, each one of which she must be seen at. There are faces to kiss; mother of the groom. There are foreign ambassadors every-where, each to be entertained, courted, or threatened. There's a new daughter-in-law to induct into the ways of the Orthodox Church (just as happened to her, twenty years before), and whose duties as bearer of tzars and progenitrix of dynasties need to be very carefully spelled out. Treaties to sign first thing in the morning, relatives to see, new alliances to be forged in the Hermitage corridors, for in the wake of weddings all the treaties change. And to complicate matters there's the rumoured Cossack rebellion, a problem with Turkey, a fresh batch of royal impostors to jail, and conspiracy and turmoil all round the court as, thanks to the wedding, allegiances shift. No, it's not always great, being Great.

But she's certainly not forgotten her French philosopher, a man whom she's been trying to tempt here for the past eleven years: ever since, with the aid of a conspirator or two, she managed to ascend to the throne. And in other respects the timing couldn't be improved on. Right now she's between Night Emperors. Long ago Sergei Saltikov, probable sire of the pug-nosed and just-married archduke, was salted away: to Stockholm, was it, or Paris? Stanilaus Poniatowski, so kindly placed in her way by the previous British ambassador, is well out of the way, having been offered the Polish throne by way of grateful thanks. With his endless bluster and promiscuity Grigor Orlov, once so fond a lover, and so very helpful in ensuring her ascendancy, has exceeded his terms and been dispensed with – the dangerous secrets he holds bought off with continued fond friendship, a pile of roubles, a vast estate, and God knows how many souls.

And since then his handy stand-in, shy young Vasilchikov, picked out from the usual source, the stock of handsome Horse Guards, has not served too well. The last few days have seen his brief contract terminated: 'I was nothing more than a kept woman,' he can be heard bleating sadly as he wanders round the court. Love-sick ambitious Grigor Potemkin, with his glorious achievements and his one working eye, is out there in Turkey, where he can be left steaming over the nougat for a few months longer. The Tzarina has found herself a window! The afternoon hours between three and six, the lovers' hours, are for the moment free. She's a studious lady and has always wanted a little patch of thinking time to spare. Of course she's dying to meet her Philosopher, the man whose library she purchased for her own.

A week after Our Man arrives in Petersburg comes the Friday masked ball at the Winter Palace, the Hermitage. He's still troubled with the colic (the malady of the Neva, apparently), but at least his clothes and possessions have been returned by the port customs. In borrowed bearskin topcoat and someone's spare peruke, he walks through the crisp winter evening to the crisp Winter Palace, a bundle of good spirits as ever. Gold coaches and huge sleds wait with their hand-slapping fine-liveried coachmen on the frosted and snow-dusted gravel. Music – all the kinds, French, Austrian, German, Italian – pours through the air and rattles the hundreds of windows along the great façade, where, in space after space, thousands of tallow candles flicker. Feathered hussars from the Empress's White Guard stand like pregnant tableaux at the many doors.

Inside footmen by the hundred, in brocaded coats and knee-britches, gather up the topcoats, the bearskins, the Paris cloaks, the Siberian furs. Ballnight always glitters, but tonight it glitters more than usual. Because of the wedding, everyone's still in town. Ambassadors, court-chamberlains, boyars, British and Swedish sea-captains, Dutch merchants, wandering harlots and courtesans, monks, mathematicians, academicians, imperial officers, provincial nobles, patriarchs and archimandrites, boyars, dwarves, innumerable court ladies from ancient to childish are all there. Gold, silver, pearl, amethyst, official decorations and sashes. Panniered dresses, elaborate coiffeurs, deep and distracting *décolletages*. Wigs, perukes, caps, shakos. Paris fashions, Cossack furs. Men dressed as women, women dressed as men.

As for Our Sage himself, he's presented himself (as is only good and proper) in his philosopher's black suit. Courtiers snigger at the outfit behind face-masks and fans. Musicians play in every corner, large sociable mobs wander the innumerable halls, one room after another, each filled with all an opulent Scythian monarch might ask for: Rembrandt nudities, Canova protuberances, Siberian wine cups, Roman busts and frescoes, oriental gems, cabinets of curiosities, strutting mechanical dolls, strange astronomical clocks. There's dancing, card-playing, pipe-smoking. There's singing of ballads, nibbling of pastries. Groups of women playing billiards, groups of men playing chess. The chink of coins from gaming tables. In one room there is French dancing, with a great billowing of skirts; in another thin girls from the palace ballet school are prancing up high on their points. The new gallery extension of the Hermitage is open, displaying the great collections shipped from Paris and Amsterdam. The place has even acquired a good French name for itself: for doesn't Her Serene Majesty's other admired philosopher, Voltaire, live at a Hermitage in Ferney, and Rousseau think away in another? Here then is hers: one of the busiest, noisiest, biggest, brightest places of retreat and quiet contemplation in the world.

He walks on. And on. Apollo and the Four Seasons – all of them aged about eleven, refined little creatures from the Tzarina's new Smolny Academy for Noble Girls – are performing an elegant masque to the music of Rameau. It could all be Venice or Vienna. Apart from the odd barbarity, it could even be civilized Paris itself.

He enters yet another room. Here his good old friend, the gallant courtier Baron Melchior Grimm − international broker of the imperial wedding, his face thick-powdered, and sporting a fine peruke from the Nevsky Prospekt − is being charming, gossiping splendidly with the inner circle of the court. His own noble host, Prince Lev Narishkin, is there too, idly wondering what happened to his best bearskin coat. They quickly greet our man.

'She's expecting you,' they say. They lead him across to the premier lady-in-waiting, the prim dark-haired Princess Dashkova, whom he remembers, having entertained her some time back in Paris.

'My dear Philosopher,' she says, 'she knows what to expect of you.' She waits a moment, then pushes through the crowd.

And suddenly there she is: a living statue in herself. Despite what the portraits tell you, she's definitely in her middle years, fiftyish or so. She's high-foreheaded, long-faced, pointy-chinned, rouge-cheeked. She's big, plump and round, but very stately and now wearing something very masculine and half-regimental; on her ripe shape it's the costume of a diva. Dashkova suddenly ushers him forward. The courtiers watch. The moment has come; he looks up, looks down, bows low, reaches out, kisses the plump imperial hand that appears before him.

'I'm French,' he says. 'My name is Diderot.'

'And I am Catherine, Russia,' she says, 'the Hermit of the Hermitage. May I welcome my dear librarian to the place where one day his books will come to rest for all eternity.'

'Yes, Your Imperial Majesty, that was truly my most wonderful piece of fortune. My pension and my Posterity. How happy I felt when you promised me that. I knew I should be happy even when I was dead. I took my lute down from the wall and sang a love-song to you.'

'My good fortune too,' says the Empress Autocratrix of All the Russias, Tzarina of Kazan and Lady of Pskov. 'Never did I think by buying a man's dusty library and letting him continue to use it I'd win so many compliments. Tell me, how do you like it, my Palais d'Hiver?'

'It's exactly as I expected,' our man says. 'I do believe I dreamt it once.'

'But you only dreamt, I built,' she says. 'In truth I build like mad.'

'You know you're now considered the benefactress of the whole of Europe?'

She nods her diamonded head: 'So they do say.'

'No other person does more for art or humanity, or more generously spreads the fine new light of reason. No one more sees the wisdom of sense. In you we have perfect proof that the light flows from the north to the south.'

'Shall we say each day in my private boudoir? Excepting weekends, feast-days, state days, and all grand imperial or religious occasions?'

'Indeed, your—'

'After lunch, I have always found that my very best time.'

The noisy courtiers round about seem for some reason to snigger.

'I'm honoured.'

'Let's say between three and five.'

'Your most gracious and remarkable supremacy,' he says, minding his manners.

'Your most grateful pupil,' says, gracefully, the most powerful woman in the world.

PART ONE

ONE (NOW)

SO: WHERE'S THE PLACE? Stockholm, Sweden's fine watery capital, laid out on a web of islands at the core of the great archipelago. Time of day? Middle to late morning. Month? Let's see, the start of October, 1993. How's the weather? Cool, overcast, with bright sunny periods and occasional heavy showers. Who's coming on the journey? I think it's best to wait a bit and see.

The fact is that the Swedish summer season – the super-physical, island-hopping, boat-building, skinny-dipping, crayfish-eating, love-feasting, hyper-elated phase of this nation's always rich and varied manic cycle – is reaching its dank autumnal end. Smart white tourboats with perspex carapaces still cruise the narrow canals of Stockholm's Gamla Stan, the Old Town. Noisy guides are megaphoning out their wonderfully gruesome tales of the Swedish Bloodbath. But now they are not very many, just an end-of-season few. On the ruffled waves of the city's inner harbours, dinghies with multi-coloured sails tack back and forth, hither and thither, up and down. But this is positively their final flurry; they'll all be winched out of the water and put into dry dock in a matter of a few more weeks or days.

In the neat windswept parks that surround the harbour, the leaves flop wetly, the last open-air coffee or sausage stalls are starting to hammer down their shutters. Here and there groups of men – some sporting summer shirts, but most in puffed-out winter anoraks – play chess with man-size pieces. Small crowds of children and various time-wasting persons, walking little dogs, gather round as they menace black with white. On the benches, at the few final tables left outside the few final cafés, hopeful people sit with their chins elevated. Blank-faced, mystical, they're staring at the sky, hopeful of gathering a last sight of that most precious of all the

9

northern treasure hordes, the sun. Aware of just how desirable it is, the sun keeps showing and then going, in a sequence of short sexy glimpses: now you see me, now you don't. It drops patches of gold dazzle onto the green-brown copper roofs and spires that cap and crown the grandiose national buildings over the water, the buildings of a big old empire: the Swedish Royal Palace, the Storkyrkan Cathedral, the Parliament Building. A bit further over in the panorama is the modernist City Hall, where the Nobel Prizes are awarded to the sound of a gunshot intended to celebrate Sweden's two most noted gifts to humanity: the sweet dream of universal peace, the big bang of dynamite.

A brooding Nordic gloom wafts through the air. Euphoria is over, winter depression starting. Yet why? Everything here is so neat, so satisfying, so wealthyish, so burgherish. Civic, that surely has to be the word. Everything suggests a common social virtue, a universal sobriety of mind, a decent respect for order, an open-faced moral clarity. Just democracy, expensive simplicity – the things of which so many people have dreamed. You'll find the same spirit everywhere you go. For instance, in the small clean efficiently modern bedroom of my nice little hotel on Storgatan, which looks out across the courtyard into the small clean efficiently modern rooms of innumerable well-fitted apartments. Both bedroom and bathroom are packed with gentle philosophical instructions – inspirations to citizenship and virtue, all couched in the liberal language of secular religiosity. 'Please help us save the world. In Sweden we love our beautiful lakes and seas and wish to protect them. Use only official soaps, and use your towels for at least two days.' 'Condoms and the Holy Bible are provided in your bedside drawer, for your physical and spiritual content and protection. Please make use of them with the compliments of the management.'

As I walk round, everything is like this. Liberal, simple, decent, without irony. The streets are clean, straight, neat, tidy. The food: crisp, clean, fresh, fishy. The coffee: dark, scented, thick, excellent. The air: brisk, sharp, pure, windy. Quality rules, yet not ostentation. It's the middle way. Nothing is too pompous, or too tacky; too blatantly conservative, or too vulgarly radical. This exactly matches what the Swedes like to say about themselves: nothing too little, nothing too much. There is plenty of wealth, but how very quietly it's spent. In the smart shopping streets the well-dressed shoppers stroll. Dark-coloured Saabs and leather-seated Volvos swish by. The cars have their lights on, the drivers have their belts on. The litres may be many, but the petrol's lead-free and the pace is sober; in fact everyone drives at a blatantly considerate, a truly *civic* sort of speed. The elegant pedestrians – tall girls in their leather thigh-boots, healthy men in their loden topcoats, universal cyclists theatrical in their arrowed helmets and Day-Glo Lycra (always in Sweden there are these reminders that it is healthy to be healthy) – stop, with the same consideration, to let them pass. Then suddenly, thanks not to some officious red light but to justice, reason, fairness and decency, the vehicles all stop in their turn. Whereat, with just the same polite consideration, the pedestrians and the Lycra cyclists, carefully, appreciatively, cross the road to the other side.

The crisp smart goods in the stores are just as well ordered, just as considerate. Don't imagine it was some chic fifties Swedish modernist with a doctorate in design from Paris who invented all these bleached white woods, pure colours, honest straight lines that deck the smart lofts of the known world. Swedish style was born from the Swedish soul: nature, the outdoors, the woods, winds, sea, rocks, spray, all of it shaped into function by the piney, craft-loving, shipbuilding, homesteading old Nordic soul. Look at it. Those carpentered chairs – so straight-lined and thoughtful. Those handmade tables – so crafted, sturdy, square-edged, crisp-grained. Those woven fabrics – bright yet so restrained. Everything modest, homely, truthful, under-stated. Yet, lest some unfortunate misunderstanding occur, all this simplicity is expensive beyond belief – especially if you're a wandering foreign tourist like myself.

But, as I'm discovering, the most expensive thing in this decent, pleasant, unpretentious liberal country is money itself. I'm in a bank in a clean tree-filled square at Storgatan, just up the hill above the harbour. An exceedingly nice bank – plain, modern, open-plan, white, computerized, smelling of fresh coffee, filled with nice people. So nice I know something is missing: the demonic rage of money, the danger of coin, not to say the angled security cameras, bullet-proof screens and Kalashnikov-toting guards that modern banking needs. The Land of the Bears is, I recall, famous for its banking. It went with a central role in the Hanseatic League, the mastery of Baltic trade, the role of financier of European wars. If my imperfect memory is right, it was Sweden that devised the notion of the National Bank. Above all, it went with a decent supply of the things money is made of: minerals and paper. To use the mineral reserves of the Upplands, the Swedes dispensed with precious metals and invented the decent plain democratic copper coin: a great invention when you wanted a loaf of bread, though if you wanted to buy something really expensive – one of those Swedish tables, for example – you had to go out shopping not with a purse but a horse and cart.

So why (I'm asking myself) am I having so much trouble in performing a normal economic transaction, a simple act of rates of exchange? I've come to this handsome blonde bank because I want to change English pounds for American dollars. In the world of money it's a normal, rational request. At a handsome blonde desk a handsome blonde teller sits, tapping away at her handsome computer console. Like everyone I've met since I flew into Arlanda airport this morning, she's serious, kind, courteous – civic, that has to be the word. That is the Swedish way. The Land of the Bears has always felt a bit like an enlightened Islington primary school, with tundra. First she asks me for my papers. Passport. Driving licence. Travel insurance. Health insurance. Social security number. Fine: I have paper, therefore I am. She enquires about the *traffik*, the *devise*, the *curso*, the *cambio*, the change I'm after. How will I pay? I hand her a splendid walletful: Visa, American Express, Diner's, Barclaycard, Master Charge, British Airways Executive Club. I have plastic, therefore I shop. But not, it seems, in modern Sweden.

'*Nej, nej,*' she says.

I offer bankcard, chargecard, Eurocard. I flash a gold this, wave a silver that. I lean forward against her scented blonde hair and murmur a splendid little secret: my pin number.

'*Nej, nej,*' she says, staring at me bemused, 'if you would like money, you must give me some money first.'

'But this is money,' I say. 'Money as we now know it.'

'*Nej, nej,* not in Sweden,' she says. 'This is not money, it's credit. I need good money. Don't you have proper English pounds?'

I look at her amazed. The year, as we've said, is 1993. This is a highly advanced nation. A glorious new millennium is to hand. Then, if computers don't crash and planes fall from the sky in the great turnover of numbers, we will all become part of Euro-Europe; that will be the end of the old age of rates of exchange. Francs will fade, Deutschmarks dissolve, escudos expire, lire lapse, the krona will crash. Even the great British pound will pass away, as in their season all good things pass away.

I for one will mourn its passing, shed a big wet fiscal tear. I madly love coin and currency, paper and print, guineas and guilders, sovereigns and sovereignties, ducats and crowns, farthings and forints, *cambio* and *curso*, cash and carry. True, here in 1993, Sweden has still not yet elected to join the European Community, but we all know it's just a matter of time. And true, with all those fir trees in the forests, all that paper in the papermills, all that copper in the Upplands, it has a vested interest in money as it always was and should be. But Sweden is modern, paper money isn't. Still, if that's what she wants, that's what she'll have. Money, yes, I remember I had some once. I dig deep into my wallet, and there it is: a small wad of British notes for general circulation. George Stevenson – Mr Puffing Billy – in his stovepipe hat looks proudly out from the fives. Charles Dickens, creator of one of the world's greatest fictional galleries of speculators and peculators, looks out from the twirls of the tens. Michael Faraday, who invented the electric lighthouse, guards the security of the twenties. The Queen is present. Nothing could be more reliable.

'Will this do?' I ask.

'*Jo, jo*, tip top, *tack, tack*,' says the teller, smiling, taking and counting them.

There's quite a long line of people standing behind me now. But this is decent liberal Sweden, so nobody murmurs, and no one complains. The teller tip-taps her computer; presently she hands me a fresh wad of notes.

'*Tack, tack*,' I say, and look. They're Swedish kronor, elegant and colourful, not what I wanted at all. '*Nej, nej*,' I say. 'It's not right. I want American dollars.'

'*Jo, jo*, dollars, *tack, tack*,' says the teller, taking the notes back. She checks them carefully, to make sure I have not done them a mischief, returns them to the drawer, tip-taps her computer. The line behind me has grown longer, reaching into the street. Nobody utters, nobody shows the faintest impatience. The teller reaches into her drawer again, counts out a few crisp American greenbacks, and hands them to me.

'*Tack, tack*,' I say.

I look. And I look again. This wad seems curiously small. In a matter of minutes, a hundred British pounds have traded into forty American dollars, a very remarkable rate of exchange.

'I gave you a hundred, you gave me forty,' I complain. The line of people waits.

'*Jo, jo*,' says the teller.

'It can't be right.'

'*Jo, jo*, it's right,' she says. 'Tax. You made three changes. Each time you pay a tax.'

'I didn't make three changes, you did.'

'But in Sweden everything is changed through the krona.'

'Why is it changed through the krona?'

'Of course, so you can pay all the tax.'

Now in Istanbul or Athens, even in London's Edgware Road, this would look extremely suspicious. But this is Sweden: the higher society, the moral kingdom, the land of liberalism and utter honesty. I glance round. The line behind me reaches right across the street and is blocking the traffic; in fact this part of Stockholm has come to a total standstill. No horns bleep, nobody utters, no one even coughs.

'I don't want to pay the tax.'

'Everyone likes to pay tax.'

The teller smiles at me, the line of people behind me nod in agreement, all with that beautiful, open, Swedish reassurance that tells me money belongs to none of us, is granted on loan to us from the mother state. So don't we feel that much more human and decent, that much more . . . civic, when we know we're being swingeingly taxed?

Now what, you could fairly ask, am I doing here, in the world's most moral kingdom, trafficking British pounds for American greenbacks? Sweden lies on no familiar route from Britain to America. But America's not where I'm going – or not for many pages yet. In any case America long ceased trading in greenbacks. Even plastic is nearly finished; money in America is already virtual money, post-money, non-specie; it's plastic, smart chip, computer debit, electronic cash. But I'm on my way to the true land of the Almighty Dollar, the real nation of the greenback, at the far end of the Baltic: the CRS, what's left of the Russian Union and the great empire of the tzars. To prepare my journey, I have carefully read, on the morning flight over from Stansted, a book by a famous eighteenth-century traveller there, the ubiquitous Comte de Segur, French ambassador to Catherine the Great just before the French Revolution – which to her eternal disgust and dismay he warmly supported, at least for a while.

Even at that date, he was struck by the unusual nature of the Russian economy. 'Here one must forget the rules of finance one learns in other countries,' he noted. 'The mass of banknotes, the realization that there are no reserves to back them, the use of strange and unusual coinages, the kind of thing that in other lands would bring immediate collapse or revolution, here cause no surprise at all. The great Empress Catherine could, I've no doubt, turn leather into money should she wish.' Well, *plus ça change*; as it was, so it is now. To this day the rouble is a strange, only part-convertible currency, a set of roguish numbers, a con man's fancy that has never truly replaced barter in silks and camels, icons, part-worn dresses, Turkish drugs, old lampshades, surplus nuclear missiles, loaves and fishes, live or dead souls. In the hard heyday of Communism, the special shops for the nomenklatura traded, of course, in dollars – which then generally drifted westward to Switzerland or bought fine real estate in Nice. Now, in the fine new free-market era, when the nomenklatura prefers to see itself as the mafia, no smart Russian hotelier, sommelier, blackmailer, bribe-taker or capitalist oligarch would dream of trading in any-thing else. Avoid the rouble; it's dollars or nothing. That's what all the hardened travellers say.

And, someone has carefully warned me, it's best to carry your dollars into the country with you. These days nobody in Russia knows what money is worth; they just know it's a mad and ridiculous invention no one can get enough of. That's why it will be difficult to make a fair and reliable exchange in the grand and noble banks of Petersburg, and probably not even on the Russian ferry I'm booked on and which will be taking me there tomorrow night. Which is precisely why I'm standing here in the blonde bank at Storgatan, evidently rescuing without knowing it the entire Swedish tax system and its fine welfare economy. I take my tiny wad of dollars and stuff them in my pocket.

'*Tack, tack*,' says the blonde teller, looking at me ever so sweetly.

'*Tack, tack*,' I say just as sweetly back, and walk out: out of the nice blonde bank into the fine bourgeois air; past the patient unending line of stalled philosophical customers which now extends almost as far as the harbour; into the tree-filled square at Storgatan, now completely gridlocked with polite Volvos, feeling different, poorer, wiser on the instant, as, for some reason, foreign travellers often say they do . . .

TWO (THEN)

On Friday, 11 June 1773, a big-browed grey-haired well-built man of nearly sixty, with a very mobile face, a wry amused expression, a bit of a cough and what he likes to call an amiable stoop, rides out of the rue Taranne, in the quarter of Saint-Germain-des-pres in Paris, in a hired four-horse coach with a yellow-coated postilion. Who is he? He's been called, by everyone including himself, 'The Philosopher'. Where's he been? Everywhere in the world, in his own busy mind at least, and all of that without ever once leaving France. Where's he going? By a less than direct route, to St Petersburg: the great new city on the Neva, often known (but what northern city with lots of water isn't?) as the Venice of the North. After all, he's the Philosopher. And he's heading, as a great thinker should, for the greatest imperial court of the day: the court of Catherine the Second, Tzarina of the Russias, soon to be called the Great. For the moment at least, she's resting – between lovers, they say. What better time to catch up on the newest, most advanced ideas of this thoughtful, reason-inspired, light-filled, positively electrical new age?

Over the last few days he's made the most meticulous preparations for his journey. It's the greatest he's ever taken: the greatest, given his annoyingly considerable age, he's ever likely to take. He's packed shirts and suppositories. He's filled up his writing case, packed a shoulderbag tight with nice new notebooks. He's written his will, left instructions for dealing with all his property. He's made exact, detailed, cunning arrangements with his secretary, Posterity (also called M. Naigeon), about what it must do with his papers: those innumerable papers, philosophical reflections, medical meditations, poems and plays, stories that are not stories, essays that are not essays, reports on drains and sanitation, accounts of the great artistic salons, fantastic travel sketches, dreams of unknown lands and noble savages, those playful works of pure pornography set in brothels and convents that spin out of him in endless creative euphoria. Truth is, Posterity is quite as fickle as princes and as careless as secretaries, and it certainly won't do what he's asked it to promise. Such is the way things are written in the great Book of Destiny above. But at least Posterity doesn't put you in jail. Under princes, he's already served a term or two.

The previous night he's organized an emotional and deeply moving scene of farewell. He spent most of the evening weeping buckets with his ill-tempered, ever-sewing wife – the Great Particularist, he likes to call her – and his fond, dancing, piano-playing daughter, whose recent expensive marriage and huge dowry is the unspoken reason for his journey. With them he has contemplated to the point of extreme despair all the terrifying risks that lie ahead of him: shipwreck, coachwreck, brigands, cholera, fleas, starvation, war, famine, getting arrested, getting lost, getting drunk. A couple of friends call by, and distress suddenly leaves him. Our Philosopher is a man who gets euphoric on sociability. Drink appears, the piano tinkles. The whole evening brightens. As the drink flows so does his famous talk: of life and death, mathematics and astronomy, destiny and drains. It flows like a torrent, for half the night. Meaning he's almost omitted to pack, virtually neglected to sleep. Now the yellow-jacketed postilion has come: early, far too early, it's still hardly dawn. He's left the apartment with a frantic rush and hardly a connubial kiss – not knowing what he's remembered to bring with him, what he's forgotten to pick up, where exactly he's headed, what's happening next . . .

Luckily the postilion is one of those sensible and well-organized modern servants, full of their own ideas, the kind he writes books and plays about. He knows: he's going to the Hague, over the lowland borders, across the Austrian lands, a four-day post by way of Brussels. And there he knows he'll be welcomed on arrival by one of the dearest of his various dear old friends, the Prince Dmitry Golitsyn. Dear Dmitry is Russian. In fact he has very lately been Her Imperial Highness's ambassador in Paris – until the two courts quarrelled, his titles were rescinded, the Great Imperial Mother shifted her man to the Netherlands, into a more sober, comfortable and duller world. Now he sits in his ambassadorial house on the Kneuterdijk, surrounded by high winds and the stout burghers of the Hague. But, as his letters confess, he's sadly missing Paris, and his dear old friend. For in Paris the Philosopher and ambassador have had the most wonderful times together: chasing women, buying art till it turns into a thriving business, becoming the best of friends, talking of grand rational dreams.

Each has always helped the other. When the Prince felt it necessary to secure himself a prosperous marriage to the usual stout Prussian Princess, the Philosopher assisted. When this meant dealing with an awkward encumbrance – a very desirable but no longer desired dancer at the opera – the Philosopher did his persuasive best. And when the Prince needed to recover some family portraits he had unwisely given the singing girl in better days, our Denis the Thinker came up with the answer – the kind of answer that displayed his crafty arts at their best. He devised a wonderful stratagem – a 'mystification', as he likes to call it – and put it into play. The dancer's one of those advanced Californian types, a dedicated narcissist and hypochondriac, a mirror-gazer, a preener, a therapy-guzzler, the sort who'll gladly devour the advice of any passing guru. An operatic dancer surely deserves an operatic drama, so our philosopher devises one. He hires a handy middle-man, a fellow named Desbrosses, and kits him out as a Turkish necromancer with a turban. For good measure, he also awards him a medical doctorate from Tübingen. Desbrosses calls on the dancer at her apartment, and quietly listens to the torrid tales of her troubled soul.

Soon he's able to diagnose the cause of her problems. Evidently some objects in the room are emanating 'simulacra', dangerous rays – or, as we say back in dear Byzantine old Turkey, bad feng shui. Probably it's the portraits on the wall. The only way the poor girl will be back in perfect shape is if the offending pictures are restored to their owner at once. Our dancer buys the therapy wholesale; only one thing goes wrong. Desbrosses goes home and promptly commits suicide, over some quite unconnected matter. The scheme fails, the simulacra cause no more trouble, the dancer is soon restored to health and doing her dance with a new partner. Golitsyn has lost, this time. But our man has what he wanted. Surely there's a wonderful plot here, for a play, an opera, a book – to be called, let's say, 'The Mystification'. He sits down and writes it, as he writes down everything. The fact is the whole world is a mystification, a place of plots and conspiracies, all of them seeking to be written. Indeed if you're just a little super-stitious and fatalistic – like, let's say, that fat postilion in his yellow tabard, sitting cursing his horses up there on the box – you could even imagine that all of life itself has been written down or is being written by a divine providence up there in heaven above, and our human problem is to figure out the mystifying plot devised around us . . .

Oh, see: here we are in the Hague. A sea-blown town of trotting carriages, big-windowed embassies, sombre bankers, sober merchants, neat well-appointed brothels. Its trades trade with the Indies, the East, the Baltic; its diplomats sit sadly in little square houses, seared by the sands of the blustery coast. When our man arrives in the post-chaise, Prince Dmitry is on his doorstoop, ready and waiting. Beside him's the pretty, witty German wife the Philosopher has found for him, not as wild and risqué as the dancer from the opera, but with better social connections. They take him indoors and offer him everything: comfortable room, writing desk, personal servant, a bottle of Dutch spirits. But spirits are what the Prince is lacking, as he frankly confesses at dinner that night. He's missing Paris, missing his friend, missing their pleasures and one of their favourite pastimes, purchasing vast and expensive works for the Tzarina. This mystifies Our Philosopher, who justly observes that these Flemish lands are exactly where most of the boodle they bought in Paris was painted to start with.

True, admits the Ambassador, but since he came to Holland nothing has gone well. He's lately made the most wonderful and expensive acquisition: the glorious Braamkamp collection of great Flemish Old Masters. Unfortunately, up in the inhospitable Gulf of Finland, which all good men should avoid, the vessel carrying the treasures north to Her Sublimity has foundered, while the ship's pious captain was diverting his attention into praying to the good Lord above. The whole boatload of wondrous paintings now lies at the bottom of the Baltic. Dmitry has destroyed the pride of the Renaissance, won the eternal contempt of art historians everywhere and the contempt of Posterity, emptied the Russian treasury, earned the clear disdain of his Tzarina. 'Well, I shall just have to get on without them,' she has bitterly announced to her court at the Hermitage.

Our Philosopher does his best to be cheery: what else are good friends for? 'It might be worse,' he says, as the German Princess plays pleasantly on the spinet in the corner. 'There are plenty more Venuses and Bathshebas where that lot came from. Here in the Lowland they all paint like crazy. Anyone will do you an Annunciation. Apart from growing tulips, it's all they ever do.'

'I don't know why, it's not a cultured country. Not a bit like Paris.'

'For one thing it isn't run by kings and venal priests.'

'It's run by bankers.'

'And publishers, printers. A land of learning and freedom, my friend. A land for philosophers. Descartes, Locke, Spinoza.'

'But you haven't even stepped outside and looked at it yet.'

'I don't need to. I know it has learning, liberalism, art and banking – the four most necessary things in the world. And I notice the women all seem fat and cheerful.'

'If you like fat.'

'I do.'

'I prefer thin.'

'Why did Her Mightiness send you here?'

'You know why. Because without these stinking Dutch canals and these stinking Dutch bankers our city on the Neva just wouldn't exist at all.'

How true. How very true.

For didn't the whole thing start as a dream here, when the young Peter the Great (great already, for he rose up six feet eight in his boots) arrived on his Great Embassy for youthful rest and recreation? A boisterous young man who broke windows, turfed friends, acquaintances, even total strangers into hedges, he drank and whored with the best. He came incognito and in disguise, even though he stood higher than anyone and had a pronounced facial tic, and his retinue of a hundred servants, six trumpeters, two clockmakers, four dwarves and a monkey, suggested to the shrewder observer he might be a person of consequence. In Amsterdam he studied astronomy and anatomy, found out how to dissect a corpse, was taught how to cast metal, shave a face, pull teeth (the teeth, indeed, of anyone unlucky enough to be to hand). He acquired the trades of carpenter, boat-builder, sail-maker, became noted for his vast and indiscriminate curiosity ('What is dat?').

When he returned to Russia, became Tzar, defeated the Swedes, retook the eastern Baltic, and decided to build a triumphal capital on the Neva, staring dangerously out through storm, ice and foggy winters at the tempting riches of the West, it was Amsterdam he tried to build. Peter's city would not be another Scythian hotchpotch: mud-based buildings, leaking hovels, bearded boyars, rooting pigs and starving serfs. It would have not just cathedrals and monasteries, fortresses, prisons and arsenals, but canals, palaces, academies, museums, and stock exchanges, the glories of trade and war. He summoned Dutchmen to dig out his canals and embankments. When these seemed smaller than the ones in Holland, he had them filled and dug again. Meantime as the new city began to rise, Dutch ships carried the bricks, Dutch painters decorated the salons, Dutch bankers provided the ready. Swedish slaves and gulaged Russian serfs might have dug the foundations, raised the roofbeams, perished in the Finnish swamp-lands in their hundreds of thousands. But the peerless new city, which some began to name the city of bones, was raised not just on drowned skeletons but jolly Dutch guilders.

'Which is why I'm here, stuck in the windy Hague,' explains Golitsyn. 'The game's started all over again.' Our man grasps the point at once. What did for huge, big-booted Peter can never please Her Empress Autocratrix. If Peter built in timber, she'll build in stone. He dug out ditches, she'll raise up palaces and promenades. He borrowed guilders in thousands, she'll borrow in millions. He was Great, she'll be Greater. He bought Dutch paintings, she'll buy collections, art by the shipload. And everything has to be backed by those same Dutch bankers, with their black suits, white ruffs, Lutheran hats, warted faces. For the Tzarina shops — shops as only a great tzarina with compliant bankers can. She'll shop till Golitsyn drops. There's no doubt about it: if the car boot sale, the garage sale, had already been invented, the Sublime Mother would have been among its first and warmest devotees. Even when the great shopaholic future unfolds, in days and stores yet only vaguely plotted in the Book of Destiny above, Imelda Marcos will still prove stingy, our Duchess of York a crass collector of airmiles, in the grand comparison. Here it's shoes and shawls, there it's amethyst and gold. It's clothes and cosmetics, gems and gewgaws, porcelain and pewter, buttons and bows.

But above all things it's the higher arts. 'It's not really love of art,' the lady honestly admits. 'It's pure and unvarnished greed. In truth I'm more of a glutton than a taster.' Which is why, when a collection — of anything at all, discovered anywhere at all — comes to market, she has it purchased, gift-wrapped, crated, shipped home. The Tzarina follows, as only she can, the first and only true law of shopping: value comes from who buys, not what's sold. The stuff may be bricolage, bric-a-brac, no worth at all to start with. Her mere act of patronage, the simple fact of possession, turns vulgarity into grandeur, debris into dream, dreck into collectable, dross into gold. Her emissaries buy everywhere; we're looking at two of them now. Twenty years into her reign, three truly enormous palaces have grown too small to hold the boodle. Which means more new commissions: palaces, museums, academies, libraries, theatres and opera houses. Which means the Queen has long been collecting not just things but people: architects and sculptors, shapers of silver and setters of stones, mathematicians and marquetry-makers, singers and dancers, writers and thinkers, tragedians and comedians, craftsmen and castrati, milliners and cutters of clothes, not to say the generals, military engineers and shipbuilders needed to defend them. And, like the painters and the furniture, when she calls they come: north, far north, to that strangest of all cities, up there on the inhospitable Neva on the edge of the swamps of Karelia, to a vast imperial building site less than fifty years old.

She's a cunning clever queen, without any question. As she shops and builds, she calculates and thinks. Like an earlier queen, Christina, at the further end of the Baltic, she's an honest blue-stocking: a splendid learned lady with a fine European education. She's arrived in the winter snows from one of the back courts of German Europe, a small-ranking Russian princess who, still only fat and fourteen, has married a prince: the mad little soldier who will in time become Peter the Third. Once enthroned as his tzarina in dirty old Moscow, it has taken her no time at all to deal with this plodding marital encumbrance. Finding, as only a clever and ambitious princess can, sponsors and conspirators, guardsmen and lovers, she manages a grand palace coup, displacing her unpopular husband to prison and becoming sole mistress of the Russias. Not much later comes Tzar Peter's strange and fortunate death, from a sudden attack of the haemorrhoids. Now she's Empress Autocratrix of All the Russias, Tzarina of Kazan, Astrakhan and Siberia, Princess of Estonia, Livonia, Karelia, Dame of goodness knows where. When rival Romanovs appear (as they do so often) they are perfectly likely to suffer the same fate as her spouse, and probably in the same prison. There is, for instance, the mysterious 'Prisoner Number One', clearly a perfectly valid pretender, an entirely genuine impostor, for whose strange maddened end she expresses deep surprise and accepts no responsibility, none at all.

But in a woman of such huge charms and splendid talents these little tricks and contrivances can always be excused. True, she seems to have adapted quite easily to some of the harsh Russian ways, but she still preserves the high European graces. She's a popular princess, an enlightened empress, especially when seen from a distance. She has Enlightenment tastes, she listens to the messages of reason, she's in tune with the newest thought of the age. She's a creature of destiny, dream and desire: a true queen of hearts. She takes lovers from everywhere, her Night-Emperors: burly brute-lovers for the body, more aesthetic lovers for the mind. Meantime, along the ever improving banks of the Neva, rotting Petrine wood turns magically into long-lasting stone, and once mean streets open out into the most inviting *prospekts*. Soon there's a university, an Academy of Arts, another of sciences; an Italian theatre, a great observatory, a Temple of Minerva, a library, even a mysterious astronomical clock whose interior can be entered to disclose the inner workings of the unmistakably rational universe. She more than reads; she thinks, studies, argues. She's drawn to grand ideas and learning; she looks to Paris and the great *Encyclopedia* itself. No sooner has she taken power than she writes warm letters to the makers and shakers: Voltaire and Rousseau, d'Holbach and d'Alembert, the people who think new thoughts not just for Paris – where court, church and censor are all too ready to burn their books or stack their authors in prison – but for the self-redeeming progressive cosmos itself.

And, truth to tell, in the course of her great Enlightenment shopping spree she has purchased our Thinker himself. 'Which is why I too am stuck now in the windy Hague,' he thinks: as Dmitry drinks, the German princess clangs away on her spinet in the corner, playing a bit of Lully, a bit of Rameau; and the east wind blows, and the northern sea-waves crash incessantly outside . . .

THREE (NOW)

ANYWAY, now I'm properly bankrolled (with all this geld I could probably buy myself one whole Russian hamburger), I shall start to enjoy what I'm really here for: the Nordic charms of Stockholm itself. As I walk away through the tree-filled and now completely gridlocked square, ripe scents in the air soon tell me I've found what I'm looking for. On the far corner is the city's ancient food and fish market, smelling richly, wonderfully of a plenitude and plurality of aromatic full-bodied things: what fish, what olives, what coffee, what caviar, what cheese! The whiffs draw me at once. I walk inside, past lighted stalls, gleaming with dead-eyed silver fish, blood-reddened with country meat, twinkling with fresh ripe vegetables. At a neat little food counter I repose myself atop a mushroom of a stool and eat the local speciality, Baltic herring. I scoff the crisp fresh bread, I drink a (non-alcoholic) beer. Then I look round with interest at another local speciality: those tall, leggy, lithe, blonde and wonderfully well-dressed girls who sit further along the counter – sexually serious, light-skinned like pure cream, summer-bronzed.

I have, let me tell you, perfect credentials for my curiosity. That's to say, I'm a writer: a professionally observant person, one of those collectors of life's little data, an avid thinker of thoughts and a watcher of things, not least big well-dressed blonde Viking girls. I'm sitting there watching with all the manners of a person with an idle and uncertain temperament and a day or so to waste. For the thing is: I've set off on this voyage to Russia a day or so earlier than I need to, and I'm not even quite sure why. But the truth is, I've been feeling pretty gloomy lately: not sure about my life's direction, not clear whether I've been doing things right or wrong. I seem suddenly to be growing much older than I ever meant to be, leaving everyone around me looking foolishly young. Time idles for them; for me it seems to pass strangely quickly. Summers grow more precious, winter seems a terrible curse. A world that used to be solid and sensible, well planned and properly run, feels strangely sick with childishness, decadence, pointless unrealities.

And, though it's just early days, I don't think I much like the look of the new Naughty Nineties, with its lazy decadence, ideological vacancy, consumerist ethics, empty narcissisms. People are self-creationists; drunk on drugs and aimless shopping, they pass by in the streets with pins through their noses, nails through their navels, clowning with their bodies. The seasoned, reasoned, puritanically serious world I've taken as history since the fifties seems to be wearing out. Newly bereft of ideas and a clear political order, it seems to have given itself over to nothingness, froth, senseless self-pleasuring, drab eroticism, licit illicitism, populist emotions, media-fed public moods and crazes. Meantime the millennium that's rising so confidently from the old Christian calendar reminds everyone that generations, cultures, dynasties, social systems are changing. Well, with time comes age, of course; with age comes a kind of depressed and resigned fatality. Suddenly it seems as if everything that's happening was already written, in some great Book of Destiny up above.

At any rate the point is, then, that I'm feeling oddly anxious, deeply grey of soul. And if gloom is what you have, and you're not sure where to take it, then let me advise. Marbella won't help, but there's no doubt Sweden – decent Sweden, serious Sweden, liberal progressive Sweden, anxious Sweden, the land of virtue and grievous moral pain – can be warmly recommended. Don't misunderstand me. I've always loved Sweden. I truly love its winter-warm stuffy apartments, their crisp furniture, their huge wood-burning stoves. I like the Lutheran afterglow, the universal air of decency, community, moral sacrifice. Like the Hanseatic trading ports, the old warehouses, stone arsenals, brackish briny harbours, tarry merchant houses, fish smells, grey waters, blustering Nordic airs; like the leggy blonde Viking girls. Finishing my snack in the busy market, I leave it and its bright row of blondes to walk down the dusty hill and into the city's watery hub. I walk through the harbour parks, the waterside boulevards, the smart *fin de siècle* apartment towers, the inland lakes criss-crossed with concrete bridges, the copper-towered buildings of the old town. I wander the gusty, drizzly waterfront, sit down on a bench to watch the Munch-like lovers crossing the bridges, and observe the intense contemplative players of chess as they slowly move their pieces.

From here, I can see, across the bridge on the harbour island of Djurgarten, some elegant new building, one of those endless modernistic galleries or museums that are springing up everywhere, fresh-formed and concept-designed. Then I suddenly know what it is; and with that an old and well-known northern story suddenly comes back to me. In the days when the Swedish empire presided over the Baltic, when its huge armies marched off down the Elbe as far as Prague, King Gustav II Adolf chose to commission a very great battleship. It would be Number One: the world's grandest ship of the line. There'd never been anything like it. Deck upon wooden deck it rose, a skyscraper of a vessel, tarred and feathered, high as a prince's palace, heavy with gold decoration, copper cannon, masts and rigging that reached the Nordic clouds. He named it, of course, the *Vasa*, after his grandfather, the hero who had made Sweden a nation and a power in the world. In 1618 it was launched, here in the harbour in front of me. It cast its moorings and set off from shore; its overloaded decks were packed with admirals and aldermen, courtiers, courtesans and priests. Guns fired, fireworks cracked, flags waved, church bells rang, bishops blessed. As the crowds cheered, the ship toppled offshore, turned on its side, sank to the bottom. The churchbells ceased, the bishops fell silent, the crowds wept, the dignitaries aboard drowned in public sight, an empire plunged.

When I last came to Stockholm, quite some time back now, this early version of the *Titanic* had just been fresh-craned from the water. Timbers black and filthy, its hulk lay on a mudflat by the island, preserved by chemical sprays. But history these days is a theme-park. Nothing is wasted. These are the days of the modern museum, the open-access library, the multimedia experience, the virtual reality ride – high-tech simulations of the way things once might have been in times when people were naïve enough to think they were real. Now over there, as I look through the trees, is the Vasa Museum, complete with a Vasa Experience, built round the old rotting hulk. I rise to my feet, cross the windy bridge, walk through the park, buy myself a ticket for the grand old tragedy. Hundreds of tourists, Japanese, Korean, American, await admission. In these millennial times, all the world likes to attend the drowning of a ship. A young female attendant with a black eyepatch stands in the lobby. For some reason she stops me, offers to steer me round herself. At her side I walk through the great restoration: by computer displays of ships and seafaring, a crackle of multi-lingual tapes. We wander through the disinfected hull: over the great poop, with its regal decorations, through low-roofed gun-decks packed with heavy cannon, past stacks of retrieved water-bottles, rotting uniforms, sailors' canvas shoes, leather buckets, deckmen's thimbles, balls of stone and lead.

My one-eyed guide is pleasant, serious, moral, instructive. Civic, that must be the word. As we walk through the sea-darkened timbers, stinking of preservatives, she philosophizes Swedishly. On the rise and fall of empires, the vanity of human wishes, the delusions of kings and princes, how she and I are here today but gone tomorrow. I nod agreeably as she tells me the sea is a very beautiful thing, but a place of danger, and the Baltic the most dangerous place of all. She says it's a seaman's graveyard; over the centuries thousands of ships have foundered in the great archipelago, while captains who lost their vessels were hanged from gallows along the shore. When our tour is almost done, she gestures through the tinted windows at the harbour waters beyond. Great Baltic ferries sail close by: huge horizontal office blocks, casinos, fun-palaces, packed with sinners and illusionists, seeking life's eternal duty-free. But, she says, looking at me seriously, we are never free of duty. What we are looking at, out there in the seaway, are just the modern *Vasas*, waiting to take the plunge.

As I'm intending to sail off on one of these floating coffins tomorrow, this isn't quite what I need to hear. '*Tack, tack*,' I say hastily to my one-eyed Virgil, and leave the Vasa Museum. I walk down wide windy Strandgatan, then across the harbour bridges that take me into the old town, Gamla Stan. More guides are waiting, keen to show me the scene of the great Swedish Blood-bath, where forty loyal burghers were hacked to death by the

Danes. But Nordic gloom has gone far enough. I prefer to walk on my own, think my own thoughts, down the wet cobbled passages, past the high merchant houses where grain from Prussia met copper from the Upplands, the cloths of Flanders, the furs of Novgorod. They're all trinket-shops now. The sun has gone for good, the seaborne wind come up. Rain, end of season, the bank and the museum, blonde bankers and one-eyed guides: all do their spiritual work. I walk collar up between high-sided churches and palaces, and start to wonder. What on earth − or for that matter off and beyond it − happened to poor old René Descartes?

Maybe you recall the story? I thought I did, though as things turned out I didn't, or not as well as I might. It's a well-known fact that princes and philosophers have consorted together for just about as long as time can remember, with much desire to mix intelligence with power, but not necessarily much success. Aristotle tutored Alexander the Great. Socrates taught virtue to the gilded youth of Athens, if with unhappy personal results. Plato sought a philosopher-king to guide the nation; the one he served soon sold him into slavery. Noble Seneca taught justice and clemency to the Emperor Nero, though to remarkably little effect. Francis Bacon, who took all knowledge for his province, served James the First of England, Fifth of Scotland: 'The standing is slippery,' he warned. Leibniz attended on Peter the Great to spread the spirit of reason; but this did not stop Big Peter killing off his rivals or having his own son hacked to death. By the great Age of the Enlightenment the custom was universal. Reason and humanism were the principles of the age, mind showed its power over God, matter and state. Priests were in discredit, philosophers were in the ascendant. Great kings and queens listened solemnly to tiny thinkers and poets. No European court was complete without its dancing master, astronomer, kapellmeister, map-maker, its physician, mathematician, and its philosophe. How else could the Enlightenment world grow truly enlightened, a monarch become wise, the earthly Utopia be brought into being, than by taking the highest metaphysical advice?

When Frederick the Great, a small man who hated his militaristic father almost as much as he loathed his militaristic wife, took power in Prussia, he saw himself as the true enlightened monarch: the Philosopher-King. When not taking Silesia, losing his fortune, winning his victories, marching his goose-stepping soldiers up and down the Brandenburg streets, he was no classic tyrant but a triumph of civilization: thinker and talker, patron and poet, composer and editor, flute-player and pianist, a prince among statesmen. He nurtured great Bach ('give me concertos'), rejected petty religious bigotries, refused to use Christian symbols, wrote learned tracts, sweet flute concertos, and some unbelievably dreary pornographic verse in French. He too yearned for his own philosopher, and called Voltaire from France to become, as he put it, his Talking Bird and his Singing Tree. How charmingly it all went to begin with! 'One thinks boldly, one is free here,' foxy Voltaire announced in delight when he settled into his fine pavilion amid the high minds, rustic splendours, wild woodlands, great vine gardens of Sans Souci, on the banks of the Havel near growing Berlin. The summer court was glorious. Tinkling fountains and belvederes, a Chinese pagoda topped with an umbrella-ed golden Confucius, bands and barracks, music all hours, intense and philosophical dinners under the lantern roof – for Frederick indeed dined only with men.

A world-famous relationship, it's remembered still. New and re-tarted Potsdam, again a summer adjunct to a winter capital, succours it. Today you'll find the Voltaire-weg leads into the Schopenhauer-strasse, which ends up in Hegel-Allee, which once pointed the way to Karl-Marx-Platz, now the blind alley of Uncertainty Square. You could even call it the world's first great creative writing class: for, day after day, again and again, the writer-philosopher went over the king's unfortunate and often depressingly pornographic poems, trying to mine them for faint traces of literary merit. The months passed, and the years, until it became apparent that the first happiness was not destined to last – not after the sage-laureate began falling out with the King's other academicians, and then overheard his generous monarch remarking, 'I'll need this chap for a year at the most. First thing you squeeze the juice out of the orange, then you toss away the peel.'

Voltaire, a vain, sharp-toothed, angry type, was no monarch's orange. After three troubled years he resolved to preserve his pips. He haughtily handed back his court titles and honours; soon he was quietly taking the quickest way out of town. But power is power, and thinking isn't; so it all ended in tears, of course – with the Sage arrested at gunpoint in Frankfurt on his homeward journey, charged with breaching his contract, engaging in illegal financial transactions, running off with some of the king's unspeakable poems. Yet it simply proved the rule of Enlightenment times; prince and philosopher were bonded to each other. 'I was born too soon,' said Frederick unapologetically, 'but, happily, I have seen the immortal Voltaire.' An absolute monarch needed an intellectual absolution. Every king or empress sought a philosophe: each needed the absolute homage of the other. Dear Didro, Denis Diderot – and he, by the way, is the chief reason why I'm here in Stockholm – thought for Catherine of Russia. D'Alembert, Condorcet and Rousseau all had need to pass on the lore of reason and human freedom to any who would govern, not least Jefferson and Franklin, makers of the First New Nation.

Naturally the day would come when – largely thanks to all these rational courtly speculations on liberty, religion, humanity, reason – the great chain of being would snap at last. The kings and princes would mostly disappear, often bloodily and irrationally, in some frenzied and thoughtless (or thoughtful) moment of mob rule. On the other hand, the philosophers survived, more than survived, to become the wisdom of the next new age. They mostly outlived the bloodbath, sometimes they were its greatest heroes. They prospered and flourished. They turned reason into will, will into being, being into nothingness. They enlightened and illuminated; they disputed and critiqued. They considered mind and matter, state and person, history and fatality, reason and madness, order and chaos, the limits of our language and the limits of our world. They looked deep into darkness, and they hungered for the light. They existed without being, they were without existing. They spoke, yet they also knew whereof to be silent.

And with thinkers as with chefs and milliners, or wines and cheeses, the most important rule was clear. Anyone could think anywhere – given the time, the space, the mental machinery. But the fact remained that the truly great performers, the top of the crop, *la crème de la crème*, were always assumed to be French. And today, though the kings and princes have nearly all been deposed and are departed (mostly for Lisbon or Gstaad), the philosophes still go on. For even modern democracies need their sages, and modern persons the newest modes of thought. As it was so it is; however many fish swim in the great world of think-tanks, the largest, most shark-like, most powerful are still generally French. Before World War II finished, a desperate America, cut off from thought by the recent hostilities, flew Jean-Paul Sartre by bomber to New York. Simone de Beauvoir soon followed, drawn by such American wonders as Nelson Algren and the electric chair. Onward into our own age of philosophical cafés, and personal thought-trainers who'll advise whenever you've a window in your corporate day. For how else could Americans know their postmodern condition, the strange anxieties of their unbearable lightness of being, their subjectless cogitos, their strange virtuality, without a Foucault, a Derrida, a Lyotard, a Baudrillard, a Kristeva to advise them, a philosopher come by transatlantic jumbo to court?

But who was the real leader of the great procession? Who was it first brought power and Francophone thought together? The answer is perfectly obvious: it was grand old René Descartes. The year, we may recall, was 1649. The place was Amsterdam, in the Dutch Republic, so long a wet and fishy haven for displaced and unhappy thinkers – the Pilgrim Fathers, the Spinozas, the John Lockes. Its universities were free in spirit, its publishers were plagiaristic but politically open and generous. Descartes was under attack in his French homeland, assaulted by priests, bishops, the Pontiff himself for his speculations on the powers of the human mind. Here, amid rank canals and bustling merchant houses, he could live quietly, nicely. He managed a discreet amour, he even fathered a secret daughter. He conducted small medical experiments on whether animals had souls, supplied with offal by the butcher who lived so conveniently downstairs. Soon he was able to show the human creature was animal too, but a special animal, endowed with reason – a splendid animal who could feel, speak and reason, discern the difference between truth and falsehood, was possessed of the right to know, all thanks to the benevolence of the Great Creator and the splendid workings of the pineal gland.

Like all great thinkers he won many fond admirers, swarms of philosophical groupies. And one was right here, where I am now, in chilly Stockholm. Her name was Queen Christina, twenty-three years old and well into her reign. She was a spendthrift, hirsute, stoop-shouldered well-read lady, who affected the wearing of men's clothes and combed her hair only once a week. Thanks to the benevolence of the Great Creator and her own pineal gland, she had been granted a devouring need to know. And she was taken by what, thanks to her generous interest, would prove to be René's last book, the charmingly titled *Passions of the Soul*. No sooner had she read a draft of it than she wrote him a fan-letter, demanding more information, a photo. René, never a sluggard in the matter of correspondence, responded at length. It was a fatal kindness; it so often is. Before he knew it a fine Swedish ship with an admiral on board had appeared in the Amstel harbour to collect him, at royal command, and bear him northward to the Swedish court.

A naturally retiring man, still occupied with dissecting his offals, René declined as politely as he might. As he whispered to friends, he had no wish at all to go to the Land of the Bears. Unfortunately, in Amsterdam, all was no longer going well. Even here, in the great *Aulas* of Amsterdam and Utrecht and Leiden, the winds of a new political correctness were growing. René's view that man invented God with the reason God had given him was provoking the annoyance of the freshmen. Soon the professors had ceased to speak his name, and before much longer his books were disappearing from the syllabus. René was a wise old thinker, and had seen these warning signs before. He burned many of his papers, made his will. Then he went out, bought an elegant court dress with fine ruffled sleeves. The admiral had left, but he went to the harbour and boarded a ship for Stockholm, setting off after all for the Land of the Bears.

Unfortunately it was no longer the best of seasons; he had left the whole thing much too late. The east winds were blowing, the seas were raging, the voyage unusually took an entire month. This may or may not have been due to the fact that Descartes, ever the scholar, decided to teach the captain the newest arts of navigation, cosmologically invented by himself. 'The man's a demi-god,' declared the awestruck captain, when he finally decanted, or perhaps decarted, the savant on to the Stockholm harbour wall. Then there were other problems. The Queen's interests had shifted just a little. Now she was out of philosophy and into ballet – the sprightly step, the upsprung toe. What's more she was busy, due out of town for a while to settle some unfinished diplomatic business left over from the Thirty Years' War. Left to his own devices in the chilly residence of the French Ambassador – it stood where I am standing, right here in the middle of the Stockholm Old Town – René tried to follow the absent Queen's instructions. He attempted to write a ballet, but found the idea was something of a contradiction in terms. Instead he wrote a play about two princes who thought they were shepherds – a well-known confusion in all the royal courts of the day.

No wonder. Not all was well at court, as he found when he went in his new ruffled sleeves. In the Queen's absence, René's arrival had become a matter of dismay to all courtiers present: the theologians, astrologers, astronomers, mathematicians and medical men who always surrounded the monarchs of the day. It didn't help that the Queen had asked René to devise a new Swedish Academy, recommending its members, writing its statutes. So jealous was the general envy of the foreign upstart that, eavesdropping on their conversations, he discovered all the courtiers were discussing was whether or how to murder him. René went home and wisely added a clause to the Academy statutes saying no foreigners should be admitted, above all not himself. By now deep winter had come: Nordic winter, chilly and hard. Old men said it was the worst in living memory, as old men always do. Shivering in his room at the ambassadorial mansion, Descartes now deeply regretted his errand. 'It seems to me men's thoughts freeze here, just like the water,' he sadly reported home.

Then, in the darkness of January, the Queen returned to court. She thought again of her philosopher, decided to put him to use. Like another great Snow Queen, Our Lady of the Handbags, three centuries later and in another part of Europe, she needed no more than three hours of sleep a night. She rose at four, and her morning toilette took absolutely no time at all. So, each morning at five, our good philosopher was summoned to the palace for a five-hour seminar on the passions of the soul. He was no normal early riser; in fact he was a well-known slugabed. But each stark morning, long before the sun rose (if in this godforsaken country it ever did), he rose himself, put on his nice new ruffles, and walked in black dark over slippery crunching ice to the Royal Palace, ready for his five-hour session with the hirsute and far from well-bathed queen. By the end of January he was visibly shaking with fever: I think, therefore I freeze. Soon he was bedbound, refusing the aid of the doctors the Queen sent to him, knowing they probably shared the murderous jealousy of their colleagues. When he was young Descartes had had the idea that, by thoughtful endeavours, it was possible for a philosopher to live for ever. It wasn't true. By February, mind and matter were seriously diverging. 'Alas, my soul,' he said to his closest companion, 'it is time for you and me to part. Try to bear the separation with courage.' He died before the month was over. Some blamed the poisons of the court physician; others blamed the flu.

And then? Now what happened next? Standing here, in the cold of old Stockholm, I try my hardest to remember. The Queen, I recall, was contrite, and demanded every honour for her thinker: the father of the cogito, the inventor of the passions of the soul. As I recollect it, he was buried with state honours and eulogies somewhere here – surely in the Storkyrkan Cathedral. There were, though, a few small problems. The Queen herself was now in the process of becoming a secret Catholic, and some blamed Descartes. Not long after she abdicated, rode off to Rome in the costumeless costume of an Amazon, and settled in the Vatican. Her monarchical ambitions were by no means over. She sent her royal c.v. to most of the European nations and states; none accepted her well-intentioned offer to rule despotically over them. She took to hanging around the Vatican, quarrelling to the last with the great pontiff, who wanted her out of town. Finally, just as warm-blooded René met a frozen death in the Land of the Bears, the Northern Ice-Lady met a warm one in the Eternal City, arguing to the last with His Everlasting Holiness about those worrying passions of the soul.

That's all I remember; all I think I remember. But the great philosopher dying of cold in the interests of thought has always managed to move me. Now here I am in Stockholm Old Town: gloomy, at a loose end, a whole afternoon to spare. I decide to track down Descartes's tomb. For the next several hours, I do just that. I start my quest at the logical place for a state burial, Storkyrkan, which raises its great high-spired bulk at the core of the Old Town. In its noble space I discover royal tombs, fine chandeliers, a quite splendid Saint George and the Dragon. But though I look round everywhere, I see neither hair nor hide of the thinker. I move on and on, from church to church in the Old Town. Soon I'm wandering the whole city, tripping from island to island, going from this high-sided Lutheran church and chapel to that. I gaze on an infinity of cold monuments, a surfeit of funerary inscriptions, a whole handbook full of scan pinewood pews, stone statues, Latinate mottos, slate-filled boneyards. Between big Swedish gravestones I halt black-robed pastors, skull-faced vergers, Bergman-like widows in eternal weeds. They all long to show me the site of the Swedish Bloodbath. Not one of them knows where to find the resting place of poor René Descartes.

Mystification overtakes me. My instinct for detection grows. My investigative blood runs warm. Walking through an afternoon of drilling rain, I spread my Holmesean net ever wider. I scan maps, hunt clues, follow every hint. I stop perfect strangers, tour guides, American tourists, determined to find out the facts of the case. I'm sent to the Finnish Church. To the German Church. To the Russian Church. To the Kungholm Church, which looks promising, but isn't. To some church on an island that can only be reached on a little puffing steamer, and holds yet more royal tombs. Remembering France and Catholicism, I go to the Church of Maria Magdalena; not here. For all its liberal morality and sublimated lust, Sweden stays a religious country. And there's really no end to its churches, graveyards, tombs, effigies, epitaphs, its kindly but uninformative pastors, its weary widows in weeds.

By now the wind's blowing up, the cold's coming down. And I've seen most of Stockholm: not just Gamla Stan, but the functional modernities, the out-of-town shopping centres, the blank pedestrian precincts that surround it on the hills. The one thing I haven't seen is a single trace of Descartes. The creator of the metaphysics of human presence, the founder of the great I Am, the prophet of the modern soul, the man who gave us doubt, anxiety, mind over matter, who taught us to question, investigate, observe, is notable only for his uneffacing silent absence. Of the thinker's thinker, there is neither tomb nor trace, effigy or epitaph, residue nor relic, sign nor signification. I'm confused, I'm engaged, I'm seriously dismayed. Could it be that something a little strange and fantastical happened to the late excellent René Descartes?

FOUR (THEN)

THIS ALL GOES BACK ten years now, to another time: the heyday of the great book itself. 'ENCYCLOPEDIA: Noun, feminine gender. The word signifies unity of knowledge,' our man wrote then. 'In truth, the aim of an encyclopedia is to collect all knowledge that now lies scattered all over the face of the earth; to make known its general structure to those among whom we live; and to transmit it onward to those who come after us, our Posterity.' It was the truly grand *projet*, the Book of the Age, the great narrative of all things known and thought, and nothing in the universe mattered more. But writing the book of the age was to prove dirty, ill-paid and bitter work; dangerous and persecuted work too, with court, church and censor rightly suspicious of every tendency, every word, every hidden hint. And if there's also a sharp-tongued wife who's always complaining about the condition of literary poverty, and a decent dancing child of a daughter who when she reaches the age of sexual reason will require a handsome dowry, then our dear Denis the Daydreamer will need to do something quite serious to survive . . .

Why not, then: why not let considerate husband and admiring father despoil the philosopher and man of letters? For his richest treasure lies right in front of him – in the grasp of his own two hands, or piled up there on his desk, or stacked round the walls about him. His library – 2,904 leather-bound volumes – is among the finest of the day. In fact it's nothing less than the library of the *Encyclopedia* – which makes it the library of the Enlightenment itself. He buys all books, he reads everything, he translates many languages. He grabs up every kind of learning, classic and modern, philosophic, medical, mechanical. He accumulates every printed wisdom. He corresponds with everyone of interest. And he's annotated the books, all of them, in his own small hand, with his own large mind. Some of these volumes contain a brand-new book of their own, an entire supplement written crabbedly into the margins or across the type. And hasn't he in turn, using the books, himself written the bulk of the book of books, the *Encyclopedia* itself: a work he's struggled with, suffered with, nearly rotted in jail for? Isn't it time to put it all to market?

No sooner thought of than done. It's not so hard to work out who might buy. The notion has only to be mentioned to his dear, dandyish, tuft-hunting old friend Melchior Grimm − fat dapper traveller, visitor to every court in Europe, cultural correspondent to royalty, marriage counsellor to the aristocracy, escort agency, whisperer of secrets, sponsor of little Mr Mozart, patron and critic, supplier of the latest Parisian thoughts and notions to all the finest European gentry − than a deal is dealt. Grimm has only to drop one of his graceful, witty, superbly well-informed notes to his old and no less widely travelled friend, Baron-General Ivan Ivanovitch Betskoi of Sankt Peterburg. He serves the great Tzarina as chamberlain, court adviser, purchase-master, and − at least according to one of the innumerable gross rumours that surround her − her mother's lover, and he depends for his cunning political insight on the wit and wisdom of Melchior Grimm. Betskoi recommends, of course. 'Buy,' he then whispers in the Empress's ear, 'it will show you are a lover of reason and everyone will admire you for it. Especially the French.'

But the great lady is, as always, wonderfully clever and ingenious. She does more, far more, than that: more than a chancellor might recommend, a philosopher imagine, a maker of mystifications ever devise. 'It would be a cruelty to separate a wise man from his books, the objects of his delight, the source of his work, the companions of his leisure,' she pronounces. She buys his library, for a remarkably generous price (15,000 livres). She also refuses delivery, and instead appoints our man his own librarian, at a salary of 1,000 livres a year. With the graceless consent of King Louis, she even makes our man court librarian to the Hermitage − and all this without him ever leaving his room. And so his books will stay on his walls, support his wisdom, accompany his leisure, require some wifely dusting, for the rest of his mortal days. Only then will they be crated and shipped to their own library in the Little Hermitage; and the deal will fully be done.

Our man can only feel deeply grateful. Indeed he makes sure no one now or in the future will ever doubt the joy he feels in this amazing benefaction. 'I prostrate myself at your feet,' he writes in one of the world's warmest thank-you notes. 'I stretch out my arms to you. I long to speak to you, but my mind has shrunk to nothing! I am as emotional as a little child! My fingers of their own accord reach out for an old lyre, of which Philosophy once cut the strings! I unhook it from my wall! Bare-headed, bare-chested, I feel myself impelled to joyous song! To You!!' True, there are little local difficulties, as occur with any great court bureaucracy. A year on, Denis the Philosopher is still struggling in deep poverty, and politely writing to complain that not a penny of the promised money has been paid. But, grand as usual, the Tzarina has made perfect amends. She not only clears the blockage, fires the chancellor, remits the money. She actually pays our man the next fifty years of his salary in advance (50,000 livres), making his presumed lifespan a healthy one hundred and four.

Grateful as ever, he's written a warm ode in her eternal praise. He's offered his respectful services in all directions, done everything he can to repay the debt. So, even while up on the Neva the world's strangest water-city grows and grows, the architects, engineers, artisans, actors, economists and even the generals of Paris keep on turning up daily at his door. It's his task to vet them, sift them, crate them, send them north. When Catherine suddenly acquires the idea of a most enormous statue of homage to be raised to her predecessor Peter, he finds from his encyclopedic list of contributors a co-operative sculptor, Etienne-Maurice Falconet: perhaps not the best, or the most level-tempered, certainly the cheapest to hand. When books and manuscripts circulate in Paris suggesting the Tzarina has been guilty of shameless crimes, the liberal philosopher takes it upon himself to try and suppress them. 'It's really bizarre the variety of roles I play in this world,' he reflects.

And, in thrall to the world's greatest shopper, he shops. How he's shopped! With or without his two greatest friends, big Golitsyn, little Grimm, he's scoured all the grand arcades of Paris,

41

tripped in and out of all the secret doorways of Saint-Victoire. Print-shops, galleries, garrets, ateliers, workshops, salons, auction-rooms: he has scouted them every day, shop-shop-shopping for the great Tzarina. He buys vast shelffuls of books; he gathers up prints and bibelots and necklaces and knick-knacks, he gobbles whole collections of *beaux-arts*. Feeling a little flush now, he even treats himself a little: to a beautiful new dressing gown, which sadly fails to suit him, for he is not himself at all a grand man. Meantime all over Paris the art prices start to soar. Auctions become battlefields. Prints sell like tapestries. The most seasoned collectors withdraw wounded from the fray. When Gaignat – a former secretary to Louis XV – dies, our Philosopher tips off the Tzarina the man has collected a magnificent library without knowing how to read, created a great art collection without being able to see anything in it more than a blind beggar. Buy, she says. He buys. When the great art collection of Louis-Antoine Crozat is offered in the market, our Philosopher-Fixer is first one at the door. He drives the hardest of bargains, devising another of his stratagems, another great 'mystification', running round Paris to divide the various heirs from one another with cunning mischievous rumour and gossip.

Soon Leonardos and Van Dycks, Raphaels, Rembrandts (*The Danae*), Veroneses, Durers, Poussins, Titians, five Rubens sketches – seventeen crates in all – are making their way north to Petersburg's Imperial Palace. Now *le tout Paris* is furiously complaining: patrons, politicians, tax-farmers. Thanks to this unfair northern competition, the art market has gone mad. They will say the same of greedy Americans a hundred years later, greedy Japanese a hundred years after that. They'll be saying the same in England not much later, when the glorious contents of Sir Robert Walpole's debt-ridden Houghton Hall, destined to deck the new pavilion in the British Museum, are handed over to good Mr Christie, auctioned to the usual Russian buyer (absent), crated, shipped off up the Baltic. It takes a sage like Denis to explain these things properly. As he explains, art follows power, there are laws of history. 'How things have changed,' he declares. 'We sell our paintings and sculptures in peacetime, Catherine buys them in the midst of war. Now the sciences, arts, taste and philosophy have left for the north, and barbarism and its consequences retreat to the south.'

Which is why for the last ten years he's done everything a true courtier and a devoted librarian can possibly do for his patron. Except, that is, for one thing: the last, the greatest, hardest service. Again and again the summons has come, ever more imperiously, inviting the philosopher to crate himself up and make this journey north.

'It is not that Didro would be coming to settle in Russia,' the lady carefully explains. 'He would be doing something very much finer: coming to court to express his gratitude.'

Year by year the invitations have grown more pressing and precise. He's been urgently asked to bring all his friends, ship his relatives, take the whole project of the *Encyclopedia* northward with him.

Similar summonses, he knows, have gone to his fellow philosophes – Voltaire, d'Alembert. All have sent homage, but displayed strange reluctance actually to go. No doubt bruised by his Potsdam experience, now happy in Ferney where he has set up his own private court, crusty foxy Voltaire has announced himself perfectly willing but found a charming and cunning excuse. He too writes a florid poem in the great lady's honour ('You astound the wise man with your wit, / And he'd cease to be wise the moment he saw you') and explains that, while too busy to visit the court while he's still alive, he'd be over the moon to do so the minute he's dead – 'Why should I not have the pleasure of being buried in some corner of Petersburg, where I could see you passing back and forth, crowned with laurels and olive branches?' Offered a palace and fortune to go to court as tutor to the young archduke Paul, d'Alembert is more graceless, publicly telling a friend: 'I am far too prone to haemorrhoids; they take too severe a form in that country, and I prefer to have a painful bum in safety.'

Our man takes a different view. He's never believed in travel, would stay home if he could. But he's given far too many hostages to fortune. 'I love to see the wise man on display, like the athlete in the arena,' he has announced. 'A man only recognizes his strength when he has the chance to show it.' That's why, for years, he has not been so much refusing as deferring and excusing. 'I shall do what you expect of me,' he faxes north, 'I repeat my solemn oath. But so much, so very much, to do.' Being our man, there always is. Four books of engravings and two supplements to the *Encyclopedia* to finish; in the ever-changing universe, knowledge is growing apace. A short novel about a servant whose fate has already been written in the great Book of Destiny above to get on with, as soon as he can find enough time; as well as a dream-like reflection on human existence and psychology posed round the slumbering figure of Jean d'Alembert, his friend the great philosophe with the painful bum.

Then a more delicate matter: 'I am attached by the strongest sweetest feelings to a woman for whom I would sacrifice a hundred lives if I had them,' he advises the Tzarina through his old friend Falconet, now irritably sculpting away in Petersburg. The delicate fact is that the woman he would go to jail or watch his house burn down for is not his wife, the Great Particularist, now getting cantankerously old, but Sophie Volland, his sweet clever mistress. Still, in this demanding world there are some invitations that cannot be refused, some deferrals that cannot be deferred for ever. A generous empress requires her gratitude; promises are promises. The time has come to . . . well, go.

He goes. But how typical that he chooses to take the route of indirection. Which is why he's here in Holland, the land of free trade, free thought, Protestant instincts and inexpensive gin. It takes but a day or so with his charming hosts to decide he likes it. He likes these long low fields, grinding wooden windmills, endless sand-dunes holding the human fort against grey northern water. He has never before seen Neptune's vast empire, the Ocean. Unlike almost everything in the world, it never comes to Paris. So the first thing he does is to visit coastal Scheveningen. There he is, a grey sparkling man in a grey wig, gazing out on the equally grey and not so sparkling North Sea. He loves it: 'The vast uniformity, accompanied by a certain murmur, invites reverie. It is here that I dream well.' This soon has him reflecting with fraternal warmth on fish: 'The soles, the fresh herrings, the turbots and perch, what they call "waterfish" – these are the best fellows in the world.' He likes the people, plodding wooden-footed through the streets. He finds himself delighted by Dutch men ('full of republican spirit

44

from highest to lowest'), decent pipe-smokers quite unlike the snuff-taking French, red-faced men who care not a scrap for style and rank. No doubt for purely literary reasons, he even more admires the women. They have the hugest breasts and buttocks he has seen. Yet somehow they appear seductively modest, as French women only do when they are returning from confession.

Soon he's nicely settled in: wig on floor, pen on desk. Within days he's off writing yet another book or three. He's hardly got here and looked out of the window before he produces a brief guide to Holland. He works on his running tale of the travelling master and his roguish servant, who reads his fortunes and misfortunes in the great Book of Destiny above. He starts another story in dialogue about meeting the nephew of the famed composer Rameau. He produces a commentary on a work of Helvétius, thoughtfully adding a deft little dedication to Catherine II. He writes about actors and comedians, considering the paradox that great actors display most passion when they invest the least; already he's invented Method acting. He slips out to meet the Dutch professors of Leiden, the cheerful little heirs of those who betrayed Descartes and dislodged him from their liberal republic just about a century before.

They greet him warmly, take him to dinner, fill up his wine glass, delight in his curious medical questions, enjoy his wit and teasing, admire his republican, atheistical cast of mind. He travels to Amsterdam, that bookish city, to buy more notebooks and meet the publishers. Some already publish his books; others, for the purposes of mystification, or just the avoidance of censorship, are purported to. Like most travelling writers, he's arrived in town with a brilliant idea. Why don't they undertake a collected edition of his works (if only he could remember what he's written, and what he's done with it now)? When the edition appears a year or so later, half the books in it are not by him. All's well here then. All's very well.

Until . . . one day a summons arrives on a very touchy matter. It's a message from little Frederick of Prussia, now known, since he slaughtered his flute-playing way through Silesia, as the Great. He has heard of our man's journey in the usual fashion: through the endless gossip of his good friend Melchior Grimm, who is even now at Potsdam collecting up some marriageable little princess to take her on to Russia. The Philosopher-King observes that if our sage is also travelling to Petersburg, he will surely have to pass by way of Sans Souci. He therefore issues a polite command: come to court. Now it so happens our man is no admirer at all of the Philosopher-King. In fact he has abused him in print on several occasions, as a cloth-headed tyrant and slaughterer masquerading as an enlightened thinker. Worse still, he remembers what happened to Voltaire (a much-loved friend, even if he has never met him) when, two decades earlier, he answered just such a summons from Potsdam on the Havel.

Admittedly Voltaire was in disgrace in France as usual. Small wonder the most famous court in Europe – with its 150,000 oversized hussars, operas and concerts, pavilions and vineyards, trumpets and violins, and its all-male dinners in the company of the king – at first seemed to him a pleasant carefree paradise, a genuine Sans Souci. While his miserable queen did the court-work and entertained foreign ambassadors, His Highness sat amid gardens and vineyards and talked of music and art. But that was before the philosopher saw His Majesty burn one of his own books in the public square, before those bitter public rows over share-certificates, pensions, honours; before the gunpoint arrest in Frankfurt accused of poetic larceny, before he was forced to return his philosophical pension and then driven into present Swiss exile. There's is even a private note come from cunning Grimm warning our man to be careful at Potsdam. With his friendly open manners, he is even more likely than Voltaire to put a foot wrong. So, sagely, our sage declines – unfortunately creating an insult that will have to be paid for in the future. As His Sagacity will duly discover, the fatal words are already being written in the great Book of Destiny above.

Meanwhile, up in Sankt Peterburg (the Venice, the Amsterdam, the Palmyra, the Wherever of the North), doubt, distress, alarm are growing. Six months have passed, the red carpet has been long unrolled, the welcome drinks poured. But where's the great philosophe? *Où est notre* Didro? One day in August, a carriage, a vast sprung Berliner, rolls up to the embassy in the Hague. It's the grand private coach of Prince Alexis Narishkin, chamberlain to the Russian Imperial Court, sometimes known as the buffoon of the Winter Palace. His European travels have been diverted to capture our man and take him northward; in they both get. The weather's nice, the carriage stout. But what lies ahead is a real dog-leg of a journey, since at all costs they need to avoid Berlin, where diatribes against our man are already being distributed in the streets. Which way did they go? I'm not quite sure. They both have severe colic in Duisberg; they certainly turn up in Leipzig, another bookish city, the Saxon city of Bach and Schumann, the Paris of the East. Not much earlier Goethe had studied here: 'Paris in miniature,' he called it. And, when one day in the future he sits down to write his *Faust*, he'll send the errant professor by magic-carpet to the student taverns of the city, where, with the help of Mephistopheles, his body can explore its desires, his mind risk the most wonderful wanton thoughts.

Our man rolls up there with Narishkin; they like the look of it too. They taste its Lutheran flavours, they trip round the same student taverns. They call upon the great professors, attend the lectures and the Bach recitals in the church. Soon, wig off, pen out, the Philosopher is writing, writing. Within days he's become a local fixture – famous for wandering galleries, parks and *Aulas* wigless, in dressing gown, nightcap, yellow slippers, affably talking to students and professors about his newest special subject, atheism, and all that with Narishkin's enthusiastic and drunken support. Strangely, by an odd little turn of fate's wheel, up there in heaven above, Posterity is lying in wait here. One day, the posthumous text of the book our man's now writing – *Rameau's Nephew*, it's called, the best thing he will ever write – will also make a journey to the Hermitage. Thanks to a venal rector at the university, or maybe a German soldier, the draft will then be smuggled out again, to Germany and the great writer Schiller. He will pass it on to Goethe, by now himself a court philosopher at none-too-distant Weimar. He'll love the book, translate it into German, publish it here in Leipzig, and so secure its fame.

Then the manuscript will oddly disappear, and a forged French version will emerge. Hegel will admire the tale, for its invention of the nephew, the first 'modern character'. Then so will Marx, and so will Freud – and thus it will go on. One day they will build

Karl-Marx University here, and give the top of its skyscraper the appearance of a half-open book, in memory of all the books that have been opened here, and the many more that have been closed. But Our Man's tale is eternal: the lovely dialogue between a peripatetic chess-watching Paris philosopher and his famous double, an idle, chimerical, flattering parasite, the useless nephew of the stiff-legged great composer Jean-Philippe Rameau. In fact it's a debate between Moi and Lui. 'I let my mind rove wantonly,' the philosophical Moi of this most pleasing of tricky stories confesses. 'My ideas are my trollops.'

In Leipzig, and later at the grand court of Elector of Saxony at Dresden ('the Florence of the Elbe' as Leipzig is 'the Paris of the Elster'), our man's current ideas prove to be the most glorious and alluring of trollops. Unfortunately they are so buxomly tempting, so seductive to the students, so radical and atheistical, they soon have him in serious trouble with the court authorities. Once again it's time to move on.

Taking, of course, the longer route – how wise they are to avoid Berlin, for the Philosopher-King is raging wildly, and writing scurrilous articles about our man for all Europe's magazines under a row of easily cracked pseudonyms – they roll onward. Here is Pomerania, here is Poland. Now and then they call on one of those small impoverished castles that litter the countryside, rural seed-beds that provide nubile princesses for the grand courts, ensuring the continuance (or otherwise) of monarchs, prince-palatines, tzars. But most of the time it's flea-ridden taverns, terrible roads. There are plagues of mosquitos, hordes of special gnats only known in Poland. Problems with toothache, problems with brigands, problems with floods. Innumerable gastric colics, searing the gut – 'Imagine if you can the state of a man tormented by violent colic travelling over the worst roads. A knife shoved in the intestines could not hurt more.' For who will ever know just how much gut-wrenching diarrhoea has been traded in this world for the international traffic in learning, the world-movement of the higher thought?

For four days they do not eat. Pigs grovel. Dirt-caked peasants groan and labour. Groaning haycarts hung with tatty children trudge. Well-poles creak. Brats scream, dogs howl, donkeys brawl.

48

Ducks croak, geese cackle, Prussian cavalry threaten and maraud. Meantime, careless with goods, ignorant of the little stuff of daily life, our man leaves belongings everywhere. He misses a nightshirt in Saxony, a wig in Pomerania, his slippers in Poland. Hats, notebooks, slippers and linen all have to be gone back for and retrieved by weary servants and postilions. Then somewhere, quite unnoticed, they cross a highly mysterious border. Europe becomes not Europe. The world subtly changes. The post-horses grow more scrawny. Now even time is different; somewhere or other eleven human days have disappeared from the western calendar and spiralled away into the strange wastes of the cosmos.

Never mind; they're travelling in a crazy hurry now. It's only days away from the young Archduke Paul's wedding, about to take place in Petersburg. Narishkin, as court chamberlain, is commanded to be there. They ride on, day and night, forty-eight hours at a run. As the carriage jolts, as north and east get nearer, the wind gets colder, the winter comes down, the Sage and Narishkin talk furiously. Or not quite. It is the Sage who talks, Narishkin who listens. He talks a blue streak; this is a man who has been known to speak without stopping a whole day and night. He laughs and he weeps. He slaps his legs, and everyone else's. He shouts loud, he whispers low. He reflects at length on . . . well, everything reason can reflect on, which is everything. On Michelangelo's great dome for Saint Peter's (never seen it, knows all about it), the best system of underground sanitation for a modern city, the role of the naïve in art, the means of deception in acting, the paradox of identity as proven by the existence of Siamese twins, the function of statues, the correct and elegant construction of reliable chairs, the perfect add-up or computing machine.

Glancing round, at mountain and flatland, bog and salt-marsh, pig-pen and well-pole, at the suffering lands of Poland, lusted over by just about everyone except the people who actually live there, at the rocky outcrops of Baltic coast at Konigsberg, he takes out his notebook – then another and another. He jots down plans, schemes, even the odd bad dream, the odd comic poem. In truth he's now busily inventing Russia, whose border they will soon shortly reach at Riga. And he's inventing it not as it is – huge *versts*, vast permafrosted steppes, white nights, fattened boyars, big-whiskered monks, fur-clad cossacks, life-weary serfs, onion-topped chapels, broken roads – but as it might be, a great moving Enlightenment dream. He plans buildings, draws whole cities, devises political constitutions, new dance academies and cadet schools. Brooding grimly on human wrongs, he invents human rights. He wonders whether big-boots Peter really put Petersburg, the new capital, in quite the right spot. Surely, he says, the heart is misplaced when it's put on the end of a finger, a stomach is attached to a heel.

He starts to construct a vast and visionary memoir for the Empress who, in that same city, he will at last be seeing shortly, delineating the ideal rational nation, serving everybody's interest, that an enlightened despot like Her Imperial and Autocratic Majesty might best have. 'A society should first of all be happy,' he sets down as golden rule number one. Seizing benevolent Narishkin's arm till the blood-flow halts, he debates everything in the universe, past, present and future. He considers prince and state, reason and madness, order and flux, acting and genius, divinity and self-creation, male and female, marriage and divorce. He writes poems for postilions, and lyrics for pettable chamber-maids. When Narishkin, tired of the jolting, sick with the tooth-ache, stabbed by the colic, stops arguing, he simply argues with the next man to hand – who happens to be himself. On he rolls, and on. On he writes, and on.

Soon twenty, forty, then sixty notebooks are full. After six bumpy weeks of travel, toothache, lost wigs and nightshirts, painful flea-bites, gut-wrenching colic, pinched maids, castled cities, fresh duchies and margravates, crashed coaches, lost coachmen, broken carriage wheels, new and chilly seas, changed borders, occasional poems, he is still he, entirely MOI. It's Narishkin who is no longer Narishkin. When at last they ride back into Russia alongside the bleak bay, cross the River Dwina, and enter the narrow streets of old Riga, he's turned into someone or something else: Lui himself, Diderot's Double.

FIVE (NOW)

ANYWAY, enough of my small Cartesian dilemma. Darkness is falling, and there's an exciting night out in Stockholm to enjoy. I return to my hotel for a quick change of clothes; my evening has already been spoken for. Tonight I'm to be entertained to a fine Swedish slap-up by none other than Professor Bo Luneberg: the man who's been kind enough to fly me out to Stockholm on this interesting Baltic junket, the precise details of which seem rather to have slipped my mind. Bo Luneberg, let me explain, is a very old academic friend of mine. Or perhaps it would be truer to say I've known him over many many years. I've met him time and again at various academic conferences, heard him speak, in his dry, edgy expert way, at a variety of sumptuous, well-catered and pretty high-level international seminars right across the world. We've kept in touch, exchanged our printed thoughts, traded our off-prints. What Bo and I are, to express it correctly, is colleagues.

Luneberg follows what's nowadays become rather an uncommon trade, though it once used to be universal. He's a grammarian – teaching scientific English, the structures of human grammar, the nature of artificial languages here at the Royal Technological University. This is important, because now computers need all this, if not human beings. But that isn't all. Bo is also a sober-suited academician, and in Sweden this is a very important office indeed. For the Swedish Academy (which, confusingly, was started by Gustav III Adolf in 1786, meaning that René Descartes' plans for it can't after all have played much of a part in its founding) is one of the world's most powerful institutions – and all on the basis of a simple activity. The academy awards prizes. It awards famous prizes. Prizes worth a million dollars, prizes that keep Sweden in the eye of the world. Yes, my old friend and colleague is one of those eighteen dark-suited highly secretive scholars who each year, in some literary vault full of books and busts above the Stockholm Stock Exchange, cast their careful eyes over all the imaginative writings of the whole world, considering who shall receive the Nobel Prize for Literature. Occasionally he even calls me up to consult me on their choices – though, as far as I can remember, no recommendation I've made has ever been accepted, and no possible winner he has mentioned to me has ever actually been laurelled. He's a man of very wide acquaintance, extensive travel, massive reading, curious learning, strange gossip, obscure discretions – in fact a little Melchior Grimm. And if anyone in the world knows the true story of what happened to Descartes, this would have to be the man.

Our rendezvous is fixed for seven, on the steps of the National Theatre, which faces out grandly over the now dark, wet, windy harbour. I arrive a little early, and stand waiting under the statues of the Swedish playwrights, looking out as bright-lit evening ferries glide by in the distance. Inside something by Strindberg is playing; but no doubt it always is. The City Hall clock strikes, its bells peeling across the water. Luneberg promptly appears, his grey hair neat, wearing his big-framed glasses and carrying a small black umbrella. He seems his usual sober self, except today he is clad in a Burberry sports jacket, which suggests either a strangely relaxed frame of mind or a gesture of politeness to a British visitor. He's not alone. With him is a tall, leggy, handsome woman, blonde and middle-aged.

'Hey, hey, my old friend,' he says, shaking my hand, slapping my shoulder, tapping my chest, and introducing me to his companion, his wife Alma. She looks me over with haughty suspicion. I can understand why. The word 'novelist' must have been used in describing me, because it often has this effect. Then I see she is actually carrying a copy of one of my novels – which no doubt she will ask me to sign later if I prove to be an acceptable sort, and otherwise not. With the warmest apology, she explains that she would have liked to ask me to dinner, but unfortunately Swedes only entertain real friends in their houses. In any case, she understands, I am a writer, and will surely want to go somewhere very bohemian. Happily she knows the perfect place.

The perfect place is a café-restaurant a block or two round the corner. It's one of those old-fashioned, panelled artistic cafés in the *vieux art nouveau* style. There are caricatures of writers and painters, portraits of actors and singers, framed on the walls, and many prints of eighteenth-century scholars, all of them looking weighty in their wigs. Several depict that low-cut Swedish nightingale, Jenny Lind, mouth open as usual. There are sepia photographs of a bearded Strindberg, showing him sitting in the café, bored and waiting for service – pretty much like ourselves. Neither the room, the cracked leather chairs, nor the waiters, who wear faded black suits and overwashed white aprons, have changed much either since the last century so creakingly turned. At the white-clothed tables a few gentlemen, nearly all middle-aged, suited, and trim-bearded, sit writing with biros over cups of cold coffee. With the benefit of the doubt, I imagine they are authors, journalists or scholars. Two elderly men play chess in a corner. The waiters, standing in a corner, go on chatting together idly.

'So bohemian, yes?' says Alma Luneberg joyfully, waving gaily at the extremely sombre scene.

'Very,' I admit.

'Usually there are many writers here, but they must be indoors tonight,' she says.

'It is a little wet,' I say.

'They say Strindberg often came here to write about his fruitless search for attention,' says Bo.

'I can believe it,' I say, as the waiters fade from sight.

'And where Lagerkvist wrote his famous work, *The Hangman.*'

'Yes, I can believe that too.'

Two noisy drunks appear suddenly in the entrance, suggesting the promise of a change of mood. However they are quickly cornered, counselled, then summarily ejected by a group of what appear to be freelance social workers.

'Welcome to Stockholm,' says Alma. 'Now shall we try to enjoy ourselves?'

Meanwhile Bo takes out an asthmatic nasal spray and refreshes his nostrils before interrogating me on various academic matters, mostly to do with the recent divorces or the sudden gay outings of a number of common professorial friends. He seems oddly preoccupied; but then, as Alma explains, he should not really be wasting his time here in a café at all. October is the Nobel Prize season. Bo should really be reading a stack of foreign books, or feeding highly misleading disinformation to the world press.

Suddenly a waiter drifts lethargically over toward us, bringing a much-thumbed, leather-bound menu with a picture of an agonized Strindberg on the front for us to study if we care to. By way of peaceful Nordic revenge, the Lunebergs in turn steadfastly ignore him. For a moment I entertain the immoral thought that I might ask the man for an ash-tray, but in this country the risks of massive liberal opprobrium always seem far too great, as in California. Brushing dandruff off Bo's lapels, Alma leans over and asks me whether I am enjoying Stockholm. My opportunity has come at last. So the following conversation ensues:

ME
Actually I've spent rather a philosophical day—

SHE
You went to see the Vasa, of course—

ME
I did, of course. But I seem to be caught on the horns of a
Cartesian dilemma—

HE
May I tell you you are looking pretty tolerably well for a man
of, what is it, sixty plus?

ME (*lying*)
Well, not quite—

SHE
I know your age. It is printed right in the front of your book.

HE
We must not always believe what we read in books.

ME
Especially my books.

SHE
I only like proper books I can believe in.

HE
However, let us go to business. First let me recommend the excellent herring.

SHE
Believe me, if you have it, the taste will stay with you for as long as you live.

ME
But I already had herring at lunchtime. No, I think I'll try the pasta. And may I have a bottle of beer?

A beat. Shocked faces.

SHE
A bottle of . . . beer?

HE
Nej, nej. We are *alkoholfri* here. Drink is a very big problem in Sweden.

ME
What, getting hold of it, you mean?

SHE
This is not Finland. We are a Viking people, not stable. Drink is very bad for us. It is the same with strong coffee. If you have a wild temperament, it is not a good thing. Bo, really, you have dandruff on your jacket again.

ME
Water then, please.

SHE
And herring, you say?

ME
I thought I asked for pasta.

SHE
Water is an excellent choice. But I really think if you come to Sweden you must absolutely try the herring—

HE
A Cartesian dilemma, you say? The mind–body problem,
I suppose you mean—

ME
Yes. Only the problem is my mind and his body. I've looked round everywhere and I can't find it.

SHE
Your mind?

ME
His body. I always thought Descartes was buried here.

SHE
Jo, jo, you are perfectly right.

HE
Well, half of him is perfectly right.

SHE
How can only half of him be right?

HE
Of course. Half can be right and half can be wrong. As you know, Descartes died here, and Queen Christina ordered he should be buried in the Royal Cathedral. So I hope you went and looked in the Cathedral?

ME
I did. And he's not there.

HE
Nej, nej. That is a Lutheran Catheral. He was a Catholic. Also he had many enemies in Sweden. They would never have allowed it for a moment.

SHE
You should have gone to the Catholic church, of course.

ME
I did. He's not there either, is he?

HE
Nej, because the Catholics thought he was a freethinker. The Vatican banned his works. Finally they had to bury him in an unconsecrated graveyard with the suicides.

ME
I can imagine in Sweden that's quite a crowded place.

SHE
Well, our weather does not suit us. Really we were born for bright skies and sun, only we don't have them here. In summer we try hard to be happy. Only in the winter do we remember how very terrible life really is.

HE
It's the same graveyard where Olaf Palme was buried. You must go there.

ME
And then I'll find Descartes' tomb?

HE
Nej, nej. They dug him up again. He was taken off to Copenhagen. In a brass coffin two and a half feet long.

ME
He was quite a lot bigger than that, surely?

HE
But most of him was missing. He had become a kind of secular saint. People had been stealing his bones.

ME
So I need to go to Copenhagen?

SHE
Yes, of course you must, it's a beautiful place. Only he is not there, of course.

ME
Quite. Of course.

SHE
The French were afraid the British would steal him, to create
a political embarrassment. So they had him dug up again and
put him in a coffin to take him to France. But when it arrived
the customs wouldn't admit it.

ME
Drugs?

HE
No, books. Atheistical books. Coffins were often used to
smuggle in contraband. But finally they let him through and
he went to the Abbaye de Saint Victoire. The freethinkers
tried to hold the new burial, but the church prevented it.

ME
And that's where he is, the Abbaye de what?

HE
No. Not at all.
(*He raises his glass, of water.*)
May I propose a toast to welcome you to Sweden. *Skal!*

SHE
Jo, jo, skal!

ME
Yes, indeed, *skal!* So – where is he now?

HE
He was dug up in the Revolution, when the abbey was
destroyed. The revolutionaries wanted to put him in the
Pantheon. Soufflot had just completed it as a state tomb for
the old regime. Now the Jacobins decided to fill it with their
heroes of reason. Mirabeau, Rousseau, Voltaire.

SHE
Maybe you remember the great procession when they moved
the corpse of Voltaire? The coffin was two storeys high. They

performed all his plays in the streets. It took over seven hours for the cortège to pass through the heart of Paris.

HE
It was meant to display the triumph of reason. Do you know in the Revolution even Notre Dame was turned into a Temple of Work and Reason?

SHE
Lenin did the same thing with the great cathedrals of Petersburg. You will be seeing them very soon, don't you know? When we make our wonderful trip to the far end of the Baltic.

ME
Good. But are you really sure Descartes is in the Pantheon? I don't remember that at all.

HE
Nej, nej. Voltaire was, yes. The ashes of Rousseau. But when Descartes got there he was rejected. Some of the Jacobins were also anti-Newtonians. They refused to let him in.

SHE
A bit like Lundkvist. One of Bo's colleagues on the Nobel Prize committee. He always refused to admit Graham Greene.

HE
Not because he was not a Newtonian, Alma.

SHE
Nej, nej. Because of all those immoral fornications.

ME
Right, so we've got Descartes being turned down for the Pantheon. What did they do with him next?

HE
They left his coffin out in the Garden of the Museum of Monuments.

SHE
Oh, see! There is also a very good pickled saltfish, if you prefer something entirely different from the herring.

ME
No, thanks. And that's where I can find him now?

HE
Nej, nej. The museum was closed down after Napoleon. So they moved him again and buried him in the Latin Quarter. The church of Saint-Germain-des-Pres.

ME
Which is where I can find him?

HE
Well, whatever is left of him. Only one or two bones. Most of him had disappeared by now. You see, each time there was a new coffin, new *pompes funèbres*, new elegies, new coats of arms. Each time they opened him up he got a little bit less. People took his bones away. After he was dug up in the Revolution, his skull was cut into tiny pieces. To put into rings and give to philosophers.

SHE
Wouldn't you love one? A piece of the famous cogito?

HE
Except be careful. They are probably not genuine. You see, there were actually two skulls of Descartes. The other was discovered right here in Stockholm, some time later.

ME
So which one was genuine?

SHE
The Stockholm one. We know it was his, because it had his name on it.

ME
Good. Then presumably I can go and see it.

SHE

Nej, nej. We sold it, for a very good profit. To the French, of course.

ME

Of course. So where is it now?

HE

In the Museum of Man in Paris. You will find Saint-Simon on one side of him, and on the other the bandit Cartouche.

SHE

So you see, even though it is very hard to be alive, it is sometimes even harder to be dead.

HE

However we should not be talking of this at all. It is completely the wrong story. I didn't ask you to come here for Descartes at all. I invited you here at our expense to be part of the Diderot Project.

ME

Yes, but I don't understand what you're intending with this Diderot project. And to tell the truth I'm beginning to like the Descartes story even better.

HE

You have no choice. As Diderot's Fatalist would say, it is already written in the Book of Providence above. You are in this story, not that one. It is already decided for you. So here are your tickets for the ferry, and your visa to enter Russia. The ferry is called the *Anna Karenina*, by the way.

ME

Good. I love a literary ferry. What will we do in Russia?

SHE

We follow the Enlightenment Trail. You remember how Denis went as a philosopher to Catherine's court?

HE

There will be eight of us altogether, by the way. Some

excellent people have agreed to take part. We meet tomorrow at two o'clock, in the Stadsgardeskajan Terminal. Just pick up a taxi from your hotel—

SHE
Oh, and don't pay too much. Swedish people are very honest, but they like to take away your money. I simply hope it is able to sail, and there isn't a very bad problem.

ME
Yes, so do I. These ferries really are safe, are they?

SHE
Of course, they are unsinkable. Nothing ever goes wrong in the Baltic.

HE
You've written a paper, I hope? We are expecting the most excellent papers.

ME
I don't think you even mentioned that when you invited me to come—

HE
You must write one. We hope to publish them in a book afterwards. I booked a conference room on the ship. You realize the Baltic is the perfect place for a seminar?

ME
Oh yes? I was hoping to see it, actually. I've always longed to sail through the great archipelago. It's beautiful, yes?

SHE
Of course, it is very beautiful. That is where is born our savage Nordic souls. I expect you will see it, through the portholes, while we are listening to the papers. In any case you are a seasoned traveller, it says so in your book. Perhaps you will sign it for me. We have all the signatures. Nabokov, Bellow, Brodsky, Morrison. You see, you are truly in Nobel company.

ME (*signing*)
I feel very honoured. Shall I put your names?

SHE
Please don't write anything else. Just your name. It will be
more valuable like that when we want to sell it.

ME
There then. So what did you mean when you said you hoped
we'd be able to sail?

HE
Oh, don't you consult your daily journal, or watch the
excellent CNN? There's an extremely serious crisis in Russia
right now—

SHE
Yeltsin dismissed the Duma. Now they are shut up in the
White House and there are tanks outside. Maybe there will be
a bloody Communist coup. Bo, you have dandruff on your
jacket again. I do hope you are not losing your beautiful hair.

ME
Oh. What do you think might happen?

HE
Maybe they will shut the border. Just as they did before, in
1917.

ME
You mean we could be shut out of Russia?

HE
Or in it, of course. That would be very much better. Then we
would have plenty of time for our project.

ME
Our project?

HE
The Diderot Project. To track down what has happened to
all our friend's books and papers after they went to the
Hermitage. You know that story, of course.

ME
The Empress bought his library, yes?

HE
Absolutely. And they still keep finding new material. Maybe
we will discover a whole new novel or something.

SHE
Or a fresh work of philosophy. Some of his love letters to his
mistress—

ME
Fine. Or maybe they'll just put us in jail.

HE
It's possible. Tell me, do you care for opera?

ME
Very much.

HE
They have it there, you know. Kirov and so on.

ME
I heard.

SHE
It will be such an adventure. Maybe you will even be able to
write a book about it. I believe you said the herring?

I have the herring, of course.

SIX (THEN)

BUT IF IN RIGA the weather has been brisk and stormy, by the time they approach the Northern Palmyra – the chill capital, the heartland city so strangely stuck out here like a painted nail on the end of a whore's frozen finger – it's colder than the very deepest hell. They've spent unending days clattering over broken, sledge-battered roads by the Baltic that seem to lead only to the polar ice-cap of the world. The speed of travel has hastened each single day. The imperial wedding is fast approaching (Archduke Paul will take Princess Wilhelmina of Hesse-Darmstadt for his lawful wedded archduchess); Narishkin, the good chamberlain, has a court reputation to maintain. By the time the splattered battered carriage rattles up to the black gates of Sankt Peterburg, tugged by shaggy Russian stage-horses, our man's feeling more dead than alive. He's iller with colic than he cares to admit, blear-eyed with sleepless nights of journey, worried about wolves and bears. His backside hurts like fury; heaven knows what's happened to his night-shirt. As for his wig, that went missing some hundred leagues back – somewhere in Europe, sunlight and the past.

The day on the true calendar is Friday, 8 October Gregorian. Here they call it something quite different. Somewhere in the lost days between two calendars his sixtieth birthday has spiralled into the void. Or perhaps the whole thing's the other way round, and he's going to be sixty twice, giving his miserable ageing a double birth. No doubt now in charming Paris it's still autumnly mild; leaves hanging yellow on the plane trees, light evening shawls for the painted ladies strolling through the Palais Royal to the opera. Not like that in Catherine's strange capital. The first winter snows are already starting to fall, the temperature is slipping, the day is so drearily downlit it looks remarkably like night.

Freezing and shivering, hacking and coughing, the Philosopher stares through the icy mud-splattered screens of Narishkin's bouncing Berliner as it trundles down the new-built granite English quay.

Trade flourishes to great effect offshore (he notes this in his notebook). High-rigged ships of the line, lumbering merchant tubs, fat barges lie roped at their moorings between the marshy islands. Rows of masts flutter their pennants at the Exchange Wharf on the far shore, Vasilyevsky Island, where European manufacture is being off-loaded on to Russian mud. Dirty loggers' barges, drifting ferries swirl about in the muddy floody Neva. This is just a wide shallow flow crossed by one rough bridge of floating pontoons – though, as stakes in the water show, other bridges are a-building. Over the water the thin spike of the Peter and Paul Fortress, where past imperial corpses lie, rises gold and glittering from the brown reeds of a wind-blown marsh.

Then, on this side, the city. A city that's been built from nothing, over the course of, out of the stuff of, his own lifetime. A new European capital, that just appeared like a mirage when no one was expecting it at all. Our Philosopher gazes: this place! He's already dreamt it, sketched it, mapped it, rebuilt it over and over. What's strangest of all is the real thing does look imaginary: everything fragile, fleeting, shifting, just like a dream. It's been planted on nowhere, except under-salinated Baltic water and Finnish fen, autumn fog and winter ice. It's shaded by chill Northern light. Everything here – idea or reality – was imported from somewhere quite different, probably devised for somewhere quite different. Its polyglot people – Scythians and Slavs, people from the fur-clad choruses of Rameau's operas, exotic foreigners of every kind – have come here from everywhere too, imported by fiat, threat, servitude, patronage, favour or inducement. Its building materials have all been carried in, log by log, stone by single stone. True, they're rebuilding Paris now, altering London, changing, they say, the face of Vienna. But this is different. This northern Palmyra has been forged from all the different fashions, torn from all the tastes: Italian, German, Dutch, French, English; romanesque, classical, oriental, baroque. Everything's mixed together, turned into opera, stage-set, travesty, pastiche. The result is nothing short of novelty. At the age of sixty, he's ended up in the world of Baltic Baroque.

They trundle on, into the heart of the new capital. Everywhere huge palaces, shining yellow, pink, blue through flaky veils of snow. Some are cracking already; some stand in Venetian fashion with their ground floors rotting to decay in swirling water; some are already sliding back into the universal mud. Many are illusions. Baronial façades are stuck on hovels, classical pediments deck the fronts of wooden sheds. Rag-wrapped workmen swarm over unfinished stucco, scramble up rocking scaffolds with half-trimmed stones. All this is rising – when it's not falling – over rough-hewn canals being edged with granite, whose water, gelid with cold, looks like damaged marble. And while this goes up, that, thanks to the divine impatience of the Tzarina, is already coming down. There has been fire and flood through the city already, and some buildings are blackened ruins. Roads are being carved, shops and warehouses rising everywhere. They're turning old wood into fresh stone, taking down huts to put up palaces, half-dismantling the not long-built Church of Saint Isaac to turn it into something other. New architects replace old, Italy remodels what Germany started, high classicism contests with fussy baroque.

Squads of thick-coated soldiers march, green-coated horse-guards ceremonially ride. The place resembles a huge military and naval barracks to which, in careless profusion, palaces, churches, academies have been wildly added. Noblemen's carriages clop through grand unfinished squares, or roll down wide new *prospekts* that run for miles in straight lines to some distant nowhere. Merchants and foreign seafarers sit talking and trading in coffee houses; paupers and beggars huddle under buildings; decorated vermilion-cheeked tarts strut through new arcades. The place booms like a workshop. Crafts, trades and manufactures prosper, as our man, son of a provincial cutler, can see with half an eye. Shoemakers tap, blacksmith forge, ropemakers weave. Huge sleds heaped with produce or vast blocks of ice are manhandled through the streets. Sheep and goats are herded along embankments; ambassador's carriages with frog-coated footmen stand outside grand buildings. Strange flaring lamp-posts, burning some kind of rank hempseed that scents the whole city.

Banners wave everywhere. To Narishkin's bouncy and braying pleasure, they have managed to arrive precisely on time. The imperial wedding will take place tomorrow, Saturday, when the Archduke Paul – the bitter neglected son of the Tzarina – will unite with his princess, one of three bright German sisters he has been granted his choice of in the usual way. Our Philosopher can take personal pleasure in the matter. This angry little bridegroom is the royal pupil his friend d'Alembert had once been summoned north to tutor, till his fear of the haemorrhoids put him off. As for the timely union of dynasties Prussian and Russian, well, every detail – the presentation of charming portraits of the three young princesses ('I'll take that one – I think,' the Grand-Duke has said, 'no, the other . . .'), the terms of the contract, the collecting up of the chosen bride-to-be from the court at Sans Souci, the delivery of her person to Sankt Peterburg all intacta – has all been managed through the matchmaking and couriering abilities of his old gossip of a friend: dear squat-faced, court-loving Melchior Grimm. Meaning that, wonderful to say, he must already be somewhere in town, taking one arm of the journey while our man has taken the other, and now waiting to meet and greet, embrace and toast him with his familiar frog-like joy.

So, as he rides on through the city, there's no way our philosopher can resist a sentimental tear or two. It's all so strange, so surprising, so fantastic; yet so exactly what he expected, a mystery of a city, polyglot, multi-cultured, a city that seems to express every fancy yet has acquired no firm shape. Having lured its citizens, its styles, its tradecraft from everywhere, planted them down in this frozen Utopia, it has allowed them to be the best or worst of whatever they are. But if this banging, clanging place is a fantastic invention, a reverie, a dream, who's the dreamer? First a tzar, of course, then a great tzarina. But others can claim some credit. Didn't he – along with d'Alembert, the thinking man's mathematician, and grand old Voltaire of Ferney – raise altars of homage here, pursuing their conviction that power and light, the electricity of reason, the bright brush of reform, would spread enlightenment downward, from the north to the south? Hasn't much of this dream been dreamt in clever critical Paris, smarting under its divine disappointing kings, witty corrupt courtiers, lawyers, priests, tax-farmers, its elderly unphilosophical God? In fact (and fair's fair) hasn't much of it been dreamt by him, sitting in his old dressing gown at a writing desk in the rue Taranne – the place he wishes, as colic stabs once more, he was sitting at right now?

So, if they're expanding Rastrelli's fine Winter Palace (it shines pinkly and wonderfully in sight now, further along the Neva bank), tying vast baroque wings together with huge display galleries and strange hanging gardens, isn't that because he, on paper, thought up much of the scheme? If these galleries are a-building because thousands of crate-loads of art, tapestries, collectables, general world-finery can't wait to be displayed, hasn't he filled hundreds of the crates? If buildings need the best architects, sculptors, carpenters, hasn't he personally interviewed and recommended most of them, not to say the mathematicians, musicians, generals, comedians and tragedians who fill their rooms each night? If the city is creating new arcades, streets, squares, didn't he sketch them? And if the whole grand plan is to be capped and crowned with a vast new statue, to be raised up high in Saint Isaac's Square . . . well, isn't that an invention sprung from his own mind too, devised amid the dusty books of his Paris study – with dear Étienne-Maurice at his side?

Falconet, Falconet! His dear, his companionable, his ever amusing, his sweet-hearted old friend! No sooner does he think of him than a fresh tear springs to his eye. He just can't wait to see him; he'll hug him, embrace him, kiss his cheeks, weep in his arms. And when they come together once more – kind master, fond pupil – he doesn't mean to ask for much: just a fabulous welcome, some herb tea, a syringe to help the colic, an ordinary bed for the night – and then all the other nights he'll be in the city till his philosophical services are done. Well, why not? Didn't he, in a sense, invent Falconet too? When that angry young man was no more than an indigent maker of small busts and sculptures for the art-salons of Paris, he chose him out, wrote him up constantly in articles, praised his works to the skies. When Catherine needed a fast-track Michelangelo, he promoted his talents – though, true enough, it helped that he offered himself cheap. And when the scale of her scheme for a grand new statue for her grand new city grew evident, it was master and pupil who sat down in his apartment and dreamt it together – the ideal triumphal figure, classical and allegorical, Big Peter the Horseman, rearing up high and mighty over the streets and waters of his fantastic city, just as he had in life.

Which reminds him. He can't wait to see the statue either; the whole vast and terrible thing must surely be nearly finished by now. The truth is, our man dearly loves statues. He seeks them out, plans them, imagines them. Didn't Plato say each human body is both a sign and a tomb? In a godless world, statues are our one ideal Posterity – what we should be aiming for, an apotheosis, a final and complete granite selfhood, created by art from the fast-shifting fluidity of our material being. They're the figure for what, in our best moments, we aspire to be: the perfect epitaph, the last tableau. Art at its highest, motion in stasis, life held in marble, biography done in bronze. To please the great Tzarina, Voltaire wrote a thousand pages of the history of Peter the Great. With our man's instinct for art's pregnant moment, Falconet's gift for know-ing the limits of tensile bronze and stone, they can do the whole thing in one shot.

So, day after day, they've together planned the ideal statue, the ultimate heroic hieroglyph. He still remembers every fine detail of the splendid plan they drew. Peter on his horse, high-rearing and betoga-ed. Around him fur-clad figures of Barbarism pay fealty to civilization and greatness. Popular Love there too, making obei-sance, naked and freely extending her arms and her charms. Beneath him, the female form of the Nation, outstretched and adoring, supine in yielding gratitude. How long ago was it? Could it be nine years? Nine years since he last saw the sculptor, and argued so wittily that the sole goal of life was Posterity (Falconet disagreeing with him as usual)? Nine years since the young man set off north in the diligence, accompanied by twenty-five articles of luggage and a pleasant, clever seventeen-year old pupil called Marie-Anne Collot, also carefully selected by him by our sage? And here they are already. Falconet's house and big wooden atelier have not been hard to find. The Tzarina has housed him within sight of her own pink Hermitage, right on grand Millionaya,

Millionaire's Row. The Berliner stops, he gets out, another spasm jabbing his inside. He claps the knocker. The door swings open . . .

. . . only to reveal that something's badly wrong. Nothing is as he's been expecting. Falconet stands there all right, stiffly holding the door. But why no grand welcome in the entrance? Why no laughter to greet him? Why no loving embrace to enfold him as he walks inside? Why no shout of filial joy from Falconet, no fond kiss-kiss-kiss from Marie-Anne? Even the long-expected, the so-much-desired bed seems not to be on offer. Falconet, standing there rigid, is grotesquely explaining that his young son has just arrived from London, where he's studying (what? Art, of course, naturally . . .), and has bagged the spare room already. It strikes our Philosopher something in his manner – an unease? a dismay? an embarrassment? a distance? – suggests the pupil is no longer delighted to see his wise master, the creation no longer feels at one with his creator. He's reminded Falconet never really was a warm man. He's temperamental, tempestuous, jealous, a man who appreciates nothing that's done for him and is quite easy to cross. Oddity. Disappointment. Rejection. Total and utter mystification.

Fortunately Narishkin's carriage waits still. Chastened if not hurt, our man makes some quick cold farewells, gathers his spirits and his cloak together, gets back in. By slippery squares and glassy embankments he trots back to Prince Narishkin's grand palace. It's nothing to be sneezed at, not even with this bad cough, in this tightening cold. More than a just reward for all the duties Narishkin has played as court clown, chamberlain, playmate, pandar, it stands in grand decorated classical nobility on the corner of the square opposite Saint Isaac's Church, only a step away from orthodox worship, just a muffled assignation away from the Hermitage, and right opposite the spot where, as it happens, the Bronze Horseman is meant to stand. Good Narishkin is, as ever, his clownish hospitable self. He offers a bedroom, in fact a choice of several tens of them, some once used by the Tzarina herself, for purposes not clear. There's a helpful bevy of servants. A comfortable much-needed commode. A hot Dutch-tiled stove, a cold thermometer, proudly announcing a temperature well below freezing. Family portraits, of boyars with unbelievable hats and no less impossible beards. All a good man might need for the rest of his stay, however

71

short or long it might prove to be. He's here at last, in the chilly city. He's comfortable. He's cosy. He's tired. He's hurting. He's hurt. Yes, it's definitely time for sleep . . .

. . . to wake next day to the world's noisiest morning ever. The horns of the city watchmen are sounding, the bells of the church in the square exploding with sound. Within minutes cannons are blasting, bells ringing over the city of strange invention. Below the window, trumpets flare, kettledrums snarl, lines of imperial horse-guards trot with a clumping of hooves. He rises at once and goes to the balcony, still in his nightcap and shirt. Lines of soldiers march, the fountains are spurting wine. Parades of big-bearded priests strut past, and black-robed monks are swinging on the bell-clappers of all the onion-topped monasteries and churches. Beyond is the Neva, where galleys, yachts and merchantmen are flying their bunting and firing their pieces. From all directions, kings, queens, ambassadors and princelings from every state, duchy and margravate throughout Europe trot in their caparisoned carriages in the direction of the Cathedral to celebrate the great and sonorous nuptials.

Alas, despite that frantic rush and rattle of their journey, it seems neither he nor Narishkin will be attending the great and world-shaking ceremony after all. Narishkin has severe toothache, not to say the everlasting trots. As for our man, he simply lacks the clothes for it. His trunks, explain the servants, have been impounded for further inspection by the intrusive officers from the Custom House. In any case, he is utterly wigless. All that remains is to watch the ceremony with his host from his fine balcony, right over Saint Isaac's square. And why not? Nothing could be better placed. The city is all there, spread out in view. Wedding bells ring, fireworks rattle, cannons explode, crowds cheer and wave. In due time the processions return, heading for the Hermitage. And here, surrounded by a battalion of the troops from the loyal Preobrazhensky guard, are the happy couple, riding in a carriage like a little castle . . .

Inside the coach sits the grim, prim young Archduke Paul Petrovitch, all pug-nosed and skull faced. This is the bitter neglected heir who will – when this fine ceremonial day turns into another, when state wedding becomes state funeral – confront the

72

corpse of his imperial mother with the exhumed body of his murdered father (if, that is, his father really is his father, which most people including his mother would deny). Then in his turn he will be hailed as the new Tzar, crowned and fêted in the two Russian capitals. Then, four years further on still, he will be carefully strangled by his own courtiers, outraged by his excesses; many of them are riding beside him now. Next to him in the coach sits his German bride, radiant. She will take only a few years more to die in childbirth, as she seeks to deliver an infant that is most unlikely to be his. Then she will be replaced by one of her own sisters, rejected this time round.

The procession rolls on toward the Neva. Riding in the coach behind the happy nuptial couple, our man sees the one person who is so efficiently capable of making such past, present and future fortunes and misfortunes happen. This is none other than his own dear and powder-cheeked friend, the fastidious match-maker Melchior Grimm. Considering all these things, Our Philosopher reflects they're all no more than a wise man might expect. For, as he understands it, the life, pomp and motion of our passing days is just a form of stasis, one manifestation in some much larger and longer fatality which is probably already inscribed in some code or text or other. Maybe they are in the rituals of history, maybe they're deep in the dynastic spirals of genes and tissue, maybe in the laws of chaos, chance and randomness, most likely in the great Book of Destiny, which is already written or in the process of being written somewhere up there in heaven above.

Which at once reminds our man; it must be writing time. As noise explodes, the celebrations grow, bells boom, noble crowds swarm toward the pink Hermitage, he finds a desk in a quiet corner, discovers a working quill and well. Not since he left the elegant if bombarded (Frederick of Prussia again) streets of Dresden has he had the time to write his postcards home. He scribbles away in pleasure, first to his spiky wife and dancing daughter, whose baby is expected soon. *C'est moi*, he announces proudly, I have arrived. Believe it or not, I'm in the right city. Throat so far uncut, but feeling more dead than alive. Most of my things are with me, apart from a nightshirt and my favourite wig. He reports in detail on his bowels, he admits his hacking cough. He offers them a

73

promise: tempted as he might be to travel onward to the Great Wall of China, he'll return as soon as he can by the quickest route he can, the moment his philosophical duty (creating a new Russia) is through. Thoughtfully, he adds some advice to his wife on the management of her extremely uncertain temper ('Shift everything round at home, then unshift it, and shift it again, and everything will come out fine'). And then he recounts the bitter tale of the ingrate Falconet – whose welcome has been so icy, whose gratitude so hard to find. What could have happened to the fellow? What's wrong? Thanks to him, I could by now be a ragged beggar, freezing to death in a Scythian snowdrift.

Utterly delighted he'll have created a gossiping frenzy of indignation and gossip all over Paris, he picks up a second sheet. And so he sets down another letter, more reflective, intelligent, rebuking, mercurial, for this one's to his charming, his philosophical, his not always enthusiastic mistress Sophie. He tells his adventures, reflecting as philosophers have to on the dying of passions and the weariness of age. He tells of his hopes, his dreams. He signs off lovingly, to her, her sisters, her interfering mother. Much later, as the music and human noise of a grand mêlée resounds from the nearby Hermitage, he eats a beetroot dinner at Narishkin's fine table. There is a great crackle and blast of evening fireworks as he goes upstairs to his bedroom. Cannons from the warships anchored in the Neva volley out over the city as he lies down in his cold and comfortable Russian bed.

SEVEN (NOW)

NORDIC GLOOM. Middle-of-the-night, end-of-the-boat-pier, screaming-in-your-face, pure state-of-the-art Nordic gloom.

. . . I suppose it really begins to begin in that art nouveau bohemian café near Stockholm's Royal Dramatic Theatre, as Bo, his bright Snow Queen and I reach the close of our fishy and totally teetotal meal. By now the time's nearly eight-thirty, and beyond the café windows the great Nordic capital is already falling silent. The dour black-suited waiters who've been seriously shunning us all evening have suddenly grown full of energy. They wipe down the nearest tables in a frenzy, lean heavily across us to close and bolt the shutters. Then, over coffee, coffee-less coffee of course ('We are careful never to take strong things in the evenings . . .'), as Bo begins to unbutton his little leather purse and carefully count his way through the copper and paper contents ('No, do let me . . .,' '*Nej, nej*, of course we will treat you, you are a most honoured guest from afar . . .' 'What lovely herring . . .'), I learn that these two cunning Lunebergs have all the time been squirrelling away a secret from me. In some fit of Nordic communion they've silently concluded that all's not yet concluded, that this cold autumn night has but scarcely begun. Quite appreciating (Alma leans over the table to tell me) how intensely my life has been dedicated to new and dangerous art, how committed I am to the most illicit transgressions of the postmodern imagination, they wish to make a bold suggestion. Would I care for them to take me into . . . the danger zone?

I know exactly what this means. Of course I know all about Sweden's puritanical permissiveness. Still, why not? Already I can see those oiled naked bodies, the healthy Nordic frankness, the glut of glistening firm bronzed blond frames. Except, as it turns

75

out, not quite. Stockholm's hottest ticket in town proves to be a concert by a bunch of student musicians in the *Aula* of the University. Here I can encounter the work of a new generation of Nordic composers: wild postmodern conceptualists who have determined minimalism has grown far too bulky, random improvization far too regimented. Tonight at nine they mean to go probing further, to the wildest shores of silence.

'We knew you would want to go, of course,' says Alma.

'Unless perhaps your Cartesian dilemma has made you just a little bit sleepy?' asks Bo, with the air of a playful joker.

I say yes, of course — yes is what I nearly always say. To be honest, I should have known better. Years of wandering the frontiers of the transgressive postmodern imagination have taught me what its key words mean. 'Conceptual' means: we haven't thought about it much, but we're cool, we'll stay cool, and something will happen to which we can add the name of art. 'Postmodern' means: guess what, we managed to get a corporate sponsor to pay for it.

Which is why you find me, half an hour later, sitting on a hard wooden bench in a vast panelled academic hall. Given the avant-garde occasion, the audience is not quite what I would expect. It consists almost entirely of very elderly gentlemen with dark black suits, neat white beards, small state decorations in their buttonholes, and severe elderly ladies with corsages in their handsome but definitely period frontages. I shake frozen hands with a Doctor Gregorius This. I chat with a zimmer-framed Professor That. I am mostly invited to express my love of Grieg and Sibelius, though some daring soul speaks of Stockhausen. I stare up above at portraits of yet older professors and thinkers: wigged botanists, perukified classicists, grim black–clad Lutheran theologians who must have been hanging there on these academic walls for an eternity or longer. Then a small orchestra of pubescents, in evening dress, white student caps over their blonde crops, file on to the stage, bearing the usual array of musical instruments. An equally pubescent conductor makes a Swedish microphone announcement.

'He explains this is a people's creation. They have composed this work all of them together,' murmurs Alma into my ear.

'Fine,' I whisper.

'He says it is entirely conceptual and influenced by the nihilism of Kierkegaard,' says Bo into my second ear. 'The young are so clever, you must admit.'

'I certainly do,' I say.

Silence falls; the first item commences. Holding tightly on to their instruments, our orchestra of tinies sits onstage in total silence. From Alma's whispers, I learn that for conceptual reasons they mean to remain like this for as long as it takes for something random to happen. What? Well, maybe someone's mobile phone will go off. I nod. It's wonderful. I nod again. And again. Then – whether it's due to a long day of travelling or an excess of Baltic herring I don't know – at a point ten minutes or so into this adventure I nod right off, into the blessed universe of sleep. For a while vague images of blonde bronzed northern frames strangely run through my slipping mind. Then some comfortable, morphine bourgeois peace overwhelms me. When I awake, to the sound of sudden applause, I can no longer recall where I am (Arizona, perhaps?), or who I am (not me, surely?). Nor do I know what has brought the awesome artistic silence to an end. But my own loud snores do have to be a serious possibility.

Now I know. I do know. There can be no excuse. This is just no way for an honoured foreign guest, guaranteed totally *alkoholfri*, to behave. It is our duty to be open at all hours to the cutting edge of art. We should all respect the seriousness of the avant-garde, even if it has been hanging around for ever, and honour the fresh creative impulses of the young, the radical and the new. Yes, it's bad. It's a cultural sin. Quite unforgivable. Yet nothing in the world could exceed the spirit of unspoken moral outrage which, at the interval, suddenly sweeps me out of the hall and into the foyer ('Professor Erno Tikvist from the Nobel committee wanted so much to meet you, but clearly that will not now be possible'), and then fills the air-freshener-perfumed interior of the Lunebergs' long, leathery and very informative Volvo ('No smoking, no food, fasten seat belt, side impact bars, do not interfere in any way with the efforts of the driver') as they drive me coldly back to my hotel through Stockholm's silent, sober and no less rebuking streets. Bo is in the grimmest of moods, Alma even more the Snow Queen, as they decant me on the sidewalk outside the unlit lobby of my slumbering hotel.

'Now you have had such a good sleep, I think you will be able to stay up all night, and write your paper for the Diderot Project,' is Alma's parting shot as – with many warning signals, and much flashing of the red and orange safety lights plastered on each surface of the car – they drive off, considerately, into Stockholm's dark and chilly night.

I try to enter my night-lodgings, which have lost their spirit of gracious hospitality and are now completely shuttered and barred. A little random sleet is now falling, a police car patrols critically around the other side of the square. It takes me ten minutes of nervous bell-buzzing before a pyjama-ed night clerk appears (but it is ten-thirty already) and ungraciously grants me the loan of my own room-key, warning me that I may already have forfeited my right to order breakfast. I mount the back stairs – the lift is considerately switched off at this late hour – and find the way to my neat little bedroom.

'Try our elite Sex Channel!!' screams a card atop the small TV set. 'Fabulous girls! Erotic Adventures!! Brand New Positions!!! Please keep the sound low and try not to disturb your neighbour.'

Sitting on the bed, I click the channel changer, surfing past blonde, bronzed frames, booby, brandished breasts, deep-furrowed buttocks, splayed limbs, erectile tissue, micro-camera trips through inner body tubing, an improbable cavorting of mass human and animal entanglements, in search of something that really turns me on.

Then there it is at last: the real world. In a snowy square in a squat, grey, towered city, a grey-green tank elevates and lowers its gun-barrel. Finally it takes aim on a great white public building by the river, constructed according to the highest principles of Stalinesque bad taste. In the tank-hole sits an ear-flapped driver and a fur-capped captain; the tank itself looks both dangerous and decrepit. *Cameras cut:* to a wide urban boulevard: a parade of thick-coated peasants in various forms of remarkable headwear marches boldly onward, ever onward, holding high a very old red flag. They're setting buses on fire, building barricades in the wide streets. Fabulous histories! Military adventures!! Brand New Ideol-

78

ogies!!! I sit on the bed and watch, in a state of truly shameful excitement. Though the commentator's voice is Swedish, it is not hard to appreciate what is going on. *Cut to:* the interior of the Duma; the deputies banging their desks; speeches by Yeltsin's recent vice president, Alexander Rutskoi, and Ruslan Khasbulatov, the black-shirted and ambitious speaker of the parliament, who had been Yeltsin's aides in resisting the last coup, against Gorbachev. I know them well enough. For weeks they and their supporters in the Duma have been out-manoeuvring Yeltsin and his crony oligarchic government, in a great game of Russian political chess. In the last days he has reacted by trying to dissolve the parliament. They have replied by trying to dissolve the president.

Now, evidently, the end game has begun. The Duma is no longer speaking in defence of parliamentary democracy: an ancient Russian package of nationalism, militarism, celebration of the glorious KGB and a return to the discipline of the Gulags is on offer again. A mixed, menacing band of soldiers and other armed men, a sudden army, is now strutting about the White House, and piles of automatic rifles are stacked for use. *Cut to:* Man in Lenin-like posture shouting into a megaphone from Lenin's tomb in Red Square. *Cut to:* Tzar Boris, beaming strangely, and moving with that slow stately step that suggests he first learned to walk at some state funeral, as he passes through the grand rooms of the Kremlin. *Cut to:* several Russian experts in a Moscow studio, all wearing entire chestfuls of ancient military medals, and apparently explaining that this time Yeltsin has miscalculated disastrously. *Cut to:* blazered American ex-Secretaries of State in a Washington studio, telling us the New World Order that began when the Berlin Wall came down and Russia collapsed is finally over. Time to get ready; we're returning to the Old World, Cold World Order again.

It's all chaos, noisy confusion. History generally is. Yet from the confusion I grasp one sure and certain thing. To be quite frank, I have no real idea of what Bo Luneberg's much-discussed Diderot Project is; many intellectual projects tend to end up like this. All I've grasped is that it involves a sponsored journey of homage to the life of a delightful writer-philosopher whose work I know and love, a free ferry-trip to the city of Saint Petersburg

(Pushkin's famous 'shattered fragment of wanton power', Gogol's 'cloudy city' made out of straight lines, Anna Akhmatova's 'phantasmagora'), a visit to the glorious Hermitage and the library of the great Tzarina, a long serious look along the Nevsky Prospekt: in short, a solemn pilgrimage down the Enlightenment Trail to one of its prime sites. And I'm here because it is an enlightened intellectual project, because our admirable Bo can be — when he wishes — a wonderfully persuasive and learned fellow, and because I am, as I said earlier, one of those people who says yes to everything. But whatever our project is, one thing has surely now become luminously clear. This just ain't going to happen. The chaos of history is busy, far too real and present, for that sort of high-minded academic junketing. Whatever our foray to the lost world of Russian Enlightenment was out to achieve, the great laws of reason tell me it's definitely going to be cancelled.

And sad as that may be for the advancement of learning, right now this feels perfectly all right by me. I'm feeling tired, really tired, completely worn out by the events of the day — the early-morning check-in at postmodern Stansted, the briny Stockholm air, the visit to the Vasa, the long and wearying quest for Descartes, the herring dinner in the midst of an *alkoholfri* bohemia, the silent Kierkegaardian postmodern concert. I'm soaked in shame over my earlier somnolence; now I just want to sleep without sin. I'm far too drained to write an academic paper, on a subject and for some seminar occasion whose membership and purpose no one has properly explained to me. In minutes I'm undressed and safe under a vast Nordic duvet as big as a classic Amsterdam whore. Stockholm lies as enigmatically silent as a postmodern concert beyond the triple-glazed windows. In minutes more, the television set still flickering, I'm deeply, gratefully asleep. And this time without any orchestral accompaniment at all.

Morning. Here I am again. And this particular new morning announces itself with a clanging of trams, a bonging of public bells, a buzzing of planes, a honking of ships' sirens resounding from some harbour not too far away. Plainly I'm in a foreign city. Through thin pastel blinds of a tasteful design, a faint and far from confident sun is trying to shine in and awake me, with not very much success. I am, after all, a well-known slugabed. I draw myself out of the usually reassuring world of sleep and into the far from reassuring one of regular daily consciousness. My dreams overnight have not been benign. Indeed, as I recall their traces, they've been truly terrible. There have been drowned corpses, huge ship-like churches with bleeding saints, silver coffins, skulls carved by glittering knives into the most mysterious shapes. There are soldiers in corridors, gun-barrels lifting into the air. I must presume conscience is paining me, and I wake anxious, guilty, sensing I've done something wrong. Have I? Of course I have, for God's sake. Last night I slept in public in the presence of advanced creative art.

Right, so just remind me: where am I then? Stockholm, Sweden's fine watery capital. When? Early October 1993. Why? I'm travelling on the Enlightenment Pilgrimage . . . A noise disturbs me. Across the room, the TV set I've fallen asleep in front of still flickers; and I see at once that history has gone on being busy in my absence. I find the remote, flip up the sound, try to discover what's been happening. The voices stay confusingly Swedish, but it's quite clear things in Moscow have not improved. Tzar Yeltsin – there he is, a strange drunken doll-shaped automaton – has departed imperiously for his dacha outside the city, though not, it seems, before cutting off all heat, light, telephones and refreshments to the White House and leaving it in a state of siege. The deputies – there they all are – have slept on benches, lain huddled in sweaters. Bands of armed mercenaries and police guards stand waiting in every corridor, anticipating the great night-time attack. Priests, communists, old believers and eagle-waving monarchists have gathered protectively around the building. 'A terrible war is coming,' Khasbulatov has promised them.

Now, as dawn comes to the barricaded, blocked-off White House, the legislators and soldiers are rising, feisty, ripe for action, gathering round microphones, intoning baritonal songs about freedom and glory, reading patriotic poems, announcing their wish to carry revolt through to a splendid and bloodstained end. The street parades – there they are – have multiplied, in scale, vehemence, rage, violence, zealotry. Down the street the red hammer-and-sickled banners of the old Russian communism march proudly this way, trying to call back the past. Up the street the red-blue-and-white banners of the CRS march just as proudly that way, trying to figure out the future. Here again come the Washington gurus, announcing in English that Yeltsin's days are numbered, the free market era is over, and all sensible investors should start buying stock in Star Wars again.

So. I climb out of bed and walk over to the window ('WARN-ING. Do not open. This window is for your viewing convenience only'). Here in the moral kingdom there seems not a great deal to worry about. Beyond the reassuring triple-glazing, the ordinary life of a delightful, solid and wealthy bourgeois city is under way. Across the courtyard, in the window of a pleasant grey apartment block, a small girl practises the cello, as every decent small girl should. In another a short-haired small boy boots up his personal computer, and will no doubt soon be hacking into the Nikkei Index. Maids in neat black dresses dust perfectly clean windows. Gardeners in blue suits brush up perfectly neat lawns. I head for the neat sweet-smelling bathroom. I take a shower, reusing yester-day's soaking towels to announce my most sincere respect for Sweden's beautiful lakes and seas. By the time I'm done, a forbidding maid has come in with continental breakfast. It sits waiting for me on the table: rich coffee, steaming rolls, bacterially-active yoghurts, free-range salamis, bilberry juice. A note tells me that this is all organic produce, and all the animals involved were wonderfully happy until shortly before I chose to consume them.

As big bear-like history rumbles on at the Baltic's still distant other end, I sip my coffee, eat the animals, work out my own tinier, more tediously human plans. These involve changing my air-ticket, phoning my family to warn them their happy respite is over, packing, finding a taxi, heading for Arlanda and home. Plainly, no one possessed of logic and reason would be heading for Russia at this moment. But a scholar is a scholar, academic duty a serious matter. So first I pick up the telephone, dial 9, and call the Technological University to secure Bo's personal confirmation that the Enlightenment Project has gone onto hold. The person I talk to is not our professor himself but one of his fluent and friendly secretaries. She tells me that (even while I've been waking, showering, snacking) the good professor has already been in, taught two classes, failed an incompetent student, marked a heap of essays and returned them, answered his correspondence, examined a doctoral thesis on Swedenborg, spread several false rumours to the press about the Nobel Prize, picked up his umbrella and gone off again. No one in the office seems to be quite sure whither, but gossip says that his steps lead eastward, and probably to Russia. No one is any surer when or if he will be back – though he is advertised in the corridor to deliver an important public lecture on the matter of the diphthong in just over two weeks' time.

What does it mean? Could the Diderot Project truly be happening after all? Putting departure plans on temporary hold, I wander off into lovely Stockholm. The weather still stays nicely warm for the season; we may all expect a pleasant, crisp, sunny day. I do a little domestic shopping, and pick up a few high-priced Nordic artefacts to show *frau* and *kinder* I really have been away, and not just hiding in the attic upstairs. I go down to the waterfront, to inspect the busy ferry traffic. I watch the men play chess, and let my thoughts rove wantonly. For literary purposes, I revisit the food market: cold herring, non-alcoholic beer, leggy girls. I return to my hotel to check on my messages and then check out. There are no messages; no word has come from the battalions of the Enlightenment. I shall simply have to assume that, despite the bloody collapse of the state, the coming of a terrible war, and other such local difficulties, our Diderot trip to Russia is on after all. I summon a taxi, put my luggage into it, and ask for the ferry harbour. The driver of the Volvo ('No smoking. No eating. Fasten seat belt. This driver never carries any change'), a voluble Turk, tells me that, even in this land of liberal decency, he and his kind are illiberally called 'blacktops', and constantly urged to go back to where they came from. This does not deter him from charging me a truly Swedish fare.

I unload my luggage into the middle of a drab, noisy, crowded, arc-lit concrete plain. The Stadsgardeskajan terminal is a thriving commercial madhouse. Freight-wagons shunt, huge refrigerated trucks fume, sea-gulls scream, seeking a passage to the distant sea. Cranes heave, vast orange containers swing high above me, sheds of warehouses ingest and disgorge. Vodka from Novgorod and Ikea chairs from the Upplands meet sound-systems from Korea

83

and hashish from Pakistan. The sea stinks vigorously of oil. Along the dockside, beyond the terminal buildings, stand the Baltic ferries: vast floating hotels, each one lit up like Christmas, huge metal jaws jammed wide open to consume the long lines of cars, buses and container trucks waiting in rows on the concrete. Foot passengers swarm from buses and taxis and head for the wooden terminals. Helsinki, Tallinn, Riga, say the signboards. Walking under the arc lights, I look for the Russian ferries. I doubt they will be sailing; and yet, it seems, they are. At the entrance of the terminal shed is a big destination board: SANKT PETERBURG, it confidently declares. And beyond the customs shed a huge white ferry lies at the dock, pulsing away at its moorings, all ready for afternoon boarding. Only one problem. That's not the right ship, the *Anna Karenina*. It's an older, sharper, more aggressive sister vessel, the *Vladimir Ilich*.

And it's now it really comes. Gloom, I mean: pure, deep-in-the-forest-on-All-Fool's-Night Nordic gloom. But let me explain to you (as they so love to say in Sweden) the reason for my sensations of utter despair . . .

As I think I said already, I'm a writer: in other words, the sort of person who, by nature, love, vocation, motivation, prefers writing to doing, meditation to action, fiction to history, dreams to the world. For – let's admit it – fiction is infinitely preferable to real life, which is a pretty feeble fiction anyway. As long as you avoid the books of Kafka or Beckett, the everlasting plot of fiction has fewer futile experiences, dull passages, worthless days, useless contingencies than the careless plot of reality written in Destiny's book above. Fiction's people are fuller, deeper, cleverer, more moving than those in real life. Its actions are more intricate, illuminating, noble, profound. There are many more dramas, climaxes, romantic fulfilments, twists, turns, gratified resolutions. Unlike reality or for that matter history, all of this you can experience without leaving the house or even getting out of bed. What's more, books are a form of intelligent human greatness, as stories are a higher order of sense. As random life is to destiny, so stories are to great authors – who (despite modern theory) really exist, and provided us with some of the highest pleasures and the most wonderful mystifications we can find.

And few stories are greater than *Anna Karenina*, that wise epic book by an often foolish author. For, as Lev Tolstoy told us himself, history is a deaf man who answers questions nobody wished to ask in the first place. As he also said, history – the Napoleonic stuff, leaders, generals, great conflicts, revolutions and grand destinies – isn't true history at all. That's lived in the heart and home, in happy and unhappy families, among the trivialities and the dull domestic detail. In the end it is lived only in the self, the only place where anything's really ever lived. Yes, Tolstoy was an annoying old prophet, who died in his eighties at an obscure railway station, following the fate of his most famous character, as if that too were written in the Book of Destiny above. It's because the perverse old man was so right, and modern history feels so wrong, that I'm here in the first place. For several weeks I've been looking forward to sailing the seas on the *Anna Karenina*, along with the great quadrille: Levin and Kitty, Anna and Vronsky. When Bo Luneberg summoned me wet from my English bath with his mysterious telephone invitation to join his Diderot pilgrims, it was the name of the boat we'd sail on that made me say 'Yes.' (Even though I often do, as I rather think I said.)

Yet now, instead of sailing in the grand presence of fiction, I'm fated to sail aboard history: grim Mr History himself. Vladimir Ilich! The man who for our dying century made the whole notion of history so undesirable, made it not just unattractive but unwise even to get out of bed. I can see his sharp face now, up there on a bronze plaque just below the bridge of this smoking white ferry. There are the foxy features, beard thrust out arrogantly, one arm thrown out in the famous pose, pointing the way to the triumph of history he means to soak in as much sacrificial blood as possible. This man was once a musician, a man who read books and wrote them, till the dream consumed him. Riding his closed freight train to Petersburg's Finland Station, he felt that History was dawning, and nothing now could wait. He became prophet of turmoil, a Robespierre to Rousseau, a Danton to Diderot. He turned reason to passion, reform into revolution, progress into pogrom, betterment into bloodbath. Before long he was grand high executioner:

hangman to the kulaks, murderer to the gentry. Politics, he explained, was simply the art of banging people over the head.

True, he had very little time. The brain in his head was rotting from within. When he died in the house at Gorky, they cut out the precious cerebellum, to study the biology of his genius and compare it with all the great brains in pickle. The surgeons who examined it discovered the truth (the great thinking machine was rotting), but did not dare tell it. That was the greatest poisoned chalice: Lenin's rotting brain. He was god for a generation; the folklore celebrated his super-human triumphs, his strange charisma. It was said he could perform miracles, save lives by touch, had a golden arm. His enemies were everyone's enemies; by definition, those who survived were friends. But for several years now it's seemed his day was over. We belong – at least till these last few days we thought we did – not to the Age of History but of the End of History. Ours is no longer a time of ideology; in fact it's the Age of Shopping. Politics have turned into lifestyle, Star Wars to Nintendo, history into retro. For years the statues have kept tumbling, one by one. Iron Feliks, Feliks Dzershinsky, the man in the big dark overcoat, was winched from his perch outside the Lubyanka and sent to the scrapheap where he consigned so many; may he never come back. Vladimir's tricky big-booted secretary, Stalin, lies broken stone and metal in weedpiles outside a hundred cities, dismantling, deconstructing, defacing.

So how does Ilich – perhaps the man of our century I dislike most, though for some reason his bust still stands on my British mantelpiece – survive? His face still stares off the rouble. His brain, cut into little strips, went adrift in the medical laboratories, but his waxen body still lies saint-like in the tomb in the Kremlin Wall he never wished to occupy (save for three weeks every summer, when he goes to the country for rest and rewaxification). Teams of embalmers sustain the holy relic, which many think still alive; eight assassination attempts have been made on the waxen corpse. True, Vladimir's Kremlin statue is already back in Gorky – and, if Tzar Yeltsin survives the next few days, Lenin's waxwork Posterity could soon be facing meltdown. The city he gave his name to (the city it seems I will be visiting shortly) he came to reject and punish, starving its people. He moved the capital back to Moscow, leaving Leningrad to sag on its watery Baltic foundations. No wonder its people voted to take back the name old big-boot Peter ('What is dat?') gave it two centuries ago.

Which is why once more it says SANKT PETERBURG here on the Stockholm ferry pier — just as it must have in the tzarry days before 1914. And yet somehow Vladimir Ilich, Lenin, is firmly with us still: his name on the bow, his mask on the bridge, casting his foxy, fierce political gaze over the Baltic travellers as he must have done through all the years since. I can't really think he likes what he sees. I've toted my luggage into the wooden terminal now. The place is packed, the crowd pushing forward, shouting, heaving cases, waving tickets, flourishing passports. And this crowd is a crowd from the End of History: no doubt about it. First comers are the Japanese, led by a guide holding high a yellow flowered umbrella. They arrive in a line, dressed in black and white, each with a little Lycra backpack, rolling wheelie coffin-suitcases across the rubber flooring with the noise of a regiment of tanks. They pause, photograph the universe, then move on. Next come the Germans, executive-class, huge-bodied, very present; their hair blow-dried, their socks of silk, their shoes of crocodile leather. New Deutschmark adventurers, they are plainly looking for the new opening to the east. You can easily tell them from the Swedish businessmen — who are quieter, shyer souls, smaller-boned and bodied, with lighter briefcases, thinner shirts, plainer shoes, lesser ambitions, commercial fingers half-burned before they start. The Americans, of the usual backpacking kind you find every-where, trekking through the galaxy, carrying their rough guides, baseball caps on backwards as if this way were just the same as that, listening to native hiphop through earphones plugged into their mastoid bones. A group of grey-haired American widows, all dressed like golfers, cruising the world for eternity, happy to be free of matrimony at last.

Last — Lenin watches in total incredulity — come the new big spenders: the Russians themselves, ever criss-crossing the Baltic on an unending buying spree. They're late, of course; when you're out of Russia every economic moment counts. Like the great Tzarina, they will purchase anything just because it exists — though for them the rule is the pinker the better. Toted on their shoulders, as after some massive adventure in rape and pillage, are all of the following: electric guitars with western plugs; boxes of soap; automatic sewing machines; Black and Decker garden strimmers; huge table lamps with art nouveau shades; electronic keyboards; whole cartons of jars of instant coffee; huge cardboard crates of Wash and Go; AIWA CD players; Barbie dolls in their booby American sex-uniforms; large dinosaurs from Jurassic Park; pocket calculators; bleepers; fax machines; electric mowers for imaginary lawns. They wear a trophy piece of everything: pink designer sunglasses, some with the labels still dangling; brand-new trainers from Adidas and Nike; baseball jackets celebrating American teams; big baggy Bermuda shorts. They've triumphantly plundered Benetton T-shirts, Gucci loafers, Vuitton-style handbags, Pierre Cardin-resembling shirts. Lenin stares blankly over their heads – surely hoping for some even more future future, where none of these things could be happening. Formalities to board are starting. We're all jostling aggressively forward, talking, shouting, moving toward whatever lies ahead: customs, passports, immigrant, history, Lenin himself.

But what can have happened to Bo? I look back over the tumult of moving heads, uncertain whether to board or no. Suddenly there he is, entering the terminal at his usual slow, affable professorial ramble. He's carrying his small umbrella, sporting his Burberry jacket, looking round with his kind academic smile. Behind him comes icy Alma, in a large suede coat and a fur hat like a rabbit, evidently clad like Lara for the Russian winter. She seems to be a beast of burden, for her arms are filled with cardboard boxes and a stack of files. Luneberg walks along the line of jostling passengers on the further side of the metal railing. He halts, unfolds and holds up a large handwritten sign. DIDEROT PROJECT, it says, and it works wonders. From here and there in the pushing crowd, a small group of devotees begins to detach itself, waving, gesturing, struggling through to reach him. I am one of them, of course.

Luneberg dismantles the railing and allows us to join him, greeting his small flock of philosophical pilgrims one by one. Meanwhile Alma has opened her cardboard boxes to reveal the familiar goodies of an academic congress: plastic wallets, name-tags for our lapels. Then she hands out little treats: tickets for shipboard meals, entrance tickets for the Hermitage, tickets for our cabins. I look around the party: nine of us. Each single one seems to know Luneberg perfectly well (but then we know he knows everyone); none of us seems to know any other. Who are we all then? How did we come to be here? What are we all doing? What is this about? Luneberg, affable as ever, shows no sign of any explanation. Nor does he perform the usual social offices. It's down to us to introduce ourselves to ourselves, inspecting each other's name-tags, offering small self-announcements and handshakes.

Who's here, then? First, there's Anders Manders. Finely trimmed blond beard, freckled skin, firm face, eyes of a limpid blue. He is, he explains, a Swedish diplomat who was once a counsellor in the Leningrad embassy. Sven Sonnenburg: thin-faced, must be in his forties, dressed in faded denim overalls. He shyly explains that he's a carpenter who specializes in the making of tables. Birgitta Lindhorst: big, red-haired, busty, early forties, quite wonderfully dressed. She, it turns out, is not just personally but professionally huge. For she's a diva, an international soprano who has just been singing in *Eugene Onegin* at the Stockholm Drottningholm Theatre in the course of a world tour. Agnes Falkman, tall, Nordic, beautiful, with a blonde chignon. Also in denim overalls, though hers are of the designer kind, plastered too with all the usual messages of concerned protest – against air, water, earth, fire, food, smoking, cars, cattle, men. She works for the Swedish trades union movement, which, as everyone knows, runs the country. Then a guest from America – Jack-Paul Verso, in Calvin Klein jeans, Armani jacket, and a designer baseball cap saying I LOVE DECONSTRUCTION. I know his type at once: he's a funky professor. In fact he's Professor of Contemporary Thinking at Cornell, author of that well-known book *The Feminists' Wittgenstein*. I've met him before, heard him lecture at some Californian conference or other, talked to him at some punch-drunk Gay and Lesbian Cash Bar in the hotel foyer. He's trouble, the American academic high-flyer type, intellectual adrenalin personified, always push-push-pushing to be where it's all at. And then, finally, there's Lars Person. He says he's a dramaturge from the Swedish National Theatre; he has a big white face, a saturnine black beard, a bohemian's floppy blue hat.

A very mixed salad of people to be interested in Denis Diderot, I murmur to Verso – who just happens to be standing beside me.

'Oh, come on now,' he says, 'that guy was interested in every who, which, why, what and however that ever existed or might exist in the world. We're just the kind of crew he might have expected. You know, I only have one little problem with all of this. Just what the hell is the Diderot Project?'

'You don't know?' asks Agnes Falkman.

'I sure don't.'

'Does anyone know?' asks Birgitta Lindhorst.

'I imagine you are not asking me,' says Anders Manders diplomatically.

'Something to do with furniture,' says Sven Sonnenberg.

'I don't think so, it's about theatre,' says Lars Person.

'Hey, Bo, come on, explain,' says Verso. 'Just what the hell is this Diderot Project?'

'In a few days' time, when we are all having interesting experiences in Russia, all you wish to know will be fully revealed,' says Bo.

'And then I know you will agree we have devised a very interesting adventure for you,' says Alma.

'Great,' says Jack-Paul Verso.

'Just tell me, please, who in the hell was Diderot?' asks Birgitta the Swedish Nightingale, turning to us all.

'He was a philosopher of the so-called Enlightenment,' says Verso.

'A writer of stories,' I say.

'Also a playwright,' says Lars Person.

'Did he like women?' asks Agnes Falkman.

'Oh, sure, he definitely liked women,' says Verso.

'And tables?' asks Sven Sonnenberg.

'He kinda liked tables too,' says Verso.

'What about music?' asks Birgitta.

'He was completely fascinated by music. He wrote a whole book about the nephew of the composer Rameau.'

'Jean-Philippe Rameau, the inventor of modern harmony?' asks the nightingale. 'Rameau who made operas about the winds and the torrents and the spheres?'

'That Rameau. But the book's about his clownish nephew, who's the classic confidence man.'

'Excuse me, I hope you're all realizing that our leader Bo has gone on board already,' remarks Lars Person.

And so he has. Our leader strides on ahead of us, through tickets and customs, passports and immigration: Diderot sign held high over his head, Alma with her boxes in frantic pursuit. At the formidable sight of his professorial demeanour, all officialdom seems to melt away; his path is smooth. An uncertain rabble of international pilgrims, we heft our luggage and follow, off and away on the Enlightenment Trail. We march through the halls of the dusty terminal, out on to the quayside, smelling of ship's oil. We climb up the ship's loading gangway, heading for the open port. Ahead of us go the Japanese, pulling their wheelie coffins, the Germans, swinging their contract-packed briefcases, and the crowd of Russians. All loaded with their trophies of the modern shopping mall.

The moment we pass through the ship's side Russia lies waiting: hospitable, noisy, confusing, just waiting to pounce. Balalaikas cluck, samovars bubble, fur-hatted boyars leap. Big-booted cossacks are already performing some Siberian version of the limbo dance. It's this way to the casino, that to the duty-free. Here is the Caviar Heaven; there's the Turkish massage. Heavy fur-hatted stewards wait in a row to take away our luggage. Pink-cheeked stewardesses stand in white overalls, like a bevy of bright Russian dolls, ready to lead us off to our cabins. Down a deck or several, to a long passageway where a row of metal cabin doors stands open, as in some carpeted modern penitentiary, to receive the newest intake of inmates. The cabin I've been assigned to is unquestionably modest. In fact it's no more than a neat green box with bunkbed, washbasin and a tiny shower room off it. It's an interior cabin; so we can take it for granted I shan't be seeing much of the Swedish archipelago, the glories of the Baltic or anything other than a swinging shower curtain from here.

There's a tap on the door. A girl – wide-faced, fair-haired, very red-cheeked – enters, wearing white overalls.

'I am Tatyana,' she says warmly, 'do you expect me to do something for you?'

'And where are you from, Tatyana?' I ask her politely.

'I am Tatyana from Pushkin,' she says. 'Do you like me to bring some tea?'

'Yes, I'd love some tea.'

Tatyana disappears just as quickly as she came, and I hang up my topcoat, take a book or two from my shoulder-bag, put down my conference wallet. There's a tap on the door.

'Come in, Tatyana,' I say.

A big Cossack wearing fur hat, robes and boots comes in, hefting a big pile of luggage.

'Bagahsh,' he says.

I look: so much of it, so much. Expensive labels on expensive cases say expensive things: München and Gucci, Wien and Versace, Venezig and Orient Express, La Fenice, La Scala, Bayreuth, Festspielhaus Salzburg, Covent Garden. My luggage? – this is not my luggage. I've somehow acquired all the possessions of a rich travelling princess, ended up in some strange and operatic world.

'Wait a second,' I say. But the man has gone, leaving me with all these wonders, but no sign at all of my own cases: seedy, yes, but my own, and containing everything I, a simple bookish man, ever live by: books, notebooks, memoirs, a packet of tobacco, Marks and Spencer's socks.

There's a tap at the door. Sven Sonnenberg enters, looks round.

'My luggage, not here?' he says, and goes at once.

Another tap at the door. Tatyana is back, carrying a glass filled with mysterious brown fluid freshly drawn from a handy neighbourhood samovar.

'Tea,' she says, as I look at it suspiciously. 'Do you like something in it?'

'I think so,' I say.

Tatyana disappears again. A tap at the door, and Agnes Falkman stands there.

'What has happened to Sven Sonnenberg?' she demands.

'He came here looking for his luggage.'

'Where?'

'He's gone again.'

'That one is impossible,' says Agnes Falkman, and goes.

Another tap at the door; and Tatyana reappears, with a small unlabelled bottle in her hand.

'I think you will like this,' she says, pouring a generous measure into my tea.

'Vodka?' I ask.

'*Da, da,*' she says.

'I'll have some if you take some with me,' I say.

Tatyana slips into my shower room, reappears with another glass, and sits down with me on the bunk.

'You said you were from Pushkin, where's that?' I ask her, as we raise our glasses to each other.

'Oh, don't you know?' asks Tatyana. 'Pushkin is place.'

'Where is the place?'

'Very near Sankt Peterburg. A long time ago it was called Tsarskoye Selo.'

'You mean where Catherine had her summer palace?'

'A very great palace for the tzars. The Germans lived there and then bombed it, but we put it back again. It is still there.'

'The palace with the Amber Room.'

'*Da*, but the Germans took it away, in the war.'

'Didn't it come from Germany in the first place? A gift from Great to Great, Frederick to Catherine?'

'Yes, but you know it is Russia's. It was for the tzars. It belongs only in Pushkin.'

'So how did the place come to be called Pushkin?'

'You don't know about Aleksandr Pushkin, our great poet?'

'Yes, of course I know about him. He wrote *The Bronze Horseman*. And *Eugene Onegin*.'

'Pushkin was born at Tsarkoye Selo. He went to the Lyceum. He was our best poet, also an enemy to Nicholas the Tzar. In Stalin times we liked better to call it Pushkin – because it is better to be an honest poet than a wicked tzar. You agree?'

'Certainly I do.'

'Good. You like more vodka?'

'Please. But this time let's not bother with the tea, shall we?'

Another tap on the door. The Swedish nightingale stands there – filling, no, more than filling, the doorway.

'I think maybe I have your baggages,' she says.

'And I do believe I have yours,' I say.

Birgitta steps in, and eyes my little tryst with interest. 'Are you really drinking vodka?' she asks.

'Wait, I find you a glass,' says Tatyana, diving into the loo.

'Who is your friend, this charming little young person, your servant?' asks the nightingale, sitting down heavily on my bunk.

'That's Tatyana from Pushkin,' I explain.

'No, no, it can't be, I am Tatyana from Pushkin,' says the nightingale.

'You're Birgitta Lindhorst from Sweden,' I say. 'It says so on your . . . on your lapel.'

'Yes, but at Drottningholm opera just now I was Tatyana from Pushkin.'

Tatyana reappears and hands the nightingale a full glass. '*Da?* You sing in Tchaikovsky's opera? *Eugene Onegin?*'

'Ah, you understand, do you, my little darling,' says the diva.

Tatyana sits down on the bunk, which trembles dangerously.

'Don't you know it, the opera *Onegin?*' she asks me. 'Perhaps you remember the wonderful song of the letter? —

' "I'm writing you this declaration / What more can I in candour say? / It could be well your inclination / To scorn me now and turn away," ' the Swedish nightingale suddenly trills, her voice booming off the metal walls.

'Yes, Tatyana's letter,' I say. ' "Tatyana's letter lies besides me / And reverently I guard it still / I read it with an ache inside me / And cannot ever read my fill." '

A tap on the door. 'Would you guys just mind turning the volume down a little?' says Jack-Paul Verso, standing there in his I LOVE DECONSTRUCTION cap. 'I'm trying to finish a paper on my laptop next door.'

' "Why ever did you come to call?" ' asks the Swedish nightingale, looking him in the eye and hitting full volume. ' "In this forgotten country dwelling / I'd not have known you then at all / Or known this bitter heartache's swelling." '

'God, I know that, *Eugene Onegin*,' says Verso. 'The greatest verse-novel ever written.'

'And the greatest opera,' says the diva.

'The greatest everything,' says Verso.

'Are you people all teachers?' asks Tatyana.

'Oh no,' says the diva. 'What does it say in *Onegin*? "God save me from the apparition / On leaving some delightful ball / Of bonneted Academician / Or scholar in a yellow shawl."'

'What have all you guys been drinking, shampanski?' asks Verso.

'No, no, vodka,' says Tatyana. 'You like me to get another cup?'

'From your hands, my Russian honey, I'd drink anything,' says Verso, appreciatively. 'Who's this?'

'I am Tatyana from Pushkin,' says Tatyana, as she reappears with another shot.

'No kidding?' asks Verso, sitting down. 'That's weird. Because that's the one thing I really want to do on this trip. Go to Pushkin and see that fantastic Summer Palace. The Chinese pavilion, the ice house. The trouble is I don't know Russian. I need some really smart Russian guide to take me around.'

'I can take you there,' says Tatyana.

'If there's not a revolution,' I say.

'Life in Russia is always a revolution,' says Tatyana. 'Who cares? If you want to go, we can go.'

Another tap on the door. It's Anders Manders, dapper, suave, every inch the counsellor. 'I'm looking for our stewardess,' he says. 'There seems to be no towel in my cabin.'

'Oh, pardon,' says Tatyana, getting up.

'You're the stewardess?'

'This is Tatyana from Pushkin,' says Jack-Paul Verso. 'Sit down, my friend.'

'And this is just like an opera at the Kirov,' says Birgitta.

'I hope we're all going to the Kirov,' says Manders, sitting down on the bunk. 'Excuse me, is that good Russian vodka I can smell?'

'I get you another glass,' says Tatyana.

Another tap on the door. And who else can it be now but Lars Person, still wearing his big floppy hat?

'I thought on a Russian ship there would have to be a party,' he says.

'I get one glass,' says Tatyana.

'Stay right there, Tatyana from Pushkin, I'll bring some from my cabin next door,' says Verso.

Just then a siren blasts and sennets, high above us. The ship's engines begin their classic bump and grind.

'Hey, listen, we're going to Russia,' says Verso, raising a finger.

'Russkaya,' says Tatyana, lifting her glass to us.

'Russkaya,' says *omnes*, sitting in a long row on my creaking bunk.

You know: I'm starting to think there could be something in this Diderot Project after all.

EIGHT (THEN)

WHAT WITH MATCHMAKING, feasting, titivating, powdering, dressing up, ushering, bowing, scraping, charming his way round the court, what with all these problems of menus and venues, and this whole strange business of human self-presentation and entertainment, in which he so delights, Melchior Grimm, maker of history, has really been most remarkably busy. Which is why it's not until a week or so after the imperial wedding, his duties all accomplished so flamboyantly and so publicly and so much to the satisfaction of *le monde entire*, that he has the chance to call on his dear old friend at the Narishkin Palace. He still basks in the nuptial journey, the matrimonial glow. For just as our man has performed one arc of a great journey from Paris to the north, so he has performed another: riding from Paris through the Low Countries, taking in a court here and a court there, passing through Potsdam to flatter an emperor and collect up a little princess, and so ending up in front of the icons and archimandrites of the Orthodox altar as the wedding vows are exchanged.

'My dear good fellow,' he cries, proving himself just as warm a man as Falconet has shown himself cold. 'My dear fellow,' our man cries, as they fall all eager into each other's arms again.

'We remained a long time hugging each other, letting go and then hugging again,' he will write home that night to the Particularist. Of course. They are two fond old brothers, French and German, who over the many long years in Paris and the countryside have been together to concerts, castles, galleries, salons, house parties, libraries, brothels and wine-shops. Over times almost too long to remember they have kissed each other's mistresses, assisted each other's finances, found each other commissions and other prospects, joined in each other's conspiracies and mystifications, published in each other's journals, written each other's books. One is little, the other is big. One is fat, the other is tall. With his fine brocade surcoat, his silk stockings, his usual flush of rouge on, Melchior is total joy. Sankt Peterburg feels better already. Perhaps he did the right thing in coming here after all.

And Melchior — what are good friends for? — is as bitter in his indignation at Falconet's manners as he is himself. The fellow, he has to acknowledge, is a sourpuss, a temperamental wretch, a cruel rogue. And yet, he wonders, with that courtly wisdom for which he's famous, is it possible that this all has something to do with the strange matter of the, you know of course, the Horseman, the issue that has been pulling Sankt Peterburg apart for so long? We must never forget — or so says Melchior, sitting there in his frogged coat by the rancid stove, cleaning out his long fingernails with a silver pen-knife — that courts are strange fickle places, hard for an artist to live in. What suits everyone one day is suddenly, well, quite out of court the next. And Sankt Peterburg can be a dour discouraging city, even worse than Potsdam. Just the kind of place where even the strongest and sanest of men — and nobody ever accused Falconet of being that — could be driven to despair.

For, as Melchior reminds him, it's a whole nine years since Falconet came to the city where life is always sink or swim. For nine years he's been working, carving and shaping, casting and smelting, under the eyes of the world's most imperious empress. For nine years strange crowds made up of sleek and well-dressed nobles and drab serfs and beggars have been pushing into his atelier uninvited, staring grimly at the mysterious maquette in the making. No one has ever expressed an opinion; not a soul has shown even the faintest smile of approval, the entire capital preferring to remain totally dumb on the matter until her serene imperiousness has declared herself ready to speak. Setback has followed setback. Thanks to incompetent workmen, the whole studio has burst into flames more than once. Foundries have imploded, and two statues at least have collapsed on themselves.

And, for all her western ways, the lady has proved a very hard taskmistress, as — Grimm adds grimly — only she can. In fact relations between patron and sculptor have deteriorated badly. Falconet's studio stands in window-shot of the Winter Palace; but he's no longer asked to court. Communication is now managed by chilly ukases on her side, irascible tirades on his. At first greatly charmed by her fine French artist, Sa Majesté has somehow cooled. Some blame this on the fact that she may have developed more ambiguous feelings about her great predecessor, now that (with whatever shows of reluctance) she has been asked to consider donning the mantle of Greatness herself. Whatever the reasons, she's apparently been setting Falconet the most impossible of tasks. Take, for example, the awkward matter of the inscription. For reasons already cited, the original 'For Peter the Great from Catherine the Second' has begun to lose its appeal.

'You mean, greater does not bow the knee to the merely great?' suggests our man.

'That's it exactly,' says Grimm. Happily some tricksy court diplomat has found the right form of language. 'Peter the First and Catherine the Second' is what the plinth will now pronounce.

And take the matter of that plinth itself. Her Splendidness has demanded the biggest granite base in existence – and this despite the fact that among the bogs of Petersburg any stone larger than a pebble is in seriously short supply. Finally she has decreed the choice herself: a large boulder of fifteen hundred tons she noticed once on her travels, stuck deep in the ground twenty miles away and across the Finnish border. Naturally, what a tzarina wants a tzarina gets. But the task of dragging half a Finnish mountain twenty miles across marsh and bog has not been simple. It's taken a year, required the energies of hundreds of horses and thousands of human pushers, demanded the invention of an ingenious little railway made of logs and brass balls. Then, as if this were not enough, Voltaire has suddenly taken to writing grandly from Ferney, adding his sage's mite of enlightened advice. It seems that in his view the statue shouldn't be erected in Petersburg at all, but somewhere else – Constantinople. A journey to Byzantium is no easy project for a Finnish mountain, especially as there is another problem: Her Highness would have to invade Turkey and occupy it first.

'That's Voltaire, he turns up everywhere,' murmurs our man, impressed.

There's more. In fact all this is as nothing compared with the argument the statue has spawned at court over Peter's physical appearance and character – of which, it seems, everyone has a totally different memory. Some recall him as under six feet tall, while others are quite certain he was over seven. Some claim he was always moustached and trim-bearded, but others pronounce him clean-shaven at all times. Should he have boots on (he generally did)? Should he wear a uniform? Maybe a boyar dress of Russian furs (but he did want them abolished), maybe a Roman toga (a fine form of dress, but rarely seen this far north)? Should he hold a sabre in his hand (he did make great use of one)? Better a legal scroll (he sometimes believed in the law)? The plan of his city (he did kill many people to create it)? And how should his facial expression be depicted? Should he be scowling fiendishly at Sweden, his old, defeated, yet still threatening enemy, always blocking off the other end of the Baltic? Should he be haughty, grand, triumphant, a soldier who was also a man of civilization, art and commerce? Should he be Peter the Absolutely Terrible, a Scythian scourge bringing fear and trembling to the entire world to the west? How about Thinking Pete, a reflective enquirer, asking for eternity, as he so often liked to do, What is dat?

No wonder Falconet has refused to dress the statue with a recognizable face, especially since Betskoi has demanded that the figure should be looking proudly at the Admiralty building, the Peter-Paul Fortress and the twelve colleges he founded on the opposite bank, something he could only manage by means of a very pronounced squint. Worst of all, there's been the dreadful problem of the snake.

'You surely don't mean my snake?' asks Our Philosopher, looking seriously worried at last.

For his snake it most definitely is. It was he, back in Paris, who first imagined an allegorical serpent lying beneath the hooves of Peter's great horse: the pregnant image, the perfect symbol.

'Symbol of what?' asks Grimm, looking at him amused.

'Good crushing evil. Humanity mastering nature. Reason triumphing over envy and ignorance,' explains our man.

'Unfortunately the Tzarina feels it might be misread,' says Grimm. 'She thinks it might be seen as the Russian ruler crushing the Russian people. Such is the slippage of signs in this country. I rather think Her Highness is right.'

At any rate, the snake, it seems, has resulted in one of those imperial letters of instruction that, by the same slippage of signs, may not quite mean what they say.

'There's an old song that says, if it is necessary, it is necessary,' the Empress has written to him, in her gnomic way, in her own fair hand. 'Let that be your answer regarding the snake.'

So, by the time Grimm has picked up his tricorne and strolled off back to drinks and canapés at the Hermitage, the Falconet Mystification has grown considerably. In fact our man's seriously alarmed. He can hardly wait to leap to his feet, grab up someone's bearskin coat, and walk through Saint Isaac's square to the log-built atelier on the Millionaya, to discover what's become of his splendid nine-year-old dream. The atelier proves a most strange and remarkable place. In the snowy courtyard outside, a regiment of cavalry officers clatters and drills, each man taking turns to ride the Empress's own horse, Brilliant, to the top of a vast sharp-angled stone plinth. The sculptor himself stands watching, evidently to see what daring positions a horse and rider can achieve before they tumble to disaster (as, it turns out, several have). The two friends embrace, but Falconet is still sullen. He leads our man inside the smoky den. Here, furnaces blast, smelters sizzle, plaster-moulds seethe. A large general wearing a crown of laurels struts about irritably – waiting, it seems, to perform the role of Peter the Great's stand-in, impatient for principal photography to start.

In the centre of the studio stands a vast stage draped with a waterproof canvas. Sweet Marie-Anne Collot comes over and joins them, clad in great leather pinafores. Falconet nods an order to his ragged band of workmen. They scramble up the scaffolds; the cover flies off. Beneath it is a vast plaster maquette. A flying horseman, the man almost indistinguishable from the horse, rears up on the brink of a vast plaster cliff. The thing's not finished, in fact, it's nowhere near. But that's Peter all right: crowned in laurels and three times lifesize, as if in real life the man wasn't already big enough. Our man stares up. As a construction, it is amazing. The whole thing is unreal, pushed beyond all the rules of form, the laws of gravity. Horse and man are strangely backweighted, held to earth only by the horse's hind legs and twisting tail. But whatever's happened to the meaning, what has gone wrong with the sign?

The snake remains, true, twisted beneath the horse's hooves – though now it seems to be removable. The face is faceless, blank, expressionless (and so it will remain until the very last minute, ten long years from now, when, as it is written, Marie-Anne will hastily sculpt the features on the night before the statue goes up). As for the cunning allegorical content (our man remembers every detail), that has quite dropped away. Barbarism is no longer present. Popular Love and the Spirit of the Nation – what has become of them? It seems they have been discarded: for something quite other, some raw and plastic simplicity wrested directly out of the sculptural materials themselves. Classicism has quite disappeared, along with the art of allegory. Everything's replaced by something different: looser, stranger, more tempestuous, haunting even, weirdly sublime. Some strange power – can it be Russia? the Tzarina? the shifting soul of Falconet himself? – has altered everything. This is not at all what they meant in Paris. This is not the statue of their dreams . . .

At once our philosopher comprehends everything. Nothing could be clearer: the ungrateful welcome, the friendless friendship, the already bagged bed, the faceful of sullen expressions and angry embarrassed looks. This man is afraid. Nine years' work, and here comes Teacher; and Teacher ain't going to like it, ain't going to like it a bit. Teacher stands back. He reflects, considers. He turns in his mind the strange paradox of sculpture, which he's spoken of many times, in fact to anyone who would listen. Sculpture is the highest art; it's also the deepest craft. It does not embody realities, depict known myths. It finds itself within the objects of its own use. One should not (he has often said so) suppose that inanimate things lack living characteristics. The world is one. In wood, in stone, in clay, there are vital secrets; and art is craft, a skill in chiselling, shaping, working out the secret of the life within. That is the paradox of art: an imitation of reality that upturns the reality, finds the single pregnant instant, the *coup de théâtre*, the great *découpage*.

He looks again. He thinks, like the critic he is, of the power of the patron, the hunger of the audience. But he's not just a critic and a teacher, a creator of creators. He's a creator himself, after all . . . He turns to the bulky, sour-faced sculptor. He takes him in his arms.

'My dear fellow,' he declares, 'I always used to think you were a young man of the very highest talents. Didn't I always say so, when I reviewed your work in the salons, all those years ago?'

'You did say so, monsieur,' says the sculptor. 'How else do you think I ended up here in hell, doing this?'

'Well, may I drop dead on the instant if I thought for a moment you ever had a conception in your head like this strange beast here.'

'You don't approve?'

'Do you know, I could grind this up and eat it.'

'It's that bad?'

'Not at all. There's nothing I would love better than to be a statue just like this myself. Only without a horse, perhaps.'

'So you do like—?'

'I love it, my sweet young friend. It's quite original, it's quite sublime. It's a wonder.'

'You mean it?'

'I'm a professional critic, remember. It's not my way to say nice things often.'

'My dear kind friend.'

'My dear friend too,' says our man. 'You're making a master-piece. And you can quote me on that wherever you like, to whomever you like. Now then: I've said what I've said. And as soon as I meet the Empress I shall tell her what I think.'

When at last they let go of each other, even sullen Falconet is smiling. As he usually does in the end, our man has found his way to the perfect flattery. He's passed on a generous, a fraternal, a perfectly intended compliment to another. And he's no less found the way to keep a big piece of the praise for his own splendid judgement and himself.

'And how is my dear darling Marie-Anne?' our man asks now, reaching out and hugging her too. Soon all three of them are in the most enormous tangle. 'What became of my wonderful fond welcome to Sankt Peterburg?' Our man booms, 'Kiss kiss kiss.'

'You're truly welcome, *maître*,' says Marie-Anne, giving him the kiss kiss kiss. 'Do you know, one day I would like to make a bust of you myself?'

'And so you shall, my dear one, you shall.'

'In that case I would like to make one too,' says Falconet, holding the Philosopher in his arms.

'Both of you? A statue for me, then? Well, why not? I deserve it.'

'These days everyone gets one,' murmurs Falconet.

'I know, we'll make it a competition, master and pupil,' our man says. 'And then I shall decide which one's best. Or maybe we'll ask the Empress.'

'You haven't met her yet.'

'Tomorrow night, at the great party at the Hermitage.'

'You're invited?'

'Of course. Everyone is,' says our man.

'Except me,' says Falconet.

Meanwhile, up on the scaffold, faceless and unfinished, Peter astride his snorting house stares out over the talking heads at the big blank wall of the studio. One day he'll have all the Baltic to look at with imperial menace. He'd better get this right . . .

NINE (NOW)

A LITTLE LATER. Pleasant civic Stockholm is gently slipping away behind us into the chilly clear late afternoon. There it goes: the copper-clad spires of Protestantism, the great granite halls of liberal democracy, the big-roofed palaces of a long-lived monarchy are all floating off in our rich oily haze. I can see the tall shaft of Storkyrkan Cathedral, where they tried but failed to bury Descartes; I can spot the modern brick pile of the City Hall, where they award the Nobel Prizes to the famous and the totally forgettable. A fine view of a web of urban motorways, a towered spectacle of welfare high-rises stacked on the hillsides above. The urban buildings go out of view. We're looking at small rocky bays, threading between rocky and tree-fertile islands, with neat waterside houses, each with a boat dock, a white motor cruiser, a blue and white national flag flapping away on each separate pier-end, each a little free state on its own. Bright-sailed dinghies tack in the water, performing another regatta: back and forth, hither and thither, this way and that.

'Now we're in the archipelago?' I ask. Beside me is the red-haired Swedish Nightingale, who has generously agreed to come with me up here, to the high empty bridge deck, to watch her native city slip from view.

'*Nej, nej,* those are dangerous waters, wild and lonely and truly beautiful. Here you are still in Stockholm. Those houses were once summer cottages. Now they're all thermalled and belong to commuters. In summer they go to work in their motor boats. In the winter when the ice comes they go on their skates, with a briefcase under the arm. You will know the real archipelago when you see it. It is very dark and strange, that is why we like it.'

We stand together, staring over the side. The red sun's sliding, the skies have cleared from Prussian to bright blue, the wind's faintly rising, sweeping across our faces as we look out. Here on the bridge deck the cruise has scarcely started. The swimming pool is drained and empty, the scatter of wooden deckchairs lacks its cushions. A cossack swabs the deckboards with mop and bucket. Beneath the bridge-house where the captain stands in his huge white hat, staring out through formidable binoculars, there is foxy Lenin, impassively, emptily, bronzily brooding over us all.

The red-haired diva seizes my arm. 'Is it true you are quite clever?' she asks.

'No, you're confusing me with someone else,' I answer.

'It doesn't matter, at least you are a professor. Quickly – tell me something about this Diderot. So I will not look all the time like a silly fool.'

'Well, in a word: French philosophe, the son of a knife-maker in Langres in Burgundy. He was going to be a priest, but he married a sempstress. Went to Paris, worked as a hack and teacher, wrote a funny dirty little novel called *The Indiscreet Jewels*. Travelled to Petersburg in 1773. Which is why we're here, I presume. Died suddenly of an apoplexy while eating an apricot at his own dinner table, 31 July 1784. Wrote the big book that changed the world.'

'Surely not another book that changed the world?'

'Yes, the *Encyclopedia*. It ran to twenty-eight volumes, something like that, with hundreds of articles and plates. It was supposed to sum up the knowledge and the progress of the age.'

'Did it?'

'Oh yes. It was the Bible of the Age of Reason. You read it and the whole meaning of the world changed. It was the spirit of knowledge, the power of philosophy. The authorities tried to suppress it. That just made it more famous.'

'Why was it so important?'

'In the old world you consulted the priests. In the world of new science you consulted the philosophers. Philosophy became a great occupation, there were philosophes everywhere, remember. Voltaire, Hume, d'Alembert, Condorcet, Rousseau.'

'So why are we following Diderot?'

'I'm not sure. Maybe because Diderot was the most interesting and engaging of all of them. At least that's my opinion. Wilder and more generous than Voltaire. Much much wittier than Rousseau.'

'That can't have been hard. Why don't I know him?'

'In his day he was mostly famous for talking. His finest books weren't printed until many years after his death. They turned up all over the place. Maybe there are still some that haven't been found. I seem to remember that's why I thought I'd like to come on this trip in the first place.'

'They could be in Petersburg?'

'Very likely.'

'Don't expect me to read thirty books.'

'Oh, nobody ever reads the whole *Encyclopedia*. Except maybe a few experts on the Enlightenment, like our funky Professor Verso. It's a random mixture, filled with articles on everything. Love and windmills. Liberty and the prophets. Priests and prostitution. How to build a cheese factory. How to design a chair.'

The nightingale looks at me very doubtfully. 'You mean he wrote about all of those things?'

'Not all of them. Voltaire and Rousseau and d'Alembert wrote some of it. It was a team thing, a lot of other people were hired too. But he gave the whole thing the impress of his mind. It was always Diderot's *Encyclopedia*.'

'I don't want to read that,' says the nightingale decisively. 'Can't you find me something easy I can read?'

'The novel in dialogue, *Rameau's Nephew*,' I say. 'One of the finest books ever written. Goethe said so. And Marx and Freud. A book written against itself, about a character who speaks against himself.'

'Rameau was bitter, mean and dull,' says the nightingale. 'They said he had legs like corkscrews and thought only of himself. But he was very clever. Have you seen his opera-ballets? They're all about the four winds talking to each other. All serpents and kettle drums, no big roles.'

'Rameau may have been mean and dull. But his nephew wasn't.'

She looks at me. 'Did he really have a nephew?'

'Yes, he did. Another musician, but a very bad one. An inspector of Dancing Masters. He even wrote a piano piece called "The Encyclopedia".'

'Maybe that is why Diderot liked him.'

'Diderot didn't like him. He was fascinated by him, as a disturbing human specimen. I suppose he must have seemed his perfect opposite. A confidence man, a deceiver, a transgressor.'

'Like Sade?'

'Yes, a kind of friendly Sade. Manipulation, mystification, fancy footwork — those were his tactics. The book's in my luggage, if you want to read it.'

'Very well, my darling, if you say so,' says the diva, completely losing interest. She pulls her wrap round her shoulders and looks out over the rail.

I gaze over her ripe and formidable proportions. 'You know Bo very well?' I ask.

'No, do you?'

'Just the way professors know professors. We meet at conferences and send each other papers. Then we disagree, which gives a reason to hold more conferences.'

'I don't know him at all,' says the diva, 'but in Sweden he is very important. Of course in Sweden all professors are important.'

'So I gather. Not in my country.'

'But Bo is more important than most. He is an academician, a man of power, a trustee of the Royal Opera. I think he is a trustee of everything. He visited my dressing room at Drottningholm and told me I should be on this voyage. He knows the people at the Kirov, the Maryinsky. But now he tells me I should give a paper.'

'He said that to all of us.'

'Very well for you, you are a teacher, you know how to. Maybe you even like it.'

'Not that much. It's what we do.'

'I don't like it at all. I don't speak thoughts. I sing them.'

'Good, I long to hear them.'

'But look out there. This is not a place to be thinking about papers.'

It's not. Now we're really sailing on. Weather's changing, landscape's changing. Nice autumn evening, still with a touch of

summer. Wind up harder now, sun starting to dip down. The seas
have widened, the water turned soft and pearly grey. Little islands,
tiny windswept bays, are appearing. Suddenly, from just above us,
a blast of hideous noise. She seizes my arm, I grab her shoulder;
the ship's siren is sounding off. From over the water, it's answered,
answered again. Like a convention of echoes, siren after siren is
sounding. The diva runs to the rail.

'See, they are coming, the great floating coffins,' she says.

I go to the rail, lean out at her side. There down the sea-lane,
between the channel markers, a row, a fleet, of high-sided, steel-
jawed monster vessels sails toward us.

'What?' I ask.

'The evening ferries into Stockholm,' she says. 'They come in
every night from all over the Baltic. Helsinki, Visby, Kiel, Oulu,
Riga, Gdynia, Tallinn. Oh, and Sankt Peterburg, of course.'

The first of the ferries is abreast of us now. They sail by one by
one, monster floating hotels: the *Sibelius*, the *Kalevala*, the *Con-
stanin Simonov*, the *Estonia*, the *Baltic Clipper*. They rise up deck
after deck to strange-angled funnels, passing close enough for us to
see the last drinkers toping in the bars, the last gamblers risking a
final chance in the casinos, the late duty-free shoppers gathering
up their final bottle of Givenchy, an extra Famous Grouse. People
are waving from the rails. Up on open-boat decks people in
topcoats and parkas lie in stupefied rows: these must be the last
drunks from Finland, staring up into blood-red sunset and mystical
oblivion. Then the flotilla sails on toward the smoke-plumes of
Stockholm. The quiet sea is ours again.

Half an hour later. We're still on the high boat deck. She's
pulled her wrap tight round her, I puff at my Danish pipe, a small
philosophical tool I rather like to carry. Red sun dropping away
now, water pearly grey, bird-whitened rocks and islands everywhere in the water pearly grey too.

'And now this is the archipelago, my darling,' says the red-
haired diva. 'A hundred thousand drowned islands. This is where
comes the true Swedish soul. It's a terrible and wonderful place.'

The islands spread everywhere: some wind-worn, barren, white
with guano, others with piers and ochre-painted chalets. Here and
there nets hang on gantries, black smoke-houses steam away on

wooden docks. Juniper, bilberry, dwarf pine grow in the crevices, small funnelled ferries punt about. To me this is the stuff of old Ingmar Bergman movies, the ones where cowled, creased-faced priests wander the shoreline, wrecks litter the rocks, middle-aged men are wracked with violent lust, young summer love affairs are a prelude to winter pain.

The diva, staring out at the grey naked islands, is suddenly telling me everything about them. They're where she spent the summers of childhood. Here's where her destiny was written, here was born her complex Swedish soul. Somewhere out there Strindberg had gloomy imaginings in a cottage by the water. Painters of grim naturalism painted dark fisher paintings on the rocks. Soon we're getting in further: naked swims in the cold cleansing Baltic; crayfish feasts on the rocks; fishermen sailing out by night in their lamped boats for herring and sea-pike; most of all the unforgettable bitter-sweet affairs of young love.

'I have only to think about it, and it makes me oh so happy and oh so sad,' cries the diva.

'I know, I know,' I say sympathetically, looking out over the rail as the rocky archipelago flows by. I have of course been here before. I know from old these wonderful, grandly expressive nightingales, with their boom, their bosoms, their bravura. I know these depthless, spirit-searching Northern souls. I know this school of grim-sentimental Bergman-ish reminiscence. And I know very well it's just one short step from here to dead lost loves, deflowered virgins, singing skeletons, ghostly drowned sailors emerging dripping from the sea, Father Time on a dark forest path, bearing his hourglass and his fatal scythe.

'Let me tell you my sensations of despair,' she's saying. And now she's explaining success is a strange delusion, her international fame a mere toy. She's confessing how truly unhappy her life is, how worthless the life of a great diva is, how unfulfilled her destiny. Then, for some reason she puts down to her fiery temperament, we find ourselves discussing together the best way to go about murdering her husband.

'If only we can decide on the perfect way,' she says.

The problem is, I gather, that opera singers have been taught so many: poisoning, hanging, beheading, boiling in oil, knife, asp-bite, it's all much the same to them.

'I know, I know.'

'First, though, we must find him.'

'I know, I know. Where do you think he is now?'

'Of course, with his whore in Milan, the nasty little rat.'

'What is she like?'

'Just a contralto. Poison is far better than either of them deserve.'

'I know, I know. I know just what you mean.'

'But ask me all you like, my dear little darling, I could never really use a knife on him. It's just too horrible.'

'I know. I know.'

'What do you two think you are doing?' asks a sharp, policing voice from behind. Luckily it's not Lenin; there is Alma Luneberg, rabbit-hatted, looking angry as only a Snow Queen can.

'We are enjoying ourselves,' explains the diva. 'And I am trying to explain to this poor English man about our true Swedish soul.'

'And don't you know the Diderot people are asking what has become of you?'

'No, my darling. I wanted him to see the archipelago.'

'You didn't examine the programmes I gave you in your wallet? Don't you realize the Diderot Project is already starting to begin?'

For once even the great diva is silenced. We turn away from the grey rocks and the even greyer water, and follow the Snow Queen down the companion way and below.

Strange. During our brief absence the entire ship has changed. What was once a lobby or a half-empty arrival platform has somehow become a total way of life. It teems with tourists, bursts with noise and shouting. Glasses clink, casino wheels spin. We pass the busy Duty Free, the crowded Beauty Expensive. We pass the Blini Bar, the Caviar Cavern, the Vodka Den, the Russian Bathhouse, the Turkish Massage Parlour, the Lubianka Fitness Centre, the Odessa Casino. But modern life is not all pleasure and shopping; it's commercial, corporate, and capitalist. Somewhere on the promenade deck behind the Fitness Centre is the Conference

Centre – silent space filled with telephone links, photocopiers, fax-machines. In glass-walled seminar rooms corporation executives are already down to business. In a room labelled SIEMENS, a band of German and Russian businessmen, many of them ladies, all in suits, are already head to head: flipping flip-charts, showing pie-diagrams, faxing faxes, fixing floppies. And a few steps more beyond capitalism and commerce lie intellect and reason. The seminar room beyond is clearly marked DIDEROT PROJECT.

Here a small welcome reception seems to be taking place, and all for our little band of pilgrims. In a quicksilver change of role – for she's now adorned in a short black dress and white frilly apron, just like a servant from a Noel Coward comedy – Tatyana from Pushkin stands in the entrance, holding out a large tray of canapés, another of fluted glasses of pink Russian shampanski. Jack-Paul Verso is energetically chatting her up, in his sharp Manhattan here's-how-to-work-a-room fashion. In the middle of the space is Anders Manders, with his clipped blond beard, talking to Lars Person, wearing his diabolical black one. There's Sven Sonnenberg in his torn, stained worker's denims talking sombrely about some deep matter of existence with Agnes Falkman, who wears a cK designer version of the same thing. As we enter, both looking a touch shamefaced, Bo Luneberg looks up crossly. But what, his expression seems to say, can you expect of a flamboyant and narcissistic diva, and a writer-type who falls asleep at a postmodern concert?

Tatyana comes over to us with pink champagne, plates for the canapés. Now that his party's complete, Bo goes to the middle of the chamber, claps his hands, calls, 'Now may we please to begin?' The Diderot Pilgrims fall silent. Bo raises up his glass.

'Welcome. We all have a glass of this fine Russian champagne, jo? Let me make a small toast, then. To the Diderot Project.'

Our glasses all go up; 'Skal!' 'Diderot,' 'To old Denis,' cry the pilgrims.

Then, as Bo seems unwilling to say any more, we look around at each other. It's Jack-Paul Verso who frames the collective question. 'Bo, someone has to ask this, so let it be me,' he says. 'Why have you invited us? What the hell is this Diderot Project?'

Bo looks us over with polite compassion. 'Ah, you are wondering why you are here? Why you are chosen, and so on?'

'Yes, Bo.'

'A singer, an actor, a carpenter, a diplomat, a writer, a philosopher and so on?' Bo removes a little card from his jacket pocket. 'I can best answer by quoting some words Diderot wrote in his famous *Encyclopedia* – in fact in the entry called "Encyclopedia". Maybe you remember how he explained the task. It is, he tells us, to bring knowledge together, expose all superstition and error, demonstrate truth, use only the evidence of our senses, assign a proper cause to everything, and take each thing only for what it is.'

'And that's all?' says Lars Person.

'However, at the end of the essay,' Bo goes on regardless, 'he utters a solemn and beautiful warning.'

'A very beautiful warning,' adds Alma. 'The day will finally come – our philosopher goes on to observe – when knowledge will have grown so extremely fast no one individual or system would ever be able to grasp it. So he explains.'

'It's here already,' says Verso. 'It's called the World Wide Web.'

'Allow me to quote his words. "If we banish from the earth the thinking entity, man—"'

'Bo, I think you mean person,' says Agnes Falkman.

'*Jo, jo*, I think I do mean person. "If we banish from the earth the thinking entity, person, the sublime and beautiful spectacle of nature will become a sad and vacant scene. The universe will be hushed. All will be a vast solitude, an empty desert where events and phenomena make their way unseen, unheard. That is why we must put ma—, put person at the centre of our encyclopedia, and give him her true place at the centre of the universe.'

'A beautiful warning,' says Alma. 'And this explains it, the Enlightenment Project.'

'We will again put person at the centre of the universe.'

'Sounds great,' says Verso. 'Now may we have some more champagne?'

'Help yourself, please,' says Bo. 'Within reason, of course.'

While Tatyana goes round refilling our glasses, I can see Sven looking at Bo as if confused. 'This is why we are here? On this boat?'

'*Jo, jo*, Sven.'

'Why we are going to Russia?'

'Just trying to make the universe human again,' says Alma encouragingly.

'I see,' says Verso. 'You aim to bring back the Age of Reason and hoped we'd help in some way?'

'*Jo, jo.*'

'But I am only a simple craftsman,' says Sven. 'I make tables.'

'Don't think for a moment that is simple, Sven,' says Bo. 'Diderot never thought that. He believed in tables.'

'I work with my hands,' says Sven.

'And I with my voice,' says Birgitta.

'We're bringing all human knowledge together?' asks Manders. 'In how many days?'

'Six,' says Alma. 'Three going and three coming back. Remember, God made the universe in seven.'

'But he must have planned it out pretty carefully beforehand,' says Lars Person.

'How do we do it?' asks Sven.

'We talk together, we share our crafts and our professions and philosophies, just like the *Encyclopedia*. We give papers,' explains Bo.

'Papers!' cries the Swedish nightingale.

'Then the papers will make a book, and the government will print the book, and give us a grant for it,' says Alma.

'Oh, those beautiful words,' says Verso. 'A government grant!'

'I understood we were visiting the Hermitage to see the Voltaire library,' says Anders Manders.

'I thought we were making a visit to the Maryinsky Opera,' says Birgitta Lindhorst.

'I thought we were going to collective farms to meet workers' representatives,' says Agnes Falkman.

'I was told our trip was something to do with furniture, we were going to Russia to look at tables,' says Sven Sonnenberg.

'And all in good time,' says Bo. 'But first we give papers. That is why we have this very nice conference room to ourselves.'

Lars Person is looking at me with his amused and diabolical expression. 'Only really boring professors give papers,' he says. 'Don't you agree, professor?'

'*Moi?*' I ask.

'Yes. I know you're sometimes a boring professor, but you also write novels and plays, I think. So which do you prefer? Giving papers or telling stories?'

'If I tell the truth, I much prefer telling stories.'

'I don't see why,' says Agnes. 'Papers are useful and stories tell lies.'

'But lies that help us find our way to truth.'

'I love it,' says Birgitta Lindhorst. 'Why don't we all do it?'

'Tell lies?'

'*Nej, nej,* Sven, tell each other stories,' says the Swedish nightingale.

'*Nej, nej, nej,* we are here to do something useful, Birgitta,' says Agnes. 'As Diderot once observed, "To know how to bake, we must first put our hands in the dough."'

'In the dough?'

'Didn't he also observe, "We present things as if they were facts to show there are things we think we know. But we also present them as stories to show how it is we find out."'

'What, Diderot said this?' asks Alma.

'Yes,' I say.

'Where?'

'I don't remember.'

'I am sure we all agree we want papers,' says Agnes. 'I think there is a consensus.'

'I don't think you are right, Agnes,' says Lars Person.

'Of course there is a consensus,' says Alma.

'No, because some of us want papers and some of us would rather have stories . . .'

'In that case we must take a vote,' says Agnes.

'*Nej, nej,* it is not necessary,' says Alma, 'I am sure we have a consensus. Do we have a consensus?'

'*Jo, jo,*' says Agnes.

'*Nej, nej,*' says Lars Person.

'Then I think we must have a meeting to find out how to find a consensus,' says Bo . . .

Jack–Paul Verso turns quietly to me as the argument rages. 'Great, I think that's quite enough Swedish democracy for one evening, don't you?' he murmurs. 'What say to a Jim Beam in the Muscovy Bar? Is it a consensus?'

'*Jo, jo,*' I say.

Strange how the life of ships can alter so suddenly, how many different little worlds one single vessel can contain. Up aloft we've left the gallant band of Swedish pilgrims, discussing reason and trying to resolve the difficult problems of a liberal democracy. Two decks down in the Muscovy Bar minds are turned to other matters entirely. The *Vladimir Ilich* is well on its way now, its engines thumping and surging noisily as, driven by some wild homesick appetite, it drives on through the archipelago toward the wider Baltic and home. The noise onboard is just as vigorous, as the ship's returning Russians take charge of the bar. Balalaika music twings merrily from the loudspeakers; bottles and glasses smash their way along the bar. Chatter, shouting, singing, laughter surge from every table. Small gaming machines have somehow appeared, and goods and chattels are passing quickly every which way and that: Barbie dolls, Western CDs, mobile organizers, mobile phones, whole hams, entire cheeses, silk scarves, old socks, strangely shaped brown-paper parcels, sinister black plastic sacks, passports, stamped documents and, for all I know, lists of dead souls are trafficking from hand to hand.

To make sure the mood of Slav euphoria never for an instant diminishes, big-necked waiters in their Russian ruffles are shuttling at speed between the tables and the bar, bearing life-giving doses of shampanski or vodka. The rest of us travellers watch bemused. In the further corner the Japanese tour-groups all sit huddled together, wearing their little backpacks, looking at the spectacle buddhistically and aiding their contemplations with glasses of iced Suntory scotch. Huge and Hanseatic, the German businessmen are exchanging thrilling tales of massage and sauna and soaking down vital cognac. The Swedish businessmen, discussing welfare reform, are drinking small glasses of Ukrainian sauterne. Hats still on backwards in the most senseless of all human gestures, the American backpackers are working their way through the educational pages of the *Rough Guide to Novi Zembla* as they tip back can after can of Bud, crushing the containers flat in their huge mitts when they've done. As for the American widows, they look happier than they must have been in the rest of their entire lives, as they flirt unashamedly with these same big Russian waiters.

As for me, how crazy I was to spend all that time in Stockholm trying to traffick rates of exchange with that nice blonde teller in that nice blonde bank. Because here we're right in the world of funny money. What was I thinking of? This is a Russian ship, after all. The waiters, rushing round the tables, are happy to pocket anything that vaguely resembles currency, valuta, at all. Russian roubles, Ukrainian hryvnia, Hungarian forints, Swedish kronor, German Deutschmarks, it's all the same to them. Chinese rinimbi, Thai bahts, Slakan vloskan, Cambodian wong; if it clinks or crackles, it pours straight into their wallets.

'*Skal!*' says Verso, raising the huge glass of Jim Beam on the rocks his dollar has bought. 'You know, there's just one thing that worries me about you, professor.'

'Oh, what's that, professor?'

'This Diderot quote of yours just now. Papers and stories. I haven't read every single word the guy wrote in a far too productive lifetime, I have to admit. But I don't remember him saying that.'

'All right,' I admit, 'maybe he never did actually say it. But it's the kind of thing he would have said. I mean, surely?'

Verso eyes me appreciatively. 'Okay, my friend, now I understand you. You're able to quote our man perfectly, even down to the things he never said at all.'

'That's it. I'm a writer. I compose falsehoods. How about you? You're a truth-teller? A philosopher? An expert on Diderot?'

'No, not quite. I'm a modern philosopher. Or maybe a postmodern philosopher, if that's not a contradiction in terms. I can lie better than you. And I'm an expert in refuting Diderot.'

'I see.'

'I deconstruct, you see. That's how I keep my cat in pet food. And I especially deconstruct the Grand Narratives of the great Age of Reason project.'

I take a glance at my *confrère*, stuffing down a bowl of cashews. He looks pleasant enough, in his designer T-shirt and his Gucci loafers, but I know him for what he is. Somewhere in there I sense the Paglia Syndrome, a big show-off's desire for celebrity thinking and intellectual trouble.

'You're an enemy of reason, is that right?'

'Sure I am,' says Verso, tapping his I LOVE DECONSTRUCTION cap. 'Just like any reasonable person. Aren't you?'

'No, I'm not. I'm afraid I'm just another old liberal humanist.'

'Tough,' says Verso, 'but let me convince you, if I may.'

'If you must.'

'I never lose the chance to deconstruct a little as I go along on my happy little way. So let's just see how we hammered all the nails into the Enlightenment coffin, shall we? First of all, reason turned out not to be reasonable, right? In fact it led straight into the French Revolution, the first encounter with the historical bloodbath and the great wasteland we call modernity. So we get Vico and his dispute with the idea of rational progress, Kant and the critique of pure reason, showing we never know anything with pure objectivity, Schopenhauer proving it's not mind but will we think with. Then comes Kierkegaard and the leap in the dark – no way of knowing being from nothingness, or the either from the or. Followed by Nietzsche and the complete triumph of the irrational. Worried yet?'

'Very.'

'Great. And you've still seen nothing yet. Soon comes Heidegger and the collapse of all metaphysics. Then Wittgenstein and the whereof we cannot speak let us be silent. Which leads by way of existential absurdity and futility to where we've managed to reach right now.'

'Which is where?'

'With Michel Foucault and the total loss of the subject. Remember what he wrote in the last paragraph of *The Order of Things*?'

'No, I don't think I do.'

'Well, this is not quite word for word, but with your approach to quotation you won't mind that. Something like: "Ideas of reason disappeared from the world as fast as they appeared. Today the figure of thinking man is just a face drawn in the sand on the very edge of the waves. Next moment the tide will surge in and everything will be erased." '

'Diderot's vast and tragic solitude?'

'Right. Our man spoke wiser than he knew.'

'And you're for it, are you?'

'Naturally I'm for it,' says Verso. 'Reason's gone the same way as religion. We're way beyond the end of the Cartesian project. We no longer believe in a single continuous self. We no longer believe in thought as the way the brain works, any more than we think we live in a cosmos made by a magnificent watchmaker. All we know is the cosmos is chaos, moving sideways at fantastic speed toward an explosive and senseless destination no one can understand. When it gets there it blows up or gets turned into some anti-matter. Doesn't it give you pause? It should do. It gave Einstein pause.'

'Okay, it gives me pause too. But if the thinking subject has disappeared, the mind is finished, why do we need philosophers?'

'Ah. We don't.'

'How come you are one then?'

'I just preferred it to football.'

'And you still find a job to do?'

'Sure. We still need philosophers. Look at France. They really respect those Death of the Subject guys there. You know they let them ride free on the trains?'

'They do?'

'Sure. Beaudrillard gets to ride free on all the railroads. Lyotard was presented with his own personal box at the opera. Have another Jim Beam, my son.'

'Yes, I will,' I say. 'I suppose what I don't understand, then, is if you're so anti-reason why did you come on this Diderot Project?'

'The same reason we all came on the Diderot Project. Free air-ticket, free food and drink, free visit to Russia. What's the first rule of academic scholarship? Never, never look a gift grant in the mouth.'

'I came to sail on a ship called the *Anna Karenina.*'

'And you didn't. That's what comes of high intentions.'

'And I came to visit the Hermitage and look at the Diderot papers.'

'You could have done that on any package tour.'

'And to find out more about Diderot.'

'And why do you think Diderot himself went to Russia in the first place?'

'To perform the task of the philosopher. Enlighten the despot, spread the rule of reason.'

'And did he? No, he came for just the same reason we do. Free ticket, free trip to Russia, free food and drink.'

'I don't think so. I think he was looking for the one great patron who'd understand him.'

'Catherine, you mean? She understood him fine. She knew he'd flatter her and prostrate himself before the spectacle of power.'

'But he didn't.'

'He did. The lady bought philosophers just like she bought shoes and paintings. He was one more possession to add to her glory. And he went along with that. *Skal!*'

Verso raises a fresh glass of bourbon to me.

'So you think. It's not how I understood it,' I say.

'It's true. Or as true as any truth is true, which it isn't, of course. No, the main reason I'm here is I needed to be out of the States a while. I happen to be between marriages.'

'I'm sorry.'

'No need. They weren't my marriages I was between. Besides, every philosopher has to go to Russia. Remember Isaiah Berlin?'

'Yes. I know he was in the British Embassy in Moscow after the war.'

'And he came to Petersburg, Leningrad in those days, to meet Anna Akhmatova.'

'And they took to each other.'

'That's right. They spent a whole night together in her apartment off the Fontanka. They found they spoke the same language.'

'Amazing. I didn't think anyone spoke Isaiah's language. Except Isaiah.'

'Anyway he talked ceaselessly.'

'He always did.'

'The next morning a friend asked Akhmatova if they'd reached the great fulfilment. "I didn't," she said, "but I think he probably did."'

'Didn't Stalin put a trace on them?'

'It was a disaster for her. They say Stalin was so angry he started the Cold War. Which means there's some unfinished business left between Russian womanhood and Western philosophers.'

'Really?'

'Oh, sure. What do you think of Tatyana from Pushkin?'

'Delightful.'

'Sure, and that's just one of them. This whole ship is filled with Tatyanas, did you know that? Tatyana from Pushkin does the cabins, Tatyana from Smolensk's in the blini bar, and take a look in the duty free. Tatyana from Novgorod—'

'Do you imagine they would take my Swedish kronor here?' asks Lars Person just then, coming into the bar in his huge bohemian hat and sitting down wearily at our table.

'Anything,' says Verso. 'Your shoes if you could spare them. So, what did they decide up there at the Age of Reason Club?'

'Swedish democracy worked as it usually does. We had a discussion. We took several votes.'

'So, papers or no papers?'

'Well, Agnes voted for papers. But Sven, Birgitta and I were all against.'

'Manders?'

'He abstained, but then he is a diplomat.'

'So, no papers,' says Verso. 'Thank God for that.'

'*Nej, nej,*' says Person, 'you don't understand. I told you, this was Swedish democracy.'

'Yes? Go on?'

'Bo was chair. That meant he had two votes and the right to appoint an ombudsman. He appointed Alma, who re-assessed the voting, decided there were various procedural errors, and was given the casting vote. Now we have papers.'

'How boring,' I say.

'They will be,' says Person, 'since at nine in the morning you are giving the very first one.'

'I haven't even given my consent,' I say. 'I like to decide these things for myself.'

'I'm afraid that is not a proper attitude,' says Person. 'This is Swedish democracy. It's a system to decide what's best for other people.'

'And where are they all now?'

'Probably taking some more votes over dinner in the dining room. We can go and join them. Or alternatively we could go down to the Balaklava Nightclub and watch the floorshow. How do we decide? Should we take a vote?'

'My friends, I really don't think that's going to be necessary, do you?' says Jack-Paul Verso.

Which explains why now we're sitting at a table in the dark Balaklava Nightclub. It's smoky, fetid, somewhere deep in the lower bowels of the ship. It's later: quite a while later, in fact several big bottles of champagne later. At the dim-lit tables men are shouting and quarrelling, red-cheeked women are giggling very loudly. A small bright-clad orchestra sits onstage: guitar, harmonica, the universal balalaika. We've already been treated to a tenor whom I'd seen swabbing the deck earlier, rendering songs from *The Volga Boatman*. Then a bass stoker has offered us a sample of the many agonies of *Boris Godunov*. Between the acts the lights go up, then go down again. Each time they dip and a new sailor-performer appears, false papers, identity cards, small consumables and various banned substances rapidly pass round the tables from hand to hand. Now, once again, they dip, and a long row of leggy girls appears, bouncing on from stage left, arms on each others' shoulders, legs tossing into the air, clad in skimpy silver costumes, gold top hats, bright spangles corruscating at every nipple and crotch.

'Hey,' says Jack-Paul Verso, looking up from pouring a bottle of shampanski into our glasses, 'am I going crazy? Or can that be Tatyana from Pushkin?'

He's not, for it is. There on the end of the sparkling row is Tatyana, decked in gold and silver, happy-faced, tossing her fine healthy legs high in the air with the rest of them.

Rising to his feet, Verso claps furiously. 'Hey, Tatyana, you're wonderful! My little quick-change artist!'

Tatyana, looking bewildered, falters momentarily; then her fine legs pick up the beat again. A waiter with a dagger in his belt walks over, and Verso subsides into his chair. 'Tatyanas by the score,' he reflects in exotic delirium. 'Every single one of them a stunner. And every single one of them longing to meet an advanced deconstructionist from the West.'

'I hardly think so,' says Lars Person. 'This girl has bunks to make and cabins to clean.'

'Sure,' says Verso, 'but it's party time, and the night is but young.'

The high-stepping, all-dancing routine comes to an end. Tatyana, smiling fixedly, bounces last off the stage. Then the lights dip completely. The entire place grows silent, watching the daggered waiter step on to the stage and switch on a TV set in the corner.

What comes on is the evening news from Moscow. There it isn't party time, and there's definitely no Age of Reason in Russia right now. An excited commentator fronts to camera; behind him is a row of soldiers and weaponed and shielded police. Marching towards them, as in the old days, comes a large, disciplined, excited crowd. They're waving the red banners of old communism, even the banners of the old Tzars; they're marching up from the Moskba river and heading for the wide open space in front of the White House. From the huge building more flags and banners wave them on. The crowd meets the rows of soldiers, who offer what seems no more than a token resistance. Paving stones start flying; the police lines keep falling back, some of the officers throwing away their riot shields and running. The crowd excitedly surges forward, breaking loose in every direction, filling the space outside the parliament building. From the square, from the window, megaphones blare, and there is a sudden surge of triumphant singing. A flight of doves is released from inside the building, to flutter high into the air. 'We've won,' cries Rutskoi joyously from the balcony. 'I call on all troops to capture the Kremlin and take the usurping traitor Yeltsin,' blares Khasbulatov. 'Victory is hours away.' The crowds turn and, driving the police before them, begin to march back into the city.

Here in the Balaklava Nightclub, all traffic and noise has stopped; we watch in total silence. Then a loud shouting erupts, and violent quarrels begin. A table is knocked over in a crash of glass. The waiter quickly switches off the TV set. At once the houselights dim, the stage lights go up. In a disordered line – they must have been summoned back quickly – the tattered band of showgirls bounces on again. Tatyana's first in the line. She and the team have done a quick costume change; now they're dressed in Russian commissar uniforms, wearing big official caps. The crowd boos, then cheers as they strip off to show they are wearing nothing underneath. It's a famous old truth, as Lars Person thoughtfully observes, that when the garments fly politics usually goes out of the window.

'But the crunch has come,' I say.

'The crunch is soon coming,' agrees Person. 'The usurper and the demagogues. It's truly Shakespearean, don't you think?'

'God, I love that girl, and all her kind,' Verso is saying meantime, staring at Tatyana, who is smiling fixedly, stripping and gyrating with the best of them, and seeing off history.

'You mean Tatyana from Pushkin?'

'Yes, let's ask her over. Maybe she can collect up a couple of her friends.'

'Not for me, I've just heard I have a paper to write.'

'Oh, come on, professor, our evening's just beginning. There are more important things than papers. Shampanski, sex, history.'

'Sorry, professor, I know if I don't go and write it now, I never will.'

A buzz of unease and political anger is passing round the nightclub; yet, somehow, the pleasures of the evening still seem to have many more hours to run. In fact, by the time I've finished paying my own share of the drinks tab to the cossack of a waiter (I have some spare Irish punts he seems absolutely delighted to take), Verso has Tatyana sitting cheerfully on his knee at the table, dressed in some quaint bird-like costume.

I set off alone through the ship. In the bars and public rooms everything is throbbing, as if an adrenalin of anxiety is passing through the whole vessel. Outside them, though, everything is quiet. In fact it's strangely quiet. Maybe the entire ship's crew have gone down below, stripped themselves to the buff in the nightclub to keep history at its distance. I can find small sign of the other Enlightenment Pilgrims either: although I do think I briefly glimpse Agnes Falkman and Sven Sonnenberg entering a cabin together, but I could be mistaken, of course. As for my own cabin, it's a silent little prison, unwindowed and gun-metalled. And the moment I enter it I regret my sudden sense of duty: fuelled, to be frank, more by a sense of sexual unease or even jealousy about Tatyana's easy compliance with Jack-Paul Verso than by a true academic passion. It's not, though, till I start to look round for my work-stuff – my briefcase, books, notes and notebooks – that I spot the huge flaw in my virtue. For the luggage that crowds out my cabin space isn't, I now remember, my luggage at all. This is soft-leather crown-emblazoned Via Veneto ware, sophisticated international-traveller finery coated with the very grandest of labels: La Scala, La Fenice, Stadtsoper, Metropolitan, Covent Garden. The luggage I need to have is somewhere else entirely. In fact it's locked away in the cabin of a very great diva.

Which explains why, minutes later, I'm marching through the ship like some burdened bellboy, toting five suitcases that seem to contain the heavy costumes of an entire opera. A few members of the crew appear and look at me suspiciously. But they say nothing, and why should they? Every single thing on this ship is suspicious. How to find her cabin? I make my way by the companion-ways: C deck, B deck, A deck. And A deck proves to be another world: there are wood-walled passages, carpeted floors. I must have found the ancient preserve of the old Russian elite and the party members. Then, from far down the passageway, I hear a noise. It's the sound of Brünnhilde in Valhalla, declaring the end of the world. As I move closer, the booming yet clear-noted song changes to something more familiar. '"To me, Onegin, all these splendours, / This weary tinselled life of mine, / This homage that the great world tenders, / My stylish house where princes dine / Is empty,"' trills a high firm voice behind a mahagony door. I rather think I've found what I'm looking for.

I tap on the door. The Swedish nightingale throws it open. Her long red hair is down now. She's looking quite grandly magnificent, wearing a soft, white dressing gown over her splendidly capacious person, and holding up a whole gold-foil wrapped magnum of pink shampanski. As for her stylish house, it isn't empty at all. A figure in a white uniform, wearing a huge cap, sits on the bed. He rises, slips past me (but after all I'm no more than another bellboy), and disappears along the passageway.

'The captain,' says the diva. 'He must go away now to drive the ship. He just came to bring me this champagne. They are such wonderful lovers of opera in Russia.'

'They're such wonderful lovers of everything,' I say. 'Sorry to interrupt. I just thought we ought to exchange our things.'

'Exchange our things?'

'Your luggage,' I say, 'you remember they left it in my cabin?'

'Oh, you have brought it? Wasn't it very heavy?'

'Very.'

'Come in, put those cases down, anywhere you like. I hope you took care of them. Do you realize there is a quarter of a million pounds of jewellery in there?'

'No, I didn't. Good lord.'

'Oh, yes, my darling, I always take it with me. And now I suppose you are expecting a little tip. Do you like a drink? Now, tell me what you think about my little cabin?'

Well . . . as little cabins go, it's certainly a nice little cabin. For one thing it's extremely big. No small cell, no windowless metal box, for the prima donna. As fits her greater fame and her larger frame, she has been given the imperial, or perhaps more accurately the Party Official suite, the ultimate or maxi-cabin. No narrow bunk bed here: instead a huge silk-sheeted double bed, luxuriously scattered with her clothing. No little metal cupboard: a vast dressing table with glinting mirrors and coloured light-bulbs, its top scattered with her jewellery. No prison-sized shower; a great bathroom off, filled with her underwear. Great wardrobes. Cushioned sofa. Flower-filled vases. Large easy chairs. A great silver ice-bucket for that magnum she's waving. Curtained portholes – and beyond them, bright in the glitter cast down by the lights of the ship, the Baltic waves gently billow and rock. A crest or two rolls by. Amid the crests, the grey granite islands of the archipelago glint in a ghostly moonlight, like the jewels on the dressing table.

'Now do you see my archipelago?' says the diva, triumphantly, bringing me a glass. 'Have some shampanski.'

In her silk dressing gown, of a kind presumably provided by the management for its most important and honoured guests, the diva, it has to be said, looks grander and more glorious than ever. There's something palatial, something imperial, in fact there's something truly transcendental, about the sheer scale and presence of her being, the bosomyness of her bosom, the booming boom-ingness of her sonic boom.

'By the way, I had the maid unpack all your luggage,' she says, sitting down on the bed and gesturing to me to join her.

'Yes, did you?'

'You will find your clothes hanging in the wardrobe.'

'I see, but why—?'

'I wanted to look in your things for that book you told me. About Monsieur Rameau and his nephew.'

'Oh yes, did you have the chance to read it?'

'A little. Till the captain came to visit me. But what a nasty book.'

'Is it?'

'It's so sad, listen to what it says,' she says, taking out her spectacles and picking up the volume. '"In Rameau we get great operas, in which we find harmony, choruses, spears, great victories, glorious ballets, grand ideas. But Rameau will simply be eliminated in his turn. And who – not even a very beautiful woman who has a nasty pimple on her nose – can ever feel as tragic as a great artist who has completely outlasted his age."'

'Yes. By his death everyone was attacking him.'

'Of course. Paris was split in two. It was the age of Gluck and Pergolesi and everyone was turning to Italian opera. Of course now he's back in fashion again.'

'Maybe you remember it was Rousseau who led the attack, in the *Encyclopedia*.'

'I know. The orchestra of the Paris opera was so furious they tried to have him assassinated. I just wish we had orchestras like that now. Musicians who care about something.'

'Postmodern times,' I say. 'Everything goes.'

'Yes, everything goes. Here, have some more shampanski, my darling. And explain me: this nephew, this fat miserable boy with no talents, why does he hate his uncle so much?'

'Why does a young person want to get rid of an old one?'

'Jealousy? You tell me.'

'The uncle was famous, one of the most famous, flattered old men of the age. And his nephew's a total failure, scraping a living off his wits. He has no reputation, no proper work. He scrapes a life by pimping and flattering, fawning on the great and then mocking them behind his back. He steals from their tables, tries to seduce their daughters. He borrows their silver and betrays them any way he can. I suppose it's what happens in a sophisticated and corrupt society, where the worst people learn how to make a parasitic living off the best.'

She pours a flowing, bubbling stream of shampanski into my glass. 'I see what you mean. The nephew's a critic.'

'I suppose that is what I mean. Rameau stood for harmony, absolute form, classical order; he stands for total discord. Rameau stands for reason; he automatically distrusts wise men and philosophers. Rameau creates a musical Utopia. He says he despises a perfect world, because it doesn't have room for utter shits like him. The only sufficient world is a corrupt one, because it allows someone like him to exist, he says.'

'But why, my darling, does Diderot like him so much?'

'I suppose because every Moi needs a Lui. He can use him to reveal the rival standpoint. Find the opposite to himself. Discover his double, his alter ego, his secret self. I'm sure our good Professor Verso would explain that Diderot was deconstructing the idea of the philosophe.'

'You wouldn't?'

'I think nephew Rameau was probably just the sort of rundown hack Diderot would have been himself, if he hadn't managed to live by his ideas and sell his library to Catherine the Great.'

'This is very interesting, my darling,' says the nightingale, looking at me thoughtfully.

'Sigmund Freud certainly thought so.'

'Sigmund thought some very odd things. Anyway, let me tell you something. I don't like that book one little bit. I liked the other one much better. The one about the servant and the master.'

'The other book?'

'In your bag.'

She's waving another volume at me, pouring me another fizzy glassful. And, you know, I have to admit it: for all her high-diva style I'm somehow beginning to feel a really warm and sentimental fondness for our dear red-haired nightingale.

'Ah, *Jacques the Fatalist*, so you found that too.'

'I found everything in the world you possess. There's nothing I don't know about you.'

'Then you're way ahead of me.'

'This Jacques, you know who he is, of course.'

'He's a man who believes in providence, and the servant of his master.'

'No, he's the great factotum. You remember the great factotum?'

'Oh, you mean the Barber of Seville.'

'Did Diderot know Beaumarchais?'

'Yes, he did. They were acquaintances, maybe friends.'

'Well, there in this book there is already Figaro. He must have passed him on to Beaumarchais.'

'Who gave him to Mozart and Rossini.'

'Which shows that your book can turn into my music. And that is why I decide I can like your Diderot.'

'Because you can sing him, you mean?'

'Of course. Here, have some more shampanski. Lie down here on the pillow and help me to drink it.'

'Well,' I say, 'I really ought to slip away.'

'Not to drive the ship?'

'To write my paper. I gather you all voted to make me speak first thing tomorrow morning.'

'But it means nothing, my darling,' says the diva, regarding me with a truly tragic air of surprise. 'Don't you know that? You are far too serious, you might as well be Swedish. Let me remind you what happened to Eugene Onegin.'

'He had to give a paper?'

'He was offered a hard choice, between solitude and love. That is how he made his truly terrible mistake.'

'Which was?'

'Don't you remember Tatyana's complaint?'

'Her complaint?'

My red-haired diva lies back on the pillow, takes a short breath, and starts again on her trilling.

' "And there beneath a Finnish sky / Amid the mournful crags on high / Alone upon his way he goes / And does not heed my present woes." You remember now?'

'Yes, I do. Wonderful.'

'And so sad. Just so terribly sad. He rejects her when in her innocence she loves him. Of course she goes and marries a very rich man. Then when he meets her again he knows how much he longs for her love. She loves him still, but now she has a terrible choice.'

'Between love and duty.'

'She struggles with herself, but she rejects him. He pleads for his cause, he confesses his errors. It's terrible.'

'A good ending though.'

'My darling, it's a truly terrible ending. She goes off to her empty fate as a wife. He remains the forlorn tragic hero. "Oh, my pitiful destiny," he cries. And on that sad sight the curtain falls.'

'Yes.'

'Now, please, have some more shampanski,' says the diva. 'See, in the bucket, there is another bottle.'

Well now: as for what happened next, if you'll excuse me, I intend to leave this whole matter right there, because, as Aleksandr Pushkin put it himself in the fine rolling verse of *Eugene Onegin*: 'Just now I'm feeling far too tired / To tell you how that meeting went/ Or what transpired from this event . . .'

It's really been a long hard day on the Enlightenment Trial: a day of meetings, a day of journeys. The *Vladimir Ilich* is beating onward through the whale-backed floating islands. Somewhere down there in the dining room, Bo and his pilgrims are probably discussing important matters of democratic procedure. Verso and Person are in the Balaklava Nightclub; heaven knows what Agnes and Sven are up to. There are mobs, guns, tanks and a curfew in the Moscow squares and boulevards, and all the evidence is the terrible war has begun. Who knows what we on the *Vladimir Ilich* will find in Russia when we finally arrive? Then the tide's erasing the faces on the beach, there's no Cartesian ego, and we live in a totally random universe of cosmic confusion inexorably tracking toward its own extinction. And, as if that wasn't enough, we've a whole day of dull papers tomorrow . . .

Still, for the moment, it's a half-chilly, half-balmy Baltic autumn night. The islands of the archipelago glitter coldly beyond the portholes. In the diva's cabin everything is made for a pinkish fleshly comfort. There's a soft silky bed, a couple of magna of champagne, a musical score on the counterpane. What could have happened next? What might have been said next? What would have been done next? I shall simply leave you to speculate as freely as you wish, only offering by way of literary assistance the one small fact that (as I think I already told you) I am one of those amiable types who, when asked, normally says yes. So I perfectly well could have said yes to this, or even that.

However it hardly matters, because the one important point, and the chief reason why this is all worth recording, is that, for the second night in a row, and for reasons that have very little to do with reason, I once again fail to write my paper . . .

TEN (THEN)

NAKAZ: THESE ARE THE RULES FOR VISITORS ENTERING
THE LITTLE HERMITAGE

Rule one
All ranks and titles shall be surrendered on entering, along with all hats and swords.

Rule two
All ambitions and pretensions, based on prerogatives of birth, rank, hierarchy or any other claim to precedence, shall also be discarded at the door.

Rule three
Please enjoy yourself, but try not to break anything, spoil anything, or chew anything.

Rule four
Sit, stand, wander about, or do anything you please, without worrying about anyone.

Rule five
Speak with moderation, and not too often, so that you never make yourself a nuisance to others, or give anyone a headache.

Rule six
Argue if you have to, but always without rage or heat.

Rule seven
Avoid making sighs, yawns, or other clear displays of boredom.

Rule eight
Innocent games and entertainments proposed by current members of the court should always be accepted by others.

Rule nine
Eat slowly, and arrive with a good appetite. Drink with pleasure and moderation, so that when you leave you can walk from the room steadily and without assistance.

Rule ten
Leave all quarrels, dirty linen, political arguments, ideologies and conspiracies at the door. Above all, remember that, before you leave, what's gone in at one ear should already have gone out of the other.

If any member of the court or a court visitor should break any of the above rules, for each offence witnessed by two others he – and this does not exclude ladies – must drink a glass of fresh water and read aloud an entire page of the *Telemachiad* by Trediakovsky.

Anyone failing three of these rules shall be compelled to learn by heart at least six lines of the poem.

Anyone breaking the tenth rule will never again be admitted to the Little Hermitage. Welcome.

It quite soon becomes a matter of habit and custom that, on nearly every non-religious non-state day of the week starting in the middle of the Russian October (which is already displaying an odd similarity to the French December), and continuing indefinitely until told otherwise, our man makes his way across the large well-ordered Petersburg streets and squares, along the canals and embankments, to the shining Winter Palace. As day follows day, it grows clearer and clearer the beautiful bright-painted building has been very well named. He's reached the northern city just in time: winter, that brisk and vengeful northern speciality, is starting its annual siege of the city with great expedition. A daily dusting of half-hearted snowflakes flutters daily around him as – in borrowed bearskin topcoat, tidy black suit beneath, wig on askew, notebooks on anything if not everything stuffed into pockets and panniers – he goes teetering off over the surface of ice, mud, human urine and rank horseshit that passes for paving in the great square before

Saint Isaac's. The cathedral church itself is chaos. It's being constructed, deconstructed, moved. Ragged frozen men work all over it, displaying that classic weary near-inertia that's the trademark of the worldwide craft of building.

Yet it must be said that Senate Square is a very fine square. It's a noble square, the very square where – one day still very far ahead, when it is faced and completed – the Imperial Mother, in homage to her great predecessor, will raise up the huge bronze statue our man had such a hand in. The day will come: but not as quickly as many, not least himself, might have expected. But who of us can possibly know what is being written in the great big Book of Destiny above? By now, of course, what was written is very clear. As the big book has it, the statue will go up nine years on from now. The year will be 1782, the day will be 7 August Old Style. Our man will certainly not be there, though he'll still be alive and well. The guards will march with lowered banners. Military bands will play. From the great podium underneath the cloth-covered statue, the Imperial Mother will bless her people, declare a general amnesty for criminals and debtors.

Across the Neva, over there in the Peter and Paul Cathedral-Fortress, the Great Metropolitan will strike Peter's tomb hard with his staff. 'Arise, great monarch,' he'll say, 'and look out over your pleasing and noble invention. For nothing you did has ever faded, nor has its glory dimmed.' Back over the sunlit water, the Empress will gesture, and the curtains hung round the statue will drop. There will be Big Peter, incredibly raised up on the back of his rearing horse, serpent between his legs, all tied to the ground only by two little hooves and the sheet-anchor of the horse's tail. His grand face, still with toolmarks on it, will come into view. He'll be looking out possessively, first across the river, toward his own bones over there in the Peter and Paul, then, more grandly, out at the Baltic and the still un-Russianized world that lies temptingly out there to the West.

All Petersburg will be there to hear the shouting. But, besides our man, it's written that another person will be absent: Étienne-Maurice Falconet, back in Paris in a rage. The big book tells us there will be a nasty argument with the Great Mother over payment of fees; it will be left to Marie-Anne Collot to complete

134

the work. That isn't all the great book can tell us. The statue itself will prosper, become a prince among statues. Blood will dedicate it, risings and rebellions surround it. Poets will write of its potent menace, its strange power to pass through the streets by night. More and more stories and myths will surround it. The most surreal dreams will be filled by it. But who now can know such things? Our Man, in his own state of being, can't. It's enough to walk through the huge cold square, brooding on Posterity and the big Book of Destiny above. For the present here-and-now is quite full enough for the asking.

Flags, buntings and banners from the recent nuptials still wave in the bitter critical wind that comes flailing off the Neva. The Neva is a strange sluggish river, bearing down fetid burdens from elsewhere, washing them up and down, here and there, suddenly falling and then dangerously rising, as if to threaten the city (as it has several times already). Its secret character, our man begins to suspect, is sinister, vengeful, pestilential; yet sometimes it glows like a magic mirror, as the big red sun, lying low, lights on it, reflects, strangely lights the imperial palaces. In front of him stands the Anna Ivanova Tower; beyond it the fine gold flèche atop the beautiful new Admiralty Building. In the city's great game of architectural chess, this matches and mates with the flèche over at the Peter and Paul Fortress, where Peter's bones lie waiting to be called. Out on the river frigates and merchantmen bob at their moorings, loading and unloading, gunports pointing this way and that. Foreign sailors already brush frost off the riggings, longing to set sail before the Baltic freeze. The carriages of foreign dignitaries and delegates clatter through the square, their noble contents sitting stiff behind fur-clad coachmen and pissing horses. But they too will soon be gone, the visitors themselves departed, the coaches replaced by sleighs, once winter properly settles in.

Our Man is walking where he walked yesterday, where he will walk tomorrow. He crosses the noble end of Nevsky Prospekt. Its fine fresh stores and new arcades are already busy, with wandering colonels, big-wigged bureaucrats, minor officers of the court, wives, mistresses, courtesans. Its great straight line points heroically to the distance, toward the marsh, sedge, lake and snowdrift of mysterious, infinitely extensive, positively illimitable Russia, spreading off beyond the senses. For all the glory of its name, that frosted open world – in these strange days of black-red sky and snow-flurried gloom – seems a less than inviting prospect. He prefers the city. He crosses the Moyka Canal, where he sees unpleasant ice-lumps from upstream tumbling furiously together before they burst into the harbour. Luckily, given this weather, it's but a bird-flight from Narishkin's mansion to Palace Square and the entrance to the Hermitage. He stares up at Rastrelli's lush façade: such a Viennese torte, a marzipaned cake, of a building. Huge guardsmen in green and red and grey-faced watchmen protect the residence, eternally standing in ground-sweeping rain-coats against autumn rain and growing cold. Now, starting to know him, they step back to let him pass.

He's coming. His notebooks on Russia – begun back in the Dutch republic, worked on in the rattling confines of Narishkin's shaking Berliner, filled out by candlelight in his fine bedroom in the palace across the square – have grown fatter day by day, filled like the crops of Burgundy geese with more and more refined and intellectual fodder. Each time he walks out, the muddy Russian reality he observes serves as a fresh provocation. His real Russia, the Russia of the mind, is growing all the time. And he's coming well-prepared. For Petersburg is full of good friends and useful warnings, so he already thinks he knows what he can expect, and what he might fear, from the Great Imperial Mother who has welcomed him so grandly, and now awaits her enlightenment within . . .

Lui, for instance, young Narishkin. Night after night, over his well-stocked table in the dining room of the huge Narishkin Palace, he's been a bubbling fount of useful wisdom. He gaily recalls past times: times when this stout and noble Empress was simply just another of those slim German archduchesses, married to just another of those snub-nosed imperial heirs. She was unhappy, bullied. She was clever, sprightly, restive, never quite sure what was expected of her from the last formidable empress, Elizabeth. She was supposed to produce an heir, yet her marriage was known to be white. Lui recalls how his own father, himself a

136

court chamberlain (Narishkins always were), realized something had to be done. He would have obliged himself; in the end the chosen solution was another of the chamberlains, the charming Sergei Saltikov, always willing to risk Siberia for a sexual intrigue. So Papa Narishkin would smuggle the archduchess in heavy disguise across Senate Square into this self-same mansion, where she could enjoy emotional rest and recreation in private. Saltikov would then come from court disguised as a woman, risking strange assaults from the ever-sparky Imperial Guards. Thus noble families have their uses. Since those days Narishkins claim special intimacy with the most private ways of the bedchamber, the unbuttoned, the so frequently unbuttoned, closet manners of the court.

'So how do I behave then?' our man asks. Lui, a courtier to his fingertips, is warm in his advice. Be as simple and natural as I am (really? – sometimes, to be honest, the man seems just another holy fool). Remember: though the outer court is grand, formal and ceremonial, the inner one is the opposite. Pomp lapses, ceremonial fades as you pass deeper into the building, until in her private rooms, where the queen bee hides, it goes altogether. Here, in the centre of the hive, a courtier pleases not by bluster or flattery but pleasantness or simplicity, not least because these are not usual Russian qualities. Never flatter – or not obviously. Never bully – she knows her own mind, a good one. Never compete for attention, or it will compete with you. Never gossip meanly; everyone else will do that for nothing. Never conspire; there are too many conspiracies already. Never presume.

You'd do best, suggests Lui on further reflection, to treat her as a mental equal, address her as one civilized and high-minded thinker to another. Remember that when she was still a newly married pubescent she loved to call herself the Little Philosopher, and sat for hours in the gardens reading the works of Voltaire – while, in his own militarized quarters, her little husband, trained as a Prussian soldier, sat interrogating rats that had strayed into the palace and sentencing their leaders to death by hanging. Take her no presents; the woman has everything except things beyond your purchase. Admit, if you like, you are an atheist (she has read your work, must know it already), but remember she's chosen to be matriarch of the Orthodox Church, and considers God Herself chose to anoint her to the throne. Laugh with her, amuse her, delight her, tell her stories: just do what you always do. But whatever you do, he warns, don't let her make you court adjutant. That means you could be in line for the post of Night Emperor. The next thing you'll find yourself having a venereal inspection with Dr Rogerson, who will provide the stiffening aphrodisiacs, before your talents are tested in the boudoirs of the two éprou-veuses, Countess Bruce and the Princess Protassov. Then you would be delegated in the Night Emperor apartments, just along the passage from the suite of her serene majesty, and thereafter enjoy a mixture of energetic night exercise and futile daily bore-dom which has already finished off several younger men.

'Dear friend, thank you, thank you,' says Our Sage. But if Lui, with his friendly chatter, has proved useful in his warnings, dear old Melchior Grimm has been truly wise, as usual. These days, his successful matchmaking finished, his diplomatic reputation vastly increased, the robust satyr has changed a good deal: he's grown rounder, fatter, more full of himself. And he's in the most wonderful of wonderful spirits, as only a dwarfish clever German from Ratisbon who has developed all the arts of French wit and manners could possibly be. The fellow is no longer hungry, he's content; been there, done that. He's no longer a philosopher, he's a universal presence; no longer out but in. What better, he says, than that the two of them have come to court together? For now the unpleasant pug-nosed boy with Saltikov's ears and all those bitter memories of 1762 have been maritally disposed of, now there's a good bed-match of Russia and Prussia, the Great Imperial Mother is free at last to do what she wants. And what she's longing for is pleasure, wit, humour, thought, art, amuse-ment, fashion, anything European; anything better than the daily round of loud boyars, boasting generals, pleading gentlefolk, pranc-ing hussars, conspiring chamberlains, flattering ambassadors, adul-terous maids-in-waiting, hirsute priests, fearsome black monks and ambitious nobles from remote provinces who've bent her ears these last ten years.

'She dreams of what she always wanted,' says Grimm. 'A clever French philosopher who will refine her mind and enhance her reputation in the drab afternoons. Then a witty German courtier who can amuse her to distraction in the calm of the evenings.'

'What? Oh you mean you, Melchior?'

'Of course me,' says Grimm. 'You bore her with your wisdom and science after lunch. Then I'll cheer her up over dinner.'

'How will you do that?'

'I sit by her side. I listen to her little rages. I encourage all her spite. Her little whipping boy, that's what she calls me.'

'Don't let it go too far. Whips can hurt.'

'She loves me,' says Melchior. 'You know I dine with her every single night at eight? She likes to have little suppers *en cabinet*. Wonderfully amusing. I wish you could be there.'

'Why can't I? Voltaire dined with Fredcrick every night.'

'It's far too intimate. A chosen band, never more than ten of us. Quite informal. We select our places at random, pop our names into someone's hat. There are no servants. We have an arrangement of pulleys and ropes, we pull up the dishes from the kitchen with our own fair and noble hands.'

'I prefer servants.'

'Not when they report everything to the head of the Secret Office,' says Melchior.

'The Secret Office?' asks our man, staring at him in dismay.

'Of course. It's the same in all imperial courts. Our Empress learned all her lessons from Paris, you know. The Russian spying service is modelled on Sartine's. Everything gets reported, every spoken word, every writing, every sexual probe, down to the doings of the monarch herself. Luckily the chief of the secret policemen is getting a deaf old man. But all the rest can hear everything, of course. And do.'

'All servants are unreliable, you mean?'

'Naturally. Everyone is a spy in someone or other's employ. By definition. A court's a conspiracy, why else would you attend it? One minute you're basking in royal favour, the next you're drowning in an underground dungeon of the Peter and Paul.'

'But not you, I hope, old friend.'

'Not me, no. I'm in very good favour. I did get that unspeakable son of hers off her hands. So that's it, you see.'

Grimm sits back: squat, powerful, self-satisfied. He's a wonderful fellow, our man recalls. For half a lifetime they've done marvellous things together. But can it be court life has gone to his head, and he's getting too big and paranoid for those shiny Prussian boots?

'You're quite sure she really does want a philosopher?' he asks anxiously.

'No one more so. She dreams of being a great despot with a huge army, a splendid mind and a glorious soul.'

'Like Frederick of Prussia.'

'Except she's much sweeter, and you don't have to sit through endless cantatas. But I can assure you she's nothing like the barbarous monarch they talk of in Paris. That's Parisian envy and spite.'

'I see she's charmed you completely, Melchior.'

'Not a bit. I flatter myself it's the reverse. I believe she loves me. You and Voltaire were quite right when you chose to call her the Minerva of the North.'

'Minerva is the owl of history that flies by night. You might be wise to fly by night too.'

'It's not my graceful body that concerns her, it's my lively mind,' says Grimm, tidying his splendid cuticles.

'Your subtle German wit and so on?'

'My wide political experience. My close relationship with everyone who matters in this world. Maybe I shouldn't tell you—' Grimm stops, looks round.

'Since we met, all those years ago, haven't we always told each other everything?' asks Our Sage.

'Very well then,' says Grimm, trimming away at his tips, 'she's offered me a great position. Chancellor of the Court. Head of the river. Top row in the Table of Ranks.'

'You accepted, of course?'

'I refused, of course. Who'd elect to be a barbarous Russian when there's the rest of European civilization to choose from?'

'You just gave me the impression that being Russian was highly fashionable these days.'

'I have quite enough to do already. Compiling our much-loved court newsletter. Introducing everyone here to everyone there. Looking after little Mozart. Visiting all my good crowned friends. In any case, I'm completely dependent on the wit and wisdom of Paris.'

'It is where all the best gossip starts.'

'The point is, I'm useful where I'm useful.'

'True,' says our man, 'half the thrones of Europe would be vacant without you. Dynasties would fade. Little German princesses would die unmarried and untouched. Cradles would lie empty. Wars would start. The map of Europe would fold up, just like a broken tent.'

'Exactly,' says Grimm, nodding, 'and the Imperial Mother understands all that. That's why she's done for me exactly what she did for you.'

'Bought your library?' asks our man, suddenly feeling a real twinge of fraternal jealousy, which only the quickest and most generous stab of reason manages to settle. 'You only have three books.'

'Given me a pension for the rest of my life,' says Grimm. 'Made me her permanent adviser, her lifetime correspondent and her roving ambassador.'

'She's making you me? She's not asked you to buy paintings for her?'

'My dear fellow, I can be just as useful as you are. I'm just as well informed. In fact better. I know what's hanging in every throne room in Europe.'

'Well, you do enter so many. But isn't it hard to see the pictures when you're always down on your knees?'

'I don't get down on my knees,' says Grimm sharply. 'She's also asked me to buy her cosmetics.'

'And who better? You do wear so many yourself.'

'And advise her on the education of her grandchildren.'

'I thought there were none.'

'Not yet.'

'Oh, you're going to have to attend to that too?'

'Very probably, if Paul is like his father. If he can't manage, there are plenty of shaftsmen waiting in the wings. Why do you think the court is full of handsome guardsmen?'

'The place sounds like a stud farm.'

'Just what it is. Anyway, my dear friend, there's no need to be jealous of me. She cares for us equally. She's proposed us both for the new Academy of Sciences. Attached us both to her Smolny School for Noble Girls.'

Our man sighs. 'But is she ready for a course in the spirit of human reason and reform? A modernized vision of the monarch and the state?'

'No monarch more so,' says Grimm sweetly. 'Louis loves his bacchanals, Frederick loves his Bach, George of England loves his roses, her Serenity truly loves her thoughts. Nothing pleases her more than to spend half an hour in meditation. Nothing makes her happier than to hear the court reader recite twenty pages of Voltaire. Rousseau even.'

'Oh my God.'

'She loves everything of his except *The Social Contract*.'

'I know the feeling.'

'She shares it,' says Grimm. 'She's just banned it from Russia.'

'Ah, I see. Your wonderfully enlightened lady is a censor too.'

'Not at all. She says she'll admit Rousseau to Russia as soon as the time's right.'

'With Rousseau the time is never right.'

'I tell you, she loves all the works of reason. She simply asks they don't defy God, offend manners, or threaten her authority.'

'Reason, but within reason.'

'Quite,' says Melchior, rising, embracing him like a brother, putting on his tricorne.

In the door he stops suddenly, as if struck by a forgotten thought.

'Something else?' asks our man.

Melchior comes back, stands close. 'As an old friend, perhaps I should warn you. Your afternoons could be interrupted by just a few distractions. Her Serenity thinks she may possibly have to go off and conquer Turkey. Maybe Poland too.'

'I see.'

'And she's having trouble with the impostors.'

'The impostors?'

'It happens every few months or so. You know how tangled great dynasties can be. Especially when they mate outside the bedclothes and engage in constant assassination. There's always someone coming out of nowhere and claiming to be true heir to the Romanovs. They usually disappear as quickly as they come.'

'I think I know how.'

'This time it's more serious,' Grimm warns. 'A man with a black beard has appeared among the Don Cossacks claiming he's Peter the Third.'

'I thought he died from the haemorrhoids?'

'He did, in prison. But this man, his real name's Pugachov, says he escaped and took a remarkable medicine which changed his height, weight and appearance. It made him forget his first language, German . . .'

'What a medicine!'

'Now he's turned up somewhere near Orenburg, and the Cossacks have started a bloody rebellion to restore him to the throne.'

'Might they succeed?'

'Not a bit of it. It's all being put down with great brutality. We'll soon hear he's been mutilated and hanged, and your Enlightenment is safe. I doubt if it will interfere with you at all. I shouldn't have mentioned it. My dear friend, enjoy your philosophical afternoons.'

Worrying, really. And there's more. No sooner has Melchior doffed and left him than there's another dreadful fuss in the doorway. The French ambassador's arrived, coughing, hawking, stifling a cold with a scented handkerchief, shouting at servants. His name's Count Durand de Distroff, a foppish, ambling, rambling sort of fellow, just posted here from the grand court at Vienna, where all his sharp-edged manners were made.

'Russia,' he says, presenting his gilded card, sitting down, 'it's cold.'

'Indeed, Your Excellency. How observant. And how kind of you to come to call.'

'His most Christian Majesty at Versailles asked me to attend you. He wished me to say how pleased he is to hear you're in Petersburg.'

'His Majesty is gracious.'

'Not exactly,' says the ambassador. 'He says the longer you stay the better. However, should you intend to return to Paris, there are a few small matters to which His Brilliance would have me bring to your attention. A few things he'd liked you to keep in mind as you debate metaphysics with the Imperial Mother.'

'Such as?'

'Who has this, who has that? Who has Poland, who has Turkey? You must know that the Empress, being born German, entertains a vulgar prejudice against the French.'

'I hadn't noticed. Every single person I've met at her court speaks the language. Half of them have just stepped right off the rue Royale. Nearly all our generals, our milliners and our chefs are here, cooking up a fortune. No wonder in France these days you can't win a military victory or get decent boeuf bourguignon.'

'It's one thing to value the treasures of our advanced civilization, another to respect our political necessities. I'm not talking millinery, sir, I'm talking the lofty realms of diplomacy. Balances of power, the future of Europe, grand alliances, and so forth and so on. We wouldn't want the Russians to turn into Prussians, would we? It's the eternal danger here. You know her Majesty's late husband was deluded into believing he was really a Prussian? He goose-stepped round the palace, he bought the guard new German uniforms and armaments. Consider, what's the point of this new marriage? – negotiated by your friend the fat German, of course. To ally this court again with King Frederick of Prussia. Probably the most dangerous man in the whole of Europe.'

'I'm no admirer of his flute-playing majesty. But I hardly think so.'

'I assure you. Frederick once slept with the Empress's mother.'

'Surely not, Your Excellency? Now her father I can believe.'

'I advise you, those two monarchs put together could outflank us completely. They'll divide Poland, take all of Asia, master the entire Mediterranean. Think what that would do to your French culture and your fine gastronomy.'

'I'm sorry, Your Excellency, I'm a thinker. I can hardly comprehend such vast affairs of state.'

'Exactly, like all you modern sages. You gladly profess political ignorance, yet you always presume to advise monarchs on the perfect society whenever it suits you.'

'I think, Your Excellency. That's what I do, all I do. I don't conspire.'

'Thought is a conspiracy, the worst there is,' says Durand. 'But in any case you have ears, do you not? And I notice you have eyes.'

'I can't believe you're asking me to spy?'

Durand taps his cane crossly: 'According to my own understanding of rational philosophy, everything depends on accumulating the evidence of the five senses.'

'In my philosophy I've always said we need more than the material evidence of the senses. We need an honest spirit and a good conscience, for one thing.'

Distroff coughs, holds up the handkerchief to his sniffing nose. 'I won't dispute with a philosopher about the proper means of grasping knowledge. All I ask is that you grasp some and take it back home with you to Paris. If it would help concentrate that tender mind of yours, I've drawn up a paper memorandum detailing His Majesty's concerns.'

'Give it to me, I'll read it and say what I think.'

'No, you will not. It's from one emperor to another. What you are expected to do is, once you have won Her Imperial Highness's total attention, slip it under her pillow.'

'Her pillow? I've no intention of getting anywhere near her pillow.'

'We know how much she admires you already. My dear fellow, remember you're a Frenchman. You come from the land of Cyrano and Casanova.'

'I understood Casanova was a Venetian.'

'Yes, but he behaved like a Frenchman.'

'So did Don Juan. And he turned out to be one more trickster from Seville. You're not asking me to behave like those people? Jump into her bed and smother her nakedness with messages of state?'

'Others have done it before for the honour of France,' says

145

Durand. 'Remember the Chevalier d'Eon, who called himself Genevieve, and got himself appointed maid-in-waiting to the previous Empress?'

'D'Eon's a raddled transvestite. I met him chez Beaumarchais, all dressed up in his pretty skirts.'

'Exactly, but he did his duty. Then when the right time came, he displayed his sweet little male secret in the Empress's bedroom. She thanked him in her usual frank way, and the fellow fashioned a brand new rapprochement between Petersburg and Versailles.'

'Extraordinary. But it can't happen twice.'

'It did. He went to London and did much the same with Queen Sophie-Charlotte.'

'I see. So now you're expecting a queer little Frenchman to become George the Fourth?'

'I'm merely explaining your patriotic duty.'

'I fear I can't, Your Excellency,' our man says. 'All I live for is to be an honest man.'

'Really? Very well, may I put it like this?' says Durand, rising and calling for his hat. 'You've already told me you intend to return to Paris. Well, His Majesty asks me to tell you he's already pre-booked a small suite in the Bastille, just in case you come home empty-handed. Leave it, that's all, and under her pillow, remember. What a vile country this is! I really can't wait to get recalled.'

'It could happen sooner than you think,' says our man, rapidly consulting the great Book of Destiny above. The ambling, rambling fop sneezes again, puts on his tricorne, goes out. Clearly it's no easy or delicate thing to be a travelling philosopher, even if this is an enlightened day and age . . .

And all that's just his prologue, the prelude to the action. But now the time's arriving for his play . . .

ELEVEN (NOW)

ODD. HOW VERY ODD. I'm waking again; it's another autumnal morning. But this time the room I'm in is rocking heavily. Beyond its large portholed windows I see the fast-moving white-caps of a frantic, angry Baltic sea. Noise grates from everywhere: those ceaseless bangings, creakings, groanings and grindings that form the unique soundtrack of a big ship under way. The massive silk-sheeted bed I'm in is empty: empty, that is, except for my own soft naked self. Empty too the whole grand stateroom – which is surely not the cabin I was assigned to when I boarded the vessel yesterday. In truth I can't imagine how I happen to be lying here; though a large silk nightdress and three large empty champagne bottles in a flooded ice-bucket offer a very faint clue.

Excuse me while I rise in my naked splendour and take a quick look around. Ah. Over here, it seems, I've acquired a large and steamy bathroom. With your permission I'll disappear for the next few minutes and take a hasty shower. There: that's much better, isn't it? Now let's go and find me some clothes. The ones I came in have somehow disappeared: utter mystification. My suitcase lies tossed into the corner of the cabin, but that's totally empty, I see. Why don't we check these fitted wardrobes? My word, just look at that! Amazing sequinned dresses! All these flamboyant hats! These wigs, in every shade! Beautiful soft silk nightgowns! The bangles, the bras, the bustiers, the huge spare eyelashes and false fingernails! Oh, there, look, my shirts. And I notice we have our own big Russian TV set, there in the corner. Shall we switch on and find out what the world's been up to in our absence?

And not only here on the *Vladimir Ilich* has the night been taken up with mysterious and confusing events. The commentary seems to have switched from Swedish to Finno-Ugrian, not a language I've mastered, but the gist stays clear. Following the principles Vladimir Ilich historically set down for the proper conduct of a revolutionary *coup d'état* (arrest the government in power, take the post and telegraph office, the national bank, and the railway station to stop the trains) the Moscow crowds have gone on the streets, heading for their modern equivalents: the mayor's office, police headquarters, the TV building, the airport. *Cut to:* a tracked hi-jacked personnel carrier smashing through the doorway of the state TV station, reinforced by a large angry mob who are trying to battle their way inside, and a firefight begins. *Cut to:* machine-gun fire spraying across wide boulevards and fleeing crowds. *Cut to:* Tzar Yeltsin, descending at the Kremlin by helicopter. Now become Action Man incarnate, he's striding round his office and asking his generals to react. *Cut to:* Disconsolate newscaster looks at camera, says, 'The conflict in Russia has at last come to the brink', and *Wipe to black*. The station's gone off air . . .

Finland, not far away from here over the Baltic, takes over with its own live footage. A big squat newscaster in a decent suit talks to camera. There are agency pictures, a general sense of confusion. But it's early morning outside the White House. Tanks are rolling across the river and ranging up in a row outside the building, their barrels raised. Deputies at the windows, shouting down to the soldiers below. Yeltsin in the Kremlin, talking furiously, dashing to the Defence Ministry where the nuclear codes are. It seems he has called out the army, no doubt a high-risk gamble, since he can hardly know now which side his own generals and troops are likely to support. Rifles are firing, a soldier goes down, a tank shell flies and hits the White House high up, windows blowing out and . . . Just a moment, what's the time? Oh my god, it's White Rabbit time: hurry hurry hurry. I've a paper to give, and the Diderot Project starts its business in the conference room in exactly ten minutes. My paper, where is it? I'm a sound and responsible academic type, so surely I must have written it. I always write it. When I say yes to something, I do it. Just a minute, I really ought to eat something, except I've left it far too late for breakfast . . .

Off we go then, breakfast-less, paper-less, through the clanging banging ship. Stewardesses hoover away in the wood-panelled passages. Below, in the bars and lounges, noisy shouting crowds of Russians are gathered, watching the next live newscast. In the conference section, things are quieter, more studious. I find the glass-walled chamber assigned to the Diderot Project, and stare through the glass walls. Yet even here things have changed overnight; Bo and Alma must have been busy. The room's been rearranged into a large square of tables, covered in green baize. On the tables are places laid with neat new notepads, pencils, bottles of Russian fizz, large cardboard wallets stuffed with maps and restaurant tickets and marked 'Diderot Project'. And round the tables, showered, changed and doubtless breakfasted, are the Diderot pilgrims, awaiting the first speaker of the morning. Bo sits in the chairman's seat. He looks up, sees me, impatiently waves me inside. The other pilgrims look at me strangely. Only the red-haired diva, clad in black today, gives me a quick glance of complicity.

The event is in train. Bo is already speaking. Difficult events surround us, he's announcing, waving his glasses. But when the world is in chaos, all the more reason for all the more reason. When things are in confusion, there must always be those who follow the bright torch of truth. When times darken, the world needs those who can deal in clarity and wisdom, can unify anarchy and order, real and ideal, arts and science. As Bo goes on speaking, in his reassuring fashion, as if it is perfectly normal for us to read theoretical papers to one another while sailing into a revolution, I try to draw thought and idea together from the darkness of stupor. Very well, it's conference time in the Baltic; must do my best. Suddenly Bo stops, says my name by way of introduction, turns interrogatively to me. I get up and take the speaker's place. I look round at the row of stony early-morning faces ranged all round the green-baized table. I begin to speak. And this – or more or less – is what I find I have to say:

A PAPER THAT IS NOT A PAPER

How very kind of you to invite me to give this first paper, even though I wasn't even present at the time to say I was

149

happy to give it. So I do have to tell you that this paper isn't really a paper. (*BO: Oh no, I don't believe it . . .*) It would probably take several chapters of a novel to explain why I've not been able to write one. Let's just say it was due to circumstances beyond my control, and maybe my self-control. But I think the best thing I can do is to tell you a story. (*AGNES: No, I thought so . . .*) Except the story is not really a story either — because it's perfectly true, and starts from a real experience I had in Stockholm just two days ago.

Bo, you'll recall that I chose to arrive one day early, before we set off on this fine scholarly voyage. And I decided to spend my extra afternoon, usefully and philosophically, hunting the tomb of the great René Descartes. It seemed the ideal way to begin any kind of philosophical pilgrimage. After all, Descartes had asked us nearly all the questions that disturb the modern mind, and he did more than almost anyone to make sure we actually had one. He's surely a figure who lies behind our own philosopher, Denis Diderot . . . (*BO: I don't think so, surely he rejected Descartes . . .*) Perhaps. But he did understand Descartes showed us a world divided into mind and matter, and gave us the world as a living, perceiving, enquiring machine.

Unfortunately when, just about 350 years before I did, Descartes arrived in Stockholm, his own living, perceiving, enquiring machine suddenly began to fail. He soon caught a chill and died of it, at the age of fifty-six. He was buried somewhere or other in the city, at the Queen's command. And what followed next, as you explained, Bo, was a remarkable history — an odd history of posthumousness, which I've been thinking about ever since. I suppose you know the story, so it goes to say his corpse and coffin travelled widely — from Sweden to Denmark, Denmark to France. In France they went from abbey to abbey, church to church, and site to site. His bones were buried, disinterred, re-buried. He was dug up in the French Revolution, he almost made it to the Pantheon. Resting in the gardens nearby, he saw the rise of Napoleon, the advent of the Citizen King, the dawn of the Second

Republic, and so on. And each time the clock of history ticked on a bit further, they moved him from here to there.

In short the dead philosopher was unquestionably much busier, better travelled, more argued over, more problematical, more celebrated, more entertained, in every respect far more attended to than he ever had been during his rather reclusive quiet life. He became a great posthumous power. In fact both he and his famous dilemma – the Cartesian dilemma – have been buried, disinterred, scattered, venerated, execrated and generally fought over by every generation of philosophers and writers from then to this very day . . . (*LARS: It's quite true. Take Samuel Beckett for instance . . .*) And all these strange posthumous adventures, these lineages and homages and defacements, these complicated heritages and anxieties of influence began to shift my thoughts from the topic I'd first thought of for a paper ('Diderot and Postmodernism,' I have to admit), from Denis to another writer, and Postmodernism to Postmortemism. Or necrology, as the French nicely call it, the study of the dead.

Perhaps you recall that in another revolutionary year in Paris, 1968, another great philosophe, Roland Barthes, published a famous necrological essay, 'The Death of the Author'. Necrologically speaking, Barthes is himself now dead, following an odd street accident in the rue des Ecoles, quite close to the place where Descartes' remains are now buried, assuming that any remain after his endless travels. But what exactly remains of Roland Barthes, the author of 'The Death of the Author'? I suppose you could say that what he's achieved is a postmodern Posterity. That's to say, in the modern way we admire him, but we've learned to think of him as he seems to have perceived himself, as a writing, a text – a teasing text, a text that both celebrates and denies the writer who may or may not have written it. Because, as I understand it, the whole claim of Barthes' work is that a writer can only be exactly that: a text.

In other words, there isn't a she that writes it, there's an it that writes him. (*AGNES: Or mostly her . . .*) Meaning books don't have authors, they just have destinations. That's why, Barthes famously tells us, in accepting the Death of the Author we're announcing the Birth of the Reader. A book's a game, a tease, a seduction that comes from the other side of a grave. Whatever authors might think of their own purposes and intentions, the text can never become final nor the game be concluded. There'll always be more readers, and more readers mean more meanings. A text's simply a language. And language is slippage; it doesn't fix or make real anything at all. Books float off into the great utopia of language, somewhere between writing and reading. And yet what's interesting about this idea, of books as an open play of floating signs between writer and reader, isn't new at all. I can find it in the eighteenth century. (*BO: In Diderot, of course* . . .) In Diderot, yes, but also in my own favourite writer. 'Writing, when properly managed, is but a different name for conversation . . .' he writes in the glorious pages of *Tristram Shandy*. 'The truest respect you can pay to the reader's understanding is to halve this matter amicably, and leave him (*AGNES: Or her* . . .) something to imagine, in his turn, as well as yourself.'

All this set my mind going on a process this writer always used to call 'transverse zig-zaggery' . . . (*BO: In other words, the Lockean association of ideas. ME: Yes, Bo, that's quite right* . . .) And I began to turn my mind to this whole complicated question of literary mortality. Sweden and its graveyards certainly had something to do with it. So did our quest for a dead philosopher. So did Roland Barthes. I began to reflect that while in modern theory we pretend we have no need of an Author to explain our interest in books, the truth is we like to grant lives to our authors, and even view them as real persons just like all the rest of us. (*VERSO: That assumes you know what a person is* . . .) Even the critics and scholars amongst us are deeply interested in literary biographies and autobiographies, or what's now fashionably called 'life-writing'. Even Barthes finally wrote a book about this, called *Barthes on Barthes* (I admit he claimed to see himself as a total fiction). But ask any publisher and they'll tell you there are plenty of readers out there who much prefer the pleasure of reading an author's biography to the pain of reading his or her work.

(*VERSO: But biographies are fictions too . . .*) Exactly. Biographies are fictions too, and in fact they all have just one common plot and culmination. They tell us the life of the author, and then they usually tell us of the death of the author. Only when we reach the final weeks, the ultimate hours, the famous last words – Browning saying, 'More than satisfied', Henry James saying, 'So here it is at last, the distinguished thing' (*VERSO: He didn't . . .*), Gertrude Stein saying, 'What is the answer? What is the question?' and so on – can we feel the plot's complete. Yet according to my new theory of Postmortemism, the end of the story isn't the end of the story at all. It's simply the opening shot in the next story: the necrological sequel, the story of the writer's after-life, the tale of the graveyard things that follow. Wakes and processions, cemeteries and dripping yews. Obituaries, eulogies, epitaphs, inscriptions, tombs, catafalques. Statues, plinths, busts, poets' corners, writers' houses, pantheons. Libraries, collections, lost manuscripts, translations, collected edited editions, complete works (they almost never are). In other words, all the things Denis Diderot (*BO: Oh good . . . something important at last . . .*) called 'Posterity': that is, the pregnant scene for which everything in life is staged, the place where literature becomes literary, a show by a dead writer in front of an audience of live readers. In short, the shadowy theatre where we all bury, disinter, translate, interpret, study, revise, amend, re-edit, parody, quote, misquote, traduce and transcend, in a wild anxiety of criticism and influence.

Which takes us into the wonderful world of 'burlesque necrology' – where some great gothic tale of deaths, corpses, tombs, monuments, anniversaries, retrospectives takes on far more importance than the life as originally lived. Think of the great English poets. Shelley: drowned at sea, body burned to ashes on the beach at Lerici, heart returned to England. Byron: dead for Greek freedom at Missolonghi, body returned to England, offered to Westminster Abbey but refused, sent off to Newstead Abbey, statues almost everywhere except in Britain. Browning: died in his son's palazzo in Venice, still mourning Elizabeth Barrett forty years after her death in Florence, taken to the island of San Giorgio, then shipped home and offered to Westminster Abbey, application approved. Hardy: entombed in Westminster Abbey, heart buried next to spiky wife in Stinsford churchyard. And so on.

In fact the fates of writer-corpses have constantly been strange. Voltaire's corpse was smuggled out of Paris in a post-chaise sitting up, so he wouldn't suffer an atheist's funeral in quicklime. In the Père-Lachaise cemetery in Paris, the tombs of La Fontaine and Molière are mysteriously empty. In a makeshift chapel on a ranch near Taos, New Mexico, D. H. Lawrence's body, moved from Vence in France, has been plugged into the ground with thick concrete to protect him from necrophilic female admirers. Perhaps the greatest artists' graveyard of all is on the island of San Giorgio in the Venice lagoon, where, for instance, Ezra Pound lies close to Stravinsky. Another's in Saint Petersburg, where Dostoyevsky lies with Tchaikovsky and Rimsky-Korsakov. Of course we're all obsessed with the Death of the Author.

Which, by more transverse zig-zaggery, takes me back to 1968, the same year Barthes published his essay. Because that year I was present at an important literary funeral – in fact the funeral of the author I probably admire most in the world. (*ALMA: But a moment ago you said he lived in the eighteenth century . . .*) It took place in Yorkshire, Britain's largest and most literary county (the county I come from myself). If you ever go there, as you must, you'll find another significant phenomenon of Postmortemism. For just as there's literary necrology, there's literary geography. You can start your Yorkshire tour in Brontë Country, where the signs are in Japanese, go on to Bradford, which is Priestley Country (signs mostly in Urdu), then head for James Herriot Country (no people, just animals). On to Castle Howard (Brideshead Country) and to the coast at Whitby (Dracula Country). Then if you head northward you'll soon find yourself among the aspiring maidservants of Catherine Cookson Country. Go south to the Humber and you'll find an area which consists of milkbars, fishdocks, huge civic cemeteries. This can be instantly recognized as Philip Larkin Country.

My particular funeral took place in the beautiful stone estate village of Coxwold, in the Howardian Hills, midway between Herriot and Brideshead Country. The deceased had been the vicar of the parish and a Dean of York. His name was Laurence Sterne. (*BO: Just like the author?*) It was the author. (*LARS: But he died a long time ago . . .*) Precisely two hundred years before I attended his funeral. He wasn't just a very famous writer but a very famous preacher (*ANDERS: Parson Yorick . . .*) Parson Yorick, the parson from York, whom so many people came to hear they enlarged Coxwold church to fit them in. But his fame soared when he began writing a novel, *The Life and Opinions of Tristram Shandy* – so successful he was presented at court. He became famous in France, went there and to Italy. He came back and wrote a tale of his travels. (*ANDERS: A Sentimental Journey . . .*) The moment it was published he died, in March 1768, at his London lodgings in Bond Street, of the tuberculosis that always plagued him. His last words, incidentally, were, 'Now it is done.'

Sterne died almost alone; at least, he was attended by one servant, and that was it. His wife, a 'porcupine of a woman', who'd turned out to be ten years older than she said, was heading off to France along with his fortune. His excellent mistress, Eliza Draper, had returned to her husband in India. He was out of favour with the church for his work. Which is probably why only three people attended his funeral: a sailor, his printer, and a lawyer. He was buried without a headstone at Archery Fields, an overflow graveyard of Saint George's, Hanover Square. It sounds a good address; it wasn't. The graveyard was guarded by a big mastiff dog because it was regularly robbed by grave snatchers. But the grave snatchers snatched the dog, and within two days they'd stolen Sterne's body too. It was next seen at Cambridge University, on the dissecting table at a public anatomy lecture. A member of the audience recognized him, but didn't say so until after the skull had been trepanned. (*LARS: Alas, poor Yorick . . .*) Of course the university didn't wish to be embarrassed (*BO: The university never does . . .*) . . . so the remains were secretly returned to the grave snatchers, taken to London and secretly restored in the grave.

And there they stayed till the Swinging Sixties. In Britain this happened to be not only a time of Beatlemania, mind-enhancing drugs and body-enhancing sex, but a property boom. One of Britain's biggest landowners, the Church of England, decided the best way it could serve its divine mission was to put the churchyard on the market for commercial development. Happily a good man I knew, Kenneth Monkman, remembered Sterne's remains, went to the consistory court, and asked for an exhumation. When they dug the graveyard, they found bones and a trepanned skull. The problem was to be sure it was Sterne's, so they called a forensic pathologist (Mr Harvey Ross of Harley Street, if you want to know). He came up with an ingenious forensic device. In Italy Sterne sat for his bust by the famous English sculptor Nollekens, who always measured his sitter's heads with callipers. If they could match the skull with the bust, which Mr Monkman possessed, it would prove it was Sterne's. The bust was brought to the graveyard. The head grinned at the skull, the skull at the bust. They matched exactly.

My friend Monkman now had skull and bones. All he needed was a grave to put them in. Fortunately the ideal answer presented itself: an academic conference. In the summer of 1968, the University of York decided (in between the student sit-ins so fashionable at the time) to hold a great International Sterne Conference two hundred years after his death. It was like our present gathering, except instead of being held on a ship heading for a revolution it was held on the campus in the middle of one, and instead of us nine something like two hundred international scholars came. (*BO: But quantity is not always quality . . . MOI: Definitely not, but it was still a very splendid and memorable occasion. I was there myself. BO: I do hope you had papers . . . MOI: Yes, I gave one. BO: If you could do it then, you could . . .*) I had time in those days.

Besides, our conference now had more than papers. It also had Sterne's bones and winged skull. (*LARS: Which reminds me, where is Diderot?*) So we arranged a funeral, and decided to bury him in the graveyard of the church he'd made famous, Coxwold.

So, a portion of the world's thinking finest, we all met at Shandy Hall, Sterne's crazy house in the village, his 'philosophical hut', as he called it. He'd spent the profits of *Tristram Shandy* remodelling it to fit his own fantastic imagination, and now Monkman had restored it to its former glory. It was quite a remarkable occasion. The Church of England decided to let bygones be bygones, so the current Chancellor of York – his name was Canon Cant – agreed to give the funeral oration. A firm of wine-shippers, Croft's (Sterne had known the founder) agreed to ship over a case of his favourite bromide, port from Oporto. We walked in a row through the lovely estate village. We sat down among the Grinling Gibbon tombs, and awaited the oration. But – alas, again, poor Yorick. Just one important person was missing, and that was the deceased himself. By a fatal error the British will understand only too well, the remains had been assigned to travel from London to Coxwold by British Rail. Following an ancient rule, they had delivered them to a wrong destination, a village of vaguely similar name in darkest Wales. Worse still, the occasion, like Stockholm, was totally *alkoholfri*. British Rail had also been entrusted with the case of port.

The funeral took place even so. Canon Cant's obsequy was quite excellent; a crying shame Sterne himself had missed it. The skull and bones did turn up several weeks later, after having toured most of Britain. By now the scholars had returned to their distant lecture-halls, so what remained of the remains had to be reburied by a tiny handful of dedicated Sterneans, who admit to little memory of the event, since the case of port turned up too. So now, if you care to visit Coxwold, as you should, you will find Sterne's remains are now interred there. In fact you'll find two tombstones in the churchyard, one put up long ago by some friendly Freemasons, the other a new one. Incidentally, as far as details of birth and death are concerned, both are incorrect. And, sad to say, at the foot of the graves lies that of Kenneth Monkman, the only one who really knew the full story, and the greatest Sternean of them all.

(*BO: I'm sorry, but we are really here for Diderot . . .*)

Ah, yes, Diderot . . .

As Dr Johnson famously complained, *Tristram Shandy* is the oddest of books. Sterne used his transverse zig-zaggery to break every rule of the new form so rightly called 'the novel'. He left blank pages for the reader to paint in, put the preface in the middle, set the chapters in the wrong order. Consequences come before causes, and only after he's published several volumes does he say he's ready to start. Most novels then started with the birth of the hero, so he started with his conception. And it's a botched conception − by a Lockean association of ideas, Tristram's father-to-be winds the clock and makes love to his wife on the last night of the month, one thing reminding him of the other. Tristram's mother-to-be finds it difficult to concentrate on the one, as she's wondering if he remembered to do the other. So Tristram's conception is a damp squib, as it were, and he's born a botched child, an imperfect specimen. But then the whole book is a botched conception too. In fact it's all a cock and bull story, Sterne says.

But if he designed a fantastic mystification for the book's beginning, he devised an even cleverer one for the ending. He chose to conclude the book in the most striking way possible: the Death of the Author. He had congenital tuberculosis, and started the book as a comic stay against his misfortunes. He decided to keep writing a couple of volumes a year till he just dropped dead. Then the book would end, 'Now it is done.' Or that's what he thought. In 1760, 1761, 1762, his writing was well up to schedule. Six volumes were out, he'd become an international celebrity. But his health was fading, so in 1762 he decided to make his will, leave Shandy Hall, and travel to France and Italy − partly to convalesce, partly because he was hoping to donate his porcupine wife to Europe in the interests of greater integration. Before he set off on his strange and irreverent Grand Tour, he decided to send the six volumes to the French writer he admired most. And he happened to be Denis Diderot. (*BO: Ah . . . at last . . .*)

Diderot fell in love with the book. He told all his friends Sterne was the 'Rabelais of the English' and this was 'the craziest, wisest and greatest of all books'. Seventeen hundred and sixty-two was, as so often, not really a great year to be English in Paris. The Seven Years War was ending, and the French were just losing their two Indies – America and India – to the British. Their overseas empire was dying, the much-resented Peace of Paris about to be signed. None of this improved Franco-British relations (they were soured for generations). Still, nothing ever did. The French became deeply Anglophobe, and soon, through the playwright Beaumarchais, they were sending arms to American Revolutionaries and making national heroes of the electric Ben Franklin, the great George Washington, the splendid Thomas Jefferson. It proved a dangerous strategy, for in supporting the American revolutionaries the French court was encouraging the coming of its own. But that was ahead, this was still the Age of Reason. And, as you know, the French generally forgive writers and philosophers, people like us who rise above local difficulties and are citizens of the world . . . (*ANDERS: Let's hope this is true in Russia . . .*) And in any case Sterne was Irish . . .

So, after all, 1762 turned into a good British year in Paris (a city which looked, said Sterne, a good deal better than it smelled). David Hume, like some fat Cistercian, was on the staff at the new British Embassy. Edward Gibbon, the man who was still scribbling the great book of empire that he had dreamt of on the steps of the Capitol in Rome, was there, charming his way all around town. So was the actor David Garrick, a very good friend to Sterne. Sterne's fame had gone before him, and soon he too was 'shandying around' all the salons in his drab black suit: meeting the learned doctors of the Sorbonne, flirting with the ladies, becoming a friend of Diderot's atheistical friend d'Holbach – that great protector of wits, he called him. Before long he'd converted Parisians to the new philosophy of 'Shandyism'. He had Garrick read a play of Diderot's to consider staging it in London, though Garrick found it far too French: ''Tis love love love throughout, without much separation in the character,' he observed shrewdly. And in turn he encouraged Diderot to study Garrick's acting performance, which led him to write a very important treatise on the matter. (*LARS: Ah yes, I know, I know – The Paradox of the Comedian . . .*)

But the great moment came at the end. Sterne was invited at the last minute to give a sermon of dedication for the new chapel in the British Embassy. It was of course a grand occasion, with princes, courtiers and ambassadors, bishops and priests present. And the philosophes were out in force as well. Hume, who worked in the Embassy, was there, and so were his friends d'Holbach and Diderot. Unfortunately Sterne seems to have decided to give a sermon that wasn't a sermon. (*BO: Ah, yes, now we know . . .*) He chose to preach on a very odd text from Hezekiah – an 'unlucky text', as he admitted later. It concerns the rather remarkable miracle where Hezekiah put all his concubines on display, and this makes the sundial, affected as it were by Viagra, mysteriously move by ten degrees. The princes and priests were scandalized, and thought it no way to dedicate an official Parisian residence, however protestant. (*ANDERS: I would think it was ideal . . .*) The philosophes, of course, thought the sermon was admirable. Half of them were former Jesuits anyway, and it seemed to them that if only they could preach from the altar like this it might even be worth believing in God.

And Diderot, feeling he'd found a soulmate, promptly decided to write a novel in the manner of *Tristram Shandy*, using the same techniques . . . (*BO: Transverse zig-zaggery?*) The book, he said, worked as true creativity did: 'By long observation, consummate experience, tact, taste, instinct, a sort of inspiration; by a long and awkward march, by painful fumbling, by a secret notion of analogy derived from an infinity of observations, whose memory gets wiped out but whose trace remains.' He particularly liked one delicious touch, Uncle Toby's famous groin wound, which makes his amours a problem. Because of the wound, Toby is forced to explain everything else he knows, like the events of the Siege of Namur, in encyclopedic detail – literally, for Sterne got his information from the great British encyclopedia of the day, *Chamber's*, which Diderot tried to translate. (*BO: It started the* Encyclopedia . . .). The odd sexual joke seemed the source of a new way of storytelling, and that started Diderot off on his own book. For Sterne, this would create a remarkable paradox – one he could never know about. His aim was that *Shandy* would end with the death of the author, a totally fair surmise. 'Now it is done,' were his last words; and some people think he meant his book. But it wasn't done. Diderot had begun to continue it, and would for years after Sterne's death.

But Denis being Denis, the book that started out this way turned into something quite different. The wounded Uncle Toby turns into a fatalistic servant, bold enough to tell his master the one reason he'll be remembered is because he had such a famous valet. (*BIRGITTA: Ah, my darling, I know what it is. Jacques the Fatalist And His Master* . . .) The servant became a significant figure of the day, in fact finally became— (*BIRGITTA: Figaro, of course. I told you that*). So we can say Sterne turns into Diderot; who turns into Beaumarchais; who turns into Mozart; who turns into Rossini. He also turns into Proust and Joyce, Beckett and Nabokov, and thus an essential part of our own literature. Instead of writing a book nobody would remember, because as Dr Johnson said nothing so odd can live long, he became the source of a whole tradition of stories, plays, operas – a classic case of Postmortemism.

But our Diderot really wouldn't be Diderot if he didn't make his book new. Sterne asked many of the great literary questions, and that's why we love him. Diderot asked a great many more. He added fresh tricks, postmodern diversions, all sorts of new games to play between the writer and the reader. It's always been said his book has four characters – Jacques, his master, the writer, the reader – and no one can tell which is in control. He adds lots of mystifications and oper-atic strategems, like the tale of the vengeful Mme. de la Pommeraye. But one thing clearly carries on from Sterne. Just like *Shandy*, Diderot's *Jacques* doesn't conclude. No one really gets anywhere, beds anyone, or discovers anything. After all, the only complete story is written in the Book of Destiny above, Jacques says, and who can possibly know how that will end?

So Diderot recommends we finish the tale ourselves. But then, when he checks the manuscript again, three endings have suddenly appeared. One has popped out of the pages of *Tristram Shandy*. Can it be plagiarism? Perhaps, he says – 'Unless this dialogue between Jacques and his master actually pre-dates that book, so that our good master Sterne is the real plagiarist. But this I doubt, because of the high esteem in which I hold Mr Sterne, whom I distinguish from most of the writers of his nation, who steal from us first and then insult us.' (A charge, incidentally, I'd like to refute here and now. I never steal. I simply inter-textualize.)

Diderot tells us a tale with no ending still has to end somewhere, like everything else in the world. That applies to Sterne's book, his own, and me now. So that's all I have to say in this paper that wasn't really a paper. Except for one thing. While he was in Paris, Sterne sent to his London bookseller for some books by British authors (Chaucer, Pope, Cibber, Locke), to be put to his account but sent elsewhere, 'for they are for a present'. The books were a gift for Diderot, and crossed the channel to join his library. But this was the library Diderot was in the process of selling to Catherine of Russia. So, when he in his turn suffered the fatal Death of the Author in 1784 (that's the date claimed in all the encyclopedias), all his books, including those Sterne gave him, went to Russia and joined the library in the Hermitage, which I believe we will soon be privileged to see, so maybe we'll be looking at them soon . . . (*BO: Well, perhaps, nothing is certain . . .*)

And then, as I understand it, many of Diderot's manuscripts went to Russia as well, including the wonderful *Rameau's Nephew* (*BIRGITTA: If you say so . . .*) and the still unfinished text of *Jacques*. Later on, through all sorts of strange channels, these works which weren't published at all in Diderot's lifetime began to reappear in Germany and France, and began to be published, but in very confused editions. People still wonder whether there are more manuscripts in Russia (*BO: I don't think so . . .*) but maybe when we arrive in Petersburg we'll find out more about how the story that never finished went on— (*ANDERS: Except have you seen this morning's news? . . .*)

And that's all . . . oh, except for one last thing. Sterne's books went to Russia, but what about all the books Diderot gave to Sterne in return – his own writings on art and philosophy? Well, they found their way back to England, and so back to Shandy Hall, Sterne's little philosophical hut up in Coxwold. But once Sterne had died the house ceased to be a rectory, and then it fell into total decay, until Kenneth Monkman found it and restored it. He also began to rebuild Sterne's lost library, and that's where I saw some of those books, though most are still missing. That was in 1968, of course. The year of the Death of the Author, and also the year I turned up at Shandy Hall to take part in a literary funeral where the corpse totally failed to be present . . .

So, Bo, I'm sorry. But that's all I can do by way of an ending, and all I can do by way of a lecture. I'm so sorry your first paper wasn't really a paper . . .

TWELVE (THEN)

CROSS THE GREAT COURTYARD, go from out to in. Past those shining hussars in their imperial green and red uniforms, into the first formalities of the court. Climb the great stone stairway; face a young court chamberlain. Announce name; hand over borrowed bearskin coat to one of the furry servants in their ruffles and their smart satin knee-britches. Check self for appearance in the vast Siberian mirrors, which hang everywhere in the most inordinate numbers. Adjust the brand-new wig, purchased at great expense from the best perukist in the rich arcades along Nevsky: imported from Paris, or so the man says, but here the shopkeepers say that about all they sell. Dust off wig-powder from the old black philosopher suit. Pull up the stockings: a shame about the holes, but there's no Particularist here to mend them. Follow the little page, walk through the imperial labyrinth. Down the vast corridors along the Neva side, windows overlooking the harbour, across at the fortress, where the imperial dead are buried after they have done their living. Observe the drilling soldiers, the swirling waters, the endless swaying masts.

Glance up at the great paintings, relishing the sweet fact that most of them you know already, for you were present at their purchase. Consider again the huge nakednesses of the great Rembrandts. Observe the barbered spiky faces of the Van Dycks. Notice the whirlpool pudding of the Assumption of Caravaggio. Swell to the glow of the Adoration of Rubens. 'It is thanks to you, my dear friend,' he has once assured Melchior Grimm, in the frankness of public print, in the pages of the court newsletter they have written together, 'that I have come to understand the magic of light and shade, that I become familiar with colour, acquired a wonderful sensuous feeling for all the fleshly tints.' Yet now, amid the familiar colours, the tricks of light and shade, the swathes of active flesh, he now sees other things – new things, things he has never seen before, not even in the great salon exhibitions of Paris, which he's reported in print over so many years. He halts a moment before Clerisseau's sketched meditations on the ruins of Rome, paintings of the kind all emperors need to remind them of the inexorable laws of decline and fall, civilization and disaster. Again before a splendid-looking ironworks by Joseph Wright of Derby, a glorious depiction of the great art of manufacture, stinkingly alive with all the industry it shows, quite worthy of his own encyclopedia. Again before a notably fleshy statue by Canova, a bust by the Englishman Nollekens, even a head or two by fierce, isolated little Falconet. A cabinet of toys. Another of painted and silvered Easter eggs. A fine display of human teeth, extracted in the best interests of learning by Peter the Great himself . . .

But wait. Just a minute. Sitting with his head bowed in an enormous chair over there – isn't it, surely it's, no, it can't be . . . Voltaire??? He's not sure. He's loved, often hated, the wicked old fellow for all his adult life. Everyone links them together, sometimes imagining the one is the other, or the two are one, like the name of some . . . well, Metro station – Diderot-Voltaire. But in truth the two have never met directly; person to person, as it were, self to self, face to face. One's always been in exile while the other is at home. So they have Boxed and Coxed, and their intimate relations are all on paper; the actual meeting has been consigned to the great plot of Destiny, still printing in the big book above. It will come, he knows it will. But not here, surely? What can he be doing in the Palmyra of the North? Is it possible his own journey has drawn the clever octogenarian fox out of his rich Swiss lair? Surely not. Arouet is far too old, far too clever, and at Potsdam he's learned the sense of paying his homage and radiating his influence from the groves of a safe republican retreat.

Surely it's a haunting. Yet there he sits: woolly-haired, clad as for one of his own dramas in a Roman toga, vain-looking as ever, usual impish grin all over his face. Better move closer. Yes, it's Arouet all right: the grand old master, the creator of roguish Candide and the wise but innocent Zadig. It's glorious Voltaire; but not the man in the flesh. His living, pulsing meat is still doubtless at Ferney, among the cow pastures, pouring out those innumerable tracts and fictions, those novels and histories and dramas, that even put his own prodigious production to shame. There he'll be, raging and conniving, protesting and mocking, infuriating priests and kings, looking after his great brood of tip-tapping watchmakers, entertaining all those innumerable guests for whom he puts on dramatic performances, wryly observing the decline of France. He's not flesh, he's stone. Not a man but a statue has travelled. What sits here is a complete simulacrum, a life-size likeness, Voltaire confronting Posterity already. Then it comes back. It's the image done at Ferney by dear and distin-guished Houdon, who's also sculpted Our Sage himself, if not so wonderfully.

So, large as life, though a good deal quieter, the Second Sage sits there four-square, squatting in his own favourite armchair. It's an ugly fellow, it has to be said. 'My trade,' he has pronounced, 'is to say what I think. What trade is better?' And there he sits as he will continue to sit, ever present to the Empress. So it is written in the great Book of Destiny above. It is also written that, as times change, as Russia swells, as revolutions happen, as Vladimir Ilich pushes out his beard, this statue will move. From Petersburg to Petrograd, Petrograd to Leningrad, and then to Moscow when the Prussians come again. It will be heaved out of windows, thrown aboard trains. The same with his library, which will come to this Hermitage to sit with Our Sage's own. But that is later; the point is he's here, determined to be present as our man meets his empress. Mischievously grinning, staring with that critical, almost obscene little glance of his, he watches stonily as our man walks on on his suddenly more nervous way . . .

Down the mirrored and art-filled corridor, walking behind the little page. Past a line of silent hussars, on toward the intimate apartments. Out there in the checkerboard city, it seems to be freezing hard; here he suddenly finds he is passing through hanging gardens. Lush real flowers bloom and fade, amid a sward of bright green lawn. Here indoors one can see small gravelled walks, a neat grove of evergreen trees. In the branches bright, feathered song-birds from the tropics flutter and chirp. Rooms lie off the corridors, filled with people. In one a crowd of young women in men's clothes are playing a game of billiards. In another courtiers in silk are playing at games of chess. And Lui is right; as one goes further the court inclines ever more toward the informal. Cooks walk by, carrying grinning dead fish on platters. Children romp, dogs bark.

A court lady appears, wearing a shift, and carrying an open slop-pail. It's the Princess Dashkova! These two have met before, in different circumstances, when the lady came to Paris once. There's pleasure, delight. They embrace. She hands over the stinking pail to a grenadier, she brusquely dismisses the page. Then she leads him toward the inner sanctum, the private sitting room. In the doorway a bustle of courtiers, guardsmen, footmen, counsellors, tiny pages. Generals and dwarves, mob-cabbed housemaids and imperial favourites, all flit in and out. On the far wall there hangs a great painting: the Imperial Mother herself, dressed in male regimentals, sitting aside her great horse, Brilliant, on which Falconet has mounted Peter the Great.

Beneath the simulacrum there sits the real thing. She's big as big, clad in a shot-silk, low-necked day-dress. There's a grand jewel at her shoulder, a large sash cast across her noble bows. Two huge-eyed English hunting greyhounds lie lethargically beside her on the large throne-like couch. There are nuts and sweetmeats on the table; a samovar noisily bubbles in the corner. She looks up, smiles. Her face is quite plain and rougeless. He halts, he bows, bends over as far as, a gentleman of sixty, he is able. The imperial hand comes out; he reaches to kiss it.

And so it begins. And so it will continue – day after day, for week after week to come, as is written in the great Book of Destiny above:

DAY ONE

HE stands, in his black philosophical suit. SHE sits. HE reaches out to kiss her hand.

HE
Your most serene and magnificent imperial mightiness . . .

SHE looks highly irritable.

SHE

For heaven's sake, my dear Mr Philosopher. Don't you know
you are now in my private apartments? Can't you read the
notices on the walls? Have none of my chamberlains explained
to you that this is a place of superior equals – where when you
enter, you set aside your hat, your rank, your flattery and your
sword . . .

HE

I never did bear a sword, Your Imperial Highness. An
umbrella, perhaps.

SHE

Set aside whatever you like. But let's abolish all these puffs and
titles and little flatteries.

HE

Excuse me, Your Majesty, I am French, and have hardly ever
left the city of Paris. I'm afraid I only know the manners of
Versailles.

SHE

Oh, do you go there often?

HE

Rarely, Your Highness. If not never. Perhaps you know our
present king is no friend at all to philosophers. We worship in
quite the wrong church.

SHE

I know he bans your books and drives his talents into exile.
That's why I invited you to my court.

HE

And who could be more sensible of the honour?

SHE

And yet it's taken you, what, ten years to get here?

HE

Work, Your Highness. I do think very hard.

SHE
And the mistress you couldn't leave – she's well?

HE
As well as can be expected in my absence.

SHE
Well, I hope you're well accommodated. You mean to lodge
with Monsieur Falconet, do you not? I trust you'll remind
him that when a monarch commands, an artist obeys. Your
friend's a problem. He takes too much time, he spends too
much money, and he won't listen to what his empress has
to say . . .

HE
I fear the fellow's French, Your Highness.

SHE
It's no excuse.

HE
And art has its own reasons. I assure you that when the
Horseman is unveiled, you'll step back in total wonder. You'll
catch your breath, leap high into the air. It's a masterpiece. In
fact you may quote me . . .

SHE
Oh yes? And why should I?

HE
In any case, he hasn't received me. I'm the guest of Prince
Alexei Narishkin, who so kindly brought me from Holland,
at his palace at Isaakiyevskaya Ploshchad.

SHE
Ah. You speak Russian?

HE
Indeed I do, Your Highness. And now you have heard the
whole of it.

SHE
The Narishkin Palace, I know it very well.

HE
It has the most splendid ceilings.

SHE looks at him suspiciously.

SHE
So I believe. And a magnificent view. Which I hope to extend substantially in the course of your stay.

HE
My stay, Your Highness. Do you suppose it to be long?

SHE
I hope so. What is the matter with you, Mr Philosopher? You are jiggling up and down very uncomfortably.

HE
A small matter, Your Highness, to do with thinking. My thinking. Usually I think wonderfully well on the wing, like a little bird. But my journey here has taken me some months—

SHE
Because you took your time about it.

HE
I have ridden for weeks in a springless carriage. Now I can hardly speak for the state of my spine and my buttocks.

COURTIERS snigger.

SHE
You have a bad back, sir? Piles, perhaps?

HE (*hastily*)
No, Your Majesty. I definitely don't have piles—

SHE
For goodness sake, why are you telling me this?

HE
I know in the presence of an imperial majesty it's always proper to stand. But my experience of the dialogues of the best philosophers is that their thoughts generally come best when seated . . .

170

SHE

Ah. You want to sit down, is that it?

HE

Only if Your Majesty thinks I am not requesting some
improper liberty.

SHE

I thought in your philosophy liberty was never improper.
Look, Mr Philosopher, if you want to stand, stand. If you
wish to sit, sit. But for goodness sake do the one or the other.
Which shall it be?

HE

Sit, Your Imperial Highness.

SHE

Very well. Find the philosopher an armchair, someone.

*An armchair is brought. HE sits, removes some rather unusual knitted
gloves, rubs his hands vigorously.*

HE

May I tell you how much I like Sankt Peterburg? Quite the
most magnificent city I have ever visited.

SHE

How many cities have you visited?

HE

None other, it's true. Apart fom Paris, of course.

SHE

And now you are going to tell me how deeply it has pained
you to leave it. That is what all Frenchmen say. How strange
it never keeps them at home—

HE

When a great monarch calls—

SHE

. . . there is profit to be had from it, isn't that right? I should
say you were very well out of it. I know our cousin King

171

Louis likes to put his great philosophical minds into jail with great regularity.

HE
And give their books to the hangman for burning with even more regularity. That is why his wise men must search out their wise monarch elsewhere. That's why our eyes turn so fondly to the wonderful Amazon of the North.

SHE
And do you really think a philosopher has anything of use to say to a monarch?

HE
Surely. To whom should he address himself if not to a noble sovereign? We must always remember philosophy can never be a power of itself. It can only share itself with a sovereign power, like your noble majesty, and speak for reason and the spirit of humanity.

SHE
How?

HE
As truthfully as truth will permit. As wisely as wisdom will proceed. As reasonably as reason can devise.

SHE
And would you speak against the sovereign?

HE
If the sovereign so wishes.

SHE
And why would a sovereign wish it? Philosopher, ask yourself this. Any fool can understand why a travelling philosopher, an ill-paid man at best, should have reason to seek the patronage of a monarch. But why should a monarch seek the views of a philosopher? As a thinking man, would you truly advise it?

HE
I can only say, Your Highness, that I did not come to you on

my own account, I answered a summons. Look at me, my
lady. I'm simply a poor fool, a strange old person who plays at
philosophy in a Paris garret.

SHE
Well?

HE
I possess a restless mind, which teases me all the time with
ideas of goodness and virtue, humanity and liberty, reality and
appearance. I ask myself how the universe works, and how we
understand it. I reflect on human nature, and what's true or
good or beautiful. I examine the world, and our purpose in
it. I speculate on dreams and fantasies, follies and grandeurs.
I ask how great acts are done and fine and noble things are
achieved. I consider how reason can advance us towards peace
and decency. Sometimes I conceive the most glorious new
societies, sometimes I contemplate the follies of old ones.
I reflect on life – as if my own life depended on it.

SHE
As well it might. Life – that's a very serious matter.

HE
I argue with myself. I talk to myself, and everyone else too.
Sometimes I feel quite divine, sometimes I feel quite absurd.
I talk all the time to others. And I never mind being denied
or refuted, because I'm always denying and refuting myself.
My aim is the quest for truth, not the announcement of it.

SHE
Of course it's easy to dream of fine new societies or create
glorious notions of progress, when your head's lying on a
downy pillow.

HE
I'm quite aware of it. I deal in reveries, you deal in realities.
That is why the thinker needs a monarch.

SHE
And the monarch a thinker?

HE
Without reveries we would never improve the realities. It
may be we never will. All we seek is the one wise and perfect
monarch who will listen . . .

SHE
And if she does listen, just what would she hear?

HE
All I wish is to perform the office of philosopher before your
eyes. I should behave quite unlike a priest of religion, pursuing
you with divine commandments and eternal truths. I'm an
honest thinking man, which means I don't know any. I shall
forbear from asking you to turn your soul toward the
contemplation of eternity, since I know of nothing that's
eternal. I work by reason and by speculation.

SHE looks at him.

SHE
I understand you are an atheist, the man who believes in
nothing.

HE
Precisely. But I disbelieve with the very greatest conviction,
Your Highness.

SHE
So is your morality the same as a believer's?

HE
Why not, if one is an honest man?

SHE
Do you practise that morality?

HE
Like many of us, I do my best.

SHE
You don't rape, don't murder, don't pillage?

HE

I promise you, very rarely.

SHE

Then why not accept religion?

HE

I did. I was a little priest myself once, a would-be Jesuit. But I saw religion was just like marriage, it brought joy to a few and misery to many. For some people it's a way to perform good deeds they would have done anyway. For others it's just an excuse for evil.

SHE

So a philosopher's a failed priest?

HE

You can call me a priest without a religion, a prophet without a message, a thinker without a system—

SHE

In that case you seem to be of remarkably little use.

HE

I work by reason. The reasoner asks questions. I should like to be known for my questions, not my answers. Praised for making people think – not telling them what they should think.

SHE

But you do wish to be praised? Vanity, Mr Librarian.

HE

It's what I share with kings. Why else would they create huge armies, build vast cities and put up statues to themselves?

SHE

You'd ask questions? What kinds of questions?

HE

I've spent my life dreaming with eyes wide open. I ask myself, how we come to be in the universe. How we might understand it by understanding ourselves. How human beings can learn to advance and prosper, grow free of false ideas, superstitions and despotisms. How they can discover life, liberty, the pursuit of happiness—

SHE
Oh, now, sir. If you do that, might human beings not decide to get rid of the monarchs you're so keen to advise?

HE
Surely if people are educated and enlightened, the first thing they'll want are great leaders who'll bring out all that's noble and reasonable in them.

SHE looks at him.

SHE
Mr Philosopher, I do wonder if you know life? I can show you people who are eternal unchangeable brutes.

HE
They are not properly educated, Your Highness.

SHE
I can show you highly educated brutes. I can show you the vilest thugs with doctorates from Tübingen.

HE
Those are people who have learned to study but not to reason. They're not true philosophers, madame.

SHE
I'm not sure I believe in the reasonableness of reason.

HE
I admit it, I'm not too sure either. We know even the reasonable man does wild and involuntary things, because we're all creatures of passion as well as common sense. I can only tell you I would rather have good sense than not have it . . .

SHE
You admit you cannot rely on human nature.

HE

I admit man is animal as well as human. He's prey to fantasy, madness, erotic delusion, atrocity. He gets sick with envy, sharp with malice, hungry with lust.

SHE

So reason betrays us, telling us what's not so? I'm no longer sure I want the company of wise and reasonable men.

HE

Indeed. But if you don't, you will never be anything more than a child.

COURTIERS snigger.

SHE

And if I'm happy to accept that fate?

HE

Then you'll suffer from your passions and be bored by your pleasures. You'll act by instinct, not by sense. You'll be gross and despotic, not wise and serene . . .

The COURTIERS stare.

SHE

Really, sir?

HE

Knowledge is a long journey. Some get a little way, some go a good deal further, a small few progress very near to the end.

SHE

I think you would like to turn the whole world into an encyclopedia. And all its citizens into Diderot.

HE

Why not? It could do no harm.

SHE

It's enough. I've a delegation of Turkish suleimans now. I don't want them to find me talking to a philosopher.

HE
No, marm, not bellicose enough.

HE rises, kisses her hand, turns to go.

SHE
But you will return, at the same time tomorrow, and we will start in earnest, Mr Thinker?

HE
I will. Yes. Good day. Your most Serene and Imperial—

HE disappears through the door.

END OF DAY ONE

THIRTEEN (NOW)

I DON'T BELIEVE THIS. I've done it all over again. The disaster's clear, my error's apparent, the moment I finish delivering my . . . whatever it was I gave them. I look around the table: Bo is sitting silent in the grimmest of professorial poses, Alma has become ever more the frozen Snow Queen, her expression made of ice. Agnes Falkman offers me a glance of sharp political protest; Sven Sonnenberg is now a man as close to sleep as a man can be without actually toppling from his chair. Anders Manders looks at me with diplomatic quizzicality, Jack-Paul Verso simply keeps his head down, scuffling through his own notes as he prepares to follow on. Only the Swedish diva and Lars Person show any sign of having enjoyed my . . . whatever . . . at all.

Tapping on the table, Bo finally delivers the verdict. '*Nej, nej,*' he says, 'I am sorry. But this is not at all what we mean in Sweden by a useful conference presentation.'

'Oh really? No?'

'I am afraid it is all too British. Too playful.'

'No theory,' adds Alma.

'Not really grounded in any fundamental concepts.'

'In Sweden we are not tellers of tales or makers of anecdotes,' confirms Alma.

'In any case our grants demand monographic papers that we can publish in the proper journals,' says Agnes Falkman.

'But I loved it,' says Birgitta warmly, 'I thought it would make a rather good opera.'

'But we did not come on this journey to make a rather good opera, Madame Lindhorst,' says Alma. 'The problem here is that already it is ten o'clock in the morning and we do not have anything at all to discuss and attack. This does not permit a true dialogue, a proper critique. This is . . . nothing more than a story.'

There's a tap on the door, and Tatyana comes in. Today, in another quick and vivid change of costume, she's back in her white chambermaid's uniform, a little white scarf wrapped round her hair. Her cheeks are bright red; she beams, and bears a tray with a coffee pot and cups. As she walks around the table, putting out the cups, I notice her throw a significant glance at Jack-Paul Verso, who looks up and gives her a smile. Then it occurs to me that Agnes Falkman is glancing quite romantically at Sven Sonnenberg, who has been roused from his somnolence by the offer of coffee. I glance at Birgitta, hoping that she'll glance at me; but am I right in thinking that now she's glancing curiously at the deep-bearded Lars Person? At any rate the mysterious chemistry of conferences has already begun, as it always does, sooner or later.

But, whatever the chemical reactions taking place, Bo Lune-berg means just now to have none of them. He taps firmly on the table with his pencil. 'Our programme is all exact, we must all keep to it,' he says firmly. 'Professor Verso, I have no doubt you will now be able to lead us along the correct academic path? Of course you have a paper?'

'Sure I do,' says Verso easily. 'I sat up the whole of the night writing it.' As he says this, it seems to me he casts a little wink at Tatyana.

'That is excellent,' says Bo.

'Here it is,' says Verso, reaching in his briefbag, and taking out sheets. 'If you'd just pass them around, Bo, and make sure everyone here has a photocopy . . .'

Bo hands round copies of his lecture, which is titled 'All You'll Ever Need to Know: How the Modern Mind Works'. I can't help noticing that a tiny piece of print in the top corner from a photocopying machine says, curiously, Toronto, 3 May 1990.

'And now, Professor Verso, if you wouldn't mind taking over the speaker's chair?' says Bo Luneberg, looking gratified.

Verso comes over and changes places with me (and isn't that a rather curious grin he gives me?). Tatyana puts the coffee pot on the table, and departs with a lovely smile. Verso taps the table, and begins to offer our pilgrims what, if I had spent the night in the correct fashion, I should really have offered myself: the first proper paper of the Diderot Project.

FOURTEEN (THEN)

DAY TWO

HE comes from the ante-room, wearing his black philosopher's suit. It still seems to cause amusement among the beardless BOYARS, pantalooned CHAMBERLAINS, tousled CHAMBERMAIDS, bewigged HUSSARS and black-cowled MONKS who keep wandering freely in and out. His armchair awaits him. SHE, wearing a military sash, is standing looking out of the window.

HE
Your Most Munificent and Glorious . . .

SHE
No, no, Doctor Didro. How's your backside today?

HE
Better for your concern, Your Serene Highness.

SHE
I see there are ice-floes today on the Neva. Soon it will freeze over. First the Neva, then all the Baltic waters. Then we shall all be marooned here together for the winter.

HE joins her at the window.

HE
I really don't think so. The sea temperature isn't low enough. And there's no moisture in the atmosphere—

SHE turns and looks at him.

SHE
You're a meteorologist then? And a prophet too? Evidently
there's no end to your accomplishments.

HE
It's true, I'm both those things. But then I've tried to be
almost everything. I've studied and written on many matters.
Weather, watermills. Beauty, ecstasy, perfection. Bees, sexual
pleasure—

SHE
For or against?

HE
For, madame. God—

SHE
Against, no doubt. Humility?

HE
Yes, I wrote on that too once – and I'm very proud to admit
it. I produced an encyclopedia, Your Royal Highness, a big
book of universal knowledge—

SHE
I'm well aware of that, Mr Librarian. You may recall I offered
to publish it for you here in Riga. When you had got yourself
into so much trouble at home with your popes and priests and
publishers—

HE
Priests, of course. One quarrels with them all the time. I have
to. As I told you, I was a little priest myself once. Popes I
don't know, and shouldn't care to. Publishers are amongst the
boldest, the wisest, most generous of all humankind, risking
their fortunes for our opinions. That is, so long as they don't
keep too much company with princes, priests, or popes. Or
bankers or the lowest tastes of the people.

SHE
You wrote on sovereigns. What's your view of them?

HE
Ah. Well, in my view a truly enlightened sovereign would be
the most finest and most beautiful thing in the entire story of
the world.

SHE
Better than a water-mill?

HE
Of far greater utility, Your Imperial Majesty . . .

SHE goes and sits down on her sofa, and looks at him.

SHE
Tell me, sir, have you read my 'Great Instruction'?

HE
The 'Grand Nakaz'? Of course. The state censor banned it in
Paris. I read it immediately.

SHE
And your opinion?

HE
I thought it was a . . . really great instruction. I admired it
profoundly. A model for all civilized societies. Such a pity
the Great Instruction's only a Faint Suggestion.

SHE
I'm sorry?

HE
I understand you've yet to put it into practice.

SHE
That will happen, when the time comes. Mr Philosopher, my
country is my greatest experiment. I mean to be careful to see
it is a good one.

HE
Then you make an ageing thinker very happy. I've always
known the time would come when Enlightenment would

sweep down from north to south. Already you're turning the rest of Europe into a wilderness of pagans and savages.

SHE
You think so?

HE
Good men will deify you in your own lifetime. Sages will prostrate themselves before you in delight. I myself long to the toes of my boots to be of service.

SHE looks at him.

SHE
I think you already have been, Mr Librarian. You have only to look around you.

HE looks gratified.

HE
True. I can't tell you the joy I feel when I raise my eyes to your Rembrandts and your Rubens, and think the taste they first delighted and ravished was mine. The pleasure when I look and see the drawings in my notebooks turned into real buildings and palaces.

SHE
It pleases you.

HE
It's exactly like waking from some disgusting and deliciously erotic dream, only to find the whole thing is quite real after all.

SHE
Have you quite done?

HE
Not at all. The dream has hardly begun yet. I can assure you there's plenty more where that came from . . .

SHE
What do you mean?

HE reaches into his bag and his pockets. Notebooks and papers tumble everywhere.

HE
See. My plans for Russia. Sixty notebooks of them. I've been writing them down ever since I left Paris.

SHE
No wonder you took so long to arrive.

HE
Plans for a university. The organization of a police force. A scheme for a city, rules for a guild of crafts. A class in sexual anatomy for the improvement of young girls. Plans for education, toleration, emancipation, legislation. A law on divorce. I'm for it. A law on gambling. I'm against it.

The COURTIERS are laughing.

SHE
You have been busy.

HE
A scheme for creating a Russian bourgeoisie, done by importing Swiss. A plan for preventing a revolt of the serfs . . .

SHE
Ah! How would you do that?

HE
Abolish serfdom. Within minutes you'd have no further problems with serfs.

SHE stares at the ever-growing pile of notebooks.

SHE
Such a pity we have only a few short afternoons. I am an empress. I have other things to think of than you.

HE
Perhaps, to make sure neither of us waste precious time, I might write you a memorandum every day. Then, if you were to rise a little earlier than usual—

SHE

Mr Philosopher. Each morning I rise before five. I do four hours of papers and red boxes before I take black coffee, which is my only breakfast. Then I see my generals and counsellors. I settle petitions, resolve church affairs, since I happen to be the grand Metropolitan. I issue laws. I check the safety and borders of my nation. I see ambassadors, deal with foreign monarchs, threaten the Turks. I eat lunch.

HE

I understand, Your Highness.

SHE

Affairs of state are onerous, but I usually manage a reading hour. When noontime dinner is done, and half this court is sleeping, playing games, or enjoying sexual adventures, I choose to relax a little with a few dear friends, or perhaps improve my health, mind or spirit. I mean these hours now, Mr Librarian, which you may consider yours. I trust you mean to employ them wisely and well—

HE

So do I, Your Imperial Highness. I have considered it.

SHE

Well, away you go now. Send me your paper tomorrow. And I will read it and tell you exactly what I think.

HE

I can ask no more, Your Grand and Imperial Mightiness—

HE rises to go to the door. She calls after him.

SHE

Oh, and you are completely wrong about the Neva, Mr Philosopher. I have discovered experience always outdoes theory. And I've lived here now for twenty years. When the sun goes red like that, the Neva is always going to freeze—

END OF DAY TWO

FIFTEEN (NOW)

ALL YOU'LL EVER NEED TO KNOW
Jack-Paul Verso
Dept. of Contemporary Thinking, Cornell University

Hi there! Good morning, my friends. As you can see from the printout I've just put in front of you, the paper I've written is called 'All You'll Ever Need to Know'. Maybe before I start out you'd like a brief personal explanation of why I chose that particular title. I picked it because I happen to be an Encyclopedia Kid. What's an Encyclopedia Kid? You'd know the answer to that right away if, like me, you'd been a poor kid in the Bronx, growing up in a high-rise apartment on an old urban block. It was a neighbourhood of tough kids, and we kids all looked the same. We attended the same public school, we ate the same hot dogs, went to the same ball-games. We looked the same – but we weren't. Because in any good ghetto, there are the street dudes, the ones who know all the action, the ones who by age six are already stealing autos and dealing crack. And then there are the four-eyes, kids with big spectacles and little muscles, who get up at four to deliver the papers, and sit reading books when they go to the beach. There are the little Capotes and the little Einsteins, the ones whose parents want them to be musicians, lawyers, brain surgeons. These are the encyclopedia kids.

Why encyclopedia kids? Right, take me. My parents were third-generation Jewish immigrants who'd come from Lithuania, somewhere right out over the Baltic there. They were observant, they were ambitious, they prayed in the synagogue for only one little favour: give us a Mozart in the family. They bought me a junior cello. They taught me chess. They put science journals under my pillow. In those days the salesman used to wander round the apartments looking for parents like mine with kids like me. They were selling encyclopedias, and we were the perfect market. They brought *The Book of Knowledge*, amazing stuff, all about how to build a submarine or make the perfect brownie. But the great one was the *Encyclopedia Britannica*, which was in thirty-two bound buckram volumes, came with its own bookcase, and cost over a thousand dollars. But, as the salesmen said, it was all worth it, because the *Britannica* didn't just contain knowledge. It contained All You'll Ever Need to Know.

So I was a natural encyclopedia kid. The odd thing was I didn't have an encyclopedia. Every week I could hear my poppa at the door, arguing with the salesmen. 'You think I'm dumb?' he'd say. 'Some Britannico. I know where you fellows make these things. They make 'em in the stockyards of Chicago, aren't I right?' And right he was, because by the time I grew up the *Britannica* was an all-American project, printed and published by the University of Chicago. Which was fine by me, but not by my pop. 'Jackie,' he'd say, 'you hang right in there. Homework isn't all. One day I'll buy you a hundred per cent echt Britannico, the kind they made back over there in Britain, not some lowdown fake they fix up on Michigan Drive.' Then one day he came home with it. I have no idea how did it, how many dollars he paid. He must have trawled every used bookstore in Manhattan. But there it was, twenty-eight volumes in their own wooden bookcase, not the American 13th but the grand old, imperial British 11th. 'Now you learn what there really is to learn,' he said.

He was right, because that set made me special. Okay, all the other four-eyes on the block knew all there is to know. But I soon knew more than that. I knew all there was to know once: when the Great War still hadn't happened, when women didn't even exist yet, when you were being educated to rule an empire that stretched over a quarter of the globe. TV may not have been invented. Nobody had figured out E equals MC squared. You went around without a Freudian unconscious, but, when push came to shove, you knew things that could astound. For example, I can advise our last speaker there's no mystery about where Shelley's heart is buried. It's in Bournemouth. But did he also know that heart-burial is a cardinal sin, anathematized by Pope Boniface VIIIth in the thirteenth century? And if you want to know the first man in England to carry an umbrella regularly, I can tell you. Mr John Hanway acquired the habit on his Grand Tour, when he realized what protected you against the sun could also protect you against the rain. And, Bo, if you think this is a little irrelevant, let me tell you John Hanway was an almost exact contemporary of Denis Diderot, meaning he could have carried a rain umbrella too.

But this wasn't all. From the encyclopedia I learned all about encyclopedias. As you'll all know they began spreading across the European nations in the seventeenth century as a result of the explosion of knowledge. The first alphabetical English encyclopedia was by Ephraim Chambers, started in Edinburgh in 1728. When the French decided they should have one, they simply took Chambers' and started to translate it. But the project ran into difficulties, the first French editor broke his leg falling down a hole, and so the project was handed on to two young philosophical hacks and wannabes, called d'Alembert and Diderot. They at once saw the problem. Start an encyclopedia and it's hard to stop, because knowledge keeps expanding to fit: new science, new mechanics, new philosophies, new political viewpoints, new discoveries. So they devised a fresh, *très grand projet*, as advertised in 1750. They'd provide a total system of modern knowledge, framed around the three branches of the great tree of learning: Memory, Science and Imagination, otherwise history, philosophy, poetry. They'd include invention, science, medicine, the crafts and the technologies. And they'd augment it with constant supplements that would tell you, in continuous supply, All You'll Ever Need to Know – Then, Now, In the Future.

Naturally the *très grand projet* just grew ever grander and grander. They gathered up all the latest philosophers – meaning the general thinkers and writers, like Voltaire, Rousseau, and d'Holbach. They toured round Paris workshops to see how the various crafts were performed, they went to new factories to see how steel or electricity could be produced. They made crafty craftsmen reveal their working *secrètes*. All the time, the list of subjects grew bigger and bigger and crazier and crazier. They had articles on Adoration and Anatomy, Bees and Beauty, Cookery and Electricity, Forges and Fornication, Jesuits and Jansenists, Magic and Masterpieces, Salt and Superstition, Vice and Voluptuousness. The state grew worried, the church grew worried, and soon the books were being censored and banned. As a result the entries began to get even stranger and stranger – because the Reason crowd had to find weird new ways of slipping their arguments in. All Europe joined in the game of censorship and secret information, and sure enough the *Encyclopedia* became the most controversial, the most important, the most necessary book of the Age of Reason. As you rightly told us, Bo.

The trouble was the project simply spread and spread. Soon they were revising the entries even before they were written, or planning new printings, or selling off new rights to new publishers who then created completely different versions. Knowledge was changing and developing at such remarkable speed that nobody knew how to keep the thing up to date. Then to make matters worse a new generation of philosophes started to dispute the original entries. So the project kept growing and growing, and costing and costing, and the subscribers didn't know what they'd let themselves in for and the printers kept getting into trouble, and there were plagiarisms and pirate editions, and so on and on, until the whole thing then got caught up in the complexities and terrorisms of the French Revolution.

All this was watched with some amusement by a certain Mr William Smellie, of Anchor Close in the Haymarket, up there in rational Edinburgh. In 1768 he determined the Empire should strike back, and he started up the project that made me what I am today: the Scottish encyclopedia that he chose to call the *Encyclopedia Britannica*. Unlike the French, who were now trying to invent even more complicated trees of learning to fit all the elements into, he stuck firmly to the good old alphabet. And, unlike the French, Smellie knew how to pass on what he was doing to Posterity. He vowed to produce edition after edition, supplement after supplement, revising, developing, but always sticking to the original plan and hanging on to the alphabet. And that's what they're still trying to manage up there on Michigan Avenue right now.

So encyclopedia followed encyclopedia, right into our own postmodern times. But what about our friend Diderot? Well, from the very beginning he knew there was a problem, and he brilliantly realized what it was. The simple fact, as I know myself, is that All You'll Ever Need to Know today isn't All You're Going to Need to Know Tomorrow. If the human mind kept on ticking, reasoning, discovering, if science kept investigating, if the globe was being circumnavigated and new societies discovered, if knowledge kept on exploring even at the eighteenth-century rate, the day would come when you'd need a book bigger than the universe to store everything known about it. What's more, it would be impossible to amend old knowledge with new knowledge. And no single individual, no one map of learning, no perfect tree of knowledge, would ever be able to hold the great think together. Reason would go cosmic. The whole thing would implode as a result of its own investigations. In fact, the perceiving mind, the dear old cogito, the thinking human person, would dissolve – creating, as you reminded us yourself, Bo, a whole new age of darkness, in which all knowledge would be available, but nobody could ever possibly know it.

In fact the tide would sweep in and the whole Enlightenment project would simply destroy itself. The result, as Mary Shelley and Foucault both tell us, would be the end of the humanity of knowledge, which would exceed and then manipulate its creator. It didn't mean science, discovery, data would cease. Quite the opposite. They'd multiply at such a chaotic rate they'd pass beyond the province of reason, the bounds of the book, the unity of text, the reach of the human mind. Machines would be able to provide information to each other. We'd acquire a random and ever multiplying set of signs, signals, systems that lay beyond any philosopher, any philosophy, any encyclopedia – exactly our problem at this moment, Bo, now we're off on the Enlightenment Trail.

But don't think Diderot was beaten. He found the answer to this too, toward the end of his life. What was really needed, he said, was a thinking machine, a machine that could do its own computations and outrun the human mind. With the result that, sandwiched amongst his many other activities – arguing, talking, buying pictures, writing essays, poems, plays, stories, travelling, conspiring, producing pornography – you'll find that he set out to imagine a complicated calculating and coding machine for the convenience of soldiers and politicians. His thinking machine in time became the Babbage Machine, the great numerical calculator. And that became the Turing Machine, which in turn became the mainframe computer, which in turn became the same desktop or laptop PC, available from a neighbourhood store near you so that you too can process words and numbers, or rather let them process you.

And this is why – and I'm very sorry about this, Bo, but it's got to be true – we no longer live in the Age of Reason. We don't have reason; we have computation. We don't have a tree of knowledge; we have an information superhighway. We don't have real intelligence; we have artificial intelligence. We no longer pursue truth, we seek data and signals. We no longer have philosophers, we have thinking pragmatists. We no longer have morals, we have lifestyles. We no longer have brains that serve as the seat of our thinking minds; we have neural sites, which remember, store body signals, control genes, generate dreams, anxieties and neuroses, quite independent of whether they think rationally or not. So, starting from reason, where did we get? We have a godless world in an imploding cosmos. We have a model of reality based on a glorious chaos. We have a model of the individual based on biological determinism.

So now what's All We'll Ever Need to Know? We need to know there are machines that are cleverer than we are, so none of our systems of knowledge function as complete explanations of anything, and our understanding is always a partial phenomena. Knowledge exists independently of the thinking mind, which we don't really have anyway. What do we have left, then? Perception and data. We see; it is. Our data comes from any source, human or artificial, and easily processes itself into something else or spirals away into some other system. It comes in any form: word, book, symbol, icon, visual sequence. It can jump from code to code, language to language. It needs no thinker, requires no author. Anyone can have knowledge without knowing a thing, except how to switch on a machine that supplies it. You buy brains in a box. You have access to all knowledge and remain in a state of total stupidity. Switch on, log in. This is all you'll ever need to know. Isn't that right, Bo? (*BO: Nej, nej, no it isn't. I completely object . . .*)

I thought you might, that's why this isn't my paper. (*BO: This isn't your paper?*) Who needs a paper? You have a print-out already. I thought what I'd do is comment on the paper of the previous speaker . . . (*BO: But no, we already agreed . . .*) I've every respect for our colleague here, even if he is white, male and British. But this morning he treated us to a total mystification, and I think we should deconstruct it. (*BO: Nej, nej . . .*) Sorry, Bo, I'm a deconstructionist. Let's deconstruct . . .

Let's start with today's number one mystification. You may have noticed how our speaker began by misrepresenting the splendid intentions of Roland Barthes in his indispensable essay, 'The Death of the Author'. Okay, I know what I'm saying can sound illogical, because what Barthes says is we don't have any way of *knowing* an author's intentions. True, but I think we could just agree that when he wrote his essay he had no interest in graves, bodysnatchers, or corpses that fail to arrive on time. When he talks about the Death of the Author, he's telling us there are no writers, only writing, because writing is trapped in language and is not attached to a real world. So what he's talking about isn't the Death of the Author. It's the Death of Authority. In other words, he's doing for all of us.

Leading to the second mystification. Our speaker offered to distinguish between a paper he didn't give and a story he couldn't tell. Suggesting he understands the difference between papers and stories. (*ALMA: But of course there is a difference. That is why we complained it was not a paper.*) Okay, what is it? (*ALMA: Papers make statements and stories make fantasies.*) You mean, papers make truth claims and stories make fiction claims? (*BO: Yes, exactly.*) I'm afraid there isn't a real philosopher who could agree with you – not in America, anyway. (*SVEN: But that is just America . . .*) Right, let's take what we heard this morning. What was it? A paper, or a story? (*AGNES: Of course it was a story . . .*) Did it make truth-claims, or fiction-claims? (*BIRGITTA: I have no idea, I just enjoyed it . . .*) What did it sound like? A witness statement, right? I did this, I went to this funeral, and so on. There was an 'I' in it, so you thought it sounded true. Like my story about being an Encyclopedia Kid – which I just made up, incidentally. (*BO: But this is absurd . . .*)

No, it's a question about the state of intelligence in the age after reason. Look, let's just suppose my name is Detective Inspector Gervase Hawkeye of New Scotland Yard. I've been presented with a worrying case-file: it's the case of the Strange Death of the Author. It seems the victim, a British guy called Sterne, has just come back from Paris, where another author has been stealing from his work. Next thing he's found dying in his London apartment, crying, 'Now it is done.' My duty is quite clear; I need to know what was done, and who did it. Consider what happened next. Our guy is given a hasty funeral, with no headstone. Within hours the grave is opened, and the corpse is on a table at Cambridge University, where they take off the top of the skull. Then someone claims to identify the victim, so the body is taken back to the graveyard and buried again. Years later, the body is dug up again, and only identified when some guy comes along with a marble bust. Frankly I've never heard a more suspicious set of circumstances. I decide to investigate the case.

Right away I seem to get the breakthrough I need. We have a new statement by a highly reliable witness, a college professor, no less. He knows where the corpus delicti now lies. He saw it reburied, in some place called Coxcomb in Yorkshire. What's more, he can claim some two hundred other witnesses, all of them professors. There's even a canon from York Cathedral called Cant. Canon Cant? Okay, it still sounds convincing, until I check the file more closely. Our witness has attended a funeral, sure. Except the corpse has gone walkabout in Wales. He wasn't at the real ceremony at all. The actual burial occurs several months later, when the witnesses have all left, except for a few who were so full of sauce at the time they can hardly be expected to testify to what was happening. So what do we really have here? More suspicious funerals than Agatha Christie ever thought of. A respectable academic witness who, along with two hundred other professors, is quite prepared to take part in a funeral that didn't happen.

Now let's ask this: what is the real purpose of a funeral? To bury a known corpse, confirm the person is dead, and show the body has been interred, so the heirs can profit and the tax authorities can dive in. Therefore I have to ask myself, as an officer of the law, just why are all these academics so obviously conspiring together? My friends, I suggest we take a rather closer look at our witness. I put it to you he's provided no evidence at all to show us Larry Sterne's body lies in that grave. I put it to you there's nothing to show that if a body was ever buried at that funeral it was Sterne's at all. I put it to you his whole story is a continuous spiral of lies and deceptions. In fact I suggest to you this supposedly trustworthy professor is simply not what he seems.

So what is the real purpose of this mystification? In my opinion, your honour, our pleasant professor is actually part of a vast cunning academic conspiracy, the like of which the world has rarely seen. It spans several centuries, it takes in many parties. I won't mention the Freemasons, the Illuminati, or the Templars. However, our friend did refer to Mozart, who of course died himself in suspicious circumstances – as Aleksandr Pushkin was to establish in his famous play *Mozart and Salieri*, a very remarkable portrait of the murderous jealousy that can be felt by one artist for another. (*BIRGITTA: I always thought that was because Mozart revealed all those Masonic secrets in* The Magic Flute . . .) Maybe. The fact remains that Mozart's death remains mysterious to this day. So does Sterne's. Which is why I start to ask myself – could it be that what was sauce for Wolfgang Amadeus was sauce for Larry Sterne?

Members of the jury, I ask us to consider again this apparently amiable professor who spoke to us all this morning. Isn't it now clear that every single thing he said to you was exactly what he described himself as being interested in – a cock-and-bull story, a fictive tissue of lies? In fact I suggest to you that this guy is the front for a ruthless band of people who, over generations, have every need to hide the facts about the true life and death of Mr Sterne. Why? Maybe the answer lies in our friend's own inadvertent words. Sterne was a famous and successful writer – great enough to go to court, rich enough to invest in property. Yet, even before he was dead, he was already forced to watch his work being re-used, recycled, plundered and plagiarized, a process that still continues. How do we prove a crime? Means, method and motive, right? Maybe today we'll never really know what happened to Sterne in Paris and London. But we do know there's hardly a serious writer of fiction then and now who didn't somehow benefit from his death, and whose plagiaristic impulses and artistic jealousy were enough to lead to murder. My good friends, isn't it obvious that – along with many other persons unknown, over the generations – the professor who sits so innocently among us is in fact a liar, a rogue, and a guilty party in the case of the Mysterious Death of the Famous Author?

BO looks at VERSO, utterly mystified.

BO
No, Professor Verso. I don't think he meant that. He meant to tell us a true story.

VERSO
Ah. So you're saying there are true and false stories.

ALMA
We all know the difference between fact and fiction.

VERSO
Okay. What are stories of fact? Histories, biographies?

BO
Scientific documents, medical papers, contracts, treaties—

SVEN
Manuals, instruction books, all those things.

VERSO
Encyclopedias? Works of philosophy?

AGNES
Yes.

VERSO
The Bible, the Koran, the Torah?

BO
In a sense.

ALMA
Of course. I don't understand what you're saying.

VERSO
Let's take the things we call fictional. What are they?

BO
Novels, poems, plays. Comedies, tragedies—

ALMA
Fantasies, fairy stories—

VERSO
Take Diderot, then. He wrote works of philosophy, encyclopedias. He also wrote plays, novels, stories. Are they all the same kind of thing, or are they different?

BIRGITTA
You're explaining that papers and stories are just the same?

VERSO
I'm saying they're just two different systems for making narratives and organizing language. Some of them we call true and some we call fictional. And I'm saying that Diderot seems to have understood that too. Which is why a lot of his writings aren't statements but stories or plays or dramatic dialogues with conflicting opinions.

BO
I really don't see what you are trying to prove, professor.

VERSO
I'm saying the categories you're using don't exactly work. You see truth statements and fiction statements. I see different ways of systematizing thought and language. Some pretend to be true and some don't. But maybe you remember what Diderot said about the task of the philosopher: 'It can be required of me that I look for the truth, but not that I should find it.'

BIRGITTA
So papers and stories are really just the same?

ALMA looks at her angrily.

ALMA
Of course not. You can get a grant for one of them but not the other.

VERSO
Sure, they're functionally different. But the truth is all of us, historians and scientists, philosophers and actors and novelists, we're all really in the same boat.

BO
Then it is not this boat, I hope. Professor Verso, really. You have not helped us at all. You are confusing us further. If we listen to the two of you this morning, we will not have a Diderot Project.

VERSO
Oh, I think you might have something else. A real Diderot
Project.

ALMA
Bo, don't listen. This is a disaster.

BIRGITTA
I think it is very nice. I always prefer stories.

ALMA
Don't you realize you are all behaving like very wicked
children? If you start talking in this way, you could spoil the
entire project. All this is your fault.

ALMA turns fiercely on MOI.

MOI
I had hardly anything to do with it.

ALMA
You had everything to do with it.

BO
Please, please. Let us try and stay calm. It is not quite the end
of the world. Not yet. I suggest we take a break for today
and consider how we want to use our Diderot Project. But
remember, if your attitude is merely cynical, we may not be
able to continue—

SVEN
You mean we won't be able to go to Petersburg?

BO
Of course we go to Petersburg, Sven, we have no choice,
I cannot turn round the ship. But we won't have a valid
project. Our researches in print will prove unproductive. Our
grant will be threatened, and there may even be no book from
it. Now, Alma, come. We will go to our cabin—

ALMA
You see what you have done, all of you? You see?

BO and ALMA depart. Omnes look at each other.

ANDERS
Oh dear.

AGNES
This was terrible.

BIRGITTA
Maybe we shouldn't have—

LARS
It's okay, my dears. Bo will come round to it all by the morning. He's used to these things.

VERSO (*to me*)
I hope you didn't mind what I said about you. It was all in the highest interests of philosophical thought.

MOI
I almost agree with you. In fact I might well have said almost the same thing myself.

VERSO
Only you couldn't, could you? Which is exactly why every Moi needs to have a little Lui. Let's go and see what's happening in Russia. Feel like a Jim Beam in the bar?

'Was there really a Canon Cant?' asks Verso, as we squeeze ourselves a place at the packed tables in the Muscovy Bar.

'There really was,' I say, 'but then don't they say that truth is stranger than—'

'What's stranger than what?' asks Verso, turning his eyes, with the rest of the shouting crowd, to the TV screens. Something new is happening in Mother Russia. In the windswept square outside the Duma, the tanks that have been slumbering have now raised up their barrels. In sudden sharp bursts of smoke and flame, they're firing blast after blast. Their shells implode against the huge white building, and its turrets and cornices come crashing down. In moments the building's ugly white bulk is white no longer. Marble and granite topple, and tongues of flame and thick smoke come snaking up out of its windows and scorching their way up its walls. There is firing from the windows, from the strange army gathered inside. 'Jesus, it's happening, this could be real history,' says Jack-Paul Verso, sitting down to watch.

Window after window blows out. Reels of office paper, the core currency of bureaucracy and democracy, come scrolling out of the window holes and down the building's side; they stay there waving in the winds, like someone's uninscribed banners. All the time the shells keep firing, firing. The White House, which Yeltsin had defended two years earlier against one coup, has become the victim of another. It's becoming a grey sepulchre, a pyre ready to burn, another state building sacrificed to keep the state. In front of the White House bodies are falling: protesters, onlookers caught in the cross-fire. Now white flags begin waving from the window cavities; the firing halts for a moment. Meantime, in a gilded state room in the Moscow Kremlin, Tzar Yeltsin is smiling at the cameras. His hair is grey, his face is very flat, his eyes are beaming.

'He believes he's done it,' says Verso; and maybe he has. In a slow procession, deputies in jackets, white shirts, informal sweaters are coming from the burning building. The cameras zoom in. Their looks are defiant, their hands held high. Like so many Russian political adventurers before them – Pugachov and Petrash-evky and Prisoner Number One – they have tried and failed, and fallen for the moment to the upstart tzar. Who knows if it's the end or the beginning, if they're finished for good or back tomorrow. For no end here is ever the end, and many strange things are written in the great Book of Destiny above.

In the Muscovy Bar everyone is shouting and quarrelling – everyone, that is, except for a couple of men who are quietly playing chess in one corner. The ship is in the fast-sweeping Baltic waves now, luffing and troughing its way homeward to Russia. Verso gets up suddenly, and there, I see, is Tatyana from Pushkin, cheeks heavily rouged, wearing a low-cut peasant dress. Verso takes her to the bar for a drink. And I take the chance to slip away, down the passageways, up the stairwells, wanting to find again the elegant and mysterious cabin in which I rather think I must have spent last night. I find my way to it at last, up on the bridge deck.

A pile of luggage stands in the companion-way outside. It consists of my own suitcases, all neatly repacked. A copy of *Jacques* lies neatly on top of it all.

I tap on the door. It's Lars Person who opens it, as I suppose I might have guessed. His hat is off, his shirt is open, he's holding up a foaming flute of pink shampanksi.

'I was hoping to see the diva,' I say.

'I'm so sorry, but Madame Lindhorst is really very busy right now. She needs to arrange the details of her Russian schedule. Also I think she has to write her paper.'

'Oh, she's writing a paper? On Diderot?'

'I think something about the rogue servant in theatre and opera. Figaro, Cherubino. And since I'm a theatre expert she's asked me to join her this evening and help her to write it.'

'I thought we wouldn't be going on with the programme? I thought Bo had decided we're not having any more papers?'

'Then maybe her paper isn't really a paper. At any rate she wants you to know she is busy. Definitely very busy. I hope you understand. Your luggage is out there.'

'Yes, I think I understand,' I say. And, picking up my luggage, I leave the huge magic cabin and make my way to my own windowless metal cell down below.

SIXTEEN (THEN)

DAY THREE

SHE sits on her throne-sofa looking at a sheaf of papers through little spectacles. HE comes in, shivering and rubbing his hands hard. SHE looks up.

SHE
What's the matter, Mr Librarian?

HE
It's freezing hard out there. The Neva seems to be icing over.

SHE
Exactly as I told you it would. Now then, sir, this paper.
I take it this is your first memorandum?

HE
Indeed, Your Imp—

SHE
Entitled 'The Daydream of Denis the Philosopher'?

HE
Yes, Your Maj—

SHE
One half of it flattering me quite disgustingly. And the other half shamelessly abusing Frederick of Prussia.

HE
It's an expression of my homage. As you can see, the improvement of Saint Petersburg has become my waking dream.

SHE

But not just Petersburg. The whole of Russia. You're the new Gustav Adolf. You seem to want to occupy my entire nation.

HE

To set it free and make it foremost among nations. But not with my troops. Only with my mind.

SHE

I'm beginning to see the imperial nature of your mind.

HE

It's only a mind, Your Highness. It's right here in my head, open to your constant inspection.

SHE fingers the memorandum.

SHE

I've always found dreams – even daydreams – very hard to inspect.

HE

I couldn't agree with you more. And that's why I've made such a study of them.

SHE

Ah. Now you're a student of dreams. And you also believe in sybils, do you? Witches? Divination by animal intestines?

HE

No. I have no interest in what dreams say, or how they prophesy. I'm concerned with what they tell us about mind and consciousness itself.

SHE

And naturally you've written an important article on the topic—

HE

A little book, marm. *The Dream of d'Alembert.* You know d'Alembert? My friend and fellow, a founder of—

SHE stares at him angrily.

SHE

Everyone in Russia knows d'Alembert. I offered him the post of tutor to the Archduke. He didn't just refuse me, he made an obscene joke to Voltaire. Who told me at once.

HE

About the piles? D'Alembert's a man of the greatest sensibility. He's always worrying about his arse.

SHE

Then he had the gall to ask me to free some French prisoners I'd taken. That man is never to be mentioned in this court. Never. What did you write about him?

HE

If I told you, I'd have to speak of him.

SHE

I know that, sir. I'm demanding that you speak.

HE

Well then . . . I decided to *become* his dreams. I simply entered his mind and put my ideas into it. Then he very kindly dreamt my own ideas when he slept.

SHE

You put his dreams into his head? How?

HE

I pointed out the contradictions in his philosophy. Then I sent him to bed. I placed his mistress there, a clever girl called Mam'selle de l'Espinasse, and his doctor, Doctor Bordeu.

SHE
Well?

HE

When he began to talk his thoughts in his sleep, and did various instinctive and revealing things with his unconscious body, she made notes of his words and Bordeu examined his thoughts and explained them—

SHE

But, monsieur, you couldn't possibly *know* what he dreamt.

HE

I knew his dreams would answer my thoughts. But it didn't matter. The main thing is to show thoughts work like dreams, and dreams are sleeping thoughts—

SHE

I don't see the point at all.

HE

A dream's the result of sensory stimulation. It responds to the stimuli we're usually aware of, but it's an involuntary response. That shows the self has a conscious and an unconscious or involuntary form—

SHE

Yesterday you said everything depends on reason. Now you're saying just the same about unreason.

HE leans forward in enormous excitement, slapping her thigh heartily. The COURTIERS observe.

HE

Clever of you, Your Highness. Which is why wisdom must often take on the appearance of folly or delirium if it's to be properly understood.

SHE

Yesterday you arrived with a sackful of reason. Today you come with a cartload of madness.

HE

Reason and delirium, dream and fantasy, Your Highness. In all of them one thing seeks to connect with another. Imagine the mind as a spider, spinning filaments. If we master them, keep them in shape, we are thinkers. If we let them spin and weave, then we are dreamers—

SHE holds up her hand.

SHE

Mr Diderot, tell me. Do you really intend to behave like a madman in my court?

HE

Whenever it might be helpful or instructive.

SHE

Very well. You trespassed into the dreams of d'Alembert. What did you learn?

HE

I learned to disprove Descartes. Descartes thought mind mastered the universe. D'Alembert rambled from thought to thought, and learned thoughts come unbidden.

SHE

He learned that? Or you told him that's what he thought?

HE (*smiles quietly*)

It's true. I wrote it down. I made it into a story.

SHE

So that's it. You didn't create his dream at all. You simply invented it.

HE

I'm a maker of stories, Your Highness. But I did prove there is a wild flux of human consciousness. And no one thing we possess and can call our self—

SHE looks at him, very displeased.

SHE

Mr Philosopher. I am myself. In fact I'm more than myself, I'm the state. The sovereign person.

HE

Who authorizes this person?

SHE

I do. I am the author of myself.

HE
In that case you're a despot.

SHE
Now, sir, be very careful—

HE
We are all despots, or try to be. We try to dominate our own existence, to claim the right to a self. Yet surely we know our real existence is different – a world of shifting cells, jangling nerves, fermenting, growing and dying? Of course we attempt to spin some sovereign self from within, just like little spiders. And then we construct a spider king and a spider god—

The COURTIERS laughing and jeering.

SHE
And this is reason?

HE
My kind of it.

SHE
You contradict yourself. You say there's no self. Yet you firmly insist on your own opinions.

HE
Wisdom lies in contradiction.

SHE
You'd contradict me?

HE
If you permit it, as a wise monarch would. Otherwise I shall contradict the one person who always permits it. Myself.

SHE
I think that's enough for one day. Indeed I wonder if it's not too much.

HE (*rising*)
So, tomorrow, may I send you another memorandum? A small one? How to create an honest police force?

SHE
Yes, sir, now just go—

END OF DAY THREE

SEVENTEEN (NOW)

A BRISK FRESH NEW SEA-DAY. And here I am, strewn out on an ugly canvas deckchair, wrapped up in a thick anorak, shrouded tight in a hired rug, up on the bridge deck of the *Vladimir Ilich*. Vladimir's bronzy face squints inquiringly out from the bulkhead behind me as I recline, overlooking the book I'm trying to read. The ship itself has grown curiously quiet, even a little mournful. On this our third day out, the weather is cold, dampish, briny, sharpened with a definite, wintry Baltic chill. Vague mist wanders over the water, appearing and then dispersing, as if unsure of its real intentions. The sea beyond the ship-rail has a moderate but unmistakably stomach-churning swell. No coastline is now visible on any side; the Baltic is big, after all. The wide seaway we're sailing is busy with big-bellied Russian factory ships, their funnels tricoloured in pre- or post-Marxist livery. All of them seem to be running westward toward the world's richer economies. Meanwhile we're beating eastward, to political turmoil, economic crisis, maybe a new civil war. To the south are the Baltic Republics, those lively and likeable nations Stalin required, with his usual Georgian charm, to 'request admission' into his union of socialist republics, and which have now managed to break loose from the cruel contract in a fresh northern configuration. And somewhere off to the north, shrouded inside a long low fogline that makes everything invisible, must be Finland and the port of Helsinki. For me it's another of the world's great cities, and another place of which I've come to grow very fond.

Shrouded and shivering in my deckchair, I try to read. I'm reading, again, *Rameau's Nephew*, the book which our splendid diva dumped in the passage outside her cabin, having firmly dismissed it as annoying and unpleasant. But is it really? Not a bit of it, not to me. In fact I'm hooked as soon as I take up again that familiar opening: 'Rain or shine, it's my usual habit each day around five to take a walk round the arcades of the Palais Royal. Meantime I discuss with myself questions of politics and love, taste and philosophy. I let my mind rove promiscuously, setting it free to take in whatever idea happens to settle first, however wise or stupid. My ideas are my trollops. I chase them just the way the rogues and roués pursue the over-dressed and bright-painted whores in these Paris arcades – following every single one of them, finally lying down with none. And when the weather becomes a little too cold or rainy, I resort to the splendid Café de la Régence, and sit down to watch the experts playing their games of chess.' Next thing there arrives the egregious nephew who makes the story: 'One day I was there after dinner, watching hard, saying nothing, when I was accosted by one of the oddest fellows in our country, which has never been short of oddities: a man who has no greater opposite, no better double than himself.'

'Hello there,' says a voice. I look up from the fluttering pages of the book to see someone swaying toward me along the rail, his body blown violently this way and that by the sudden variable gusts of wind. It's Anders Manders, fine and dapper, an expensive woollen raincoat blowing all around him, his ears capped with a hat of real fox fur. Thus far on this voyage Manders has been no kind of oddity at all. He's been one of the stronger and more silent members of our party, charming, reassuring, the perfect gentleman diplomat, another man who watches hard and says nothing. Even the dour Sven Sonnenberg – a man who seems to think of nothing else in the world but tables, whose mind itself seems a perfect tabula rasa – has, over the group meals we've started taking together in the ship's huge dining room, proved fierce and alive in defence of his craftsman's passions. He's criticized my imitation leather watch-strap, looked contemptuously at my plasticated shoes, dismissively examined my imperfectly crafted pipe. Lately, though, he's been talking only to Agnes Falkman, our reforming feminist and union organizer, who seems to share with him some deep Swedish love of working with the hands.

Today, though, our party seems to have disintegrated completely. Thus far (and it's almost lunchtime) Manders is the only member of the group to emerge into the light. The fact is, an unfortunate Baltic chill has fallen over the whole Diderot Project. What's more, it's presumably been caused by the two papers Verso and I gave (or more truthfully failed to give) yesterday. Yet I still can't convince myself that's the true or only explanation for the note of moratorium that's now fallen over our entire adventure. Our fine conference room two decks below now stands locked, empty, unlit. There's been no further talk of papers. The philosophical pilgrims themselves have all somehow disappeared, just to be spotted now and then at the end of some long passageway in our perfectly comfortable floating hotel. The Swedish diva seems to have retreated for good to her elegant cabin on the captain's deck, no doubt unaware of my odd fits of jealousy, with or without the company of Lars Person, who has become almost invisible too. Jack-Paul Verso can be glimpsed occasionally, though he seems to have given up lap-tapping his laptop and devoted himself to chasing an endless tribe of laughing Tatyanas all over the ship. Today I've seen Agnes Falkman only once, emerging suddenly like a drowned creature from a very thick coating of mud in a chair in the Beauty Salon. Umbrage presumably taken, Bo and Alma Luneberg are just nowhere to be found. Out of the group of nine we began with, Manders is all the society there is left.

'Very fine book, I know it well,' he says, smiling affably, wiping off the next deckchair with an old Russian newspaper, and glancing over my shoulder at my reading as he sits down.

'I'm glad you think so,' I say. 'Tell me something, have you seen our grand diva this morning?'

'No, but I shall see her tonight,' says Manders. 'We've made a little appointment to have dinner together, alone.'

'So she's not with Lars Person then?'

'No, I saw him drinking alone just now in the bar. She's surely not been with that boring fellow, has she?'

'Yes, last night, I thought.'

'I really doubt it. They're old Stockholm enemies. They never do get on.'

'So is anything at all happening on the Enlightenment Trail?'

'Not too much now. Professor Bo has locked himself away in his cabin with Alma.'

'My fault. I feel extremely guilty about that.'

'I assure you there is no need. Unless guilt gives you pleasure, as I know it often can. All this fuss he's making is just a fine excuse. Professor Bo knows an opportunity when he has one. Now he can sit down and do what he likes to do best.'

'What's that?'

'Becoming a factotum. Making arrangements. Bo is a true meddler, a trader, a mixer, a fixer.'

'Really?'

'Professor Bo knows everyone, and everyone knows him. He's on the Nobel Prize Committee, the Olympic Committee of literature. That opens every door to him, and places him among the great councils of the world.'

'What's he up to in his cabin?'

'I expect telegraphing and telephoning, sending his messages and his proposals and his fixes back and forth. Washington and Paris, Stockholm and Rome. And Petersburg, of course. He knows Petersburg very well, it's quite clear. These international operators are the true salt of the earth, you know.'

'What about the Diderot Project? Is it still on?'

'Oh, I think so, even more so. Why not? A little row about papers, it happens at every conference.'

'I mean the news,' I say. 'Did you watch the television news this morning?'

For today the world of Russia looks even more troubled. Cameras panned across a blackened, burnt out White House, its windows gone, its walls licked with smoke scars, its parliament silenced and done for. Now angry crowds are massed everywhere under their tricoloured or red banners, and tanks are still rolling heavily through the streets. Bodies are rushed away on stretchers. In Moscow overnight a night curfew has been declared. Only Tzar Yeltsin seems unconcerned. There he is on television, stiffer and scarier than ever, like a grand yet undoubtedly powerful automaton: Papa Russia.

'Friends, I bow my head in warm appreciation to the Russian people,' he says, solemnly bowing down his silvery nob to camera.

'Yes, I saw it,' says Manders, looking amazingly unconcerned, as diplomats often do. 'Things are plainly getting very interesting. Don't you want to go to Russia?'

'With the country in such a crisis I'm honestly not too sure I do.'

'But when could it be more exciting?'

'The middle of a revolution doesn't seem the ideal time for going on an Enlightenment Project,' I remark.

'A very bad attitude,' says Manders. 'For one thing, whenever you come to Russia it's going to be in crisis. Because Russia always is a crisis. Then I thought the Enlightenment was a revolution in itself. Reason has always been a source of trouble and difficulty. It always was and it always will be. This is what your friend the nephew is telling you, there in your book. Philosophy and virtue are perfectly all right in their place, but they have nothing much to do with anything. Remember what the nephew says? It's very nice and respectable to think and discuss ideas and go to pleasant salons, if you're a fine philosopher. But if by occupation you're a worm, then you have to spend most of your time crawling. And you also rear up in anger and revenge when you get stepped on.'

'True, of course,' I say. 'You know, I remember going to a conference in the Canary Islands once.'

'You academics, it's always a conference,' says Manders, amused. 'It was pleasant, was it?'

'Not exactly. This was back in Franco's time, and there was a student rebellion, a militant campaign for Canarian independence. I knew there was something wrong when I landed at the airport and the professor wasn't there to meet me. Instead there was a group of students who seemed to have their jackets pulled up over their faces. They said the professor sent his warmest apologies, but unfortunately he was hiding up in the hills with his wife. He hoped it wouldn't interfere with my lectures, and I'd be able to give the conference without him. As I was the only outside speaker, this wasn't too encouraging. Then when I got to the university I found myself in the middle of a big student demonstration. The Spanish authorities were responding in kind as usual. There were civil guards with bullet-proofed Land Rovers and machine guns all over the university steps.'

'They let you in, I hope?'

'Of course. I was a visiting foreign lecturer. They even let in a few students, or maybe they sneaked in through the back doors. At any rate I was able to present my opening lecture. If I remember rightly, it was a radical new reading of *The Scarlet Letter*, Nathaniel Hawthorne's story about puritanism and adultery. The only thing was, right in the middle of the lecture, when the argument was getting interesting, some sort of gun battle started outside. Then a few bullets came in through the windows and flew across the room. The students were very good really, and kept on listening fairly patiently while I explicated the significance of Hester Prynne as a symbol of natural passion. But I frankly have to confess to you the lecture really wasn't one of my best.'

'I can imagine.'

'Still, we had a very useful discussion period. Then when I left the students who were protesting outside had disappeared. Except a couple of them lay dead on the steps.'

'Oh dear.'

'That evening some of the professor's students drove me up to some bar high up on a remote mountain top so I could meet him. He was in extremely heavy disguise: big hat, dark glasses, false moustache, you know. His wife was the same, actually. He was very apologetic and said he was sorry to miss my lecture, since as he was working on Hawthorne too he'd been looking forward to my thoughts with delicious anticipation for weeks. But he did want me to understand that, since he was from the peninsula and had been appointed to his job by the Franco government, he'd probably have been assassinated if he'd attended. A difficult choice, he was kind enough to say. We had a meal together and then I went back to the university residences and he pulled an overcoat over his head and went off to a safe house somewhere in the hills.'

'That was the end of the conference?'

'Not at all,' I have to explain. 'The second day was dedicated to Melville's *Moby Dick*. The troops and the Land Rovers were back all over the campus. But a few students managed to turn up all the same.'

'Naturally. For *Moby Dick*.'

'Quite. We had a tolerably useful discussion on the nature of American tragedy and the significance of the White Whale. The students were all very kind, and seemed to accept my interpretation. Then after it was over they bundled me up in a blanket and took me to the airport, so I could escape on the next plane to Madrid. Strangely enough, the professor who invited me and his wife were also on the flight, dressed as a pair of Benedictine nuns.'

'What happened to them all?'

'Oh, a few weeks later Morocco, I think it was, claimed ownership of the Canary Islands, and the independence movement changed its mind. They preferred to be Spanish after all. The professor and his wife were supposed to be Franco spies, but when democracy came they got chairs in Madrid and became quite famous. And I changed my views on *Moby Dick*.'

'Quite a conference, then.'

'As I say, not one of the pleasantest I've been to.'

'Yet at least you remember it. How many of the others do you remember?'

'All right, I admit, the ones I remember are those where everything goes wrong. Although now I come to think of it, most times I've lectured abroad there's been crisis, revolution, or something similar.'

'Really? It must be the way you tell them. So why is it unusual this time?'

'It isn't, really. It's just that as the world goes on you hope things will start to get better. We are at the end of history, after all. Anyway, maybe with all this trouble they won't even let us land.'

'True,' says Manders, 'in Russia you never, never know. They may not allow us off the ship. They may detain us in the terminal. They may admit us to the country and then refuse to let us leave. It's always this way with the Russian authorities. One day they're the nicest and friendliest people in the world. The next they're the most oppressive.'

'Depending on which party's in charge?'

'That really makes no difference. Whatever party's in charge, it's usually the same people. The most fervent former Communists now manage the free market. The people who toast international friendship and open democracy are the same ones who run the repression. The people who run the police force also organize most of the crime. It's a very simple system. Darwinian. The management of the beast. The survival of the fittest. Otherwise called riding the tiger of history.'

'I can see you know a lot about it.'

'I know everything about it. I spent five years as a cultural attaché in the Swedish consulate. I'm sure that's why Bo thought I was going to be useful on this trip. I know all those officials.'

'You were in Saint Petersburg, you mean?'

'Yes, only then it was called Leningrad. To be honest, being very ancient enemies, the Swedes have always got on very well with the Russians. One end of the Baltic always needs the other. That's why although we were western we had a high-minded pacifist policy. We let them have free run of the sea–routes, because they could have controlled them in any case. We let them fix up their nuclear submarines in Swedish ports. And the Russian Embassy in Stockholm was a very famous nest of spies.'

'I presume you got something back in return?'

'Yes. We were permitted our virtue. We were allow to smuggle people in and out all the time. Also manuscripts, scientific papers, books. That's how a lot of samizdat got to the west. And then we always had our glorious secret weapon.'

'What was that?'

'The Nobel Prize, of course. It was bigger than ten battleships. If we felt they were treating their best scientists and writers too terribly, then we could always award them the famous prize.'

'Did it help?'

'Sometimes, not always. It made them a little afraid of us. We could never threaten them, but at least we could exercise our moral opinions. And this, you see, is one reason why Bo has so much influence now in Russia.'

'Has he?'

'Yes, of course. He's been there a good many times. People understand his influence. He knows everyone at the university.'

'And at the Hermitage library?'

'I'm not so sure Bo is very much interested in libraries. His ambitions reach a little higher. I expect he's really coming to find out about the best Russian writers and do some work on the prize.'

'It sounds as if you liked Leningrad?'

'I loved it. In those days I was young and liked my life salted with a little danger.'

'They really were interesting times.'

'Remarkable, wonderful, conspiratorial, horrible times. Leningrad when it was Leningrad. Pushkin called it the city that lived underneath the water, and somehow it was. Did you never go there?'

'No. I went to Moscow once. Leningrad, very nearly.'

'Oh, Moscow was quite different. And what does that mean, very nearly?'

'Simply that the chance came my way. But then things turned out to be a little more complicated than I expected . . .'

And, as we lie there on our deckchairs on the cold quiet bridge deck, I tell Manders my tiny story about a certain Small Finnish Interlude . . .

EIGHTEEN (THEN)

DAY FIVE

SHE sits on the sofa, stitching at an embroidery frame and looking impatient. HE arrives with his stockings in disorder. SHE looks up crossly.

SHE
Late, Mr Librarian. Very late indeed.

HE
Yes. I'm sorry. I'm afraid the servants were very slow this morning.

SHE
But now it's mid-afternoon.

HE
The streets were icy. The Neva is frozen. The bridge over the Winter Canal is closed.

SHE
Sir. Servants are always late, in Petersburg or Paris. So their masters should rise early. I warned you the Neva would freeze over. In November streets are always icy and the Winter Bridge is often closed. Surely a wise philosopher, using the tools of reason and logic, can work out how to give ten minutes more to a short journey in the city, in order to meet his Imperial Mother at the proper time?

HE
I'm sorry, Your Highness. The honest truth is I had a severe

attack of the Neva colic. And I had to return in very great haste to the stool.

SHE
Cold water baths, that's the answer. Go to the public bathhouse and dowse yourself in the cold water baths.

HE
The public bathhouse. Thank you. I will indeed.

SHE
Do you know my courtiers think you are mad, Dr Didro?

HE
Just a poor clown in your service, Your Highness.

SHE
Do you know why? Apparently you have been walking around this entire city asking questions. The Secret Office is getting extremely annoyed with you.

HE
It's my occupation, Your Highness – asker of questions.

SHE
Who gave you permission?

HE
My curious mind gives me permission. If I am to give Your Highness answers about how to develop and improve her country, that's because I'll already have been asking questions. Aren't I free?

SHE
Yes, you are free. But just as you are free to ask questions, my people are free not to give answers. If that is what they happen to choose.

HE
I'm not sure they choose on a rational basis. They say that if they answer a foreigner's questions, their noses might be cut off.

SHE
Surely that's a rational basis. And have you seen anyone in
Sankt Peterburg with less than a whole nose?

HE
True, Your Highness. I haven't.

SHE
You see? So what are these matters on which you wish to ask
your questions?

HE
I've tried to ask them about education and the progress of
manufacture. Tried to discover how the economy works.

SHE
And how does it?

HE
I'm far from clear that it does. I tried to find out if there were
shops—

SHE
Of course. Lovely ones. Look on Nevsky Prospekt.

HE
I've tried to discover how many banks there are in Russia—

SHE
Then don't ask strangers, merely ask me. How many banks are
there in Russia, Dashkova?

DASHKOVA
I think . . . none, Your Royal Highness.

SHE
Nonsense. I always have money. More than enough.

DASHKOVA
You use the banks in Amsterdam, Your Highness. And the
Rothschilds in Frankfurt . . . the Fuggers in Augsburg . . .

SHE looks triumphant.

SHE
There you are then. That is what we do here for money.

HE
Banks, I truly recommend them as a stimulus to trade. If you want progress, you have banks.

SHE
Why worry about those things? You are here to think, not to become some greedy shopkeeper.

HE
I like to reflect on the greater good of Russia.

SHE (*angry*)
I think that's my job.

HE
I'm here to reason. But reason is useless without an application. It can create wealth, invention, discovery, trade and science. How big is Russia?

SHE
Do you know, when I took over the throne, there was no map of the nation in the whole court? True, Dashkova? If you asked one of the courtiers about Russia, he had no real idea of where it even was. I sent Dashkova out to buy a map for me, at a shop for sailors on Nevsky Prospekt.

HE
Splendid.

SHE
So you see, we do have shops.

DASHKOVA
Except when you found it sold maps, you closed the shop.

SHE
Don't gossip, Dashkova. Find it and bring it here.

DASHKOVA goes to the cabinet in the corner and gets out a map.

SHE
When I looked at the map I saw what we had all ignored.
Russia is the world's biggest country—

DASHKOVA
And when you saw this you decided to make it bigger.

SHE
Of course. Now look here, Mr Philosopher. I have Sankt
Peterburg, Moscow, Archangel, Vladivostok. A route by
the Baltic to the English sea, a route by the Arctic to the
American sea. Now, notice what's missing?

HE
I'm not sure I do, Your Highness.

SHE
No? I have the world's largest deposits of ice and snow, the
biggest steppes, the hugest expanse of tundra. I have the largest
inland lake. But what about sunshine?

HE
Sunshine? Ah – I think I understand. To complete the
collection you would like to have the Mediterranean.

SHE
Your excellent friend Voltaire, who always has my concerns at
heart, tells me I should take Constantinople.

HE stares at her.

HE
Voltaire advises you to capture Constantinople?

SHE
Does that surprise you?

HE
A little. Perhaps you might have read his novel *Zadig*?

SHE
Of course. I read everything he sends me. It's the tale of an
Arab philosopher who possesses great wisdom and thinks he

should be the happiest of men. Only his lover rejects him, his wife betrays him, he's sold into slavery and endures every kind of humiliation. But at last he marries the queen and establishes a great age of reason. I imagine that's why you mention it?

HE
Not really. It's because in the book Voltaire declares his love for Arab philosophy and the Musleem people. So why then would he advise you to take Constantinople?

SHE pouts at him.

SHE
You don't believe me? I'll show you his letter. He tells me to revenge the Greeks, end the captivity of the poor Turkish ladies, scourge the infidel, and restore the true Church to Byzantium. Oh, and put up my statue.

HE
We're talking about Voltaire? The great atheist?

SHE
Deist. My philosopher and distant friend.

HE
The man who hates war above everything? Who mocks the folly of killing men simply because they wear turbans?

SHE smiles at him, takes out a letter.

SHE
Read his letter, see. 'Perhaps one day you will have three capitals, Sankt Peterburg, Moscow, Byzantium. Remember, Byzantium is far better situated than the other two.'

HE
Your Highness, if I were a sovereign, I should want my generals to advise me on matters of conquest, and my philosophers to advise me on morals and metaphysics. Never the other way round.

SHE
But surely there are just wars, and moral conquests?

HE
Yes. That's always the opinion. On both sides.

SHE
Oh, my dear Mr Philosopher. You know, I am good, and everyone knows I am as gentle as anyone alive. But I just can't help terribly wanting the things I mean to have.

HE
So yesterday a Rubens. Today a Byzantium.

SHE looks at him coyly.

SHE
Maybe I should have asked Voltaire to come here instead of you. He writes to me constantly, enquiring about your progress. I think he is a little jealous of you. And perhaps just a little bit in love with me.

HE
What philosopher would not be?

SHE
Very well, sir. Now excuse me, the English Ambassador is out there, getting very impatient. Go away now, and just think what it means to be a monarch.

HE rises.

HE
I will, Your Majesty—

SHE
And remember what I told you. Cold baths. That's what we do here, isn't it, Dashkova?

DASHKOVA
Yes. Your Imperial Highness is always making us take cold baths for everything. I'll see you out, Monsieur Didro.

END OF DAY FIVE

NINETEEN (NOW)

A SMALL FINNISH INTERLUDE

Well now, all this takes us back a little, to the distant days you must also remember: days of social democracy and the dawning of the welfare state, when the charming word 'Scandinavia' aroused liberal images of democratic justice, social improvement and neat square furniture. The world was existentially divided into two polar opposites, East and West, and you were supposed to support one or the other. Travel was still exciting, and every single country you went to was different. They didn't bother to check you out for weaponry at Heathrow. All British airline pilots were called Captain Strong, you travelled everywhere like a real gentleman, the gin served in the air did not come out of miniatures. Everywhere there was a whiff of spying. At this time I was a young writer, or just beginning to think about myself as one. I'd published enough and taught enough to be able to stick 'teacher and writer' onto my passport. On the other hand I was so splendidly unknown I was totally amazed if anyone recognized my name or recalled even a single word of the various books – the youthful first novel, the odd works of lit. crit., the volumes of humour and satire – I had managed to get into rather obscure print.

One day I heard I'd been awarded a striking literary honour. One of my books, my dear first novel, was to be translated into a foreign language: something that happened far less commonly then than it does now. On the other hand, the language it was to be translated into was Finnish, which meant the people who were so keen to read me lived in a part of the world I didn't know at all. I wasn't even sure whether Finland was in Europe, or just off the edge of it – a question that, I would later discover, the Finns were constantly asking of themselves. In fact at that time I think I knew only five simple facts about the Finns. They drank. They ski-jumped. They produced remarkable architects. They spoke an obscure agglutinative language strangely related to Hungarian which nobody else could understand, not even fellow Finns. And – how I loved them for this – they were a great nation of readers. Yes, they read books, amazing numbers of them, more books than any other people: quite possibly, though I didn't quite realize this at the time, because in that land of vast forest, wide lakes, great deer ticks, huge mosquitoes, open and empty landscapes, deep and endless snow, a wintry universe of engrossed solitude where one person hardly ever spoke to another, there was very little else to do.

I imagined the Finns to be a thoughtful bespectacled people, ever in and out of libraries, constantly discussing the novels of Charles Dickens, the tales of Tolkein, modernist fragmentation in T. S. Eliot's *The Waste Land*. And then one day a letter came from my Finnish publisher (oh, what words!) with a striking invitation. He didn't simply want to have my book translated; he hoped I would fly to Finland on his invitation, meet the press, be photographed with my translator, and then take a tour to the country talking to the various literary circles and reading groups that all spoke English and gathered, it seemed, in every little town and hamlet. I read the letter; and of course I said yes. Even back in those days whenever I was asked I always said yes.

So: the place was Finland, the month was February, the time was the early and innocent beginning of the sixties. Now, as I say, to me at that time Finland seemed distant, strange, remote, as far off as Mongolia, as politically obscure as Dubai. I knew really nothing about its history: except it lay on the topside of the Baltic, whose shores at one time or another seem to have been disputed by just about everybody; that it had suffered terribly under the Russian invasion during the Winter Ski-War; that it had since then stayed free of occupation from its predatory and expanding neighbour, though no doubt at a very high price. In political terms it looked like a land suspended in history, somehow tucked in a trap between East and West in a knife-edge deal that was actually known as Finlandization. For the Cold War, at this date, was extremely cold. In fact it was a prime period of nuclear anxiety. Stalin had gone, but the spy-planes swept the skies, erect missiles pointed their warheads in every direction, the crisis of global annihilation seemed to wait there just a few minutes away, and the Cuban crisis was just round the corner.

But the grim political weather that worried everyone seemed not a bit colder than the chill Nordic winter I encountered when I set off on what was to be my first real literary voyage. I crossed the North Sea from Britain in some old propeller aircraft, captained, of course, by Captain Strong. There was a refuelling stopover at Stockholm, I recall, and we were allowed off the plane to wander briefly around the endless pornography stalls before we rose up again and began to cross over these same troubled waters, the political seas of the Baltic. Russian warships ploughed these channels, western submarines slipped about underneath the ice, spies and refugees struggled to find information or refuge. Seen from my viewpoint, a dusty plane-seat, the Gulf of Finland was just one great frozen crust. Huge ice-breaker tugs were working the waters below me, carving narrow black shipping tracks through the massive white ice-cap. The plane signs came on. We flew lower and lower, beginning our descent over a landscape that, like the frozen sea, seemed entirely without colour: spiky whiteness, conifer forest everywhere, a world filled up with snowdrift.

To me, Helsinki's tiny airport felt like a strangely obscure place. A long way away, it seemed, from any city, it was enfolded in that strange silence that somehow descends on a world of total snow. I took the slow-moving airport bus into the city, riding on ploughed-out and hard-crusted roads through thick forest, past sawmills, log yards, steaming wooden huts. When we reached the capital, Helsinki, also caught in snowfall, seemed weirdly silent too. The trams glided noiselessly along its boulevards, the cars moved without making a sound, the heating steam puffed silently from the city roofs. I found my way through freezing streets and squares to my hotel: a charming white establishment called the Hotel Gurki, which I later discovered had been used as Gestapo headquarters during the war. But that of course was twenty years before – in another time, when there were different enemies, different politics, different alliances and sympathies. It may even have had something to do with the air of comfort it offered the frozen travelling writer; my pleasant hotel was as crisply and self-consciously warm as the world outside felt cold.

I unpacked in a clean comfortable room, discovered the lift (it was called the HISSI), and went down to the lobby, where my foreign publishers had said they would come to collect me. I felt wonderfully content. To my own surprise, I was now the kind of person who had a foreign publisher, persons who would take my work to transmit it to an audience of whose nature I had absolutely no idea. To pass the time, I sat in a chair and picked up the local newspapers, provided on sticks for easy reading. Besides the fact that the pictures struck me as peculiarly bloody (horrific car crashes, people shot dead in the middle of the woods, or hanging from trees), I found myself staring at a language of total incompre-hensibility. The nouns behaved like cancerous bodies, adding syllables with careless profusion; the verbs seemed missing. The vocabulary came from ancient word-stock carelessly thrown about as in some semantic accident. Everything was prolix, random, anarchically inventive, as if the whole language was still being made up. It seemed odd to think that my own writing, with its realistic statements and social observations, could be transmuted into this, or mean anything if it was.

I read for a while, then watched as some workmen struggled to release some guests – an American tourist in plaid pants, a weeping wife – from the Hissi.

'My wife's been stuck in there two hours,' said the tourist.

'Our Finnish Hissis are excellent,' said the manager indignantly. 'They are exported everywhere all over the world.'

'Oh God, you mean I could end up in another one like that?' asked the tourist, comforting his sobbing wife. 'Why did we ever come to Europe?'

'Finland is not Europe, Finland is only Finland,' said the manager.

At this point two huge men, wearing great snow-dusted leather overcoats and vast fur hats, walked into the lobby and began looking dangerously around. They exactly resembled my idea of the Gestapo agents who had used these premises twenty years before. They went over to the desk. A moment later I heard them pronounce my name.

Then I understood. These tough guys weren't agents at all. They were publishers, from the house that meant to publish my work. It was, I discovered when they came over and led me downstairs to the bar, one of the great Finnish houses, the house that over generations had published the major Finnish writers – Runeberg and Topelius, Kivi and the remarkable Lonnrot, without whom we would never have had the *Kalevala*, and therefore not Longfellow's *Hiawatha* either. My hosts were hearty men (I have always found the Finns a warm people in a cold land) and great specialists in vodka: or rather in the amazing variety of vodkas on offer near the Arctic circle, each one of which they insisted I try. We went into the restaurant to continue the experiment over reindeer steak and whale meat. So the evening went on.

In answer to my questions, my excellent hosts told me all I wanted to know about Finland, a squeezed and flattened country that had been Swedish when it was not being Russian, and had scarcely ever been itself. They told me about the Great Wrath and the Little Wrath, the Swedish occupation, the Russian terror; about Mannerheim and their own Red Revolution, the Winter War and painful postwar loss of Karelia, the most beautiful Finnish lands of them all. They told me about life in a land of four-fifths forest, lake and tundra, about the sea, bears, wolves, trolls. For some reason just possibly to do with the unending supply of vodka, the information they gave me began to seem more and more obscure. When our meal was complete, and I had finally consumed a dessert of mysterious forest bilberries that made me feel even stranger than before, they took me upstairs again, and there introduced me to a waiting bevy of press photographers, who all took my photo for the morning papers. In Finland, they explained, it was considered extremely rude to photograph a writer when sober. Then, with the greatest kindness, considering the condition they were now in themselves, they got me into the Hissi and managed to find my room, which as far as I was concerned had quite unaccountably disappeared.

There, when I woke in the morning, it was, again, in far better condition than I was. I was in a neat modern bedroom with red iron bed, clear white curtains. A maid or warder of some kind was admitting herself into the room with a pass key, and handing me a tray with a green pot of coffee and the morning papers. On the front page of the *Sanomat*, a raddled, bloated, broken British writer, looking ninety years old at the very least, peered out over my name. The telephone rang and it turned out to be my hosts who were calling. They were waiting for me down in the lobby, feeling as fresh as daisies, ready to take me on the tour of Helsinki which I had apparently demanded of them the night before. They in big coats and furry hats, myself in a Burton's shortie raincoat, we set off into the freeze. Sliding, slithering, slipping, I walked round a city like none I had ever been in: deep-locked in ice and snow, frozen in time and space. Great winds swept down wide boulevards. Long-trailered rattling trams carved their powdery way through streets that seemed far too full of snow to allow any traffic at all.

The city itself struck me as completely charming. It was at once the most imperial and the most colonial of capitals, equally western and Russian. There were big, bow-fronted, art nouveau apartment blocks, troll-covered residences from the Nordic Revival, square blocks of concrete modernism. Great Nordic architects had done their work here: a couple of Aaltos, a couple of Saarinens, the famous Jop Kaakinen. Most were in the modern manner, yet they were covered in the most obscure of signs. They said RAVINTOLA, YLIOPPILASPALVELU, OOPPERA, MATKAILIJAYHDISTYS, ARVOPAPERIPORSSI, POSTIPANKKI, SUOMEN PANKKI, HAPPII HOTELLI, HANKKI PANKKI. We arrived at the grand Senate Square, a fine spread surrounded by domed public buildings in the style of nineteenth-century classicism: Senate, White Lutheran Cathedral, the splendid high-stepped university. There amid them in the snow, covered in evergreen wreaths, was the statue of the one liberal Tzar, Alexander II, emancipator of the serfs, the man who had permitted the Finns to express their nationhood – until, as usual, he was assassinated.

So we went on, slipping and slithering, to the Baltic esplanade. Despite the frozen weather a flourishing market was working. Vast ships stood along the dockside, the Swedish ferries: not high-sided monsters like ours, but old steamers smoking like papermills. Out in the harbour of Sandviki the icebreakers pulsed, cutting the channel open with a cracking noise like thunder, carving the boatpath out past Suomenlinna. To one side was a Lutheran church, to the other a huge onion-domed mass, the Russian Orthodox Cathedral. Huge dirty buses marked Intourist were parked all round it, and people from seaside postcards, men in suits and medals, women with false blonde hair, vast in spotted dresses, were unloading and going inside. We went inside too, to see the black metropolitans, coroneted priests, the swinging censers, the flickering candles, the worshippers kissing the golden icons.

'The Russians still come, then?' I say.

'Oh, yes,' says my host, 'we always expect them at any time.'

Finland's winter days are very short, and very sweet. So somehow it was already the middle of the afternoon, and the light was rapidly darkening. In fact it was time to go and meet my Finnish translator at a famous writers' café. We walked over to the place, somewhere near my hotel. I remember it was called the Kafé Kosmos. And, as soon as you lifted the heavy door curtain and felt the fug inside, you could sense it was exactly what it was. The walls were hung with prints, lithographs, photographs of the Finnish literary heroes: Runeberg, Topelius, Kivi, the great Lonnrot. The hot fuggy room was noisy, the tables were full. It then suddenly occurred to me (I was young then, remember) that never before had I ever seen so many writers at any one time, gathered in any one place. There they were, writers of every kind: male and female, fat and thin, young and old, well-dressed urban writers, fur-clad brutish peasant writers. Some had high intellectual brows, some had no brows at all. There were adult writers, children's writers, writers of history or biography, writers of folk and fairy tale, writers of humour, writers of Gothic terror. There were realists, and there were modernists. Literary writers who had won great prizes, commercial writers who had won great advances. Poets and dramatists. Novelists and journalists. So many writers, and only one thing in common. The Kafé Kosmos was certainly not *alkoholfri*; every single one of them was drunk.

Some were quietly drunk, and some were noisy drunk. Some were in the infernal pits of despair, and others on the soaring heights of euphoria. A Nobel prizewinner lay with his head in a toppled soup-bowl. A famous children's writer trilled to herself before a row of empty glasses. And so a deep truth struck me, for the first time but not for the last. The writer's life, now my chosen path, was not always one of delicious pleasure, eternal freedom, endless fame. It was too not amusing at all. It was mournful, self-created, lonely, an unending struggle against failure, fate, ignorance, idleness, blankness, insecurity and death. No wonder the writers of Finland felt the need to join together, raising their glasses in celebration of creativity and comradeship. No wonder their heads felt heavy with the weight of delicious thoughts. Or, of course, there could have been a different reason. After all, they were Finns.

Whatever: I'd arrived at the literary heartland at last, and I passionately felt the need to join them. I gladly took my place on the minstrels' bench, and soon we were all drinking together and telling stories, as writers so often do. Somehow, here in the Kafé Kosmos, it really didn't seem to matter that my stories were in English, and theirs were in Finnish. Many interesting things were said that day, though heaven alone knows what they were. Then, finally, in the very late afternoon, my translator appeared: a huge man, six foot or so, bearded, sweatshirted, an outdoor type, seemingly fresh from the forest. He wrote plays himself, and poems, and had translated James Joyce into Finnish. The problems of my work were, he said, modest in comparison, but he confessed he had found a few. Story fine, prose fine, but something was missing: a true intensity of soul. He'd had just the same problem in Joyce. What was wrong with western writers was they'd never probably imbibed the great Russians: Pushkin, Gogol, Dostoyev-sky, Biely. Yet Russian writing taught the true spirit of the novel: rage, extremity, wildness, passion, torture of the heart.

'You've never been to Russia, I can tell,' he said. 'I will take you. When your trip is finished, we will go.'

'Sure,' I said.

'No, forget your tour, why don't I take you tonight?'

'I don't think so, Pentti,' said one of my publishers.

'Sure. Look, it's simple. We go to the station, we get on the military train with the sealed windows. Then we go through the lovely lands of our lost Karelia, which you will not be able to see because the windows are sealed, and we wake up in the writer's city.'

'The writer's city?'

'Petersburg. The place where all writers come from.'

'It's not so simple, Pentti, he needs papers,' said my publisher.

'Bureaucrats, all that paper shit, let's just forget it, right?' said my translator, staring me in the eyes.

'But if he doesn't have a visa from the embassy, they won't let him in. Do you want him to go to jail?'

'I'll get him in. You just have to give the guards a ham or something. They haven't eaten for months. You know in Russia nobody believes in the law, and everything is for sale.'

'But the Russians don't like westerners just walking into their country.'

My translator put his huge arm lovingly around me. 'Just don't listen to any of this shit,' said my translator. 'I know Russia, all the back passages and little arseholes. I go into Russia all the time.'

'When did you go last?'

'Five years ago,' said my translator, filling up his glass and mine. 'Maybe ten.'

'It's crazy,' said my publisher.

'You know me, I'm your friend,' said my translator, squeezing me tight, 'Would I do anything crazy? I just don't take shit, that's all. Paper shit. Border shit. The world is a forest. In it a man goes where he wants to go. We're writers. The world is ours, huh?'

'That's right, the world is ours,' I seem to have said.

'Our writer wants to come,' he said. 'You see, he wants to come.'

'He's English, he's just being polite, Pentti. That's how they are.'

'You know, I love this man. I'm proud to translate him, even if his book is shit. Get him papers if you like, that's only some more shit.'

'He has a tour to do, it's all arranged.'

'Okay, and when you come back from the tour, my friend, we get on the sealed train and go to Russia, all right?'

'To the Finland Station?'

'To the Finland Station. Yes, my dear good old friend. You will never forget it. It will be the greatest experience of your life—'

'Yes, Pentti,' said my publisher.

'I know,' I said, 'I know . . .'

During that night the whole world changed. A heavy new snow fell all over Finland and the Baltic. When I woke in my red-painted, thin-mattressed bed next morning, feeling no better than I had the morning before, a strange white light filled my hotel bedroom. The maid, letting herself in with the pass-key, brought coffee and opened the curtains, revealing the white-filled square below and the great snowfall my walls had reflected. Suddenly I recalled that on this snowy day my ten-year tour round the small towns of Finland was due to begin in earnest. Then, as I drank my coffee, I remembered something else – how, in the literary glow of the Kafé Kosmos, I had agreed to go on the sealed train to Leningrad as soon as I returned. Various small problems now crossed my mind: students back home to teach, a wife and little child waiting. Still, writers are writers; the world is ours. I packed up my baggage, and went down in the Hissi. I signed my hotel bill, and sat in an armchair in the lobby, waiting for my publisher friends to take me to the station.

And the world truly had altered overnight. A new snow had fallen all over Finland. Beyond the windows, cracked ice had turned to fresh fleece, which filled every space and turned everything to the purest white. The snowiness lit up the cars and brightened the street, where Finns in big hats, great coats and boots walked by, half-bounced along by the weather. Flakes the size of cottonballs whirled past the windows, wiping away the buildings across the way, plastering a huge snowsuit on the patient hotel doorman. Whenever the swing doors opened, a howling frozen whirlwind scurried through the lobby. My publishers arrived by car, grinding through packed snowpiles in the gutter. As soon as I walked outside, the bitter wind sliced, my eyebrows froze, my face turned to a mask. My raincoat offered no protection at all, so my publishers thoughtfully took me to a great department store, Stockmann, to kit me for the journey. Winter wares – snowshoes and skis, Parkas and sledges – were everywhere on sale. Wooden stands held domed fur hats in every fashion: seal and beaver, mink and fox, wool and nylon. Soon I was suitably clad. A huge fur pelt with ribboned ear-flaps covered my ears and most of my brow. I had huge fur mittens, stout blue moonboots. 'Wonderful,' said my publisher. 'How nicely it goes with your smart English blazer.'

Helsinki train station is designed by the elder Saarinen. A noble modernistic façade makes a grand effect, though it leads to sadder and rather etiolated hinderparts, unroofed and open to swirling blizzard. Here, in the snow, a train of six very ancient wooden carriages was waiting behind a black steam locomotive, tender stacked high with birch-logs. My publishers said farewell, and I climbed aboard a first-class carriage. A metal stove steamed in the corner. A stout female attendant sat beside it issuing glasses of tea. Thick curtains hung at the misted windows. Heavy armchairs formed the seats. Slowly and wearily, the train begin heaving itself out of the station. It didn't matter; I was in no hurry, no hurry at all.

Once the train leaves Helsinki station, it's soon into the pine and birch forest that seems to cover the rest of Finland. In fact the forest comes right into the city, growing round the new apartment blocks. In moments the city becomes the country, the urban scene turning into a vast rolling forest. Yesterday's world had gone too; the overnight snow had covered all Finland with a coating that, seen from a train seat, was pure delight. Snow hung heavy on the pine and birch trees, highlighting the twigs with a precise white detailing. Occasionally branches would crack off and shatter, opening a white wound in the trunks. Everything seemed suspended – not least the train itself, which moved so slowly through this noiseless world every little scene appeared to go on for ever. There were red wooden houses, with metal ladders to their roofs. Steam rose from the big square chimneys of the sauna houses. Animal tracks ran through the drifts, birds of prey hung in the sky. Skiers made their way through the forest paths. Muffled ancient ladies stood up on the runners of high-backed sledges, pushing them along with booted feet.

In my chair in the slow-moving wide-coached train, I felt myself caught in a happy delusion. I felt in some perfect space: out of time, motion, history, politics. I imagined myself in a peaceable kingdom, more peaceful than any I'd known. Foolish and dangerous nonsense, of course. Finland was not outside history. It was a troubled, squeezed, divided, often occupied small country, still under threat. It had known the Great Wrath and the Little Wrath, its own bloody Red Revolution and the Winter War. This rail line once led on past Lahti to the lost lands of Karelia, from which the population had been expelled, to Vyborg and the Finland station. The Russian border now lay not so far ahead: armed soldiers in the watch-towers, mines and mantraps in the snow. Lenin fled here twice, disguised as a fireman on a railway engine, protected by the Finnish reds. Then in 1918 refugees from the Cheka purges had taken this same railway, carrying their fake Swedish passports and what valuables they could manage. Some had made it through the sentries, many had not. Even then their problems were not over; for half of Finland supported the Russian Reds, the other half hoped the Germans would bring a solution for their Baltic peril. Finland had never really been used to peace; it was too near Russia. 'The ghastly logic of geography,' one famous Finn noted in 1917. 'Petrograd is so close. There is blood everywhere.'

Short of the border, I got off the chugging train – at Kuovola on the Kymi. The Kymi is Finland's great logging river, and as I descended on to the bare snow-swept platform the sawmills ground and the rank papermills were steaming. In the blizzard the local schoolteacher was waiting; she didn't know me at first, so odd did I look in my fur hat and moonboots. She walked me through town, past brand-new shopping centres, to the local hotel. And there, that night, while some forty Finns sat dining rather mournfully, I rose at the table and began to read from my work. It came to seem an absurd activity, as I went through the most parochial details of contemporary English life, while my tolerant audience of good citizens – businessmen, teachers, butchers, shop-keepers, librarians – stared up at me in friendly mystification. Next day I took another train through the snow, heading northward up the Kymi past chugging sawmills, rancid papermills, the odd landed estate or so, as the blizzard deepened. So the days passed, taking on a familiar rhythm, as I zig-zagged through the freezing heart of Finland, a land of small settlements, vast frozen lakes, huge silent forests. A little train would emerge from the blizzards to deposit me at some little local capital, entirely shut in snow: Kuopio, Mikkeli, Tapiola, Jyväslykä, Kyyjärvi. Another meeter on the platform, a teacher, a librarian, a local doctor. Another hotel, ancient or modern. Another audience, gathered in the hotel dining room or some local ravintola, eating a hearty dinner while I talked and read to them my strange little tales of British life in distant industrial cities.

The towns I descended on out of the blizzard in my silver moonboots came to seem to me stranger and stranger. They were towns out of Nikolai Gogol, remote provincial outposts like those in Russia, ancient, folkish, faintly touched up with modernity, but happily and timelessly spared what had happened just over the border – the political purges, the grand electrifications, the Gulags. And in fantasy I was beginning to feel like a character out of Gogol's stories too: the wandering bureaucrat, the travelling dignitary, the confidence trickster visiting the regions from the great capital where the reins of government lay. I ride through the forests, I come to the next town, even more remote than the last one. It's called, let us say, B——. Pigs and cats run in the streets, and in the normal way everything must be as dull as ditchwater, except when the cavalry regiment is stationed or the government inspector visits. There's a town square, a local inn, a shop selling saws, horse-collars, barrels and ropes. There are a few fine-looking residences and a row of neat merchant houses, nice enough except when they catch fire, or fall in under the weight of snow. There's a mayor, a doctor, a police chief, a fire chief, a town drunk, some shopkeepers, some landowners, some business folk, some sparky little wives, and a bevy of those fair to middling gentlefolk with estates out of town who always want news of the world. The visitor descends from the capital, the best dresses come out, and there's a reception at the hotel or the restaurant. Gaiety rules for its moment, till the visitor leaves, returning to the distant bright lights of the capital, to parties and palaces, and then life goes on as before.

Everyone was extremely kind to my stories; kind to me, especially after night fell and drink began to pour. They congratulated me warmly on my good English, my little tales. 'Your book was so funny that we almost laughed,' one of them said to me. 'Do you like Finland?' 'Do you like Sibelius?' 'Do you like hunting?' 'Do you like sauna? You must do it properly, jump in the lake and roll in the snow.'

In Kuopio I went to the sauna, surrounded by someone's stout wife and gleaming daughters, who dropped me in the lake and then slapped me with birch twigs to bring me back from what felt like my final moments. In Mikkeli I was taken cross-country skiing, and had two planks strapped to my legs for a four-hour plod on the flat. In Kyyjärvi they took me elk-hunting, though all I brought down was a frozen branch or two. In Jyväskylä I went to the ski-jump competitions, where figures no bigger than dots descended from huge wooden gantries and crashed into snowdrifts. My stories seem to grow ever odder to me, my skin got drier, my voice grew fainter. The days got colder, the mercury dropped lower, and I moved onward, ever upward and northward.

At last I came to my final and furthest destination: the little town of . . . Well, let us call it O—. It lay somewhere high on the ice-packed Gulf of Bothnia, toward the Lappish lands and the Arctic circle. I had only one last reading to give; then I was off on the midnight express, back to the capital, then on to Leningrad. I was very tired now, exhausted by the readings, the generous hospitality, the sauna, the elk-hunting, the cross-country skiing. My head was blurred, my voice was beginning to fade away completely. I climbed down from the train into freezing temperatures and a whirling wind. My eyebrows promptly frosted, my face froze in a hideous grimace. My windpipe seized, I felt decidedly unwell. I looked around for the usual quiet librarian or schoolteacher, waiting to greet me. I noticed something different. Standing there on the station platform, in a veil of blizzard, was the entire town band, in their tassels and their epaulettes. It was not hard to guess what they were waiting for; the tune they struck up was 'God Save the Queen'. British flags waved. A banner was unrolled. A small girl in a white folk costume ran forward to present me with a scroll.

Behind her stood a snow-dusted row of local dignitaries. There was the town mayoress, her blonde hair drawn tight and strict, formally dressed in ermine and fur. There was the provincial governor, with a feather in his hat, the police and fire chiefs, in grand uniform, the head of the gymnasium, wearing an academic gown. And there in a long civic line were the merchants, the shopkeepers, the librarian, the fair to middling gentlefolk, the sparky young wives, the town drunk, all of them waiting to greet me. The lady mayoress lifted a sheet of notes and made a warm speech of welcome, translated for me by the schoolteacher. Then, to the sounds of 'Finlandia', we set off in procession down the main street. Frost-bitten citizens stopped and waved at me in welcome. There, out of Gogol, was the scatter of small stores, selling horse-collars and ropes. There was the little wooden inn, with chickens in the yard. Frost-bitten citizens halted their work and gave me warm waves of welcome.

Then, ahead, was a fine provincial town square, crowded with snow-filled trees. Around them stood a fine spread of metal-roofed civic buildings. A white Lutheran church, a wooden Orthodox church. A grand old-fashioned white wooden residence with smart shutters, perhaps for the provincial governor; an illuminated stone building with a clock on it that was presumably the Town Hall. In front of this stood a Lapp in blue costume, holding two tethered reindeer. A horse-drawn sleigh went by with a jangle of bells, just avoiding the huge logging trucks laden with forest timber that constantly swept at speed through the town. The band ceased, we came to a stop . . .

'But I thought this was about going to Leningrad,' says Manders.

Yes, in a moment . . . We all swept into the fine Town Hall, walked up on to the platform. Practically all of the local citizens must have gathered in the big audience that sat in front of me, evidently under the illusion they were enjoying the visit of a major celebrity (I later traced this confusion to an article in the weekly paper, written by one of the writers from the Kafé Kosmos, who had seemingly confused me with William Golding, an odd mistake to make anywhere but in Finland). The mayoress rose and made a long speech of welcome, explaining (according to the shopkeeper's thoughtful translation) how grateful they were that, of all the many towns scattered by the good Lord through the whole wide world, I had made such a point of visiting this one. Then, after reciting many lines from the *Kalevala*, she waved me to the centre of the platform to speak.

My throat now felt as if it had been filled by a thorn bush. I rose up in my silver moonboots. I croaked out a few words of grateful thanks to the mayoress and the town council, and then I began to read from my work. My voice was truly fading now; after a few moments I ground to a total halt. 'There's a problem . . .' I whispered hoarsely, and then my voice box totally seized. There was nothing to do but wave my hands in despair, look round helplessly, sit down . . . The mayoress stared at me grimly. I shrugged in despair. She rose furiously, and swept off the platform. The town band struck up 'The Swan of Haemenlinna'. The audience rose, and in moments the entire place was empty. There I was, in the grand civic room of an empty town hall somewhere up near the Arctic Circle, voiceless, a useless writer, robbed of the only thing that had brought me here in the first place: words.

I had already been told that a grand dinner and reception in the little wooden hotel across the square had been arranged that night, in my honour, or at any rate in William Golding's. I presumed the event would now be cancelled, so I walked across the square, sat in the hotel, and ordered a restorative hot drink, resigned to wait here until it was time to take the midnight express that would take me out of town, back to Helsinki and my translator. But, as I waited in the salon, something began to happen. The entire hotel began to fill with people, all of them dressed in their best evening finery. There again they all were, the leading citizens of O—: the blonde strict lady mayoress, the sly little governor, the portly police chief, the thin fire chief, the headmaster from the gymnasium, the town drunk, the fair to middling gentlefolk, the sparky little wives. Their expressions remained a little grim and dour, but it was very evident they had no intention of missing a great evening's entertainment. The band appeared, and struck up. I sat and watched them. No one came over and spoke to me at all: fine by me, of course, since I was totally incapable of answering them anyway. A bevy of waitresses in folkloric dresses appeared with huge clear bottles of vodka and went round the room. I sat in the corner and looked on with interest, knowing in about four more hours I would be out of here on the train and gone from this world for ever.

It was the close of the week, a Friday. Nobody had told me what happens to Finns on a Friday night. The truth is, they turn into different people. In half an hour they had gone from misery to good humour. Another half hour took them from grey solemnity to ravening happiness. Around the room everyone who was still upright was laughing at something.

'It's you,' explained the shopkeeper kindly, coming over to bring me a huge vodka. 'You have made them very happy. They are all laughing at you.'

'Oh really?' I attempted to croak.

'Nothing so wonderful has taken place here for many years. We met you from the train. We provided the band for you. We all came to the Town Hall.'

I nodded sympathetically.

'And then what did you give us? Nothing. You came a thousand miles and gave us nothing at all. Thank you. It made us very happy tonight.'

I nodded generously.

'On Friday night we really like to relax. To amuse.'

And that did appear to be true. Something had indeed transformed the excellent people of O—. The portly police chief was dancing on a table with the drummer from the town band. The head of the gymnasium was undressing the local librarian. The sly governor was lying full-length in a corner, surrounded by a great bevy of the sparky little wives. Only the town drunk seemed unhappy, as he wandered round the place looking sober by comparison with everyone else.

Half an hour more, and they had all gone again from happiness to near-stupor, from joy to the pits of lachrymose misery. I sat there watching over a beer; by now I'd learned the menace of the vodka. And it was now, as the band played in a confused and senseless discord, that the lady mayoress came over to me. Her blonde hair had now fallen down crazily over one eye. Her dress had split. She was smiling at me warmly.

'She wants to thank you very much for coming to our simple town,' explained the shopkeeper.

I nodded.

'She says you have done us a real honour. She has one small request of you, she hopes you will grant it.'

I nodded again, graciously.

'She would like to have a child by such an eminent person.'

I raised both eyebrows.

'It need not take long. Her house is very near. And you still have two hours before your train.'

I croaked again, pointed at my throat.

'She quite understands, but the important thing is not your throat. She does not speak good English anyway.'

The mayoress beamed, very attractively, and said something graceful in Finnish.

'She says it would be such a nice memento of your stay,' said the shopkeeper. 'When we travel we should always leave something behind.'

I looked at the fecklessly charming woman, who seemed to have become so very different after vodka time, now that her mayoral chair was off and her hair was let down, and that's why . . .

'I know just what you're going to say,' says Manders. 'This is why you never managed to get to Leningrad. For some strange reason you were delayed that night and you missed your train back to Helsinki.'

'Oh no, I did catch the train all right,' I said. 'The mayoress kindly saw me on board.'

'The town band too?'

'No, just the mayoress. She took excellent care of me.'

'So this is the famous Finnish Friday night,' says Manders admiringly. 'We know all about that in Sweden.'

'Yes, and then it was a Finnish Friday night on the Helsinki express too,' I say. 'I swear to you every single person on board, man or woman, beautiful or ugly, first class or third, from one end of that train to the other, was blind drunk as well.'

'I believe you.'

'There was this beautiful blonde woman sitting opposite me all the way, wearing long black furs and a splendid ermine hat. She spent the entire journey having a loud quarrel with her own reflection in the window. Then, when we rolled into Helsinki station in the early hours of the morning, the porters were all on the platform with their barrows parked outside all the coach doors, waiting to stack the recumbent passengers in large piles on the trolleys and wheel them out to the taxi rank.'

'Does that mean you did make it to the sealed train to Leningrad, after all?'

'Well, not exactly. My translator went, but he went on his own. They arrested him the moment he stepped off at the Finland Station. He spent the next three weeks in a Russian jail. Unpleasant, I believe, though he did say he was able to pass the time translating my book. Finally the Finns protested, or the Russians got tired of him. At any rate, they bundled him in a truck and dumped him over the Finnish border, in the snow.'

'Did the translation ever appear?'

'Yes, it did, the following year. It was very successful. The Finns read a lot of books. It's the winter, you know, when there's hardly anything else to do. The critics were very kind, and I had met most of them in the Kafé Kosmos. Some of them even called me the youthful heir of Gogol.'

'Well, you were probably wise not to go. The Russians wouldn't have let you out that easily. You were heading for real trouble.'

'I expect so, but I didn't know that then.'

'Why didn't you go?'

'Oh, didn't I say? After I got off the train from O—, I went right back to the Hotel Gurki—'

'Gestapo headquarters in the war?'

'That's the one, and the next morning I woke up delirious, with swollen glands and a raging fever.'

'Tonsillitis, no doubt. You had probably over-exerted yourself on your travels.'

'Quite. My kind publishers got a doctor who said I wasn't fit to travel anywhere and shot me full of antibiotics. After a couple of days they drove me out to the airport, and I returned to my family and my normal life. Except it took three weeks for my voice to come back. I've been to Russia since. But somehow I never did make the journey to the dandy city, always preening itself in front of Europe.'

'What?'

'That's what Gogol called Petersburg. Otherwise Leningrad.'

Manders looks at me. 'And the mayoress?' he asks. 'Up there in your Let Us Call It O—, by the Arctic Circle? Is there perhaps a little professor now?'

'No, no,' I say, feeling rather embarrassed. 'You should understand, I was extremely moral in those distant days. In those days the world wasn't a screwfest. We discussed the moral life all the time. It was when we believed in virtue, followed the good and the true.'

'I suppose we all did then. Even in Sweden.'

'Especially in Sweden. But I always felt a little rude about leaving like that. When she and the others were all being so very nice to me.'

'I hope so. The town band and everything.'

'Do you suppose she made an offer like that to all the visitors?'

'I don't know Finland all that well, but I doubt it. She was entirely taken by your charms, I'm quite sure.'

'I must admit I was by hers. She really was a most attractive woman. I was never quite sure, though, whether she really meant it or just wanted to make sure I didn't go home thinking my trip had been totally wasted. And I suppose at that time I was just too young and foolish to accept the irresponsibility.'

'You know, I seem to remember Diderot said something about all this,' says Manders, getting up and going to stare out over the rail.

'Really? I don't remember.'

'Yes, in the essay he wrote about Bougainville's voyage to the South Seas, when the French sailors met all those wonderful noble savages. I seem to recall he took the multi-cultural approach and the sexual freedom line.'

'Do what you like, you mean?'

'"Be monks in France and savages in Tahiti," that was how he put it.'

'But he did believe in the moral approach as well. The rule of virtue. Didn't he also say: "You can put on the costume of the country you visit, but always remember to keep the suit of clothes you need to go home in."'

'It's true,' says Manders.

'Anyway, now you can see why I feel such a soft spot for Finland,' I say. 'In fact to tell the truth, I wouldn't mind a bit if we didn't go to Petersburg and this ship changed tack and re-routed to Helsinki.'

'I'm sorry, I really don't think it's going to do that,' says Manders, leaning windblown over the rail.

'You never know,' I say.

'I think I do,' says Manders, looking out at the channel.

'Do you see that island showing up ahead? I know that. It's Kotlin. That's Kronstadt castle.'

I get up to look out too. A huge and battlemented land-shadow is rising from the cold oily waters in front of us, sur-rounded by a mass of moving grey ships. On the decks down below us, sensing a change in the climate, the Diderot pilgrims have suddenly begun to appear again: Agnes and Sonnenberg, Verso and the Swedish nightingale, Bo and Alma, looking happy and chattering warmly as they stare out over the side. Here, in a hurry, comes Lars Person.

'Kronstadt?' I say.

'Revolution Island,' says Manders. 'Where the sailors started the Russian Revolution. And where Catherine the Great came to arrest her own husband Peter, so she could jail him and take over the throne.'

'This means we're getting near then?'

'Kronstadt's where the old harbour used to be. Just beyond is the sea-terminal at Vasilyevsky Island. You see, you really are going to Petersburg, after all.'

TWENTY (THEN)

DAY SIX

SHE sits on the sofa. HE comes in, and looks round. Today there is no chair.

HE
No chair, Your Imperial Highness?

SHE
No. Surely you know why?

HE
Something's wrong?

SHE looks at him furiously.

SHE
The Secret Office has warned me about you. They advise me you're a spy sent here by the King of France.

HE
The King of France sends me nowhere, Your Highness. Except to his prisons now and then.

SHE
Now I understand your dreams of Sankt Peterburg. Your attacks on Frederick. You're trying to bind me to the French court.

HE
Not at all, Your Majesty. All I said was I wished you were monarch of France instead of the one we have.

SHE
You would not be the first French spy to come to court. One came to attend the last tzarina, a man dressed as a woman—

HE
That was the Chevalier d'Eon, Your Highness. Everyone knew cross-dressing was his common habit. The moment the little dragoon got back from gutting enemies on the battlefield he was back into his corsets and petticoats.

SHE
The Tzarina Elizabeth had no idea it was his common habit. She let him attend her as a lady of the bedchamber.

DASHKOVA
That is how she found out, Your Imperial Highness. But it's said once she knew she didn't discourage him.

HE
Many people were confused by him. My dear friend Beaumarchais got engaged to him once.

SHE stares at him relentlessly.

SHE
There was no confusion about it. He came as a spy and sought access to the last tzarina's body. Now you are here trying to do the same.

HE
Simply to pay my homage and share my thoughts.

SHE (*rising*)
You deny you were commissioned by Durand de Distroff, the worst French ambassador we ever had?

HE
He did approach me, it's true, but—

SHE
Approached you to do what?

HE holds out a paper.

HE

Give you this memorandum from the King of France.

SHE

And now you dare hand it to me?

HE

Yes, forgive me. But I was promised a spell in the Bastille if
I didn't put it under your pillow.

SHE

Under my *pillow*? Have you read it? What does it say?

HE

The King of France wishes to offer you all his services in
negotiating a peace between you and the Turks.

SHE

And now you're about to advise me to accept it?

HE

No, I don't think so, Your Imperial Highness. It would really
be most unwise.

SHE

No?

HE

No. I'm no diplomat, and I scarcely comprehend these things.
But as I see it, King Louis's intention is to weaken you if he
can, and drive Russia back from its new enlightenment to its
old obscurity. What he wishes is to see the three wolves turn
and rend each other—

SHE

The wolves?

HE

Russia, Prussia, Austria. Then he will strengthen his own hand
with your enemy Sweden and make his own alliance with the
Sublime Porte. But understand I know nothing about these
things. Diplomacy confuses me. I'm all innocence and
candour. I don't know how to spy, conspire or conceal—

SHE reaches out her hand.

SHE
Give that to me.

HE
Forgive me. I wish I'd never brought it here.

SHE
Surely you wouldn't conceal it from me?

HE
No, Your Majesty, indeed not.

SHE reads the king's letter.

SHE
Mr Philosopher, you really are a useless spy and a sorry patriot.
Aren't you?

HE
I hope so. I should always prefer to be a good man before I
am a good patriot.

SHE
You are right about his intentions, of course.

HE
Of course what I have said and done could be the ruin of
myself and my Posterity when I return to France—

SHE
Don't go then. Stay here.

HE
My loved ones, Your Highness.

SHE
Your wife, you mean?

HE
Her as well.

SHE looks again at the paper.

SHE
This letter. What do you advise me to do with it?

HE
It is not at all for me to say. But I do notice the day's very cold.

SHE
Our stove could do with stoking, you mean?

HE
I really don't mean anything. All I ask before I suffer a hideous traitor's fate and die torn to pieces on the gallows is that I should be the object of your trust, and not of your suspicion—

SHE goes over to the stove and puts the paper in. It flares up splendidly.

SHE
There then. You may tell your ambassador you've delivered it. Tell him too you've seen exactly what I think of it. Then tell him I have done with it just exactly what I have done with it.

HE
I will, Your Imperial Highness.

SHE
And now you know I should dismiss you from this court and send you back from Russia at once?

HE
It would be the just action of a just monarch.

SHE
However, you will stay, sir. It's your ambassador who will be departing before long. Under my pillow, did you say, sir? Well, Dashkova, go . . . Fetch the philosopher his chair . . .

END OF DAY SIX

And it's that same night, as he's lying in his cavern of a bed near the nightstove in the Narishkin Palace, that our man has quite the strangest of dreams. He's following the usual daily summons, crossing the great imperial square, making his approach to the grand Hermitage. Yet it's all in the half-light, and the place is oddly empty. No sentries are standing stiffly in the boxes, no guardsmen wait inside in the halls. No footmen stand at the top of the great staircase, no servants flit about the corridors. The mirrors reflect nothing, not even the emptiness. All the stairwells are silent. He walks alone and unattended along the many long corridors, which are lighted only by the moon. Every one of them is empty of people, except for just one. There is the betoga-ed figure of Voltaire. He's grinning, waving, rising from his marble arm-chair. His hair is white as wool, his eyes are little flames of fire. He strips off his toga, and, standing there, ancient and naked, he shouts a warning, something quite mysterious about sunshine and the Turks . . .

Up on the walls are the huge paintings he's sent in his homage all the way from Paris. But they're scratched and stabbed through, some of them running in water, others covered in thick layers of dust. There are statues along the corridor, lit up strangely by the moon. But the Canovas have lost a hand or two, and some are without their heads. Falconet's sculptured angels now have the fangs of devils, and the paintings of ancient ruins seem to have come alive. Loud rude voices are shouting in distant corridors, and glass shatters in a window somewhere close. He goes on toward the indoor garden – but the plants are all wilting, the birds do not sing. He passes all those imperial ante-rooms, and every one is empty. In one the chess pieces lie scattered across the chessboard. In another the billiard table has been draped with a huge grey shroud. He enters, as he's learned to do, the imperial drawing room. But today there is no chatter. No ambassadors or emissaries sit waiting. No courtiers stand about, no maids-in-waiting. And over the sofa her portrait has grown dusty too.

Yet, beneath it, there she is. She's lying there, head on a pillow, spread out grand and comfortable, naked. Her breasts are large and pendulous, her stomach a wide imperial tract of territory, a vast expanse of tundra. To the lover of Rubens, this is majestic grandeur. She looks him up and down, and it grows apparent that the black philosopher's suit he wears for court is missing. All the time he has been buck-naked too.

'Late again, Mr Librarian, extremely late,' she murmurs.

'Deepest apologies,' he says. 'There is fog on the Neva.'

'Come close, Mr Philosopher,' she says. 'I'm sure you know very well why you were really called here?'

'I was never quite sure, Your Imperial Majesty.'

'Voltaire would have gladly done it if you hadn't, you know that.'

'But he's eighty, and toothless. The whole world knows his stomach rumbles. And even I am sixty.'

'You are nothing, you are ageless. One day like an old man of a hundred, the next like a small boy of ten. I never know which one to expect.'

'But here, your most sublime and imperial—?'

'Why not here? Where else? It's the lover's hours. The palace is empty, there's no one can disturb us. Yes, here, sir, and now. Before all the ambassadors come fussing.'

'Yes, Your Imperial Highness.'

'You know I should really send you away at once?'

'That would be the entirely just action of an entirely just monarch.'

'Oh, come here, sir. I felt you would bring me sunshine—'

'If I do truly have your permission—'

Frankly, she spreads her legs wide. Obedient, he works himself between. She smiles gently down at him. Gently he moves forward, begins to touch the warm centre of imperial Russia. The spirit of France in him, cautious at first, begins to glow. He floats on, sailing between the twin shorelines of the estuary that is opening before him. He finds the harbour front, gets ready to dock.

'Onward,' she murmurs, drawing him in with her arms, 'remember, you have come here a thousand leagues for this.'

Now he can feel himself gliding, riding along the English Embankment of the Neva, past the spire of the Admiralty, past the Peter and Paul. He turns down Nevsky Prospekt, and now the whole of mysterious Russia lies before him, unknown, unentered, *verst* beyond *verst* of sedge and marsh and steppe. Cossack bearskins yield before French shakos. Soon his galloping European forces will take Moscow, reach southward down to the warm and sunny Caucasus, northward toward Siberia, permafrost, arctic snow . . . till suddenly he's arrested; something is pulling hard on him from behind. Four angry court dwarves are heaving at him, taking him viciously by both arms and legs.

They break open the confused embrace, they angrily drag him loose. They lift his body and carry it to the open window. Now he's hurtling out, rolling over the snowy embankment, down into the ice-crusted Neva. The ice breaks open, with the most dreadful cracking. The muddy waters gape. It's sickeningly cold down here, but also surprisingly hot. He's sinking, yet he's swimming. He's vanishing for ever, and yet he's still content. He's going downward, but rising upward. And all the time he's doing what he always does best; he's busy explaining.

'Sleep is the condition when our animal ceases to exist as a whole entity. A dream is almost always the result of a sensory stimulation. It's almost a transitory form of illness. When we are asleep, it's the activity of our own continuing consciousness that creates all these sensations we believe we are aware of. Co-ordination and subordination of the various human faculties are lacking. The master, our self, is thrown upon the mercy of his servants, abandoned to the frantic energy of his own uncontrolled activity. The self at the centre of the human web is active and passive by turns. Hence the sense of disorder so characteristic of dreams.'

'So does that mean in dreams we become completely without reason?' asks the charming Mademoiselle de l'Espinasse, who has suddenly joined them and is sitting beside his bed in the river.

'Not quite, what we are looking at is a picture of things that have been taken from experience and entirely reconstructed in the mind,' explains Doctor Bordeu, who stands with his hat off somewhere in the room. 'Sometimes these sensations can actually appear so vivid we aren't quite sure whether we're wide awake or dreaming.'

'Then surely this condition of sleep can actually be quite dangerous,' observes Madame de l'Espinasse, looking at him with concern.

'I've told him that countless times,' says Bordeu, 'but he still pays no attention.'

'What are you thinking about now, doctor?'

'I am thinking about the ways of great men, mademoiselle, like the genius Monsieur Voltaire,' says Bordeu. 'I'm reflecting on how a truly great man is put together. About how he's learned to tyrannize over his sensibility and his passions, learned to reason, become the centre of his own human bundle, control himself and everyone else around, master the masters of the world. Because those are the powers of the completely rational man. Yet, believe me, even our glorious Voltaire nightly visits the world of sleep. Even genius has its dreams and its disorders. Even the clearest mind has an unconscious stratum. Well, is everything absolutely clear now, my dear mademoiselle? Where's my hat? I'd better be on my way. I have another patient to see in the Marais.'

'So how are you yourself, Doctor Bordeu, my friend?' he asks, rising up to the surface of the water. 'And what are you doing here in the middle of the Neva with our good Mademoiselle de l'Espinasse, at this unholy hour of the morning?'

'You'll find out one day,' says Bordeu. 'But right now, if you want to wake content and whole in the morning, you'd better get back off to sleep.'

'Yes, thank you, doctor, I think I will,' he says, entirely satisfied. 'Thank you for coming. See you in the morning. Good night, doctor. Good night, ladies. Good night.'

PART TWO

TWENTY-ONE (NOW)

AND YET – despite the three days of nagging anxiety I've been suffering from ever since that night in Stockholm when I switched on the TV set and discovered Russia had returned to a state of crisis – the harbour we've just now sailed into has the appearance of being a pleasant, a normal, a perfectly unthreatening place. We've sailed the seaway past Kronstadt on Kotlin Island, its fortress buildings lost somewhere inside the mist. We've come down the estuary channel, lined with cranes and defences, where rusty-looking warships and submarines lie spliced together at moorings offshore. We've eased gently into the crane-spiked harbour, where the waters are thick, mud-marked and oil-stained. There, Anders tells me as we watch our landing from the bridge deck, is the passenger terminal that sits on the very tip of Vasilyevsky Island, and which is no distance at all from the heart of the great old capital. At first glance, seen over the water from a distance, it could not look more smart or hospitable, as good and gleaming a sample of late-modernist space-age architecture as you could wish for. Lit by cold crisp autumnal sunlight, its curves swing and surge in the hi-tech fashion, its aluminium claddings snatch at the sun. Its white cement gleams, its big windows glisten. It has all the appearance of being built at the peak of superpower assertion, when every big building was a symbol of the prevailing regime. Modernist emblems of sailing caravels mural its walls. On the building's end a sign announces, in two different alphabets, SANKT PETERBURG / SZENTPETERVAR.

In fact it's only when, siren blaring, the *Vladimir Ilich* begins to receive the embrace of shore – the dock-arms opening, the hawsers swinging over the closing gap, the shore stanchions starting to grip, the probing gangplanks swinging out over the side, the side-ramps dropping down – that some of the flaws and blemishes grow apparent. All is not quite as it seems; what can have happened here? The building is new, surely, its curved lines and modern materials belonging to recent times and the age of sixties heavy cementing. Indeed much of the city, especially this part of it, would have to be new, since most was rebuilt after the horrific 900-day siege, when German forces surrounded it through several winters and began a night bombardment, vowing to pulp the place to bits. Since then, despite the confrontations and stand-offs of the Cold War, the city's buildings have never been under any further bombardment. Yet somehow the entire façade seems bullet-pocked, every cement pillar seems part-shattered, revealing the rusting metal core. No one ever tried to nuke it, so how is it that the vast roof of titanium or whatever seems to lie just off-tilt? No one set mines here, so how come the grand windows are not just grimy but cracked and half-shattered? No one ever torpedoed the place below the waterline – so why are all the pilings bent, rotted, sagging?

What's happened? Baltic weather, vast overuse, structural imperfection, sheer neglect? Or perhaps the will to complete it just ran out, like a brilliant idea that exhausted those who had it. Whatever the reason, the grand edifice so clearly intended to welcome the impressed foreign traveller into the international joys of socialism, looks half-shattered, a little like the Moscow White House after the events of yesterday. It has the look of being utterly worn and wasted, like a raddled old whore: past it, pocked, seedy, unstable, quietly crumbling on itself from within. Whatever rises, it seems to say, also falls. Yet apart from this overwhelming sense of neglect or dereliction, there are no further signs of menace: nothing to show we're trying to set foot in Russia at the wrong time, some instant of crisis when the whole nation has again divided and dreadful events are in train. No: somnolence, rather, seems the mood; there's no heavy presence, no note of military readiness. Just this vague air of attrition, weariness, wear, of everything being dusty and defective.

'Problem?'

'No problem,' says Manders, smiling at me, and heading for his cabin; he seems to be quite right.

Music is sounding. On an elevated deck of the terminal building, which is plainly intended to have a ship-like appearance, a bemedalled band in military uniforms is performing, serenading us as we all begin to line the rails and watch the ship come into dock. But what is it they're playing: march, mazurka, anthem, waltz? It's strangely hard to tell; what is evident is that, like the building, something is just not quite right. These bandsman lack precision, if not some form of agreed musical policy. They've clearly not managed to come to terms on the length of a note or the run of a harmony. In fact, seen from a little closer, they're a rag tag and bobtail bunch altogether. They're all remarkably elderly: some must be seventy years of age, some a little nearer eighty. Those uniforms come from all the regiments, all the services: some are wearing tank grey, others cavalry green, others submarine white and blue. In fact, when you consider, they're not really a band at all. They're an imitation or an illusion of one.

And much the same applies to the soldiers we can now see down there on the dock. The usual conscript types: young, pubescent, short-haired. But, despite the talk of crisis, they're simply lolling carelessly, hanging around the stanchions, wearily smoking cigarettes, casually drinking from unlabelled bottles, their weapons lying carelessly at their sides or at their feet. Some are holding their hands up in supplication, apparently begging for gifts thrown down from the decks of the ship. And, as for the port itself, Russia's busiest, surely, Peter's outlet to the North Sea and the Atlantic, well, it has a great appearance of trade and traffic, but here too there seems to be just a touch of illusion. Tankers run down the seaway, great fishing vessels, the mother-ships of herring convoys, sit in the harbour, container ships load at the cranes. And yet most of the dockyard cranes are unmoving, the traffic doing very little. We're moored, now, in a line of ferries and cruise-ships. Yet many of these are not going anywhere at all. They're docked up for the season, and now they've turned into a row of floating hotels. Under the logos of Swiss, Swedish, German hotel chains, they lie fixed at permanent moorings, with all the familiar hotel complement on offer: doormen, porters, whores, casino girls, fronted off with a row of bouncers and armed guards.

Now shore has locked tight to ship, ship bonded firmly to

shore. The gangplanks rest in place. The universal port officials, wearing huge hats and carrying worn plastic briefcases, march aboard to do their duties. The ship has suddenly become strangely full of itself, with every deck and gangway packed tight with crowds of decanting passengers. A great many none of us have ever seen before, suggesting they have spent the entire voyage in some form of hibernation, carefully avoiding all bars, dining rooms and duty-free shops. Now they're out in huge numbers: pressing, surging, swarming, yelling to be let off. They drag along babies and dependents, carry huge packages, toss parcels over each others' heads. They heft cardboard suitcases and old boxes; they drop packages over the ship's side to waiting hands below. From both ship and shore, tannoys are blaring, filled with overwhelming Russian instructions. The gangway chains are removed; the returning Russians swarm down the ramps and into the terminal, where their own world awaits.

The travelling Baltic tourists descend rather more slowly. Off march the neat Japanese tour-teams, led by their guides, the American backpackers, all waving their maps, the blustering German execs, all looking out for pre-booked Zil limousines. But, as before, amid the noise and confusion there stands a small oasis of sanity, a little island of calm. In the ship's main lobby, where the crowds push and shove, a simple banner has been raised over a small table. DIDEROT PROJECT, it says. Beneath it stand Bo and Alma Luneberg, he having added a black woollen snow-hat to his Burberry, she in her northern furs. Our conflicts and problems have all been forgotten; Bo and Alma have re-acquired, and without the least sign of any resentment or bitterness, their traditional authority. Once more they're the good shepherds of our naughty flock. They're smiling, handing out documents, answering all our questions, reminding us about the charms of the Petersburg palaces and opera houses, the dangers of dark streets at nights, the quality of the caviar and the infinite ambiguity of the rouble.

The Diderot Pilgrims themselves – that once seriously mutinous but now totally compliant band – are also slowly emerging again from each little corner of the ship. Here come Agnes Falkman and Sven Sonnenberg. Each day of the journey we've seen less and less of them; but of each other they have clearly come to see more and more. Now they appear a quite inseparable couple. They talk to no one else, they say everything to each other. He smokes a huge self-crafted pipe, she has donned ever more radical denim and folkwear. Now decked in identical shore-gear, bobble hats, anoraks and walking boots, they're plainly longing for the rugged outdoors: a mountain to go up, a moor to stride. While they have dressed down for labour and the country, Anders Manders reappears, quite evidently dressed for town. In elegant loden coat and fine fur hat, he's ripe for the metropolis, a capital city where taste is everything and daily life is art. Yet more impressive is Birgitta Lindhorst, our splendid red-headed Swedish Nightingale. Descending amongst us from her noble eyrie up on the bridge deck, she looks quite glorious in a great golden top-coat, ready to take centre stage in whatever operatic roles this famously operatic city can offer.

Meantime over by the blini bar our funky professor Jack-Paul Verso is apparently saying very fond farewells to a whole glorious bevy of red-cheeked Tatyanas: Tatyana from Pushkin, Tatyana from Gorky, Tatyana from Novgorod, and a couple more from heaven knows where. They're laughing happily, delighting in his word-play, clutching hold of their natty little philosopher, tugging at his hands, kissing his cheeks, pulling at his Deconstructionist's hat. The demonstration of farewell is, I now gather, completely redundant. For, according to Bo and Alma, who are now giving us instructions, we are not really leaving the ship at all. Instead the *Vladimir Ilich* itself is going to become our Petersburg hotel, serve as our residence for the next few nights, until we make our return voyage. Never mind; Verso is clearly enjoying it. So, for that matter, are the laughing Tatyanas. And ah, here comes Lars Person, wearing his big hat. It looks as if we're all ready to step ashore . . .

And it's then we hear it. It comes swooping towards us over the water, like the cry of a great diving sea-bird. '*Ah, mes amis!*' comes the sound. '*Ah, mes chers confrères!*' Then we see her: standing high on an upper deck of the terminal, an extraordinary, a wonderful, a truly amazing sight. She's wearing a longish blue-and-white dress, but what a dress: light, crêpey-silky, clinging, it's in the fashion of the haute couture twenties, the style of Paul

Poiret or Coco Chanel. A big red flower is tucked provocatively into the declivities of her *décolletage*; a white fur-wrap with animal tails hangs sweetly round her shoulders. Her big face is white-powdered; across it her mouth is slashed in lipstick, vermilion red. Her hair, large and bouffant, is white as snow, and then is topped off with a straw hat decorated with false cherries. A sharp harbour wind is blowing round her, whipping the silk dress round her full figure, threatening the white straw hat. And, though she must be well over seventy for sure, she's waving and calling, waving and calling, just like a delighted happy young child. She's even unfurling, down the side of the building, a banner of welcome: to us. GRANDS PÈLERINS DE DENIS DIDRO! it reads. SOYEZ LES BIENVENUS!

Who on earth can the lady be? But no time to think about it now: we're off.

'Let us go,' says Bo, and we're all sheepishly following our leader again, walking down the gangplank. Our feet press the hard and crumbling cement of the great Motherland, where the land seems vast and the recent troubles of history seem, for the moment, to mean little. The usual arrowed signs direct us into the terminal. Outside the doors, the row of tattered bandsmen waits, surrounded by their instruments. They look older than ever, grey-bristled, sad, yet weighed with entire chestfuls of medals. They're holding out hats, helmets, kepis, asking, like beggars, for the gift of a rouble or two. They're not alone; the young conscript soldiers are at the same game, stopping the incoming passengers, evidently asking, with an odd mixture of threat and pleading, for cheap goods and gifts. The same tattered informality prevails inside the grim and cavernous terminal, where everything seems dented, battered, defective, out of true. As at the bar on shipboard, this is a world where anything goes. Rules don't work like rules; they're obstructions, inconveniences, that invite either resignation or strange devices. At the passport booths, each passport handed to the officials seems to contain a little wad of roubles. At the customs benches, every suitcase and package presented seems to need supporting by the giving of a small gift. Bo presents our papers to the soldiers in the passport booths. Manders in his diplomatic fashion talks in Russian to the port officials, evidently telling our story. Alma is digging in her purse for a pourboire or two. An odorous scent, the smell of the harbour mingled with the smell of ancient cigarette smoke and the dampness of crumbling plaster, dominates everything.

Then, suddenly, we're through, ushered by uniformed guards past the barrier, Bo and Manders having exercised their political magic. So here we are: in Russia, no, in Petersburg, which is also several other cities, Pieter, Petervar, Petrograd, Leningrad. We're in the city of writers, the capital of intense and troubled souls. My unfinished Finnish enterprise can be finished off at last. And it's a bright cold day in early October 1993 – just 220 years (as near as exactly) since Denis Diderot came to the city to offer his clever political wisdoms to a grand-fronted Empress. Russia then as now was in trouble, tugged as it ever has been between west and east, the mystic promises of bourgeois dreams and the amazing passions of the Old Believers, the strange tzars and the incredible impostors, by grand utopian dreams and the burden of those endless dead souls. Here extremity is the speciality, mysticism the rule, history the principle, a grand sense of history that can engulf continents, nature and desert, but still has trouble in struggling into humanity.

Today, at the dockside, it's the free market that appears to rule – or maybe rather it's the old world of the souk. At any rate no sooner are we walking out of the terminal than we're swept up by a turmoil of trade, a frenzy of solicitation. Everything is for sale: all the things you can think of, and then a good few you can't. Youths stand in lines in front of ancient suitcases, which are packed with military medals and lemon peelers; tank-drivers' fur caps and old postage stamps; peasant carvings and old cameras. Old women standing on squares of cardboard hold up worn dresses and old suits. There are glorious CDs of Prokofiev, and the great Gregorian liturgies. There are bronze busts of Lenin at knockdown prices, and others of the slaughtered Tzar Nicholas II. Weapons are everywhere – from small pistols and rusting hand-grenades to an entire armoured car, loaded gun-turret and all – on offer at a price marked in dollars and apparently ready to roll.

Verso and I stop together to inspect the coloured dolls, the *matrioshki*, which are supposed always to carry the latest political news. Well, for the moment at least, it's still a wooden Yeltsin that firmly encases a wooden Gorbachev and a wooden Brezhnev, and no one is yet encasing Yeltsin. On the other side of the world, Clinton too seems to be all right for the moment, holding inside himself the images of Bush, Reagan, Carter, Nixon. Helmut Kohl contains Schmidt and Adenauer. Quiet John Major boxes in Thatcher and Heath. 'Buy now before everything changes,' says Verso, taking out his wallet and virtually disappearing beneath the scrum. Following my own tastes, I look around and find exactly what I'm after. Joseph Brodsky holds Anna Akhmatova, who in turn embraces Mandelshtam, who incorporates Dostoyevsky, who digests Gogol, who has assimilated Pushkin. Pushkin opens up too, and inside him is the very tiniest and most indecipherable something. Who? Could it possibly be Diderot? Never mind. I'm here and, as they told me at the Kafé Kosmos, it's a writers' city, a set of telescoped images, illusory and ever-shifting, and yet presumably very real and just waiting for us over the other side of this vast dockyard wall.

'*Ah!! Mes amis!! Mes braves pèlerins!! Voici!! Ici, s'il vous plaît!! Bienvenue!*' The cry comes once more. And there beyond all the scramble of commerce she stands again, waving gaily, furiously at us. Behind her stands a very battered mini-bus, containing a bored and miserable driver.

'Ah, there you are, Galina!' cries Bo Luneberg, hurrying over.

'*C'est vous, Madame Solange!*' cries Alma.

The lady in Poiret, arms outstretched, rushes toward both of them.

'*Ah, mon brave savant!*' she cries. '*Mon cher cher, Bo-Bo! Et toi aussi, Alma, ma soeur!*'

All of them fall into such an operatic embrace that even our opera singer is put out:

'I thought one Kirov was enough,' murmurs Birgitta Lindhorst.

'*Et voici les pèlerins!*' cries the lady in silks, turning towards us all.

'Yes, these are our pilgrims,' says Bo. 'Now, this lady is our dear old friend, Madame Galina Solange-Stavaronova.'

'A lady we have known so many years we do not care to tell you!' says Alma.

'Hello, my darlings,' says the lady, smiling at us. 'Please speak to me in anything, I have them all, French, German, English, Swedish. But truly I love best French. French is the language of reason, *n'est-ce pas*, and reason is the language of Petersburg.'

'Really?' asks Verso.

'*C'est vrai*,' says the lady. 'During the worst of times, when we had Stalin and his stupid nasties, I spoke only French. How else could an honest person stay sane?'

'Galina, perhaps I should explain to them just who you are?' says Bo. 'Galina is a fellow scholar and I have been in touch with her these many months, from the very moment we thought of the Diderot Project.'

'*Bien sûr!*' cries Galina gaily.

'She has helped us very much and been kind enough to make our arrangements in Petersburg.'

'Your tickets for the Hermitage, your tickets for the Maryinsky,' says Alma. 'But of course you can go your own way if you wish.'

'*Pour vous, c'est mon plaisir!*' cries Galina.

'Now in her kindness she has arranged to take us all on a first tour around Petersburg and show us the Diderot Trail. I think I can assure you there's no one in the world who knows more about the culture of this very great city.'

'And that is my sweet little Bo,' says Galina. 'Always so kind, so civilized. It is true, of course. Now, I welcome you all to Petersburg. Sankt Peterburg, that is its name. I cannot tell you how I cried when they gave it back to us again. By the way, before we get on our little bus here, I tell you one thing. Most of the lady guides here – and you know we have many, they are a Petersburg speciality, every lady who is not a whore is a professional guide – will tell you the name comes from Peter the Great. *C'est absurde!* Not a bit of it! It was named for the first saint in heaven, the one who opens the door with his golden key. Now allow me to open the gate of heaven for you also. Follow me on to the bus.'

The bus is tiny and has unpadded seats, just about enough of them to take all our little pilgrim party.

'Maybe you have heard we have a political situation,' says Galina as we climb aboard. 'Once more Russia heaves, and nothing is born. My only advice: don't go all in different directions, and don't walk the streets alone very late at night. Then you will have very good luck.'

The bus sets off through the dockyard, past the various floating hotels, and passes out into the streets of the city. The view is not utopian. We're bouncing violently up and down over crane-tracks, potholes, tramlines, the wear and tear of a hard winter. None of this deters Galina who, in her soft clinging Poiret, stands at the front, addressing us all as the driver stares up at her dubiously. 'I will tell you a story of very good luck. Maybe you know, Petersburg is not always a lucky city. It has suffered everything. Flood, fire, earthquake, whirlwind, plague, all kinds of diseases. It has had repressions, rebellions, purges, revolutions. Everyone has tried to attack us, the Swedes, the Danes, the French, the Germans. We still remember the 900-day siege, when the Germans were on every side of the city, bombing us every night, and children dragged the bodies of their children through the streets to the cemeteries. How can I say luck?'

'Tell us,' says Bo.

'It was only this,' says Galina. 'The city, you know, was named again after Lenin, but he hated it, and the capital was moved back to Moscow. And that is why you don't see those dreadful pointed ministries, the silly towers, the great Marxist steeples. And even when it was bombed and we rebuilt it, we rebuilt it as it was, a French city in the north. That is our luck, and soon you will see it through the window.'

'Where are we now, Galina?' asks Verso.

'Oh, this is Grand Avenue, also called Bolshoi Prospekt.' To tell the truth, the prospekt is not impressive. We're bouncing down the dullest of avenues. People walk everywhere doing nothing very much. Children play between the tramlines, babushkas carry wrapped bundles along rough sidewalks. The aroma of dead smoke and wet oil does not fade. The apartment blocks have that battered and peeling look, the air of eternal neglect, that is the truest note of East European gloom.

'And does this mean you're going to be our guide for the whole visit, Madame Stavaronova?' asks Jack-Paul Verso. 'Because some of us may want to make different arrangements.'

'Everything is possible,' explains Bo. 'Within reason. May I explain, Galina is not our guide. She is one of us.'

'*Ah, oui, d'accord!*' says Galina. '*Je suis un pèlerin de Didro!*'

'We just have to remember Galina's warning. It's an awkward time here, so let us not do anything foolish. But for those who have questions about Diderot in Russia, Galina can tell you everything.'

'*Oui*, you see, for the last forty years I have been a state librarian,' explains Galina. 'I work with the French books at the Saltykov-Shcherdin. Perhaps you know it, this is the Petersburg Public Library. Here Lenin read the works of Voltaire. But please don't think that is why it is famous. But now, don't stare at my beauty any more. Look out the window. What do you see?'

While we've talked, our bus has switched streets, moved over a block. The scene has changed, our views have completely altered. Now we ride along a splendid waterside embankment, looking across the width of a river at another splendid waterside embankment. Near us, on the edge of fast-flowing waters, two huge and top-hatted Egyptian sphinxes sit gazing enigmatically at each other, while at the same time framing up our own view of the scene. Beyond runs the wide Neva, where white tourboats probably already filled with our own Japanese tourists are shuttling back and forth. On the further embankment rise up large towers, bulbous onion domes, fine golden flèches.

'Now you ride on University Embankment,' says Galina. 'Here on Vasilyevsky Island Peter built all his academies. Here is the Petersburg University, which I hope you will visit. Gogol went to teach world history there, you remember. His problem was only he didn't know any. There is the Kunstkammer, over here is the great Academical Clock. Now look across the river over there. Do you notice a green square? In it, something like a missile pointing at the sky? Do you know it?'

'Isn't it the Bronze Horseman?' asks Lars Person.

'*Oui, mon petit*, the statue of Falconet. Even this was by a Frenchman, you see. And now, *mes amis*, I will say nothing at all, even though you understand this is very difficult for me. But in one moment you will understand why.'

Eight Enlightenment Pilgrims, we look around, staring from

bank to bank. Only one or two of us have been to the city before, and yet everything we see is more than half-familiar, spoken of by old repute. The Kunstkammer: that was where Peter kept all his waxworks and his odd curiosities, even down to the teeth he pulled. The flèche on this side is surely the Peter and Paul Fortress, where an ancestor of Vladimir Nabokov was the governor who imprisoned Dostoyevsky. There are other flèches, other domes: the high one on the further bank, beyond the English Embankment, must surely be Saint Isaac's Cathedral. The fine façades on each of the two banks look out at each other, just like the two solemn sphinxes, shaping and enclosing a distinctive space.

At the heart of this space is the water, into which all the buildings and both embankments seem to stare. The afternoon air is feeling cold now, and the sky seems to have purified itself to a clear lucid blue. The red afternoon sun is just beginning to dip. Ahead of us a stone bridge spans the Neva, joining the facing embankments to each other. Beyond, where several rivers seem to meet together, something strange seems to have happened to the light. In the clear bright air, the river itself seems to dissolve here: turn into luminous matter, become an encrimsoned shimmer, sky, sunlight and river all disintegrating into each other. Above this floating mirror or luminescent lake stands a row of splendid buildings, linked together, and suspended there as if by the forces of a mirage. The buildings, painted in green and white, are in the classical style, simple at heart and yet highly embellished, their walls caked with baroque pilasters and elaborate window frames. The roofs are verdigrised copper, and the façades run on and on, a Turneresque battery of Venetian palaces overlooking the waterless water.

'Notice, I say nothing at all,' says Galina. 'But I think you know what it is.' Indeed we do, Galina. Though most of us haven't seen these façades before, we've also known them for ever. They're the Winter Palace. They're the Hermitage . . .

TWENTY-TWO (THEN)

'LIKES YOU? My good dear fellow, of course she likes you,' says squat big-nosed Melchior Grimm, sitting filing his nails in the grand drawing room of the Narishkin Palace, which looks out over wintry Senate Square.

'Are you quite sure?' asks Our Philosopher.

'I know it. It's obvious, my friend. She's absolutely crazy for you. I've heard her telling everyone she meets you're a quite remarkable man. Extraordinary, unique, beyond compare.'

'When did you hear her say so?'

'I've already told you that. In the same way you see her most afternoons, I see her nearly every single evening. We really love each other. We just chatter away all the time like two blind magpies. She calls me her little *gobe-mouche*. Her dear fly-catcher, her favourite slave.'

'I can see she compliments you wonderfully. But precisely what was it she said about me?'

Grimm glances at him archly. 'I'm not entirely sure you really want to hear.'

'Don't be so prim, Grimm,' says our man, impatient as usual. 'I've known you since you were an ambitious nothing, a fat boy from Germany living in that stinking bordello in Saint-Roch. That was when you were still a good friend of Jean-Jacques Rousseau, and took him round the whores.'

Grimm looks up. 'There are some old times that are best forgotten,' he says. 'Especially to do with Rousseau.'

'I forget nothing,' says our man, 'and nor does Rousseau, the vainest man in the world. I advised him to become a philosopher. I wrote most of his first essay for him and got it published. But you realize what a capital crime that is: to help someone. Rousseau's never forgiven me.'

'You always were too kind.'

'Now they say he's writing down his most intimate confessions to publish them everywhere. And then you'll suffer and sting, my dear Grimm.'

'I don't worry,' says Grimm. 'And remember, so will you.'

'Oh, come on, please, tell me what she said, Grimm.'

'Very well,' says Grimm, teasingly, 'she told everyone that after she's spent one of her sessions with you, her thighs turn all black and blue.'

'Her thighs? It's not true!'

'Of course it's true,' says Grimm. 'She says you keep slapping her legs all the time while you're talking. You may not realize it, but all your good friends will agree with her. I have awful bruises myself, just from listening to you.'

'You know that's quite ridiculous, Grimm,' our man says, reaching out.

'Get back, please, philosopher, you're doing it now!' cries Grimm. 'You always were the world's heartiest thinker.'

'I love ideas, that's all. They drive me to distraction.'

'She says she's placed a table in between you to get away from your violent ideas.'

'So she's complaining to the world I'm much too forward?'

'No, no. Really she finds you innocent, enchanting. She says sometimes you seem like a man of a hundred, sometimes like a small boy of ten.'

'Does she? How very strange,' says our man, remembering a certain dream he had once. 'And which of the two of us does she prefer?'

'Oh, the boy, no doubt,' says Grimm. 'This court's full of dotards and professional arse-lickers. What it lacks is a bit of honest truth and youthful levity.'

'Well, you know me. As I've told her already, I'm all innocence and candour. I don't really know how to behave at court at all.'

At that Grimm nods firmly. 'Yes, and there are a good many who would agree with you. You really should take a little more care with your fellow courtiers.'

'Parasites, fleas, spies, sniggerers, little automata. They're not my fellows at all. And surely if one pleases the mistress, one doesn't worry about the pettiness of servants.'

'I can see you're really not a courtier,' says Grimm. 'A court is a jungle, old friend, a hidden example of the most primitive state of nature. Far worse than the brutal world of Rousseau's *Social Contract*. These animals are always tearing and gnashing at each other. Everyone wants a prize, a flank or a loin. Everyone has to destroy those who are most in favour. You should observe me. I'm always discreet, cautious and charming to everyone in sight. Exactly as you are open, indifferent and crass.'

'You're a sneak, and I'm a simple good man.'

'Every court has parasites. Only you want to be different. You want to be pure as the driven snow. But you're simply one more little puppet in the whole outrageous spectacle. You know all your movements are watched, your friends and associates are noted, your letters are read?'

'My letters? Oh, surely not.'

'Of course. Whatever you write is noted and copied by the cabinet noir. I trust you haven't been too indiscreet?'

Our Man considers. 'Not to my wife. Never in my life have I been indiscreet with my wife.'

'But your mistress, our dear Madame Volland?'

'There I may just have told the truth once or twice. If a man can't be indiscreet with his mistress, what's the point of having one?'

'A court thrives on every single small indiscretion, didn't you know?'

'That's why I'm a philosopher, not a courtier. I talk reason, not politics or flattery. Don't they understand?'

'They understand you're in a position of influence. Shall we consider your situation? Who's for you, who's against you?'

'Very well, go ahead.'

Grimm takes out his notebook. 'First, those against you. Number one, Grigor Orlov.'

'The discarded lover. He's jealous, and what do you expect? The hours I see her used to be his.'

'Remember, no one can be more influential than a rejected

lover. She can't afford to offend him, he knows far too much. And now he's saying you employ those special hours for the most corrupt of purposes.'

'Not true,' says our man. 'I no longer risk it at my age. I've learned my lesson. I'm no longer that old buzzing, sniffing, supping high-flying insect, Grimmie. These days I'm content to rest quiet on the surface of the earth.'

'My poor fellow, I'd no idea.'

'Now now, before you start with your gossip,' our man says hastily, 'though the will may be weaker these days, I can still raise the wizard's wand quite as often as I wish.'

Grimm looks at him sceptically. 'Can you? Anyway, that's not what Orlov means. He's still sleeping with the éprouveuses, so he knows exactly how near you're getting to the noble bed of her highness. The corruption he's talking about is thought.'

'Ah, he's against it?'

'Orlov's a clever man, but he's still a brute Russian. He thinks like a beast, by instinct. And he hates all western ideas.'

'Does anyone listen to him?'

'Yes. The Archduke Paul, for one.'

'He doesn't hate western ideas. He wants to be a Prussian goose-stepper like his father.'

'It's not ideas he hates, it's you,' says Grimm. 'I see him every day.'

'Naturally, you found him the wife he lies with. Maybe he'll never forgive you.'

'He forgives me. I have his closest confidence. He trusts me because I'm German. He hates you because you're French. Also you're his mother's friend, and he hates his mother more than anyone else in the world. He says you're here as a mask to place over her despotism.'

'Evidently a bitter youth.'

'Indeed. Unfortunately Chancellor Panin agrees with him. The most powerful figure at court. He always agrees with Paul, he became his tutor when d'Alembert turned down the post. He declares you're a shameless sponger. One of that kind always knows another.'

'So that's three then? Orlov, Paul, Panin? It's not many.'

'No, look at it. Three of the most influential people in the court.' Grimm shows him the list, then gets up and cautiously drops it into the stove.

Our man thinks. 'But surely some of the courtiers are for me?'

'Yes,' says Grimm, 'Prince Narishkin says you're the wisest man he ever met. Unfortunately he's also telling everyone you've converted him to atheism. Now he's going round the court saying the cathedrals should be deconsecrated and the monasteries closed.'

'Oh dear.'

'You're lucky everyone regards him as nothing better than a court fool. Everyone laughs at him. But that means they also laugh at you.'

'What's wrong with laughter? They say it's life's best medicine.'

'Unfortunately, as with many of the best medicines, a lot of those who take them fail to survive.'

'I presume Chancellor Betskoi is for me? He brought me here.'

'He's your warm supporter. A pity so many people think they know why. They claim for his own profit he sells off half the pictures you send from Paris.'

'I don't believe it. And Princess Dashkova likes me.'

'Yes,' says Grimm, 'a shame no one in Sankt Peterburg can stand her French silks, her Irish fancies and her London airs. She'll be sent to Siberia or exile in Moscow before much longer.'

Our man looks at Grimm in dismay. 'I begin to see court life really is very confusing.'

'Precisely,' says Grimm smoothly, 'that's why my job is never easy, however you choose to despise it. You always have to watch out behind you, or you lose your income, if not your head.'

'Thank you, Grimm. You've really cheered me up. But it's always best to know who one's friends and enemies are.'

'Quite. But do remember your greatest and most dangerous problems aren't here in Petersburg at all. They're in Potsdam.'

'King Frederick. Don't expect me to admire him. He's the firebrand of Europe. All the philosophers hate him. He calls himself Philosopher King, when the truth is he's a despot and a thug.'

'The most powerful man in Europe,' says Grimm. 'You can't afford to offend him. He expects every important figure of Europe to attend his court.'

'And look at poor Bach. The Emperor soon stepped hard on his organ, didn't he? Anyway, I've thoroughly offended him already.'

'I advised you to stop over at Potsdam.'

'You told me I'd make a complete fool of myself!'

'Exactly, but better be a court fool than a court enemy. And now you see what's happened.'

'What?'

'You went to Dresden instead, after he'd only just finished shelling it. In his eyes nothing could be more insulting.'

'Well, luckily his offence is a long way away.'

'But getting nearer all the time,' says Grimm. 'You wrote Her Serene Highness a paper, did you not, "The Daydream of Denis the Philosopher"? Attacking him outrageously. It turned up in his hands within days, of course.'

'How?'

'Half the courtiers here work for Frederick, when they aren't working to enrich themselves.'

Our man sighs. 'But what on earth can he do to me?'

'Oh, believe me, everything,' says Grimm, rather unpleasantly. 'First he's been reviewing all your books in magazines right across Europe. Under a pseudonym, of course. He says your writings are corrupting, plagiarized, and totally unreadable.'

'I see logic is not his strong point. How can they possibly be corrupting, if they're also unreadable? And how can I be blamed for what they say, if I've plagiarized them?'

'The point, my friend, is that because he sees himself as a philosopher this is the most vindictive monarch in all Europe. Now he's intending to send emissaries to Her Highness to expose you.'

'As what?'

'A false philosophe. A charlatan. An atheist who went around Leipzig trying to draw attention to himself by walking the streets in a red nightshirt.'

'Nonsense, it's yellow, I can show you. Except I've lost it.'

'They've already warned the Empress you're here as a French spy.'

'The Empress knows that story already. Durand tried to make

me deliver a royal message. She put it in the stove and is sending him home.'

'Where he'll return to Versailles and tell His Christian Majesty you're a black traitor, only deserving of the gallows. I hardly think your tactics were brilliant.'

Nervous now, our man thinks. 'Oh Grimm, Grimm, what on earth should I do?'

'First, you agree to call in at Potsdam on your return journey. It's right there on the way home.'

'What? As far as Frederick is concerned, I'm a plagiarist, a charlatan, a nightshirt wearer and a spy.'

'Yes, well, I am a good friend of his.'

'I know, you're a good friend of everyone. Everyone who just happens to sit on a throne. You have no standards, no honour, no taste . . .'

'Now now, my friend, let's not quarrel. I use my talents, I don't abuse them. I attend and advise. I inform and I please. I'm a mixer and a fixer. I'm an intermediary, and to tell the truth I'm quite indispensable.'

'A spider who sits grinning in the middle of a great web.'

'Europe wouldn't begin to work without me.'

'It certainly doesn't work with you.'

'There would be no treaties, no children in the court cradles, no heirs to thrones. It would be a place of sterile dynasties, brutal tyrants and vacant palaces.'

'It is already.'

'Without me it would be a good deal worse,' says Grimm, rising to repowder his face in the mirror.

'There would be no music, no court theatre. No Gluck. No Mozart. No Diderot at the Russian court, with a nice little pension for eternity, and his posthumous reputation taken care of. Think of that. Well, now I must go.'

'No, no, Grimm, wait, my dear dear friend,' says our man, hurrying after him into the lobby. 'I can't bear to quarrel with you. I'm just anxious, that's all. I can see now I may be garrotted in Petersburg, shot in Potsdam, hanged at the Bastille.'

'As Voltaire says, that's what happens to the man of reason.'

'And I do understand now I'm not a courtier, not even a court jester. My face is just much too near my heart . . .'

'Never mind,' says Grimm generously, 'for a dozen afternoons you've kept the Empress happy, and no doubt drawn her attention away from repressing her people. What could be more useful?'

'That's something then. But, my dear fellow, tell me, what shall I do?'

'Why not let me write a little letter to Frederick, telling him you'll stop at Potsdam on the way home.'

'I refuse to stop at Potsdam on the way home. I despise Frederick and he detests me.'

'Then I warn you, he'll make your life a total misery.'

'Too late. Really. Life has done it already.'

'You're not in total misery, Diderot. Your fame is assured.'

Our Man stares at him, pained to the heart. 'Look at me. Stuck in Petersburg. Stricken with the everlasting shits from the Neva. I've offended my king. I'm cut off from my wife and even worse from my mistress. I'm surrounded with enemies. I'm struck down with the Swiss disease.'

'What's that?'

'Eternal homesickness, Grimm. I'm longing for the high mountain peaks of my life.'

'It's nothing. Every honest man is homesick. Everyone's in exile. Voltaire's in Switzerland, homesick for Paris. Rousseau's in Paris, homesick for Switzerland. People like us don't have homes. We're wanderers and vagabonds. All of which reminds me, there's something you can do for me.'

'Of course, you only have to ask,' says our man.

'Good then. Speaking of vagabonds, you remember the little music prodigy who came with his papa to Paris and stayed for a time in my house?'

'Amadeus, little master tra-la-la? The mannekin pisse? I shall never forget how you took him to Versailles to meet La Pompadour. And then he sat up on his hind legs and proposed marriage to her, even though he was only, what, six years old?'

'Well, now Her Imperial Majesty is after him. She desperately wants to bring him here to court.'

'Why not, another dwarf for the collection? That boy will come if you ask him, surely? He owes everything to you.'

'Of course he'll come. Musicians are like travelling acrobats, or philosophers, they always come. And Mozart's a jealous little fellow. He wants to drive out all the old kapellmeisters and become composer to every court in Europe.'

'I don't see the problem then.'

'The problem is the Empress. Maybe you don't know, but the lady's tone-deaf. She can't tell a harp from a harpsichord. Music is just a great braying noise to her. She always claims the only notes she can ever recognize are the sound of her dogs barking. Well, I tell you – she even loves Gluck.'

'No matter. You're allowed these quirks when you play the patron.'

'You don't know our little Master Upstart. One hint that his music hasn't been understood and worshipped, and he'll lose his tiny temper and sweep out of Russia in a mortal fury. And that will be two enemies made at one stroke. What do I do?'

Suddenly our man is all delight. His eyes are glowing, his worries are gone. 'As a good and clever courtier, you mean? An expert parasite?'

'That's right. What do you think?'

'My dear fellow, of course,' says our man, slapping Grimm's thigh. 'What you need is a nice little mystification.'

'That's it, exactly, a mystification.'

'So, first you tell Her Serene Empress it's poor Mozart who's tone-deaf. Say the poor little kid can't even hold a tune in a bucket. So how could you, an honest courtier valuing her fame as one of the age's patrons, bring an off-key juvenile all the way from Salzburg to mock her perfect pitch?'

'But she knows the Emperor Joseph admires him to heaven. And the Italian courts, and the King at Versailles.'

'All of them tone deaf too.'

'But if I say that, I offend Mozart. And that I definitely can't afford.'

'No, of course not. When you were in Paris you had his portrait painted, didn't you? Now you're selling copies of it everywhere, so of course he's got to be a genius, or your royalties go down.'

'He is a genius. What do I say to him?'

'Tell him the truth, as far as you can. Say the Empress is crazy to have him here at court. Nothing in the world would make her happier than to have his little trickiness wandering round the Hermitage. Just one problem. The weather here's so cold you can't possibly play a piano or tune a clarinet. What's the point of becoming court musician in a country where you can never play more than half a concerto?'

Grimm laughs, reaches out, embraces him. The cosmetic dust from his cheeks falls over the dark philosophical suit.

'I tell the Empress Mozart is tone-deaf!' he cries.

'Now I know exactly why I like you, Denis. Now I know why you really are my very best friend.'

'Not counting all your other very best friends? I only wish I could sit on a splendid throne for you, and you could kiss—'

'But you do, my friend, you do. The high throne of reason.'

So they go to the door together, they embrace again, fond brothers that once more they are.

'There's just one thing, my dear Denis,' Grimm says fondly, as he pulls his cloak around him and steps into Senate Square. 'That drab black suit you wear. I know it's a thinkers' suit, but I'd drop it. Try blue or red. Get something with a little gold frogging, like this.'

'Frippery, self-disguise, textile fantasy, body-promo,' says our man. 'It's the philosophy of the whorehouse. It's not how we look outside, it's the state of our souls within that really matters.'

'Not a bit. That's the problem with mind, it's all on the inside. Believe me, dress is all. You can tell that by the frowns. And you're top favourite of the court now, you can easily afford it. All the best shopkeepers will be delighted to make you over for the prestige. But remember. Top people like top clothes.'

'Ridiculous. Really? Not really?'

Well, what else could you expect from dear old, loyal old, vulgar old friend Grimm?

TWENTY-THREE (NOW)

JUST A LITTLE MORE THAN 200 years before the day I first arrived in Saint Petersburg (for remember, for all my good intentions I never did make it to Leningrad), a rather striking sailing vessel tacked up the Neva River and anchored in the harbour, which in those days – the time in fact was the high summer of 1777 – lay directly opposite the Hermitage. It was a splendid yacht, whose owner and crew proved to be British. Indeed the figure on the poop turned out to be a famous, if not scandalous, English traveller. Her name was Elizabeth Chudleigh, though she generally called herself either the Countess of Bristol or the Duchess of Kingston. And why not? She had married both of these gentlemen, though it seems without properly advising the one about the other. Her too rapid journey from Bristol to Kingston had brought her into trouble with the British courts and the British press, and she'd won a remarkable reputation back home for bigamy, imposture and false inheritance. Like many of her sort – and at that time there was somehow quite a lot of her sort – she now preferred to live on the continent, first of all in Paris, where she settled for a while, and then across the breadth of Europe.

Fatally attractive, she would never be short of reputation or company. And, since the possessions, trophies, even the platoon of servants that served her were not quite legally hers, she found it wise to carry most of her boodle with her. This is why she had commissioned a fine yacht to carry her wherever she went; now it had docked in Petersburg. The more distinguished locals soon discovered that the boat was a mobile Aladdin's cave: a floating museum of excellent possessions, a seagoing cabinet of curiosities, of whom La Chudleigh herself was hardly the least. Here, on the Neva, in full sight of the Hermitage, she entertained: quite sumptuously, according to some; quite disgustingly, according to others. Soon she was one of the spectacles of Petersburg, and had attracted the attention of the great Empress herself. This was an age of English tastes, in everything from dress to gardens. La Chudleigh sent home for more possessions, more servants, more docile English gardeners to fill the city with roses and herbs.

Before long she was a striking figure at court, the theatre, the opera: an aristocrat, a grand courtesan, a maker of fashion. The Tzarina much enjoyed her bravado, until it became just a little bit too interesting to her own Grigor Potemkin, after which she grew a little bored. But not, though, before — when a Baltic storm blew up and damaged the yacht out in the river — she granted the Duchess of Kingston, or Countess of Bristol, permission to build herself a glorious house in the English taste on the shore overlooking the Neva. It rose up, a little bit of Britain, with English gardeners and English servants. But it was a little bit of Russia too, for a large vodka distillery was set up in the grounds, doing much for her general popularity.

But of all the tastes, the fashions, the trophies that Elizabeth Chudleigh brought over with her to Petersburg, quite the most splendid item was a quite amazing silver clock. She had some time back commissioned it, in London, from James Cox, the finest of the British jeweller-watchmakers. In an age of intricate and wonderful clocks, when time-pieces were toys and fables of the meaning of the universe, this one was thought by many the finest in the world. For ease of transportation it had been dismantled, and it arrived in Petersburg flat-packed and without instructions. So when the moment came for the clock to be properly put together again, it took a Petersburg craftsman two years to link all its amazing intricacies together.

Thus a huge silver peacock made out of many separate pieces stands up on a stump amid an intricate forest of branches. Among the branches are concealed creatures of all sorts of different kinds and sizes: a cockerel, a squirrel inside a cage, an owl, a grasshopper, a lizard, a snail, and various mushrooms that conceal the dials that clock the time. When an hour strikes, a chime of bells begins to play. The owl moves, the squirrel spins in its cage, the cockerel crows, and various other actions are provoked. The peacock itself turns, bows, and spreads out its huge tail. By the time the clock was assembled again, the chimes had already rung for Elizabeth Chudleigh. She herself died back in her favourite Paris. But the clock itself remained in Russia, and it was duly acquired by the duchess's admirer, Grigor Potemkin. He was the victorious hero of the Tauride, the Empress's best general and her one-eyed lover. She gave him the greatest of gifts (the Tauride Palace, dinner services from Sèvres and Wedgwood, many thousands of dead souls). He longed to return the compliment. He acquired the Peacock Clock and presented it to her. And she placed it in the Small Hermitage.

That's why, amid a press of what feels to be a hundred thousand jostling tourists, we Diderot Pilgrims are standing around it right now. Galina has brought us here, of course. Galina has decanted us from the mini-bus in the middle of Palace Square, right beside the Alexander Column, on an old site of history: the scene where tzars more than once sent out their cavalry to slaughter their people, and where, in 1917, the commissars sent in the people to slaughter the cavalry and the tzars. The Red Revolution, it seems, is far from forgotten: another red flag demonstration is taking place in a corner of the square, watched by armed policemen. Big banners wave and loudspeakers blurt; a band of marchers sets off toward the centre of the city, shouting passionately as they go. None of this impresses Galina.

'Politics, take no notice!' she cries. 'Do not even look! Just follow me!'

And so, a small band of Enlightenment pilgrims, we surge across the square, between the menacing Intourist coaches, and storm the steps of the Winter Palace.

Except the gates today are not locked, and the doors are wide open. For something has happened to history these days. We may be at the scene of great and revolutionary events, ten days that shook the world, events that seemed so grandly historical and truly real they had to invent a new art to go with them, called proletarian realism. Naturally, since the real events were so much smaller than the events that reality required, painters, opera-makers, film-directors and the authors of works of history improved them. Even the photographs were inaccurate; it was necessary to brush out some and brush in others. This is a common problem with History, history the great power, inevitable, inescapable, progressive, written in the great Book of Destiny above. The reality frequently fails to concur with what has been destined, which makes it necessary to correct it, so that what happens is brought into perfect harmony with what is.

Odd, though, that the great inevitable machine called History should have gone on to produce what we witness here right now. For, where the people surged and the great gates tumbled, American backpackers knock back their cans of coke, Japanese tourists photograph each other standing next to something or other, and weary-looking Russian army conscripts smoke on the steps and eye up the endless supplies of young foreign girls. Inside, in the great buildings, vast tour parties sweep past each other, going in all directions, up and down the staircases, along the thirteen miles of stone corridors, into the twelve hundred rooms of paintings, objects, every kind of treasure, two million different items from all over the world. And from all over the world the people come to see them. They swarm through the Little Hermitage, the Big Hermitage, the Old Hermitage, the Hermitage Theatre, steered about in sheep-flocks by those bossy Russian guides who once used to promote socialism, comradeship, peace and world friendship and now promote Constructivist posters and *Demoiselles d'Avignon* T-shirts.

Today the world seems to be one museum after another. And of course everyone wants to see this one. Hermitage now means museum; museum now implies Hermitage. Tzar after tzar added to its boodle and multiplied its trophies. Collector after collector added their private contributions, general after general came home with more trophies. Loot from other museums came as spoils of war; while other wonderful things that were here once have been sold abroad, looted, ransacked away, shared out with other museums in Russia. But however much has been and gone, everything you can think of is somehow still here, and in the most amazing quantities. World-famous paintings hang in an unbelievable profusion. Every age and stage of art is depicted, from primitive to the highest baroque and the richest romanticism and so, in the great cycle of being, back down to primitive abstraction again. Every material, precious or semi-precious, has been mined, chipped, shaped, forged, fashioned. Every kind of human skill, craft and art has been used. Every nation and people seems to be represented. Every image and icon is kept in stock.

So history now has become a kind of noisy museum: a glittering, booming place of wonders, a scene of half-indifferent worship. Paintings and objects take the place of history and power. Tour companies take the place of popular revolutionaries, surging up and down the stairs. Indeed it can only seem as if history – for so long our aggressive and murderous master, sweeping us into ever more horror and atrocity – has suddenly become our servant and friend. No longer here to spill blood, no longer urging ideology or faith, no longer requiring death and sacrifice, no longer raging and purging, it instead deposits bright and well-lit scenes before us: glittering Fabergé and glinting Sèvres, brilliant Impressionist chiaroscuros and raw Cubist splashes, fleshly Rembrandt human puddings, strange vivid Constructivist collages.

Tired travellers look at it all, in a kind of worried desperation. Painting after painting passes across the retina, signals to the brain-cells, passes into confusion, excess, redundancy. The tourists pause a while, hunt round for the tea rooms, the chairs and the couches (and why are there never enough?). They put down their cameras, they take off their shoes. Girls chitter and chatter in front of the huge Rembrandts. Boys chase them through the endless rooms of the building, from gallery to gallery.

'And all this is simply for myself and the mice to admire,' the great Empress is supposed to have said once, in quiet satisfaction, after the great boatloads sent north by Golitsyn and Diderot arrived, were uncrated, hung on new walls that had to be built to display them. Now the collections collect the tourists in their millions, coming from every part of the globe.

'Tourists, dreadful people, please ignore them,' says Galina imperiously, ushering us all through the rooms. 'Guides, they're all terrible, don't listen to them!'

But why should we? We have our own guide, Galina, and she is clearly beyond compare. She knows everything and for some reason is permitted to go everywhere, just like some insuperable force.

'*Bonjour, mon brave!*' she cries to the guards in gallery after gallery. '*Félicitations, mon ami!*'

She opens doors in walls and we find ourselves in small offices, where curators smoke secretly and restorers paint.

'*Parfait!*' she tells them. '*Voilà mes pèlerins! N'oublie pas ton français.*'

'*Pardon! Attention!*' she shouts as she cuts a swathe through huge and well-armed tour-parties, who open up and scatter as she makes her attack.

'*Excusez-MOI!*'

And now she gathers us around Elizabeth Chudleigh's great silver peacock, indicating to other parties it is now time to depart. As if at her express instruction, the clock now starts to chime. Its mechanical motions begin, this intricacy locking itself into that. The owl moves, and the squirrel cages turn about, tinkling quietly. Then the cockerel crows, the peacock turns toward us, bowing its head low and spreading out its tail. In her silk Poiret dress, Galina stands there, crowing at us, clapping her hands loudly. The tourists who come and go, talking of Rembrandt or Malevich, listening to their imperious guides or auditing the chattering headsets, stare at us curiously, as if we are different from the rest. Indeed we are. Let them have their usual gallery narrative; we're being treated to something rather different. I think we ought to call it 'Galina's Tale'.

TWENTY-FOUR (THEN)

DAY TWELVE

It's snowing beyond the Hermitage windows. Wind is heard whistling down the corridors. HE sits opposite SHE. A rather large low table is set between them. Even so, their knees appear to be touching. HE holds a large sheaf of papers and is going through them with her.

HE
I need to know the total production of timber, grain, linen and birdseed. Imports of oil and horses. Exports of furs, metals, pottery and caviar.

SHE
Whatever for?

HE
You said you'd like me to produce a Russian encyclopedia. An encyclopedia is a book of everything.

SHE
Surely you can have far too much of everything.

HE
In life perhaps. Not in an encyclopedia. Now then. What is the landmass of your empire?

SHE
Unknown.

HE
Total income? Total state debt?

SHE
Don't ask me. Go and bother the members of the Academy of Sciences. That's why I have them.

HE
I've tried. Every time I go there they simply hand me gold medals and huge citations. But they won't actually tell me anything at all.

SHE
They're jealous of you. They think I like you far too much. Or maybe you're asking them questions they are not supposed to answer. How can I know?

HE looks at her.

HE
Questions they are not supposed to answer? What's the point of having an academy, then?

SHE
I should have thought the point was obvious. All great countries have them. In any case I want the whole world to understand my love of science and my love for learning and philosophy. Anyway, if they refuse to answer your questions, why should I?

HE sighs.

HE
All right, my dear lady, let's try a very easy one. What's the total population of Russia?

SHE
Don't you know?

HE
Some tell me 18 million, some say 20.

SHE
I can give you a list of who pays taxes. Nine million men. Women are excluded, also certain nobles.

HE

Good. The population of Moscow?

SHE

Changes all the time. Up and down. Now for instance there's
a plague. So you're very well away from it.

HE

More than Petersburg? Less than Petersburg?

SHE

Just put down a lot.

HE

Thank you, Your Highness. The population of Moscow is . . .
a lot. And this I have on the very highest authority. From the
very top. Number of Jews in Russia?

SHE

We never try to count them. But monks and nuns I can tell
you exactly. We have seven thousand monks and five
thousand nuns.

HE

Then I suggest you should have two thousand less monks or
two thousand more nuns. Then if they ever pair off—

SHE

Why would they ever pair off? The whole point of making
them monks and nuns is to stop them pairing off.

HE

It's often tried, but it's never succeeded. Sexual passions can
always break down convent walls.

SHE

How would you know?

HE

I've often tried to climb them. Monasticism's an amazing
stimulant to human depravity. No woman trembles more
with passion than an unhappy nun. And since nunneries were

chiefly devised to calm the anxieties of worried fathers, there's a plentiful supply of those.

SHE
Not in Russia. What else do you want to know?

HE checks his list.

HE
What else does Russia produce? Timber, furs, precious stones, minerals?

SHE
Yes, of course.

HE
Hemp? Mulberry trees?

SHE
Yes. And yes again. Just put it produces everything.

HE
Wine? Rhubarb?

SHE
Yes. Yes. Oh, do write down about my Devil's Grass.

HE
What's that?

SHE
That's what they called it when I introduced the potato.

HE
You introduced your people to the potato? Was that kind?

SHE
Yes. Now they grow everywhere. I require my people to eat them, too.

HE
What else did they propose to do with them?

SHE

What they do with everything. Make vodka. Surely those questions are quite enough—

SHE looks bored.

HE

My dear lady, you know I ask you these questions for a reason. I long to see Russia progress. But a nation can only progress if it uses all its resources. We cannot have true science unless we also have good manufacture. We cannot have innovation and discovery unless we cultivate crafts and skills. We cannot have good society unless people have dreams and aspirations—

SHE

Yes, I agree.

HE

What is better, a society where there is no energy or hope, where people live short lives in poverty, where all is struggle, where everyone robs each other or sells their bodies and their souls to each other, or a society of goods and talents, professions and arts. A society where people decorate their houses, cultivate their gardens, attend theatres and museums, acquire good manners and fine graces, spend and consume—

SHE

That is better. Of course.

HE

But then you must also pay the price. You will have to change your towns and cities. Create more streets and neighbourhoods. Devise more workshops, encourage more tradesmen, more craftsmen and inventions, more shopkeepers, more learned scholars, more solid citizens. Then the citizens will become burghers, and insist on governing themselves. They'll ask for guilds and parliaments. They'll demand laws that they agree with. They'll require reform, and in the end they may think they may not need a monarch at all—

SHE
Write down about our wonderful stud farms. Do you know King Frederick of Prussia buys all his stallions from us?

HE
And I'm told that in return you acquire all your best breeding mares from him.

SHE looks at him. The COURTIERS are sniggering.

SHE
Didro. Today you're being impertinent beyond belief.

HE looks extremely contrite.

HE
I'm very sorry. Sometimes my tongue seems to break loose from my brain. My thoughts come out before I've even thought about them.

SHE
Just as your hand does from your pocket. It's resting on my right thigh yet again.

HE
I regret it. I do indeed.

SHE
Now you're squeezing. Are you trying to flirt with me, sir?

HE
Not at all, my dear lady. I'm trying to think with you.

SHE
And how does this help?

HE
My dear lady, with me philosophy has never been a form of contemplation. It's an active current, an unending and torrential flowing of the mind. I don't think thoughts, I electrify them. Sometimes they pass through me with so much power I hurl my wig across the room. Sometimes, I'll confess it, they've made me squeeze a breast or slap a thigh. Still, to

the best of my knowledge, which as far as knowledge goes is among the best there is, no harm has ever come of it. No one has suffered. No one has been hurt. Yet my most sincere and abject apologies, Your Imperial Highness, all the same—

SHE laughs.

SHE
No need to be humble with me, Mr Librarian. I do believe we're two of a kind.

HE
Are we?

SHE
You have a hot head, and I have one too. We interrupt each other, we don't listen to what the other is saying. We're wild and rude, frank and open. We both say stupid things—

HE
But with one difference, let us admit. When I am rude to Your Majesty, I commit an unpardonable offence.

SHE
Only between two honest and open philosophers there can never be any offence. Don't you think that's true?

HE
Now you say it, I do believe I do.

SHE
You know, they tell me when His Christian Majesty put you away in the prison at Vincennes, you told the authorities your thoughts all slipped out without you knowing it. In which case you simply couldn't see how you could possibly be blamed for them—

HE
I told them my thoughts seemed absurd even to me, so I was not surprised they startled them. I said if they desired I was happy to deny them, since to be capable of changing an

opinion was the first mark of an honest man. They resisted, of
course.

SHE
Why of course?

HE
Because they realized they needed my thoughts exactly
as much as they needed to put me in jail for them. That
showed me what a waste of time it was trying to avoid being
outrageous. And the same must be true for here and now,
surely, my dear lady. What would be the point of carting a
poor tired Denis a thousand leagues across Europe, simply for
him to be flattering or dull or meek?

SHE rises, walks across the room, looks at him over her shoulder.

SHE
You're certainly not that. You know, I've already decided
to tolerate you. For just as long as you remain tolerable. But
please remember this, sir. You can even try the patience of
a saint. And though I may be sublime, I'm certainly not a
saint—

HE
And I hope not. I can't think of anything I should hate more
than having to discuss philosophy with a saint.

SHE
Anyway that will do. What do you have for me tomorrow?

HE
A splendid paper. A really excellent paper—

END OF DAY TWELVE

DAY THIRTEEN

*It snows even harder. SERVANTS are running in with logs for
the stove. SHE stands beside it, reading a paper. HE comes in.*

SHE
This. This . . . writing. Do you dare even call it a paper?

HE
What, Your Highness?

SHE
Your memorandum for today. 'On the Morality of Princes'.
How could you, you—

HE
I spent all night writing it. I was quite pleased with it.

SHE
I spent all morning reading it. I was completely outraged by it.

HE
Oh, Your Most Imperial Majesty! My intention was simply to
be pleasing and persuasive.

SHE
No. Your intention was to insult, offend and humiliate me.
And not just me. Every noble monarch on this earth.

HE
I really hadn't noticed.

SHE
How dare you inform me monarchs lack every restraint that
law, honour and simple decency impose on every other
mortal?

HE
I thought that was the whole point of kingship.

SHE
Not at all. As you say, it's our duty to act as a constraint on
others. But we ourselves must act under the highest constraint
of all. The law of God.

HE
Exactly, Your Imperial Highness. And that's what I was trying
to explain. My complaints about kingship were never

addressed to you. They were sent to the divinities, to say how badly they performed their office.

SHE looks at him with the greatest suspicion.

SHE
You don't even believe in the divinities—

HE
Yes I do. Whenever it suits me.

SHE
Listen. 'Jove arises each morning and looks down through heaven's trapdoor. "Oh dear," he yawns, "plague in Asia. Warfare in Germany. Earthquake in Portugal. Disembowelling in Turkey, pox across France, knouting in Russia. Well, well." Then back he goes to sleep. And this is what we call the work of divine providence in the world.'

HE
Rather good, isn't it?

SHE
That teaches us, you inform me, that the gods are shifty, idle and useless. So letting monarchs rule by divine right means they rule without any proper constraint or control. That would be an argument for not having monarchs at all.

HE
Precisely.

SHE
How can you call that reason?

HE
I call it reason, justice, decent common sense.

COURTIERS murmur.

SHE
You may not say such things, Monsieur Didro. Neither in public nor in my private court.

HE

Madam, if you would be good enough to read just a little
further, you will find I also say that, despite the indifference
of the gods to human fate and fortune, no monarch can ever
be really free to do whatever he or she wants—

SHE

Because, you say, they are also constrained by the fear of being
assassinated by their own people, which makes them a little
less vile than they would be otherwise.

HE

Quite so.

SHE

Mr Philosopher, if you insist on coming to my court and
calling me a despot, you may find one of these days, when
your head is chopped off, you're right after all. Meanwhile
I take it, like all my people, you depend on my gentleness,
tolerance, and nobility—

HE looks extremely contrite.

HE

Once more I'm truly sorry, Your Highness.

SHE

Except you don't mean a word of it, do you?

HE

What, my contrition? I assure you it's very sincere. Or my
performance of it is, most certainly.

SHE

You don't truly mean to say I am a despot?

HE

Certainly not, madame, if you order me not to—

SHE

I require to know what you truly think.

HE
Then of course I think you are a despot. We none of us
expect you to be otherwise. Why do you suppose we adore
you so, incline the head, bow the knee? Why else do you
merit universal homage? You're our most honoured divinity.
Our great Athena. Our northern Minerva. Our enlightened
despot—

SHE
What I am, sir, is an imperial monarch with the world's largest
nation to master and sustain against my enemies.

HE
And I truly understand how hard it must be, to sit and discuss
metaphysics with me in the afternoons, when only that very
morning you have had to go and pillage and dismember
Poland.

SHE looks at him.

SHE
Oh, is that it? You are disputing with me over Poland? You
know Monsieur Voltaire entirely approves of it?

HE
Monsieur Voltaire never ceases to amaze me. I presume he's
decorated your rapings and pillage with the most enlightened
of reasons? Of course. After all, he has no other reasons.

SHE
Here's his letter, see. Go ahead, read it.

HE (*reads*)
'My object, from which I shall never budge, is tolerance. That
is the great religion I preach, and you are head of the great
church in which I'm simply a humble friar. Your zeal to
establish freedom of conscience in Poland is a great blessing
humanity will surely acknowledge . . .' Oh, my dear, good
lord—

SHE
Don't stop there . . . keep on—

HE (*reads on*)
'And not only is the great Empress sublimely tolerant. She equally wishes her neighbours to be tolerant. For the first time, supreme power and force will have been exercised to establish a true freedom for the human conscience.'

SHE
There then. And don't those words come from the greatest thinker in the world?

HE
If you tell me so.

SHE
Now, now, sir. Surely you wouldn't compare yourself with Monsieur Voltaire?

HE
No, Your Highness. Not on the matter of Poland, anyway.

SHE
I believe you're jealous. I'm sure you'd have called me tolerant first, if you'd had the wit to think of it.

HE laughs to himself.

SHE
What? Come along, tell me?

HE
Sometimes I amuse myself by imagining you on the throne of France. What an empire you'd make of it! And in what a brief period of time!

SHE
I should. I should be a Sun Queen.

HE
What a truly terrible empire. I've no doubt you'd make everyone eat potatoes—

SHE
Better than lettuce. Better than starving.

HE
We would rebel and send you to rule over England. They live on potatoes there. You know what they call you in England? 'The Philosophical Tyrant.'

SHE
So you *are* calling me a despot—

HE
Why not, if that's what you are?

SHE (*angry*)
Mr Philosopher, if you had an empire to run, and I only hope for your own sake you never suffer that fate, you'd do everything just as I have.

HE
I should not.

SHE
I am what I am, and I'm extremely good at it. You should have seen Russia before I ascended. A ruinous dump of a place. And look at it now.

HE
What a wonderful difference a sudden attack of the haemorrhoids can make.

Silence in the court. SHE rises.

SHE
Go away from here. Right now.

HE rises to leave.

SHE
Come back. And what would you do then? Free the serfs, I suppose? Enoble the merchants? Create a parliament of the ranks? Remove the power of the patriarchs? Give a franchise to the people? Take away the knout?

HE
Why not implement your own Great Instruction? Surely it would be your quickest way to Posterity.

SHE

There, sir. That shows us the difference between the philosophical tyrant and the tyrannical philosopher. It would be my way to Posterity, oh yes. But not in the way you mean. It would be my quickest route to disaster, the quick way to lose my head. You're a playwright. What do our finest plays, our noblest operas tell us? The dramas of Corneille, the operas of Handel, Rameau? The greatest tragedies befall those royal heroes who seek to do most good for their people. Coriolanus, Rienze, Godunov. Because your splendid common people turn out to be a mob—

HE

Your people love you greatly, you told me. What would you have to fear?

SHE laughs, and even the COURTIERS are amused.

SHE

Don't you know in Russia the serfs hate the kulaks, the kulaks hate the landowners, the landowners hate the provincial governors, the governors hate the nobles? The nobles hate the generals, the generals hate the bureaucrats. There are thirteen levels in the table of ranks, and each rank hates all the other twelve. The church hates the army. The army hates the navy. The infantry hates the cavalry. Every regiment hates every other. Everyone spies on everyone else, including me. And each person in all Russia hates the bitter fate that binds them in duty to their loving mother-tzarina—

HE

They have only to use their reason.

SHE

Their reason! I'm the only reason there is in this whole society. Otherwise every single person longs to rob or replace or slaughter every other. I'm all that exists between the hangman's knout and a river of blood.

HE

Yes. I can imagine it's so.

SHE

Thank you. So if, as you claim, you really are wise and just, you should appreciate the value of a despot. If you knew the nature of human beings and their gift for hatred, envy and wickedness, you'd know that a society without someone like me is far worse than this—

HE

Yes, Your Highness. I confess I didn't truly consider the difficulties of power, or the grandeur of which it's capable. Indeed I forgot for a moment why I adore you. Why I travelled all these leagues to see and worship you—

SHE

So now you confess I'm tolerant?

HE

You prove it with every kindness you show me.

SHE

Enlightened? Philosophical?

HE

An adornment to human thought.

SHE

Good, sir. Now, may I suggest you go and rewrite your paper, now we've discussed it carefully, and show me again tomorrow. Good day now, Mr Librarian . . .

END OF DAY THIRTEEN

DAY SIXTEEN

HE enters, in his black suit, looking tentative and uneasy. SHE is sitting on the sofa. SHE looks at him, smiles. A large box of golden trinkets is beside her.

SHE

Ah, there you are, my good friend. Come over here. Look, what do you see? Presents . . .

HE looks into the box. It appears to be full of watches.

HE
What, you mean . . . for me, Your Majesty?

SHE
Yes, sir. You have been late for these meetings far too often, my dear philosopher. That's for you.

SHE reaches into the box and draws out a very beautiful gold pocket watch on a chain. HE looks at it. HE looks at her. HE's touched.

HE
Dear lady. Are you really sure?

SHE
Of course. You're pleased?

HE
How could I be more so? A golden hunter, Your Majesty. A watch for the pocket. To hang from a golden chain on my leaden chest. And with your own portrait, always there on the face . . .

SHE
So you accept it?

HE swings the watch against his chest.

HE
Of course. No gift could give me greater pleasure. After all, what more displays the spirit of our age, the cunning intricacy of our universe, than a watch. With this one small ticking machine we can see our place and way in the world. We see the world's not a seamless entity, but a mysterious clockwork motion that spins us in space and time—

SHE
You do consider God to be the great watchmaker then?

HE
No, I consider man to be the great watchmaker. What supreme intelligence! With what cunning we comprehend

303

how time spins in the cosmos, how space twists in time. What is the universe compared with our modellings of it. Where was it made?

SHE
This little watch? Switzerland, sir. Geneva.

HE
The Swiss, a people of great craft and independence. Some say they make the best watches in the world—

SHE
Or very near Geneva. These watches were sent from Ferney by my dear Voltaire. You know he's set up a colony of craftsmen?

HE
I heard. Eighty watchmakers all tick-tocking away in his workshops. Such a thoughtful gift.

SHE
Not exactly a gift. He sent me a crate of five hundred of them.

HE
Five hundred? Soon Russia will have more time than it knows what to do with.

SHE
I praised his devotion to craft and enterprise. In return I got this large crate of watches. And a bill for fifty thousand pounds.

HE
I'd heard Swiss time often comes expensive. Permit me to observe that with what he's charged you for five hundred watches you never asked for you could have built a battleship. Or bought half a dozen Rubens from the next impoverished English milord.

SHE
I sometimes think you're growing a little jealous of our great Monsieur Voltaire.

HE

Not at all. So what does he advise you to do with these knick-knacks he's sent you? Apart from honouring your darling Denis, of course?

SHE

He thinks they'd make excellent gifts for distinguished foreign visitors. And he tells me I could easily sell them for twice the price he's charging me—

HE

If you take his other advice and invade Turkey, you could sell his watches to the Turks.

SHE

I've heard he's already doing that himself. I hope he's charging them a good deal more than he is me.

HE

Indeed, it would be only fair. Still, now when your two armies go into battle, they should both arrive at more or less the same hour of day. But I'm sure the money's well spent—

SHE

Of course it's well spent. I owe a great deal to Monsieur Voltaire. When many in Europe were calling me an assassin, he established my reputation with the world.

HE

Not alone, of course.

SHE

I admit it. There was yourself, and others too—

HE

And this is why I'm here then, is it, Your Highness? To establish your reputation with the world?

SHE

Like anyone else, I merely wish to be understood by everyone. And how better to do it than have some wise men understand me?

HE
Wise men who are foolish enough to believe whatever you choose to tell them? Who dismiss invasion as a trifle, hanging as an incident, and write eulogies like hacks?

SHE looks at him.

SHE
Now I know you are jealous, sir.

HE
Do you? Jealous of whom, then?

SHE
Of Monsieur Voltaire. Because he loves me to distraction, and doesn't care who knows it. Because your mind's so dull and your passions so thin you wouldn't even know how to come near to him. Because every word of praise that comes from him means more to me than ten words of yours. Because his generosity and kindness are so much freer and franker than yours—

HE looks at her in surprise.

HE
You're wrong. I'm not jealous of Voltaire.

SHE
Well, he's certainly jealous of you.

HE
Is he really? The great Voltaire jealous of me?

SHE
Of course. He's at Ferney, you're in my chamber. You're younger than he is. More amusing.

HE
How would you know all this?

SHE takes out a letter from her bosom.

SHE
Here is his letter, today. Listen. 'I hear with regret that your

Diderot fell ill at the Dutch frontier. But I reassure myself he must now be at your feet, and you will know you have more than one French devotee. If there are some who will always vote for Mustapha the Turk, I venture to say there are many more who worship only Saint Catherine. Indeed our small church is becoming quite universal . . .' But this is just flattery—

HE
Yes. Go on.

SHE
'I imagine you daily, conquering the new sultan. Yet still, burdened with the responsibility of war against a vast empire, and ruling your own vaster empire . . . seeing everything, doing everything . . . somehow you find time to converse with Diderot, as if you had nothing else in the world to do.'

HE
What style the man has. How very wonderfully put.

SHE
Indeed. 'I long to converse with him myself,' he says, 'merely so I can learn all I can of Your Glorious Majesty. In fact majesty is hardly the word I mean. I would rather say "Your Glorious Superiority", which lifts you above all thinking beings.' Excuse me, then more and more flattery. But I think you see how delightfully he writes to me.

HE reaches a hand out for the letter. SHE smiles, moves away from him.

HE
But do go on, Your Glorious Superiority. What else does the wise man have to say about me? Anything?

SHE
Oh, yes. 'I ask you, intercede with Diderot for me. Surely he could make a small detour of fifty *versts* and prolong my bitter existence by coming here to tell me all he has seen and heard

in Sankt Peterburg? Or, if he will not attend me here on the shores of Lake Geneva, I only beg I might come and be buried near you, on the shores of your own Lake Ladoga. As you know, I love you to folly, yet I fear I'm in disgrace in your court. Your Majesty has abandoned me, for Diderot, Grimm, some other favourite. This would be understandable if Your Highness were a French coquette. But can a great empress be so fickle? Truly I shall never love another empress as long as I live . . .'

HE
Eighty and sick with jealousy. It's wonderful.

SHE
So if one day you leave me, you will go and visit him? And tell him that even though his Catou thinks so well of you, it doesn't mean I love him any less?

HE
Unfortunately Geneva is nowhere near Paris.

SHE
I think now he's an old man he fears you're taking his place.

HE
Yes, Your Majesty? And exactly what place is that?

SHE
I have no idea what he thinks about me, though he's known for a lusty man. But I shall write at once and say he's foolish to feel jealous, since thus far you've not given him even the slightest occasion—

HE
And assure him that as long as I'm in your court I shall strive to do everything he would desire to do himself, if only he could be here.

SHE
But you do admire Monsieur Voltaire?

HE

Admire him, I adore him. The greatest man in the world. He
has genius, merit, nobility, urbanity, sexual charm—

SHE

Then what could make him so jealous, I wonder?

HE

My dear lady, sometimes I imagine the entire world must be
envious of me. Here I enjoy your company, three hours a day.
I think your thoughts with you, dream your dreams with
you—

SHE

You're like Voltaire, monsieur, you're flattering me. It's all
I get, flattery. Never an honest opinion, a proper judgement,
a truthful feeling—

HE

Naturally everyone flatters the woman who is Russia, the most
important woman in the world. They'll pretend to anything.
Say her witches are virgins, her hags are princesses, even her
cabbages are fit to eat—

SHE

They are fit to eat.

HE

Where I, my lady, am an honest man and speak only the sober
truth. Why shouldn't I? I sit with you every day, I hear the
wisdom of your thoughts, the sharpness of your wit. I take in
the seriousness of your countenance, the purity of your soul.
I sit across the table looking at your face. I gently touch your
hand—

SHE

It happens to be my leg, sir. So you refuse to flatter me?

HE

I do indeed.

SHE

Then I hope you like the watch I gave you. Even though it came from Monsieur Voltaire.

HE

I like it the better, knowing that what once belonged to Voltaire now belongs to me.

SHE

And what does the watch say, sir? Doesn't it tell you it's time to go?

HE

It speaks Swiss, dear lady, well-known as an obscure language. I think it advises me to stay—

SHE

No, my dear friend, because I have the Swedish ambassador arriving. But bring it with you in the future and we shall listen to it again. You will send me another paper? Something I can read in my bed tonight?

HE

Indeed, dear lady.

HE rises, kisses her hand.

END OF DAY SIXTEEN

TWENTY-FIVE (NOW)

GALINA'S TALE

'*Mes amis*, thank you for listening to me while we made our little tour. But I know you are not like these other people, you have not come to be tourists. I know you are proper pilgrims, come all the way across the Baltic Sea to follow in the path of our great philosopher, the one in Russia we call Dionysius Didro. I understand some of you are interested in one thing and some another; I am sure the Hermitage can please all of you. When Bo telephoned me from his office and asked my help to arrange his little journey, I realized your tour would really have to start just here, and for an excellent reason. Where you are standing now, as you know, is in the Small Hermitage, just one little part of the great Winter Palace. And you are here because a long time ago, in the winter of 1773, when these buildings were new and most of them did not exist yet, our dear Philosopher used to come by these halls and passages to share his ideas with the grand tzarina in the private apartments down the corridor.

'Can you imagine it? Because, please remember, nothing you see is quite as it was then, and yet Didro is everywhere. At that time this was a private palace, the palace of a great tzarina, made open to the people only when a tzar or a tzarina said so. Once these rooms went from public to private, from state to household, and the better the court knew or respected you the deeper you went. Today anyone can go anywhere, without bother, unless you touch the objects and set off the alarms. Once everything in the building was arranged quite differently, as the palace of a tzarina, her workplace and her home. Then one winter night in 1837, when one of our worst tzars, Nicholas First, was in the royal box

311

at the opera, a great fire started in the buildings, and they burned for three days. Everything inside had to be carried out there, into the snows of Palace Square. The windows blew out, the chandeliers fell, but most of the objects were saved at a cost in human lives. After this, the Hermitage was rebuilt, the plan was altered, many things were changed. Again after 1917, when the tzars had been assassinated, the rooms were taken over by the people and the commissars, and the collections moved. Nothing is the same, yet perhaps nothing at all we see would be here at all, if there hadn't been that old friendship between the Empress and the Philosopher. *Da?*

'So, *mes amis*, that is one reason why I brought you here and ask you to look around. But there is another. As I told you already on the bus, I am a librarian. If you have a mind, a curiosity, an imagination, a librarian is a good thing to be. But I started work when I was a young girl and it was the very end of the war. In Leningrad this was, if you remember, a terrible time. The Germans had been driven away at last, but the city was left with many ruins. The Germans are called civilized but they were also barbarians. They occupied the Summer Palace, Tzarskoye Selo, and stripped it of almost everything, signing their names in the ruins so we could hate them. Whatever they couldn't take as plunder they were happy to burn or flatten or destroy. Every night they bombed the city with their guns: the Winter Palace, the Tauride, the Duma, all the factories and apartments. If they couldn't take Leningrad they would just eliminate it. So when it was all over, we were like Dostoyevsky's underground men. We lived under the floorboards, in the cellars, starving and struggling to keep alive.

'Even so, we tried to re-create the city as it had been, and bring its culture back to life again. Because Leningrad was always Russia's culture city, the writers' city, the place they wrote of most often and knew best. Pushkin and Gogol, Dostoyevsky and Tolstoy. Then Bely and Mandelshtam, Akhmatova and Brodsky, Bitov, they all wrote of Petersburg-Leningrad. This doesn't mean they always loved the city. Often it depressed them, defeated them, sent them to despair. It persecuted them, starved them, exiled them, left them in pain with no money and no hope. So it was the city with the darkest fears, the oldest dreams, the biggest terrors, the strangest illusions – a place of fictions and deceptions, where nothing seemed exactly real and everything was shaped by stories, books, illusions and dreams.

'Even in the bad times, I was like all Russian children, I was taught to love Pushkin and to remember the books. Maybe it mattered to me more than ever, because in that time there was nowhere to go but disappear into the books. You remember what the Underground Man of Fyodor Dostoyevsky tells us? "It's better in books, that's where life makes more sense." For me it was better in books, so I read very many. Not just Russian books, from my mother I spoke other languages, French and German. When they began to put back the city and try to bring it to life again, to put back the things there before, I went to work in the public library. And because my French was so good I was asked to look after the special collection, the famous library of the Enlightenment, the collection of Voltaire-Didro, which I think is why you are here.'

'Some of us,' says Bo. 'But go on, Galina, it's fascinating . . .'

'Well, maybe you can remember just how those libraries came here to Russia? As you can see from this place, Catherine just acquired everything she could think of that would make her Russia seem powerful or civilized, part of the new world of Europe. What she wanted she asked for, and what she asked for she got. But from the moment they crowned her in the Kremlin, she knew what she would like most, to be a philosophical empress. She called for support from the philosophes, *les lumières*, and told them Russia would now become the land of freedom, where they could hold on to any ideas they liked. They could bring their philosophical speculations. The censor would not interfere, the church would not be allowed to oppress them. Like everyone in Europe, she had come to love the great Voltaire. She corresponded with him her whole life, sending the first letter within a month of her crowning. She wrote it with a pseudonym, pretending it came from one of her courtiers who wished him to know how the Empress admired him so. At first Voltaire didn't trust her, but she never stopped. She sent him admiring letters, great delegations, wonderful gifts. She knew some of his works were banned in France and he lived as an exile, so she offered to print everything in Russia.'

'Diderot's *Encyclopedia* too,' says Bo.

'The Empress had many charms. After a time Voltaire was quite seduced. Soon he was writing her admiring letters and poems, some of them here on display, I will show you. They never met; I think she made sure of that. She knew the illusion was better than the reality. I think he would like to come, but she warned him he might be unhappy. In the end he offered to come after he was dead, a perfect arrangement: the grave of the world's greatest philosopher here at the court of the world's greatest empress. "I would rather end my days in a greater empire," he had written in a letter which she kept very carefully. Voltaire died, you know, in May 1778. So she ordered a court mourning, and distributed hundreds of copies of his works. By this time Melchior Grimm was her agent all over Europe, and she told him to go to Ferney and buy up the library, and all the letters he could acquire.

'At this time she had bought already the library of Didro, but he was alive and allowed to keep it in his apartment. Voltaire's library was bigger; it was three times bigger. He could afford everything; he was a rich man, while Didro was really most of his life a poor hack. Voltaire lived like a king in his own palace near Geneva, Didro had a small apartment in Paris. Voltaire had published hundreds of books, more than almost anyone ever; Didro preferred talking, and could never remember where all his papers and writings were. Grimm talked to Madame Denis, who was Voltaire's niece and also his mistress, and a very greedy woman. He bought the library, at a very high price − 135,000 livres, maybe ten times what was paid for Didro's. He tried to buy the papers, but most of them had already been sold to the publisher Panckoucke, who had had the idea that he would purchase all the great philosophical papers − Rousseau's in Neuchâtel, Buffon's − and publish them in Paris. But in the end he gave so much money to all the writers' widows and nieces he had to sell Voltaire's papers on to someone else, Beaumarchais.'

'Of Figaro?' asks Birgitta Lindhorst.

'*Da*, that's right. But Grimm was also told to get hold of something else; he was supposed to buy Voltaire's body too. Then she meant to build a complete copy of Ferney, here at Tzarskoye Selo, and place Voltaire's own tomb in the middle of the grounds.

Unfortunately for Catherine, at the very end of his life Voltaire decided to make a visit to Paris, where he had his famous apotheosis at the theatre, when all Paris hailed him as a great man. He died just after, and his body had to be smuggled upright out of Paris in a carriage at night, because the church wanted to throw him into the lime-pits as a wicked atheist. In the end, maybe you remember, he was buried outside Paris in a disused chapel, and later brought back to the Pantheon. So Voltaire never came here, and the new Ferney was never built. But you can see it if you like to; the plans are all here, in the Hermitage.

'But something *was* built, in these corridors here, near where we are, in a gallery overlooking the waters of the Neva. Catherine made a beautiful library. Voltaire's secretary came all the way from Ferney, bringing his books, and they were arranged in the same order as they had been in his own house. In an alcove at one end of the library, Catherine placed a seated statue of Voltaire, the famous one that had been commissioned from Houdon. Before the library was built, she had kept it here in the Hermitage next to the Apollo Belvedere. She said it was important that Voltaire looked out only on equals. At the other end of the library, there was another statue, done by Marie-Anne Collot. She was Falconet's assistant, and she married his son. She finished off the face of the bronze horseman, and many people thought she was the better sculptor. The other bust was Didro, who died six years after. So his books too came, his papers also, and they went into the same library. So right here, overlooking the Neva, was created the library of Enlightenment, the *libraire des lumières.*'

'And now are we going to see it?' asks Sven Sonnenberg, who is tightly holding Agnes Falkman's hand.

'Ah no, *mon ami*, not quite. Because nothing in this world is that simple. Nothing is where you think it is, and if it was once it has often gone. Times change, and everything happens. All that is solid melts into air. Only a little time after the library was finished the world turned upside down. The Revolution and Terror came to France. By now Catherine was getting old and frightened. She felt sure the revolution would spread to Russia. It didn't, of course, not then, it would take more than another century. But now she thought the philosophers were dangerous. She told Grimm it was necessary to identify the culprits who had caused this evil. She banned French clothes, French books, and sent all the French who supported the Revolution home from Russia. And she turned against Voltaire. When his body was taken from the chapel at Sellières, and delivered by Beaumarchais in a great parade to the Pantheon, she locked up the library. She sent the Houdon statue up to the attics and forbade anyone to look at it again. And not too long after this she died herself, here on her privy at the Hermitage—'

'But the library—' says Anders Manders.

'What happened to it? Well, in Tzarist times, it was nearly always the rule a good tzar was followed by a very bad one. Catherine was succeeded by her son, the Archduke Paul, who made such a bad tzar he was murdered four years after by his own courtiers. Paul hated his mother and the philosophes. What was surprising was he didn't destroy the whole library. But when his son Alexander succeeded, he began as a great reformer, and opened up the library and restored the Voltaire statue. That was until the armies of Napoleon invaded Russia. Now the French were Russia's enemy, so the library was closed once more. Alexander was succeeded by his brother, Tzar Nicholas, not a good tzar. He began by firing on the Decembrists, and he ran a reign of terror. It was bad for all the writers. Pushkin was driven into exile, Dostoyevsky was put in front of a firing squad at the Peter and Paul Fortress, and pardoned at the last minute. Nicholas especially hated Voltaire. Maybe you remember what he said when he saw the Houdon statue? "Destroy that grinning old monkey."'

'Was it destroyed?' asks Agnes Falkman.

'*Non, non, ma cherie*. It was just at the very beginning of its great adventures. Someone hid it, in the library, the one place Nicholas never went. Then came the fire, and everything was moved again. The next tzar, Alexander the Second, the liberator of Finland, the man who freed the serfs, decided to use the library for other things, because the collection of paintings and *objets* was now so big. He was the one who decided the library should move. It would have to go to the fine Petersburg Public Library, the place where I work now, the Saltykov-Shchedrin. He decided the Philosopher would have to go too, so they put the statue on runners and off he rode, right down the Nevsky Prospekt. Now maybe you remember what happened to Alexander? He was assassinated, by some anarchists who worked from a little cake shop, also on the Nevsky Prospekt. His successor was another Alexander, and he acquired another great library, the library of Didro's good friend, Dmitry Golitsyn, who had been ambassador in Paris and the Hague. He thought it was best if those books too went to the Saltykov-Shchedrin. But he asked one present in return. He wanted the statue of Voltaire. Out into Nevsky Prospekt the philosopher went again. Off he rolled on his runners, all the way to the Hermitage.

'There he stayed for a long while, and then it was 1917. The Tzar had created the Provisional Government and was trying to lead his own armies, the Germans were advancing on the city. It was like the age of Napoleon all over again, and the government decided it must once more protect the Hermitage treasures. In his marble armchair the philosopher set off once more, this time even further along Nevsky Prospekt to the Moscow railway station. He took the train to Moscow and spent the rest of the war in the Kremlin. By the time he returned to the Hermitage, everything was different. This building had been taken, now it belonged to the people, and the city was no longer Petersburg, or Petrograd, it was Leningrad. In 1941 the Germans were back again. Naturally Voltaire realized he had better go to the station yet again. He sat opposite Rastrelli's famous waxwork of Peter the Great in the very last train to leave Leningrad before the siege started. If you wonder where he spent the war, it was in Sverdlovsk, which used to be Yekaterinburg, and which is where the Tzar and his family were murdered. By the way, a famous party official came from there later on; his name was Boris Yeltsin.'

'So where is the statue now?' asks Sven Sonnenberg, looking a little confused.

'It's here, you can see it if you like. Except I thought you really came here for Didro.'

'Well, that is perfectly true,' says Bo.

'And of course his story was not the same at all. Voltaire and Didro were very different people. Voltaire was sharp and cunning, always guarding his fame, protecting his ideas, thinking about his editions. Didro was kind, and open, a noisy man. He liked to talk first and write after. What he wrote he changed, so in the end he had no idea which version of his writing was correct, or the one he liked best. Didro outlived the others. He survived Voltaire by six years, Rousseau by the same, and they were six very important years. He lived almost to the end of the age of reason. When his life was near the end, he recalled his promise to the Tzarina. He hired three copyists, and asked them to copy out all his papers, so there would be copies in France and others in Russia. The only problem was there were so many drafts the copyists found them-selves copying different versions of the same book.'

'How very confusing,' says Lars Person.

'It was just the beginning of many more confusions. When she heard her friend Didro was dying, Catherine arranged for him to move to a more comfortable apartment. And she sent Grimm to make sure she got not only his books but his papers. "Take care nothing goes astray," she said. "Not even the least scrap." He died in the summer of 1784. The next year his daughter, Madame de Vandeul, sent his library to the Hermitage. With it came all his papers, in thirty-two volumes and packets. The Tzarina had them put under triple key, because they revealed many details of his interesting relationship with her—'

'They were lovers?' asks Birgitta Lindhorst.

'Were they? Do you know? But there were also the other copies. One set was kept by Melchior Grimm. Some more copies went to the young philosopher Naigeon, who later published them. The daughter kept the originals for herself. And everyone assumed the moment had come for his papers to be put in order, his works sorted, and everything published, given to Posterity, exactly as he wished. Except now came the Storming of the Bastille, then the Revolution, then the Terror. Reason had turned into revolution, light had turned into torches. So was Didro a revolutionary spirit or not? Was he a founder of the new order, or its enemy? Didro was such a clever butterfly no one was sure, and they never can be. Of course, he said, he supported the American Revolution, and he spoke of wanting to see the last king strangled with the guts of the last priest. But it was obvious he didn't believe in terror and violence, he believed in sense and reason.

'So some of his works were released, but many others were hidden. The daughter stored most of the originals away and they weren't found again for a hundred years. By then they had already started to rot. Of course there were still the copies. The ones that belonged to Grimm, for instance. But in the revolution Grimm was in great trouble too. He'd been the friend of every king, prince and tyrant right across Europe. He'd arranged to marry most of them, so he was the inventor of all the dynasties now in trouble. He took the messages of Catherine the Great to the hands of Marie Antoinette. No wonder he thought it was time to pack up his things and take the coach off to Gotha in Germany, taking with him all the letters he'd had from Catherine – her letters to the Grimmalians, she called them. We know he took some of Didro's papers too, because some appeared in Gotha. But which? What about *Rameau's Nephew*, for instance?'

'Oh, your book,' says Birgitta Lindhorst, turning to me.

'What we know is that many papers were left behind in Paris. Then Grimm's fine apartment was raided by the Jacobins, and the precious things were taken. His papers were given away to various people who just asked for them. Some were by Didro. Some disappeared and have never been found, some were copied or published. *Et voilà, mon pauvre* Didro. His papers were scattered everywhere, all over Europe, in a time of trouble and chaos. It looked as though Posterity would never hear of him again. But then strange things started to happen. In Jacobin Paris, various manuscripts appeared in print, mostly from Naigeon. But some were probably the papers taken from Grimm, and others were false copies or forgeries not by Didro at all. Then other editions and texts appeared, in London, in Leipzig, in Geneva. Grimm published some things from Gotha. Then in 1807 he died too, and his papers were scattered further.

'So what about the Hermitage set of papers? Well, as I told you, because of the Revolution, everything here now had to be locked up and shut away. And here too strange things began to happen. Maybe you know how it is in libraries. People enter and exit. Scholars are not always honest people. Even with closed doors and triple-locked cabinets, soldiers in the corridors, guards at the gates, things disappear. What is there one day is not there another. The rooms were entered, books and papers removed. One of the chief rogues was the rector of Petersburg university, who took away a good many manuscripts, including *D'Alembert's Dream*, and sold them abroad for a profit.

'Soon it was Didro here, Didro there, Didro everywhere. All over Europe, in a number of languages, works under his name began to appear that no one had even heard of before. In Weimar, Schiller translated some of *Jacques the Fatalist*, and somehow got hold of a manuscript of *Rameau's Nephew*. He gave it to Goethe, who translated it into German and published an edition of it in Liepzig. A French translation was made from this, and falsely described as the original edition. But how did Schiller get hold of the book? We can't really be sure, because after Goethe had finished translating it, the manuscript disappeared. He might have got it from Grimm, of course, or maybe from Petersburg. Many people thought he had an original manuscript stolen from the Hermitage. Later another original manuscript was found, this time in Paris. You can find it in the Morgan library in New York.

'So, right through the nineteenth century, new works by Didro kept appearing. So did new versions of the works that were published already. Nobody knew which were the true originals or the false copies, no one seemed sure where they came from or how they got there. No one was quite sure if a work was complete, or this version more authentic than that one. New letters kept emerging, it always happens, and the notes he made for the Tzarina. Still these things keep on appearing. We might find a whole new book any day. And because they came out in so many ways in so many countries at so many different times in history, there could never be any one Didro. He was a writer with many faces – not only a thinker and a philosopher, but a trickster, a tease, a very modern writer. He was no longer just a maker of fat encyclopedias. He was a dreamer, a fantasist, a liar, a maker of the strangest stories.

'This was not all. Here in Petersburg we created even more confusion. When the library was moved from the Hermitage in the middle of the last century, the papers went also. Because Didro was here and talked to the Tzarina, some of his writings belonged in the state papers, and went to Moscow. Others were moved about and confused, and got into other collections. During the Bolshevik Revolution and the Stalin years, many treasures were stolen from all the old imperial buildings and sold here and there. And of course there was much more confusion in the time of the Nazi siege, when the shells fell every night over Nevsky Prospekt.

'So, of course, when I first started work in the library, after 1946, everything I found was in chaos. The great collections, the libraries of Voltaire, Didro, Golitsyn, where were they? Only when I started to search through the confusion of the library, go to the cellars and attics, did I start to find the books again. Voltaire's books from Ferney, which were bound in morocco and had his insignia. Books with handwriting by Didro inside. Papers of this, papers of that . . . more and more, gathered from here and there, locked drawers or closed cupboards. So I hope now you can understand me – Galina. You can see the work of my life, to make again the Library of the Enlightenment, to find what it was and restore it. That is what I do, and I am still looking. Nothing is done yet—'

'Really, you keep on finding new papers?' I ask, excited and entranced.

'Will we be able to see?'

'Perhaps, sometime, tomorrow if you like, or another day,' says Galina, looking far from enthusiastic.

'And which of them do you really prefer?' asks Agnes Falkman. 'Voltaire or Diderot?'

'Prefer, *mon ami*? If only we didn't have to prefer. They were two great writers, two very amusing men. They both loved reason, they both admired the new Mother Russia. They each loved the other – sometimes. They each loved the Tzarina. Both of them were as jealous as tigers. If one of them wrote an ode to her, the other had to write a lyric. If one advised her to grow cabbages, the other said please plant beans. Didro or Voltaire, Voltaire or Didro, I truly do not know. But I can tell you this. Voltaire is always French, as the French like to see themselves: clarity, wit and reason. Didro is not a French writer, he is British and German and Russian too. In Paris they call him Denis Diderot; here we have our own name for him – Dionysius Didro. He made the journey to Russia, he learned the mystery of our city. He looked in its mirror, he invented the double. He influenced Pushkin, who influenced Gogol, who influenced everyone. In him we can find all our other writers. Yes, *monsieur*, it's just like those dolls you carry.'

Galina is pointing at me. I look again at my little stack of dolls.

Meantime, like any tourists with any guide in any museum, a fair number of our pilgrims are growing openly bored.

'You have talked too long, can't we do something?' demands Birgitta Lindhorst, imperially. 'Why don't you show us the statue of Voltaire?'

'Your guide and servant,' says Galina. 'Follow me please. I hold up my umbrella. *Pardon, pardon. Excusez-moi.*'

And off, at formidable speed, she takes us through the surging mass of tourists, through the great halls and marble galleries of the Hermitage – where, as they'll tell you, you can find something of everything from every single part of the globe.

TWENTY-SIX (THEN)

OUR MAN CAN BE SEEN coming to court almost every day now. And, thanks to his black philosophical suit and his sharp distinctive stride, he seems to have grown familiar to everyone in the city. The beggars, street vendors, hussars all know him: he's the Empress's Philosopher, commonplace as the Empress's English greyhounds, who also take long dawdling walks down the streets. How much time has passed now? Five weeks at the very least. Five weeks since he got here, settled into his chill room at the Narishkin Palace, began the way of life that's now become his one and only way of life. Over that time, cold clear freezing autumn has switched to black murderous winter, a kind of winter that no man from the south of Europe, however great his perception, could ever imagine in advance. Ice in huge blocks, massive brutal lumps, rattles and bangs its way down the ever more savage Neva: shattering pilings, crashing into brand-new embankments. Parts of the river and all the canals of the city are already frozen completely. Traders shout and bargain at wooden stalls on the ice. Sausage-makers function, fires burn, toboggans and sleighs slither on the crust over deep water. The Fontanka and the Moyka, the two city canals he bridges every day, are black-frozen hard as stone.

His curiosity with what lies round him grows and grows – though it's not yet taken him out of the city into larger Russia beyond. Beyond the Hermitage lies Big Peter's Summer Garden, where it has become his habit to walk. Ever since he came, he's gone most days to think a thought or two. Here, as everywhere, ice and snow now hold sway. The garden is made of statues, long white promenades standing each side of the pathways, apart and solitary, yet all seeming to address each other. Now they've been boxed in for their own protection. His favourite, the Cupid and

Psyche (love caught in its perfect moment as it becomes revelation, illumination), has gone behind a prison of wooden shutters, to save naked innocence from the cold. Queen Christina of Sweden – a lady with a wicked smile, whose effigy interests him, she who once exchanged thoughts on the passions with René Descartes – has been caged in her own box. In the summer gardens there's only deep winter. No one there to talk to, nothing at all to say.

In Sankt Peterburg city he's wandered further and further: walking out over Neva ice to the far embankment, to inspect the curiosities of the twelve Academies or the fascinations of the Great Academical Globe, which enfolds him inside, shows the universe he belongs to in its cosmic strangeness. Somewhere out there, beyond the steppes he has not seen, the fog, ice-cap, permafrost, the ever wintering marshes, there's another and different world; we call it Europe. It's a light-dark place, of wars and hostile religions, plagues and pestilences, nobles and suffering peasants, minds and bodies, arts and music, misery and delight. It's a bright-lit theatre of comedy and tragedy, pleasure and disaster, where a single life plays all the different roles. Now it's behind him. Since the fog swirled in forever, snow started falling every single day, the long black nights took over, it's impossible to imagine anything other than Sankt Peterburg. The dream city, the place he once devised on his Parisian pillow, has grown big and true. It's so real it enfolds him entirely. It's everything he first imagined, yes, but a thousand times more. No doubt about it, it's an enormous fantasy of a city – presenting mind and spirit, consciousness and senses with a form of society that never before existed, and perhaps even now is only in its first stage of taking real shape.

In fact it's just like those weird imaginary cities that fill the devisings of the authors he loves best. Raging Doctor Swift; witty mocking Doctor Sterne; needling canine-toothed Voltaire, writers who for the service of the age invent the most grotesque worlds they can in order to shame and reform the drab and real one. Yet here he is in the middle of just those things: in a city, a capital, a court that might have served the imagination of any of them: been devised as a fresh port of destination for Lemuel Gulliver, that misanthropic unfortunate ship's surgeon, or a mad place of resort for the wandering simpleton Candide. He's been reading their adventures again, with a new sense of truth, while he lies each night in the darkened Narishkin Palace, the watchmen shout their way along the hemp-lit city streets, the guardsmen in the barracks shout drunkenly and sound alarms on their drums, the black nights grow longer and start to occupy the territory of the days.

By now he's spent over forty nights by the Neva. Yet nothing has grown any more familiar, any less confusing, unreal, absurd. If the city still seems strange, so do its people. He's in a world built and populated by fellow-Europeans – people who speak the languages he knows, wear the same kinds of topcoats and stockings, practise the same civilities. Here are watchmakers and carriage-builders, astronomers and garden designers, monks and English vicars, architects and gunsmiths, barber-surgeons and ship-masters, honest citizens of the world. There are men in fine wigs and powder, women in silks and beauty spots, speaking German, speaking French. They stroll the great *prospekts*, frequent the coffee houses, attend the theatre, opera, ballet. They draw fashion from Paris, china from Dresden, silk from Venice, spice from Samarkand. Every night is an entertainment: a festivity by Gluck, a solemn tragic opera by Rameau, a play by Racine: maybe even a piece by the brilliant hero of the age, his own Monsieur Voltaire.

This in a city that has raised up street after street of the grandest Viennese or Venetian buildings, where society goes out nightly to its treats and celebrations in the very best glitter and gold, driven through the streets by frogged-coated coachmen in castellated carriages or gilded sleds. Half of its people call themselves counts, princes, generals, chancellors or chamberlains, and many do have a place in the very long tables of ranks. There are Russian gentlefolk who've spent half their lives in Paris, Germans who've spent all their lives in Moscow; rich merchants, London fops, Vauxhall courtesans, inventors and honest artisans of every kind. Yet, when a card is played or a bet is wagered, the winner's prize often comes not in the shape of a bag of gold but a thousand human (or perhaps sub-human) souls. And for all the silks and satins, airs and graces, there are bare-knuckle fights even within the Hermitage. Now and then, even at court itself, a duel is fought, a throat is slit, an eye gouged out, a captain of guard knouted and taken off to the Peter and Paul.

Perhaps it's the same in the great courts all the world over (the Sublime Porte, the Peacock Throne); he wouldn't really know. But the streets of the town are stranger yet. Here's a new European city in the building, as Paris is building, Dresden and Berlin, London and Vienna. Everywhere there's something new. The boulevards, squares, *prospekts* are carefully planned and ruled, the mansions regulated, the gardens ordered. The great street lamps burning their stinging hemp oil strangely illuminate the city every night. Great flares on the embankments guide the ships going in and out, the streets are swept every day; prostitutes do it by way of punishment. The great arcades are full of the richest goods and pleasures; everywhere a new academy, a fresh institute for noble girls, another convent seems to open. On Nevsky Prospekt, the greatest and most obsequious shopkeepers of the world have begun to trade, selling shining new English carriages, glistening Dutch clocks, furniture with new woods from the Americas, Japanese porcelains, floating dresses from Tashkent and Muckden.

And yet, and yet . . . this too seems a mask, an illusion, disguising something entirely different. Behind every symbol of elegance there's a traffic in depravity. Bodies are sold cheaply for any purpose: serfdom, labour, sea-faring, sex. For all who stroll or strut, swagger or march, there are the thousands who tout and cringe, beg and grovel. For every grand palace housing this prince there are a thousand wooden apartment sheds, packed with screaming, teeming, fighting humanity: hovels that only the winter freeze prevents tumbling straight into the stewed waters of the canals. Winter has deepened suddenly. Stray cats shudder in their fur as they prowl through sodden streets. A smell of stale brine, like frozen bear-piss, comes unremittingly off the Neva. Snow-flakes fall always – sometimes like a constant thin powder that seems to have the power of penetrating human skin, sometimes like a spilled cartload of balled wool that brings movement to a halt. Behind the arcades, each alley and entry is filled with unspeakable things: drunken human bundles, noisily copulating twosomes, maimed beggars, soliciting tots, decaying corpses. As shopkeepers compete for custom, here they compete for sins. In a world where existence itself is criminal, criminality is a serious form of existence.

Most big booming cities are much the same, he knows. The great capital of civilization he's come from himself is capable of more than its fair share of crimes, horrors, executions. Paris and London famously stink with fetid open sewers. Venice has piss in every canal, excrement in every doorway, Lisbon shivers to its earthquakes as foundations tremble and its buildings topple to the ground. Moscow rots with disease and disorder, its buildings constantly burn or collapse. But Sankt Peterburg is a new city, a new idea. Its people claim to be from everywhere, and see the world afresh. Yet who are the true natives, the Russian people: the ones who are not émigré, Huguenot, Swiss, Prussian? Some claim they all descend from the noble Vikings, others say the Slavs. Yet half are Tartar, Cossack, oriental, speak a strange repertory of languages, write, when they are able to, an alphabet that has wandered up from a Mediterranean monastery, and which he's already begun to replan and improve. If some are freemen of Europe, hunting an opportunity, many are the slaves off the steppes, brought here by imperial fiat or obligation, herded in off the Siberian wastes. Even nobles and gentlefolk are often brute souls, brought off distant estates by draconian law to serve at court or in the army, before disappearing into war, drunkenness, exile, servitude.

The strangeness reaches the inner sanctums of the court itself. It has its fine stock of learned and judicious men, from all parts. Clever Doctor Rogerson from Scotland, court physician; wise old one-eyed Euler from Switzerland, the greatest mathematician of the age. Yet here too nothing is what it seems. As Euler observes quietly one day at the academy: 'In this country they hang people who talk too much.'

At court everything proceeds with freedom, levity, frankness, the very rules the Empress has set. Politeness and civility are watchwords; indeed Her Majesty forbids profane speech. Every few days there are polite galas, ballets, plays, where everyone dresses up to the nines, the Empress participates herself, clad from head to foot in silk and diamonds, cheeks unusually rouged. Yet every single thing hides its opposite. Behind curtained doorways, couples copulate freely, and maids of honour have little honour at all. Generals order a supply of nightly bed-companions, adultery is almost a matter of court instruction. All servants are spies, and the Secret Branch exercises a reign of fear and favour, making its own lists of those destined for a trip to Siberia or a cellar in the Peter and Paul.

So what is he doing, why is he here? Her Serene Majesty now really does seem to trust him. She respects his frank manners, takes pleasure in his flights of mental fancy. She accepts his whims, shows no resentment when he disputes with her, when he grows candid, angry, outraged. She bites back like a bright little terrier, throws his words back at him; in fact she makes it all feel like an elegant love match, a fine philosophical flirtation that can go on for hours. Most days now he doesn't even leave the small library until dinner is about to be served, by which time a posse of angry diplomats and place-seekers stands impatiently beyond the curtains, nibbling titbits, supping the universal vodka, waiting till she lets him loose. Where does he stand? It's just like a love-match, and she's both frank and deceptive, sometimes a courtesan, sometimes an uncertain young girl. She's always tempting him toward her bedchamber, conveniently tucked there just behind the library; then shutting the door with some sudden polite reasons of state as he seems almost there. A small push and . . . Does she want him, does she not? Should he do it, should he not? Is he good, is he bad? Who knows? He doesn't . . .

Going to court one day, stepping only a little aside from the usual path, he goes inside Saint Isaac's church, domed and strange-looking, a building that has always been in the process of building, ever since Great Peter dedicated it as his own. His first church in wood has come down, been moved half a block or so, risen again in stone. Yet, even as it's being renewed, it seems already in a process of dilapidation, and sure enough it will be replaced again, as it says in the great Book of Destiny above. How odd that, wherever he walks here, whatever's going up is already starting to come down. Now, staring at the images of Byzantium, the gilded altars, the dark-eyed mournful icons, the secret chambers around the shrine, our man sees the signs and symbols of a religion that's nowhere near his own. How strange the faith is, how odd the building, formlessness aspiring to form, and everything about it bent somehow out of true. Such are the floods and quakes that have already shaped the city that its shapes are already battered and shattered. Window holes gape empty, pillars bend out of line, things that are solid melt into air . . .

Reminding him of an old truth he felt once, in times when he reported Paris art and architecture for the journals of Melchior Grimm. Any true building, any successful structure, is a grand and intimate harmony, all parts and arts linking into each other according to the best rules of proportion and arithmetic. He recalls the greatest example: Michelangelo's dome for Saint Peter's, Rome. It's proof how a master, seeking the strongest shape, instinctively finds the most perfect, using all the lines of least resistance. The dome is the perfect number drawn from all the mathematical combinations. So the power of the building meets the mind of the artist who makes it, art, craft, nature and genius coming into exactness, as does the finest mathematician, the greatest clock-maker, the cleverest cutler, the perfect creator of chairs or tables. As reason rises out of animal being, progress ascends from history, so art looks onward and upward, toward the perfect dome.

Staring now at the cracked Christ Pantokrator in the church's broken drum, he thinks of Jacques Soufflot in Paris. Soufflot is an architect, maker of churches; now he's been asked to create Sainte-Geneviève's, a new church for a reasoning age, soon to be given a fresh Roman name: the Pantheon. The building's rising over the streets of Paris now, soon to reach its dome. Soufflot is dreaming of it: the lightest, purest, riskiest, most improbable. His enemies are mocking him, telling him the building will surely fall. Before he left Paris he tried to advise him: 'Think what inspired Michelangelo, the sense of line, the experience of craft. All his life he's spent trying to shore up tottering things. He's learned how to make one thing counterbalance another, how to stop a ceiling falling down. The same instinct makes the builder of a windmill find the perfect angle for rotation, the carpenter make a chair of perfect balance, the writer give his sentence perfect shape. The lesson of lessons is here, use it well. Instinct is what makes us reach out of darkness and ascend toward the light.'

Yet even this truth seems different here, as God is different too. For a lifetime he's known him, quarrelled with him over everything in the world. But in those days God spoke French. Here he speaks odd tongues and manifests himself in the strangest of forms. His saints and apostles are without number, their painted faces iconed everywhere. His priests and vicars – there, kissing the iconostasis, is one of them now – are bearded fanatics, more like Musselman mullahs than the abbés and monks he's known all his life: cunning hypocritical prelates like his own brother manipulating logic to pursue God, fame, fortune and the court. Here they're nearer a frank band of brigands, not people you'd care to entrust a prayer to on a dark night. Beyond the surface of reason and Frenchness lie the Old Believers. Beneath enlightenment superstition rages, and ghosts and visions are a matter of course. The late Tzar may well have been felled by the ravening haemorrhoids, but hardly a day passes when he hasn't been seen again: reborn, presenting himself to monks in strange visions, or interrupting the babushkas who've simply stepped out into the forest to gather sticks. There's hardly a community in the whole great country that hasn't taken a false Peter the Third to its bosom. And no sooner has one been hunted down than another takes his place . . .

I am here still, in this strangest of cities [he writes home that same day to Sophie Volland, as he sits in the Narishkin Palace, trying to understand]. It is surely a city of quite a new kind, in a nation of quite a new kind. It has a splendid court at the top, blankness and human despair at the bottom, and a small space for hope and illusion set somewhere in between. It is a great and amazing city, but one that lacks the usual tissues, the normal arteries and cartileges of true cities that have been formed out of their own pasts. I am walking up and down in my room, mechanically. Now I go across to the window to look out at the Russian weather. I see the endless torrents of snow, the raging winds and the dark skies, and I subside into despair.

Yet there is everything to make here, everything to do. I study people in the streets, I enquire of all the facts from the many academies our enlightened patron has created. As you know, I believe in a philosophy that endeavours to lift up humanity. To degrade ideas and create false societies is to encourage men to despair and vice. So I myself seek to study the foundations of a fresh human civilization – one that is free of superstition, oppressive custom, bad morals and false tyrants, yet which has not lost its roots in all that's good from the past. At any rate, I have made sixty-six notebooks, full of thoughts, ideas, my best moral hopes. Every day I improve them, every day I present my notes to her serene empress. Every day she encourages me, despite many in the court, which is good. For I truly think my notes and notebooks are needed here more than any place in the world.'

DAY THIRTY-FIVE

HE and SHE are pleasantly taking tea together on the sofa.

SHE
America. Tell me about it.

HE
Tell you what about it, my lady?

SHE
Come, you must surely have written a book about it. Haven't you written a book on everything? Surely there's very little in the world so unlucky as not to have been the subject of a book by you.

HE
I haven't written it. Yet. Of course I mean to write about it. I've been asked to collaborate on a book on the great American empire by my old friend the Abbé Guillaume Reynal.

SHE
Ah, now you are writing books with Abbés?

HE
He's a former Jesuit, it's true. But it's a courtesy title. Now the

order is dissolved he's become quite as much a deist as the rest of us.

SHE
Like me, you mean? Am I a deist, do you think?

HE
It's hard to tell. But then our discussions have hardly started yet.

SHE
You'll make me one, you mean. I don't think so. The Abbé writes books about America?

HE
This is the man who first publicly raised the great question of whether the discovery of America was helpful or harmful to mankind.

SHE
What was his answer?

HE
In the Abbé's view America is all a great mistake. He thinks animals, nature and even the sexual passions all grow more depraved and distorted the further west you go. But like any honest Frenchman he acknowledges India and Louisiana as the two great empires the French have had. And Louisiana as one of nature's greatest wonders, where the hope of mankind could be renewed.

SHE
Now lost to the British, I believe?

HE
And that might be why his views are so negative. A paradise ruled by the British hardly seems the perfect playground for the cultivation of the natural instincts.

SHE
But come along, sir, no more Abbés. Give me your own opinion. Chancellor Betskoi's been telling me that a century

from now the world could have only two truly great powers, the Russian and the American. If so I would like to be ready. I want my nation to be far better than theirs.

HE sips his tea.

HE
Very well then. Denis on the Americans. First, imagine a landscape no one has succeeded in describing before. Its lights and shades are new, its colours different. Painters take fright when they see what's in front of them. The people are strange and unusual, set in geography and nature somewhere a little astray – between the Europeans and the Asians, let's say, but with no real certainty about being either. The birds are rare and bright-coloured. The vegetables cultivated and eaten are huge and strange. The simplicities of primitive existence compete with great intellectual sophistications, often creating both amazing inventions and the oddest distortions of thought. An excess of land and the process of migration across strange and shifting landscapes inclines the people to Republican sentiments . . .

SHE
I might have known.

HE
It encourages independence of opinion, and that gives them the illusion they are all splendid philosophers.

SHE
Deists, you mean?

HE
Any form of thought thinking can manage seems to flourish there. The landscape nourishes strange and novel religions – which appear, last a year or two, then vanish, leaving only a faint trace in the history of thought. Because there are lands without law, it's possible for the people to be complete fantasists, imaginary even to themselves. They're certainly the first people to think they can live without higher law and

governance, and that life exists on this planet solely so they can live in a state of perfect self-imposed happiness—

SHE
They're wrong, of course.

HE
Completely wrong. There is no happiness. But I see no harm in trying.

SHE
So the future, sir, what's written there? Will your Indian America be French or British?

HE
French, if the French have anything to do with it. British, if the fat Hanoverian Georges have anything to do with it.

SHE
Which would be better? British or French?

HE
Let us try to imagine a British America, dear lady. They'd serve roast beef daily and there'll be great estates in the country where the hounds bark and the churchbells toll. If French, well, it will be just like Petersburg. Domes and statues, palaces and garnishes, and all the follies of fashion. Of course, if the people themselves, an impatient lot, have anything to do with it, it will be neither.

SHE
Because now they aspire to be a nation?

HE
And a republic. And because the British hate the French and the French hate the British they will be one. Each nation will arm the Americans against the other. The result is they'll have arms of their own, and they'll use them.

SHE
A republic? A people's tyranny, you mean?

HE
I do.

SHE
In fact, exactly like this amazing new Russia you are
describing to me every day in your notebooks . . .

HE
No, dear lady. More like Venice. A place where one finds
little enlightenment, much repression, almost no morality of
the official kind, and quite different vices and virtues from the
normal.

SHE
Very well, sir. In that case, do I bother with them or not? Tell
me wisely.

HE
Very well, dear lady. I'd say: bother.

END OF DAY THIRTY-FIVE

DAY FORTY

*SHE's in finery, clad in jewels, hung with orders. It has been a
day among notables; now she sits embroidering. HE sits by her side,
close. No courtiers.*

SHE
Atheist!!

HE
No no, please, dear lady. You really must not think I'm not
a religious man. In my youth I took the tonsure. If I had
listened to my father, you would have seen me in very
different vestments, with a very different haircut. You would
have had a Jesuit priest. My brother – my tonsured, cloaked,
strait-laced jackass of a brother – is one to this very day.

SHE
So why a philosopher?

HE
A philosopher is a priest who's exhausted the old religion and creates a church and creed of his own.

SHE
And your brother, what does he say?

HE
Naturally he despises me. No quarrel is more terrible than brothers who have fallen out. Mine spends his time trying to restrain knowledge. I spent mine trying to make it spread its thighs ever more freely and fully . . .

SHE
Which is why you have all the arrogance and vanity of the priest – without any of the learning, the self chastisement or the humility. This is a philosopher.

HE
I gather you don't know priests very well, my dear. Who ever met a humble Jesuit? My brother of course is always in the right. Whereas I, as a philosopher, know my opinion is entirely wrong. As is, of course, everybody else's.

SHE
So why should I sit here listening to you?

HE
Because human knowledge has scarcely started. It advances, it progresses. It disputes every day with itself. *This* is philosophy.

SHE looks at him thoughtfully.

SHE
What I don't understand is this. If there really were no God—

HE
Ah yes, well done. Please continue, madame—

SHE
. . . then how could we believe in anything at all? In the existence of the universe, the function of things, the reality of

our selves? We would be completely lost in time and space. Nothing would have a cause, a reason, or a destination—

HE
We would all be poor philosophers if we didn't consider the existence of a world without a divine intention. A world that existed not by purposeful creation but by a random evolution, or was made as a world simply by virtue of our own interpretations and understandings.

SHE
So . . . what would such a world be like?

HE
Imagine you were a pure consciousness, floating in the spaces of the sky. Then take away time, order, and consequence. The universe, the stars, all things living and dead, before us and after, swirl round us. Memory and mind are one, and before is the same as after. But consciousness is self, it has a need to know. It seeks order and relation—

SHE
How?

HE
It has the power to speak, and name things. It has the gift of grammar. At the centre is consciousness, a perceiving person, Moi. For Moi to make sense to himself, he requires something other, a Toi and a Lui.

SHE
Yes, language lets us name and explain things—

HE
But in my cosmos, it *is* only language – a map of things, not the thing itself. A Frenchman names one world, a Russian another. An astronomer can spend thirty years studying a single star. But which of us stops long enough to study himself: the thoughts of his mind, the means of his perception, the nature of his locomotion, the beat of his heart? We need

our philosophers, not to explain the universe, but to explain the self who claims to know the universe.

SHE
How? If the world isn't real?

HE
Let us suppose, my dear, that I am not an invention or product of the world. Let's suppose, and why not, the world is an invention of mine.

SHE
What then? You just dreamt it, like d'Alembert's spiders?

HE
It's possible. The world is simply what I myself know to be the case. No more and no less than that.

SHE
Really? And what about what *I* perceive to be the case?

HE
Considered from the standpoint of Denis the Divinity, what you perceive is simply one more illusion created for *me* to perceive. It would be quite logical for me to assume the world came into being the moment I came to consciousness, is my consciousness, and will cease when I no longer have a consciousness.

SHE
Yes, I've heard of madmen before. But why is your dream so superior to mine? Why are you the one for whom the world exists?

HE
Very simple. The world, I observe, is filled with millions of people. Yet of all those million I's, I am the only one with a me in it.

SHE
So all the rest of us are fakes. Scenery, illusion? Waxworks? You're telling me I don't exist at all, but you alone do?

HE

Indeed you exist, and I experience you as entirely real and precious. Just as I do history, geography, nature and the cosmos. Yet why shouldn't this entire universe – its past, its future, remote peoples, furthest cosmos – be an illusion designed to amuse me?

SHE

But you will admit *I* exist?

HE

Oh yes, you exist. But when I rise in a few minutes, kiss your elegant hand, and walk away down Nevsky Prospekt, thinking so warmly of your eternal kindness and your sweet good humour, where are you then?

SHE

I'm here, sir, believe me. And I have soldiers to prove it.

HE

And when in a few weeks I regretfully leave Russia, and my dear memory weakens and my old mind starts to fail, will you still be so then? Or will you become my life's most wonderful and greatest illusion? All I can ever know is what I'm conscious of – what happens in the theatre of my mind's existence. So when I cease to recall, what remains? And when I cease to exist, why shouldn't everything in this world halt too, since now it will be without its one essential witness . . .

SHE

And what then about your famous Posterity?

HE

It exists too. I've already imagined it.

SHE

Sir, do you ever believe one word of the things you say to me?

HE

Not always.

SHE

Of course not. One minute you are telling me there is no self. The next yours is the only self in the world. One minute the world is immaterial, the next the wonderful clockwork universe is the only thing there is.

HE

Do I contradict myself? Very well, I contradict myself.

SHE

So you keep saying. Denis, you are completely infuriating, you do know that? You call yourself the thinker. Now show me how your argument is wrong.

HE

I will, my dear, and very easily. If I really were free to invent the world, then it has to be obvious I would never have invented this one.

SHE

You wouldn't?

HE

A vale of misery? I should certainly have invented something that didn't always defeat and wound and constrain us, tie us down with laws and moralities, deny our pleasures and punish our thoughts. As a free man, I would have invented freedom.

SHE

But what would be the point? If everyone else was an illusion, they wouldn't have any possible means to enjoy it.

HE

How well you disprove me.

SHE

Do I?

HE

And how foolish my life would be, because I would never have had the imagination to have invented you. Which shows you I'm out of my senses.

SHE

Sometimes when we sit here I think you *have* invented me.

HE

But the truth is that by summoning me to join you, you actually invented me.

SHE

Sometimes I wish I'd sent you away at once.

HE

It would have been the entirely just action of an entirely just monarch.

SHE

Stay. Come with me. Today the court is empty.

HE looks at her.

HE

Your Most Grand and Imperial Highness . . .

END OF DAY FORTY

TWENTY-SEVEN (NOW)

WAKING UP on a fresh new morning, cold and yet duvet-wrapped in my now familiar cabin, I'm at once reminded by the general silence that the ship I'm aboard is sailing no longer. Now we're moored and docked it's not only the engines and machinery that have ceased to function. The entire vessel is oddly empty. Since most of the passengers went ashore to continue their onward journey, the ship, just like the other liners moored at the water-front, has turned into an exceedingly lethargic hotel – exactly like the grand hotels on the Venice Lido if you go there out of season, where the illusion of service somehow continues in a desultory fashion even while you can't see why the place bothers to open at all. Here on board, a mood of tiredness has set in. Most of the crew has gone on a few days' shore-leave. Those who have stayed behind to serve the few residentials have somehow changed in character. Lively stewards have turned into drab resentful hotel waiters, spry stewardesses into invisible chambermaids, as if the very fact of being in Russia has reminded them that a sullen hostility is the proper way of life. The bars that once pulsed with shouting and music have fallen quiet, left to the use of the odd gloomy drinker. The duty-free emporium is locked and barred, the Caviar Cabin firmly shuttered. The beauty shop retains just one magazine-addicted assistant who spends her long day doing simply nothing at all. The lounges and dining rooms have an air of dereliction, abandoned as they are to a few Japanese tourists, several tough German businessmen, and our own pilgrim selves.

And, I realize when I get down to the cavernous dining room for breakfast, some of the same dereliction is affecting our own party as well. The group at our special table seems strangely depleted – and that's surely not just because I've come into breakfast late. It's as if our serious dedicated company, which had set out so determinedly from Stockholm to take the great Enlightenment Trail, really isn't that serious or dedicated after all. The group seems to be diversifying, fragmenting, maybe even dissolving entirely, splitting into quite different directions with quite different aims. Our Diderot lovers show no signs at all of being interested in Diderot, to the point where I'm beginning to wonder whether the whole confusing voyage was ever the kind of trip I'd supposed it was – or whether it was simply a cover for some much more mysterious and masonic enterprise to which everyone else other than myself had been made party.

For instance: for the last three days Jack-Paul Verso, our funky professor, has been telling me, over the various Jim Beams we've enjoyed together in the bar, about his own intentions: his interest in studying the future of Marxist-Leninist philosophy in Russia, now that it's had to forget history and adapt to new gene-science and string theory, and the book or maybe article he means to write. Yet now I gather from the others at the table he's already done an early bunk, leaving the ship first thing in a taxi, equipped with his Deconstructionist's hat, several bottles of vodka and at least two and possibly three of his band of red-cheeked Tatyanas. According to unconfirmed rumour, they've set off on an extended excursion to the town of Pushkin (which was once called Tzarskoye Selo) and no one knows when they're likely to come back.

Then, even as we drink our breakfast coffee (awful), and finish off our morning rolls (hard), a large black Zil limousine appears in the lens of the portholes, bouncing its way along the dockside. From it descends an elegant, black-caped, barrel-chested gentleman of distinguished bearing and late middle years. He carries a bunch of flowers, and looks up at our ship, waving frantically. Not very much later, our Swedish nightingale can be seen descending the gang-plank, clad in enfolding furs, looking yet more like a grand Brünnhilde. With appropriate gestures she accepts the proffered bouquet, and extravagantly embraces and fondly kisses the caped gent, who in turn takes up front-of-stage top tenor position. Behind her, evidently playing the old comedy role of extravagantly fussy servant, comes the obliging figure of Lars Person, bearing an armful of her topcoats and a couple of vanity cases. Having taken their bows, the entire trio get into the black limo with its grinning chrome grille, which then sweeps them off in the general direction of the city. Breakfast table gossip has it she's going to attend some fabulous press conference at the Hotel Astoria, before being received at the Maryinsky Theatre – the place where, as it is well-known, all great divas now and then come to rest.

No sooner has she gone than Sven Sonnenberg and Agnes Falkman return from a trip to the bursar's office which seems to have proved very productive. Gone, apparently, is the dark age when much of Russia was red-mapped and foreigner-hostile country, and where a journey off-course would inevitably lead to arrest. Personal touring is being encouraged, so Sven and Agnes have been able to arrange to rent bicycles and mean to set off into the countryside, hoping to find brute nature, the Russian spirit, the vastness of the steppes. In his very Swedish way, Sven has become quietly excited, saying he looks forward to meeting carpenters, and examining many tables; Agnes is longing to see the amazing achievements of the Russian co-operative farms. No sooner do we see them carrying their backpacks off on to the dockside than Anders Manders rises from the table, wipes his lips, and quietly excuses himself. He would, he says, have dearly loved to spend the day with the rest of us, looking round the shelves of the public library as Galina seems to have arranged. However, embassy contacts have arranged a diplomatic invitation for him to attend a grand banquet given by the mayor of Saint Petersburg, where, over champagne and Beluga caviar, various matters of Russo-Swedish co-operation will be discussed. Such a pity; but it really is one of those invitations a poor working diplomat can hardly refuse . . .

Glancing around the breakfast table, I suddenly realize that all this has stripped our party down to the very barest minimum. In fact there are only Bo, Alma and myself left to take care of reason and pursue the Enlightenment Trail. 'I didn't realize the others had been so busy making their own plans,' I remark. 'It looks as if our party to the public library is going to be pretty small after all.'

Bo and Alma look at each other.

'*Jo, jo,*' Alma agrees.

'And what a pity we are not going to be able to spend the day with you either,' says Bo.

'Unfortunately Bo has been invited to Petersburg University to give a very important lecture,' explains Alma.

'As part of the Diderot Project?'

'*Nej, nej,* not exactly,' says Bo, taking up his paper napkin and wiping the crumbs from his lips. 'I am giving a lecture about the great Russian critic Mikhail Bakhtin and his role in the development of linguistics. I wish you could be there, but it is very specialist. Not your field, I fear.'

'It's just been arranged?'

'*Nej, nej,* this was arranged many months ago. You see, it is always my habit to try to kill two different birds with one stone.'

'It saves time,' says Alma. 'And you can use one grant for two things.'

'Or even two grants for one thing?'

'Some important professors are coming to meet us. Bo is famous, I think he is famous in every country in the world,' says Alma complacently.

'So was Carlos the Jackal,' I say.

'Pardon?' says Alma, her face freezing.

Oh dear. Once again I've managed to say the wrong thing . . .

At any rate, all this explains why it is that, when Galina Solange-Stavaronova appears on the quayside at nine with the battered mini-bus, ready to guide her little party as arranged, I am the only member of the party waiting on the dockside.

'*Salut, mon cher,*' cries Galina, waving gaily, and wearing another splendid twenties outfit, a bright-red silk dress topped off with a lopsided beret with a pom-pom. Somewhere in the background I can see Bo and Alma being met by a group of grey-haired men in dull suits and put into the back seat of an old Lada; these must be the professors from the university.

'*Mais tu es seul?*' cries Galina, red dress fluttering, emanating the most wonderful fragrance of Chanel. Abjectly, I try my best to explain the situation. Galina shrugs her shoulders and shows no sign of surprise at all. Why not? Perhaps a lifetime spent inside the bitter framework of modern Russian history creates such saintly resignation. Perhaps she simply knows the ways of academics: a careless and unreliable bunch of wonderful people, who are capable of behaving like this anywhere in the world. Or perhaps the tour was never really intended in the first place, and she is continuing the charade only as a pleasant politeness to me.

At least that's how she makes it seem.

'*N'importe, mon cher, c'est plus intime, oui?*' she cries, holding out her hands to me, and placing them in mine. 'Then the two of us can spend a very nice day together! A delightful day all on our own! Remember, you are in a civilized city, you can do whatever you like. What do you like? Maybe you want to go to Pushkin? Return to the Hermitage? Or do you want to take coffee and cakes on the Nevsky Prospekt?'

'I suppose I was really hoping to see the library.'

'Oh, you mean those Didro books?' asks Galina, as if this is a strange and absurd suggestion.

'Yes. And his papers.'

'But you really want to? You truly like our Monsieur Didro?'

'Well, yes, I do. I've been reading him again on the voyage over and I start to like him more and more.'

Galina looks at me. 'But don't you want to see the writers' Petersburg? The Pushkin Apartment Museum, the Dostoyevsky Apartment Museum?'

'Well, yes, that would be nice.'

'The Lermontov Apartment Museum, the Goncharov Apartment Museum?'

'Yes, indeed. I'm fond of visiting writers' houses. I might as well do the lot.'

'And then you will want to go to the Alexander Nevsky cemetery and put a carnation flower on Dostoyevsky's grave?' says Galina, now bright-eyed with excitement over what she's devising.

'Well, yes, naturally.'

'Also the graves of Tchaikovsky, Rimsky-Korsakov and Mussorgsky?'

'Yes. Of course.'

'Good, I think you are quite Russian,' says Galina, looking utterly delighted. 'But we will do everything properly. First we will start where everything in our city starts.'

'Where's that?'

'At the Bronze Horseman, naturally. I will tell the driver to take us there. Then I will tell him for the rest of our day we will not need his bus at all.'

'Very well, fine.'

Once we are aboard the bus, with the disappointed-looking driver bouncing us along the potholes of Bolshoi Prospekt, I ask Galina about today's news. I'm still worrying about how the Russian drama is unfolding. Galina silently raises her eyes to the heavens.

'The same. Everyone tries to betray everyone else. Russia is one coup after another.'

'But Yeltsin survives?'

'Sure, Yeltsin rules okay. He always rules okay. Yeltsin will continue to rule even when there is no more Russia to rule over.'

'You don't sound too hopeful.'

'Hopeful? Please, I am Russian. I live in a land of mad hopes, long queues, lies and humiliations. They say about Russia we never had a happy present, only a cruel past and a quite amazing future. Of course we worship another crazy leader, another false tzar. We are used to being repressed. We are the people who invented the equality of misery. All we like here is one strong man who tells us what to do. Yeltsin, well, think, he survives because everyone else is so much worse. But maybe you understand why I prefer to spend my days with Voltaire and Didro?'

And so once again we pass along the embankment by the university, and take the Palace Bridge over the Neva. Today, though, instead of going as far as the Hermitage, we halt in a square beneath the spire of the Admiralty. In a mess of touristic confusion, passengers are descending in crowds from Intourist buses. We climb down from our own. From somewhere over the far side of the square there comes a noisy crackle of loudspeakers, a great booming of voices. Another demonstration has gathered, much bigger than yesterday's. People are marching under a flurry of waving red flags, watched by police and soldiers. Then, coming from somewhere near the Hermitage, an alternative procession appears, old Russian tricolours in red, blue and white, waving, shouts and chants singing through the air. Jeep-style police vehicles buzz around them.

'Something's happening?' I ask Galina.

'Nothing is happening. It is not happening and it will not. It was Didro who said the best thing about Russia. He says everyone in Russia acts as if they live in a place that has just suffered an earthquake, so nobody can trust the ground under their feet.'

'But what are these demonstrations?'

'Nothing, I told you. This thing, that thing. The past, the future. Old style, new style. Socialism, shopping. There are always demonstrations around here. Because this used to be Decembrists' Square.'

'Where they had the Decembrist Revolution?'

'There was our famous song, "Don't you come to the square, Will you be there at the square?" Only in the end, like all of those things, the December revolution wasn't a real revolution. It was just an idealistic confusion. The nobles had gathered to stop Nicholas from becoming tzar, because they preferred his nicer brother. One problem, they were already too late. Nicholas was tzar already. And he sent in the soldiers.'

'So another bloodbath?'

'Not at first. They drove the demonstrators out on to the ice over the Neva. They didn't even need to fire the guns. The ice cracked and they were drowned. But today the square cannot be used for revolutions.'

'It can't?'

'Don't you see how neat it is, wide lawns and big gardens? Why do you think it is made like that?'

'Ah, I see. Revolutionaries never walk on the grass and the flowerbeds?'

'In Russia, they do not,' says Galina firmly. 'And now you can see him. There he is.'

I look upward. There he is indeed. Big Peter, high-hatted, trapped on his rock-pedestal, rises up high above us on his horse. He's a flowing figure, as big as can be, big as bronze and Falconet can make him, dwarfing the squat Intourist buses parked all around him, and shrinking to nothing all these dressed-up Russian wedding parties that have gathered round his pediment, to have their photos taken, somehow hoping to link their Posterity with his.

'You remember the poem of Pushkin, we all learn it at school?' asks Galina. ' "Where lonely waters strive to reach the sea, he stood / And gazed before him, mind filled with the greatest thoughts." '

He's not what I've expected; in fact he looks perfectly pleasant as he sits up there, staring out at the Baltic as if he's expecting a fresh load of pictures, rising up out of his flowing rock pedestal, more civilized in looks than I imagined, more gallant, more – how can I put it? – French. The whole ensemble is so flowing and mobile it's not hard to see why Pushkin imagined the horse leaping down from the pedestal, and Peter and his mount thundering through the streets and squares of the city, chasing the guilty, the unhappy, the anxious to their dooms.

The marching demonstrators are themselves heading for the Neva, though on this occasion they are wisely making the safer crossing by the bridge. But when I'm curious and make a move to follow the parade, Galina seizes my arm and steers me on my way.

'Take no notice, it's so tasteless. Those are two kinds of people who can never be happy. It's not important. This is our new civil war. Now this enormous building in front, with the golden dome, don't you think we really must go in?'

'Why must we go in?'

'It's Saint Isaac's Cathedral. It's the highest place. From the top you can have the very best view of Petersburg. Let's take a look. Or maybe you don't like it?'

'It's just I prefer the churches with the onion domes.'

'The Orthodox styles, of course. But this one is designed by another Frenchman. And oh, by the way, for a little fact Didro lived at the Narishkin Palace over there.'

I look across the square, but Galina is already steering me toward the church ahead.

'What other Frenchman? Was he a friend of Didro?'

'Not a bit, he lived much later. His name was Auguste Montferrand. He rebuilt the cathedral for our tzars. He wanted to be buried here, but Tzar Alexander refused him. He died as soon as the cathedral was finished, but his body went back to Paris.'

'Why did the tzar refuse him?'

'Because the cathedral finally took forty years to finish. The plans were wrong. Nothing fitted. He wasn't a true architect, but even so he built the greatest dome in all the north of Europe. You can see him still, he is carved up there on the façade.'

On the huge marble steps leading up to the cathedral there stands a long line of wrapped beggars, their hands outstretched: old men on homemade crutches, babushkas in black dresses and headscarves. Galina halts and opens up her handbag.

'I always give five kopecks, it brings us good luck,' she says.

We walk inside, hand over an entrance fee to someone, and find ourselves in a vast cathedral that feels much too big for itself. It's a great dark monster of rational baroque, a place of huge sculptures and mosaics, less a place of true worship than an opulent museum. High in the centre, above the crossing, there rises up Montferrand's vast open dome, the third largest after St Peter's and St Paul's.

'It's a pity. Until two years ago you could have seen the Foucault Pendulum. It swung here to show the axis of the earth.'

'Here? But I thought it was in Paris. Didn't they hang it first in Soufflot's Pantheon?'

'Of course there was one in Paris. But the other was here. Didn't you know Petersburg is supposed to lie on the true meridian, the heartline of the world?'

'I thought that was Greenwich in London.'

'No, this is the English, who are always cheating. Here is the real line that runs through the centre of the world.'

'What happened to the pendulum? Why take it down?'

'Perhaps because we don't believe Russia is at the middle of things any more. But you can still go up on the roof and from the top of Petersburg look out at the entire world.'

So we go up and up, by the spiral staircase through the layers of the cold rational cathedral, across the iron ladder to the balconies of the roof. I look out onto the endless rooftops of copper and tin, the broken chimney stacks, the domes of the Smolny Convent, the fingers of big buildings; then, beyond that, spreading out to the wide horizon and the still wider world, the factory chimney stacks, the grim slabs of endless apartment blocks, the thick dirty smoke-plumes rising from distant power stations, the hint of far palaces and fortresses, the grey glint of the Baltic sea.

This is what I see. It's somehow not quite what Galina sees. She sees a great city made of form and symmetry. For, as she carefully tries to show me, each part of this cunning and intricate city exactly balances some other. So two golden flèches, carefully matching each other on either bank of the Neva: one the Admiralty, the other the Peter and Paul Fortress. Two tzars on horseback, one on either side of the cathedral. One of them is Big Peter, pointing like a projectile out to sea on the surge of his great pedestal; the other is Tzar Nicholas, who slaughtered the Decembrists just on the other side of this building, a stiff straight autocrat set erectile on his highly high horse. In front of the Admiralty, a full-length Nikolay Gogol stares across at his stone opposite, Mikhail Lermontov. Down there in front of the Smolny Convent, where Tzarina Catherine Veliko took care of her noble girls, the figure of Karl Marx is exchanging glances with his old collaborator Friedrich Engels. There, glittering upside down and mirrored in the luminous water of the Neva, is a second Admiralty, a second Hermitage. On the Neva bridge, there marches one procession with waving flags, and then another procession.

'You see, we are a city of doubles,' says Galina. 'Even our most famous books are books all about doubles. Of course so was Didro's.'

True. When I really think about it, Galina is probably right after all.

And then, as we're leaving the cathedral, coming down the steps into the square, heading towards the second statue – Tzar Nicholas of the bloodbath, high on his erectile pedestal – something rather unfortunate occurs. A swarm of gipsies in bright dresses appears and surrounds me, holding out their hands. All of them are female: two adult women, and maybe six or seven girls, of all ages from four to seventeen. My hand moves toward my pocket to give them something; I'm thinking of Galina's superstition about good luck. Suddenly, screaming, shouting, they swarm all over me, the women trying to push me down, the children's hands pulling at my clothes and pushing into my pockets. The children shove and tug; as I manage to pull loose from one, I'm grabbed by the others, or hit at by their many flailing hands. Passers-by stop, tourists halt, but nobody reacts.

Or nobody but Galina. Suddenly she's in the middle of the fray: hitting, punching, slapping hard with her handbag and the guide-book she carries. Her red dress flies, her hat comes off, her hands grab. People start to come running toward us, and the gipsies give up. They run away across the square and down the gardens, in their long bright skirts, a dangerous squad. Galina helps me to my feet again.

'Truly we are a friendly city,' she feels obliged to say. 'But so many criminals now. You must try hard to be careful, *mon cher.* And watch out for those people, the police don't bother to stop them. Maybe they pay them a very good bribe. Did they take anything, your wallet, your passport? Have a look.'

I stare at the grey-haired lady in surprise, then check through my pockets. My wallet, fortunately, is still there, and so is my passport.

'No, they took nothing. Thanks to you.'

'You see! I told you if we gave to the beggars you would have very good luck.'

I don't dispute this analysis. 'You were completely amazing, Galina, I don't know how you did that.'

'You think I am too old to fight? Well, now you see, I am not.'

'I think you're the heroine of the occasion. Thank you, really.'

'Come,' she says, taking my by the arm, 'I think you need a cognac. I will take you to a very nice place on Nevsky Prospekt. You have heard of the Nevsky Prospekt, I hope?'

Yes, indeed, I've heard of Nevsky Prospekt. Writer after writer, over the years, has introduced me to it. Pushkin has told me about its elegant parade of human lives and its imperial style, Gogol has created for me its strolling absurdities: those preening clerks in their well-brushed morning coats, those chancellory clerks with their magnificent briefcases, those persons of serious consequence; those elegant women with their leg of mutton sleeves, those cavalry officers, those protective watchmen, and the proud foreign governesses, who only come out, walking their noble charges, somewhere around lunchtime. I know from writer after writer about the men with their well-trimmed whiskers and their favourite barbers, the women with their red ankles showing under white petticoats, about the topknots and the elevated noses, the fine canes, the magnificent epaulettes, the splendid overcoats, worth saving a fortune to buy. And I know, thanks to the saddened Dostoyevsky, about the many others too: the drunkards and the gamblers, the noisy rakes and plaintive whores, the superfluous, the hidden, the insulted and injured.

We walk across the square, beside a canal, past the busy Aeroflot building. The traffic noise and the human chatter promise everything: except that the boulevard Galina brings me to bears no relation at all to the scene I've imagined. True, it's broad, it's grand, but not like Nevsky Prospekt. A long straight perspective, seemingly endless, runs the length of it, from the Neva end to the distant Moscow station. High façades interspersed with churches, bridges, theatres, narrow and fade off into the blurry faint snowfall. A great surge of traffic sweeps along it; trolley-buses swish under networks of sparking wires. But there's no spirit of elegance, no touch of style, no social parade; the pedestrians trundle past us in blank solitude, blundering into each other, heads down, faces cramped, white, featureless, tight and anxious. A wet crowd smell comes off them. The shops and arcades of the imagination have gone; instead more ill-dressed crowds gather in queues and clumps outside drab storefronts that display almost no goods in their windows. Women stand impassively in doorways holding some single small possession — an aluminium kettle, a dress, a white kitten — for sale. Outside the long and rational façade of the Kazan Cathedral more beggars are waiting with their hands outstretched. Weeds are growing through the pavements outside the war-battered frontage of the Gostinny Dvor department store, the city's grand arcade where once the world's traders used to come and barter.

And when here and there you see a brighter spot, a more brilliant façade, it's nearly always a western store: maybe Benetton or Gucci or Prada. These are not shops for the passing people:

armed men, the civilian troops of some private army, stand outside in suede jackets, cradling Kalashnikovs. Just like in the old days, observes Galina; then it was dollar shops for the nomenklatura, now it's western stores for the new rich, many of them the same people. We stand and watch as the shop assistants lock and unlock the shop doors to the new glitterati, whose frank flamboyant hints of wealth and fortune – a Rolex watch, a gold necklace, Nike trainers – are to be briefly glimpsed for just a few seconds as, like the old aristocrats, they flit quickly across the pavements and disappear into a slow-moving chauffeured Mercedes, coasting down the curb. And beside the stores are the Russian banks, doors closed, protected by yet more hard-headed, thick-jacketed armed attendants.

Close to the metro station there's another angry but contained Communist protest. More crackling loudspeakers declaim, more red flags wave, more pamphlets are thrust out at the shrouded passers-by. We cross the road by the metro subway. Here, out of the blowing wind, the crowds push and jostle, stalls sell food in a stink of frying onions. There are bloodstains on the concrete, we stumble between the feet of drunks and oddly submissive children begging by the walls. We ascend to the pavement, then somehow dive downward again, into a quite different subterranean world. Galina opens a small doorway, then leads the way down a very long set of stairs. Down at the bottom it's *belle époque* Paris – unless it's turn-of-the-century Vienna or old Saint Petersburg. There's a long zinc bar, with posters from Pernod and Byrrh and Vladivar Vodka. There are Turkish wall-hangings, art nouveau lamps, plenty of chinoiserie, drawings all done in the manner of the Secessionists and the Futurists: Bakst and Klimt and Schiele. There are waiters in white linen aprons; there is warmth and noise and money. There's a flavour of taste. The people at the tables are young and laughing, a confident sure bourgeoisie of some sort, wearing western clothes, quite unlike the dismayed drab figures we've just seen on Nevsky Prospekt.

'*Garçon, ici,*' cries Galina, a little grey-haired empress, as we sit at a table to ourselves in the corner. The waiter comes at once, and quickly returns with two cognacs. Plainly this is Galina's place. The waiters know her, many of the customers too. It's evidently where she dresses for, and where she often comes. And now she's explaining that in such splendid cafés, in this very best part of the Prospekt, the very best people of Petrograd (it's not hard to see who she means) came, just as the Bolshevik Revolution, began to drink the last of the great champagnes. The dark days were about to start: the persecutions, executions, exterminations were already expected. But there was still time to buy expensive drinks at the most inflated prices, and maybe pick up a girl. Now to come here you should really have dollars, she says. At this I pick up the tab and take out the wallet Galina has saved for me.

'Please, no, put it away,' she says. 'If you pay it will be ten times what I pay. This is for me, I am allowed to pay in roubles. You see they know me here, *mon ami*. Here and everywhere. Now, drink it quickly. Are you resurrected yet, *mon ami*? Eau de vie.'

I drink, get my breath back. 'It's okay, I'm fine now,' I tell Galina.

'This place, it is my oasis,' she says, pleased, taking out a coloured cigarette and lighting it. 'I come here, I read books, I speak in French. For me this is the real Saint Petersburg. Always such a civilized city, even if it had its dark side. Always so clever, so original, so beautiful. Now, don't you agree?'

At this moment, the waiter comes back, and places two more glasses of cognac on the table in front of us. At the same time a youngish and roundish man comes to stand beside the table.

'For you from me,' he says, giving a small smile and sitting down.

I glance at Galina, who shakes her head.

'Welcome to Russia, British I think,' says the man, who wears a tweedish sort of jacket in an Englishy sort of cut. He has a clubby style of tie that goes with his somewhat Oxford shirt. His smile is brittle, his features heavily acne-ed, his hair firmly slicked down with grease. And he carries a worn leather briefcase which, with priestly veneration, he sets on his knee, and then clicks open with a hey-presto motion.

Galina looks at him dryly. '*Qui est vous*, who are you?'

'I am Ruslan Chichikov,' says the man, ignoring Galina, holding out his hand to me.

'Chichikov, please, you are joking,' says Galina.

'I don't think so. Now, sir, I know, you are an investor?'

'No, I'm not.'

'A real smart businessman, I think.'

'No, I'm not.'

'Good, I am a real smart businessman too. Entrepreneur. Joint venturer.'

'I am sure you are,' says Galina.

The youngish man takes no notice of her. 'I understand very well how it is with you, my friend,' he tells me. 'You have a project.'

'No.'

'You have tried everything. You knock on all the doors, visit all the offices, all the time you get nowhere. You can't get a single thing sewn up. Tell me, isn't it right?'

'No. Really, I'm not a businessman.'

'They send you everywhere, this official to that one. You never find the people in top job, you never find the one with the real power. Isn't it right?'

'No.'

'You can't get official permission to import or export, to start a business, open an office. Trouble with currency restrictions. Laws about hiring people. Maybe they don't let you have a Petersburg apartment.'

'I'm not trying to—'

From his briefcase the youngish man is now unloading sheaf after sheaf of typed out paper, sorting the pages into sets, pushing them into my hands. 'Every official you meet wants to have a share. A holiday, a portion of the company, seat on the board. Business here is a tricky business, right? Why pay bribes to people who have no influence? True?'

'Well, true.'

'Now then, how much do you really have to invest?'

'I'm not in Russia to invest.'

'See there. Letter from the mayor of Petersburg. Telling you who I am.'

'Amazing,' says Galina.

'Letter from the chief of the Narodny Bank. Telling you who I am.'

'But how do you know who you are?' asks Galina. 'Not Chichikov.'

'*Da*. See? Statement of property ownership, with my name on it.'

'It isn't your name,' says Galina.

'My commercial name, I work in companies, partnerships. I know everyone in this city. Officials, bankers, business types, security teams. A stranger cannot just walk into Petersburg, you know. It's the Wild West here.'

'Ruslan Chichikov, really?' says Galina.

'Ignore her. Look, I can introduce you to everyone, find you property. Arrange your imports, ship your exports. I can fix your permits, provide your protection. A businessman who doesn't understand how it works can end up in the forest with a little hole in the back of his head.'

'You don't have to talk to this man,' says Galina.

'Of course, you must, if you want to know Russia. You have capital, I have organization,' says the youngish man. 'We make it a joint venture? I take twenty per cent? Do we shake?'

'I'm sorry,' I say, 'there's nothing to shake on. I'm not what you think. I'm not a businessman at all.'

'Everyone in the west is a businessman. You read the MBA manual? Wherever you go there is always a good business opportunity somewhere. If you look for it.'

'I'm not looking for it.'

'You have plenty capital?'

'No.'

'But you do want to invest?'

'I don't want to invest. I'm a visitor, a tourist.'

'So you go somewhere. Where do you want to go?'

'I don't want to go anywhere.'

'A tourist who doesn't want to go somewhere. Maybe there's something you'd like to buy?'

'No, there's nothing at all I'd like to buy.'

'A tourist who doesn't like to buy. So you have something to sell?'

'Nothing to sell.'

'Pleasure, you are looking for pleasure. It's all here if you ask me.'

'I'm not into pleasure.'

'A tourist who is not into pleasure. Who do you need to see?'

'I don't need to see anyone. And I'm very nicely looked after.'

'Now thank you for this brandy,' says Galina. 'We go.'

The youngish man looks me in the eye. 'Oh, please, sir, make some use of me, only ask my help. I can arrange travel. Make introductions. Find you beautiful hostesses. What do you do?'

'I'm a writer.'

'Okay, maybe you need a movie crew.'

'I don't need a movie crew.'

'You like cafés, I'm sure. I show you a better café. Come with me.'

'*Alors, mon brave*, time to leave,' says Galina, taking up her handbag.

'No, wait, please,' the youngish man says very urgently. 'You write books? I can sell them for you. Only a small discount. I know every bookstore in Petersburg. They love to do me favours.'

'I didn't bring any books with me.'

'I can be very useful. I studied literature at the university. I take you to the Pushkin House.'

'No, thank you.'

'You collect books?'

'Yes, some.'

'Good. Now we do business. I can get you books. Wonderful books. Treasures, books from the imperial collections, the city library.'

'This is bad, really, it's time to go,' says Galina.

The youngish man seizes hold of my jacket sleeve. 'Give me a list, anything at all you want. I know just what to do. I've worked for Americans. I can find you anything. Tell me which is your hotel and I can bring anything there before you leave, so you don't have to pay me now. Then you can slip it under your shirts, you will have no problem.'

'Thanks, but no thanks.'

'Listen, no time could be better. In Russia right now everything is for sale. Don't go yet, listen to me, wait. There has to be something you want. Icons? Old cameras?'

'Goodbye, Chichikov,' says Galina, as we walk away from the table and head up the stairs.

'That name, I heard it before,' I say.

'Of course, don't you remember your Gogol? He's the acquirer, the clever rogue who travels round the landowners and buys up all the dead souls.'

'It's a joke?'

'In Russia even our crooks love our best writers.'

'And every café has to have a nephew,' I say.

'Well, I am so sorry,' says Galina, as we step out again on Nevsky Prospekt, 'but I just don't like you to see our bad new Russia. Not everything here is like this.'

'I'm sure of it.'

'Russia is full of good people, not like this ridiculous Chichikov.'

'He was quite amusing.'

'Then you are amused far too easily,' she says. 'When capitalism arrives, it produces only strange and morbid symptoms. You should have been here before, now you have come too late. You are visiting the ruins of a dying empire.'

'Please, wait,' says a voice behind us. The youngish man is there again, smiling. 'You say you are a writer. Don't you like to see the grave of Dostoyevsky? Not far away from here. Only the other end of Nevsky Prospekt.'

'No, thanks.'

'So let's have a drink, yes? Give me a chance.'

'Not now.'

'Then sell me something that will cost you nothing,' he says. 'Sell me your name—'

'My name?'

'I will print here on my documents.'

'Come,' says Galina, taking me firmly by the arm. In her red dress and red pom-pommed hat, she dives right into the middle of the traffic. Horns hoot, tyres skid.

'Where are we going?' I ask.

'I think I take you now to the Didro Library. You ought to see it in case our friend gets there first and it disappears completely.'

And thus, while the traffic honks and races around us, she drags me bodily to the other side of Nevsky Prospekt.

TWENTY-EIGHT (THEN)

CHRISTMAS, grandest of all the European festivals, is nearly here. If he hadn't known that already, the black nights have appeared to tell him: amazing nights that last nearly the whole day long. The Neva has become a silver, frozen-topped stream that flows and slithers through an almost continuous darkness. High in the vast arctic sky, northern lights flash down through an unrelieved veil of snow. Snow blankets all streets, squares, embankments. Icicles like swords crash from the cornices of the apartment houses above, taking a life or two every day. For several weeks now, the whole court has gone shivering about the Small Hermitage, as servants run through the corridors cradling huge log-piles to be stuffed whole into every steaming stove.

With the sea-harbour to the Baltic shut down for the winter, the Livonian routes to the south blocked to all traffic, except the lightest and fleetest of sleighs, everything – that is, all those social things we know there are in the world – has become amazingly distant, so distant that all letters, which never were easy to deliver, have practically ceased. So have the memories that went with them, so have the pleasures. New songs, new books no longer come up from Europe; now the ice-pack has closed, all is in a state of arrest, and everything waits for the spring. Cold, these deep minus temperatures, just doesn't suit him. No one could be better housed than within the comforts of the Narishkin Palace, but his body still strains, rumbles, trembles, declares its bitter resentment. He begins to wonder – exactly as he wondered on the fevered night just before he left Paris – if he was brought for a purpose, if his fate has been settled, if the decision to grant his corpse to the worms of Saint Petersburg has already been taken, and is written down in firm letters in the invisible pages of the great Book of Destiny above.

And then, one day, and quite suddenly, the entire court is absent: gone. As if on a whim, the Empress has risen, upped sticks and tailed it, dragging the whole enormous decorated apparatus with her, the twelve *versts* up the snow-packed road to Moscow, out to the new palace at Tzarskoye Selo. The great house she has been rebuilding endlessly is really meant as a summer palace, but now she has chosen to call it into winter use. Teams of carts, lines of smart coaches, hundreds of sledges, have been massed in the freeze outside the Hermitage, respectfully serviced by hundreds of hussars and cossacks, thousands of servants. They have learned all the lessons, having often made such moves before. Out has come the china and the silver, the tables and the beds, the clothes panniers and the linen baskets, the imperial commode, the royal archive, the national mint. Everyone – chamberlains and generals, court-physicians and clockwinders, assayers and dressers, cooks and laundrymen, court jewellers and police spies, the fine riding horses and the royal greyhounds – has then trotted off out of the city, escorted in their coaches, wagons or sledges by entire bobbing battalions of the cavalry guard.

Now in the huge rooms and vast grounds of a palace that bids to be even bigger and more spacious than the Hermitage, they have already taken up a new way of life. Here it's early to bed, and early to rise. There will be long snowy walks through the deep crisp winter, all contained within the boundaries of a six-mile perimeter. For exercise and amusement they will chop logs in the forest, drink hot tea in the English gardens, vodka in the hunting lodges, pursue seductions in the snowy arbours, hold their winter festivals in the belvederes. Snow has been smoothed flat for comfort, sledging slopes have been laid. Lake-surfaces have been brushed and skates have been prepared. They'll skate, they'll slide, they'll ski on the frozen lakes and ponds. The truth is that once in a while the Empress truly loves to go tobogganing; and it's this, it seems, that has shifted the entire court and administration.

They did, of course, ask him to go as well. Indeed it seems he was expected to, and possibly, by the rules of protocol, even required. But he's been able to plead his ill-health, and truly. Fed by age and rank water, the bitter colic, malady of the Neva, has been biting at his stomach ever since he came to Russia, pushing its rough-edged knife deep into his guts, firmly refusing to go away. But truth to tell, he also welcomes it. He welcomes the sudden Petersburg silence, the death of almost everything in the streets. For more than a week now, the Hermitage has rested in silent neglect. Its windows are black, its candles and lamps stay unlit. Its doors are firm-closed, its sentries stand silent and never summoned. The entire spirit of the city has wandered. The arcades too are completely quiet. No officers or countesses or governesses parade the pavements, and the shopkeepers have all suddenly lowered their prices, and are begging the world to purchase. It's all been a wonder; and he's gloriously grateful for the chance to reflect, take stock, consider, think again, and write.

So as soon as the servants bring him the commode, at six in the morning, he's up and out of bed. Soon he's sitting at his desk in the bedroom, staring out. Snow-filled square, silvery river. Unfinished church, and golden spire. He writes, he writes . . . Soon he's begun a refutation of M. Helvétius, his friend in Paris, who in all daring has claimed that man is no more than a superior animal, a creature of instinct, a greed machine, a body motored by survival and self-interest, no more. It reminds him of another voice he heard once: on a rainy day in Paris, at the chess tables of the Café Regence, when an angry idle nephew vents his rage.

'You know me perfectly well,' the composer's fat-faced, dolled-up, lank-haired relative has said to him, sitting down. 'I'm a fool, an idiot, a glutton, a madman and perhaps a bit of a thief. A real old cuss, as the Burgundians say. But why should you expect me to be humble, starve or beg, my dear sir, when the world's filled with rich fools and spendthrifts at whose expense I can live? All right, I'm a parasite. But I do have one virtue: I do by the light of reason what the stupid rogue only does by instinct. And if only I could be rich, famous, powerful, be fawned on, stroked and tended and flattered by all the pretty women, I'd be just as clever, charming and pleasant as you. No, I wouldn't, I'd be better. Much more elegant, far more clever. I'd develop the most advanced of ideas, the most sophisticated of vices, the most refined of corruptions. I'd be a true philosopher, I'd take advantage of everyone and everything. Wouldn't it be delightful?'

What should he tell them all: Helvétius, the lank-haired nephew, the police spies, the fawning courtiers who hang around only to please? That reason says that human beings, though animals first of all, do have their own special powers and splendid passions: sentiments of taste, feelings of charity, instincts of altruism, a warm admiration for virtue, the capacity to feel the most sublime and profound forms of love. And what's more they have reason itself: wise, calming, illuminating, civilizing reason. Is all that no more than nature, brute cunning, survival, self-interest, struggle, the selfish genes? No, it's only human to be a little human for once. Persons can do good, and what's more they can love good. It's not just the cunning of reason. The great Leibniz didn't think the way the great Leibniz thought simply in order to win food and shelter and mate with the prettiest of women. And surely, surely, something far more than a desire for fame, reputation, rank or profit brought his own elderly self, groaning yet bright and energetic, a thousand miles through the wasted tracts of Europe to share his highest thoughts and warmest feelings with a great empress, the shining Minerva of the North? Or is he wrong, and is reason his delusion, the folly he travels across the world to promote?

Which somehow takes him back to the pages of that other tale he's been writing: the story he worked on in the Hague, the story of the clever servant, barber, postilion, valet, and his dull master, which started when he first read the Shandyisms of Doctor Sterne. Sterne's book is there in his baggage, its covers stained and tattered from the many rains and soakings that penetrated the fabric of Narishkin's grand carriage. He picks up the manuscript again; nothing is quite right.

'Reader, excuse me,' he writes apologetically, 'I see I've totally failed to describe the exact positions of the three characters we happen to have standing here: Jacques, his master, the mistress of the inn. This means you'll be perfectly well able to hear them speak, but you won't be able to picture them. Just give me a moment, and I'll put that right.' He puts it right . . .

And so he finds himself staring at the last lap of the book, and the awful business of ending. He's thought of several already, put in a number, including one that's been lifted right out of Sterne. It still doesn't seem right. Stories don't close in life, or not till death; so a conclusion is an evasion. How should the story conclude? He looks at the river, the winter; he picks up his pen and tries all over again. There is Jacques, putting his master on his horse so he can tip him off again; there is the past, there is the future. There are many more stories to tell, but who should tell them?

'Come on now, master, admit it,' he writes:

MASTER
Admit what, you little rat, you dirty dog, you total scoundrel? Admit you're the most awful of servants, and I'm the unluckiest of masters?

JACQUES
Admit I proved my point. That for most of the time we act and do things without even meaning to.

MASTER
Nonsense.

JACQUES
Well, just think of the things you've done in the last half hour. Weren't you just my toy, my little puppet? Couldn't I have gone on playing with you for the next month of Sundays if I'd really wanted to?

MASTER
You mean this is all a game? All these troubles you got me into? You deliberately made me fall off my horse?

JACQUES
Naturally. I've been sitting waiting all day for those girths to come undone.

MASTER
You untied them, didn't you? Just to make me fall off.

JACQUES
I might well have done.

MASTER
You realize what you are, don't you? A rogue. A dangerous,
troubling, impious rogue.

JACQUES
Or alternatively you could call me a serious thinker, trying to
make a philosophical point.

MASTER
What point? Servants don't think.

JACQUES
So masters think. But it's not what I think. I think I think.
And I think you really think I think too.

MASTER
Suppose I'd tumbled off my horse just then and injured myself
seriously?

JACQUES
I was most careful. When you went arse over tip I jumped
down and caught you, didn't I? Besides, I knew there was
nothing dreadful on the cards. It wasn't written in the big
Book of Destiny above.

MASTER
I'm sick and tired of this. I've told you, there is no Book of
Destiny up above.

JACQUES
You're bound to say that. Once you realize what's written in
it for you.

MASTER
The Book of Destiny has nothing to do with it. You fix
everything, don't you?

JACQUES
Everything?

MASTER
Yes. You talk to everyone, interfere in everyone's life.

Arrange their love affairs, flirt with their mistress, fix up their marriages—

JACQUES
And cuckold them afterwards? That's what you're really afraid of, isn't it? But if that's what's written in the Book of Destiny above—

MASTER
Am I never going to be free of the Book of Destiny above?

JACQUES
No, master. Because that's where it's written that you're my master, and I'm your servant. So where are we going next?

MASTER
Don't you know where we're going next?

JACQUES
How does anyone ever really know where they're going? No one in the world, as I told you at first. So you're my master. You lead me.

MASTER
How can I, if you won't tell me where we are and where we're going?

JACQUES
Just do what's written in the—

MASTER
I have no idea what's written in the—

JACQUES
Maybe that's because no one's really got around to writing it yet.

MASTER
Who does write it, then? You?

JACQUES
I can't do everything, can I? You're the master, it's your duty

to lead me. I'm your factotum, so it's my duty to follow you. However ridiculous your instructions are.

MASTER
No, that's not what it says in the book at all. It says the master gives the orders, and the servant thinks he can choose whether or not he'll obey them, and insists on giving his own opinion whether it's wanted or not. So what is your opinion?

JACQUES
My advice? Let's go . . . forward.

MASTER
Why, may I ask?

JACQUES
Because I really see no point in going back.

MASTER
Right. But why doesn't one of us go one way and the other the other. I presume we're able to choose?

JACQUES
Not if it's written in the book above. Besides, we're bound together, like a head to a body.

MASTER
Heads do sometimes come off bodies.

JACQUES
True. But one tries to avoid that if at all possible.

MASTER
Right. So which way's forward.

JACQUES
Any way that's not back. The best line is the shortest line. As the cabbage-planters say.

MASTER
Yes. Shall we go.

JACQUES
Yes. Let's go.

'They do not move,' he adds. Then he finishes writing, folds the paper, and slips it inside Sterne's battered old book. It's one way of doing it, for the story that just won't end.

So, then, a little something – an alternative ending, a second or fourth choice – to tease the spirit of fiction and confuse Posterity. And, speaking of Posterity, it's time to go and visit Falconet again. For, despite that never-to-be-forgotten moment of rejection, when the city offered him its first and hardest hour, he has never given up on the sculptor. In fact, far too warm to stay unforgiving for ever, far too curious to neglect the drama of the great atelier, he's lately taken to seeing a good deal of his old and ill-tempered friend. And, now the Empress has left the city, and he no longer needs to spend the morning writing a paper on the improved Russian police force or the Siberian economy, he's begun wandering often to the atelier on the Millionaya, where furnaces grow red at the heart of the dusky city, and seeing how the Horseman proceeds.

It's wonderfully warm here, in fact an inferno, as casting ovens flare, furnaces bubble, and foundries hiss. Molten metal bubbles, hot torches sear. In the middle of the huge atelier the Peter maquette sits waiting, brooding, still faceless, under its massive canvas. Our man sits, or at least attempts to, in a quiet corner. A scarf knotted cavalierly around his neck (for a sculptor must always look like a sculptor, as a general must look like a general), Étienne-Maurice sits on a stool to one side of him, looking him over. And on a stool to the other sits Marie-Anne Collot, staring hard at the Thinker's other profile.

'Two statues, it's amazing,' he says.

'Be quiet,' says E-M.

'This way a little,' says M-A.

From time to time a young man wanders in. It's the Falconet boy, back from London, the cause of all the original troubles. Now, from his exaggerated gallantries, his liquidic stares, his hesitant touchings, his fumbling hands drifting uselessly here and there, it's quite clear the upstairs bed has not been wasted. M-A and Falconet *fils* have clearly constructed an intimacy. Casting a quite fresh *lumière* on the sculptor's first clumsy rudenesses, and that bitter territorial struggle for the guest-room bed.

Still, never mind. Now it's slap-slap-slap on this side of him, chip-chip-chip on that. Étienne-M plasters away on the one hand, Marie-A carves away on the other. Tossing clay and modelling stone, they're each one bringing to life a little eternal clone of the Thinker. A little Moi takes shape on the turning table, a small Lui is coming into being on the easel.

'I suppose it would be far too much to ask our Great Thinker to sit quite still just for a moment?' asks Étienne-M.

'And please do try to turn your head a little more this way,' says Marie-A. 'And at least you could put down the book.'

'I never put down the book,' he says. 'Besides, I'm trying to learn Russian.'

'Quite impossible, at your age,' says Étienne-M. 'And surely to learn grammar you don't need to bob your head up and down like that.'

'You don't know Russian.'

'You're quite wrong, I know it only too well.'

'Do you mind if I get up and walk up and down for a bit? I want to look at the furnace.'

'Of course we mind.'

'It annoys you?'

'Naturally it annoys me.'

'I thought perhaps it might put a little bit more life in it. A statue isn't the model of a corpse.'

'I put the life in it, not you,' says Falconet. 'In any case most of my best sitters have been dead.'

'I'm not surprised,' our man says wearily. 'You wear them out. And I do happen to be one of the best sitters in the world.'

'Oh, is that what Houdon says? And Pigalle?'

'Houdon has done me, more than once. I'm still waiting for Pigalle, or rather he's still waiting for me. After all, isn't the sculptor made by the quality of his sitter?'

'Not in this case,' says Falconet.

'What does Levitski say?' asks Marie-A.

A good question, for our man is also having his portrait done, for court or archival purposes, by a designated painter on the

Empress's orders. The young man is Dmitry Levitski, a Russian, one of some new breed in the making; it's his task to make sure our man will survive for good, somewhere on the long walls of the Hermitage (and in time our man will acknowledge he has done a perfect job).

'Levitski says I'm the most fluid, the most mobile, the most interesting sitter he's ever had the pleasure to work on in his life.'

'You're not even a sitter, you're a stander,' says Étienne-M. 'You're a getter-upper and a walk-arounder. It's all very well for Levitski. He uses paint, not stone or plaster.'

'What's the difference?'

'With paint he can wipe you down and rub you out.'

'And why would you want to wipe me down and rub me out?'

'Can't you imagine?'

'I do hope you're making me look like Peter. Can't we find me a horse?'

'I have no intention of making you look like people. Surely you'd like to look like you?'

'That's quite impossible.'

'Oh yes, why?'

'Because the subject I call "I" in no way resembles the object you keep on calling "you". You call me an angry man, I call me a charmer. You think I'm a chatterbox, I think I'm a sage.'

Falconet stops and wipes his hands on a rag. 'In that case, maybe you'd better chisel your own damned bust.'

'I should do a far better job of it than you, old friend. At least I think I know who I am.'

'Go on, then, tell me. Who are you?'

'A witty wise man. Certainly not that effeminate old flirt you're turning me into over there. What will my grandchildren say when they see that? I'm sending them a quick message through the atmosphere to Posterity right now: don't believe it, it isn't me.'

'Well, it will be,' says the sculptor firmly, 'just as what's under canvas over there will be Peter, and what he sits on will be the universal horse. It's not what you look like that counts, it's what I make of it. And I'm sorry, but it's my bust your grandchildren are going to believe in, not you. It's not that stuff you inspect in your mirror every morning you're going to have remembered. It's what the sculptor, the painter, the genius has made of you that will count in the ages to come.'

'But you don't even believe in the ages to come. You don't believe in Posterity.'

'I don't believe in trying to live our lives for it.'

'But you do believe in busts and statues?'

'They're good business.'

'Meaning I'm condemned for eternity to be that . . . parody of a philosopher? That smirking little clown? He isn't the least bit like me.'

Marie-Anne laughs: 'So what are you like then?'

'He's the most handsome man in the world,' says Étienne-M angrily. 'A cross between the Apollo Belvedere and Seneca. But with a bigger conk.'

Our man ignores this. 'You know what I'm like, my darling,' he says to his dear M-A. 'On any one day I assume a hundred different faces, depending on how I'm feeling and what I'm thinking.'

'Wonderful, so you need a hundred different portaits then,' cries the sculptor.

'I'm putting to you the problem of representation, old fellow,' says Our Thinker. 'The paradox of the copy. But, yes, you should be really making a hundred different portraits, if you truly want to do me justice.'

'You're not asking for justice, you're asking for mercy,' says the sculptor. 'Ignore this man whose prospects I created and whose entire life I made.'

'Indeed you did. And what, I should be grateful?'

'Ignore him, and let's both think now, what am I really like?' he says to Marie-Anne. 'I suppose I'm serene and dreamy, yet at the same time tender and passionate. I have bright lively eyes. A broad forehead, a head just like a Roman orator's.'

'Seneca.'

'I have, as you know, a very warm and instinctive nature, just like the simple spirits of the golden age.'

'He's a marble faun, then.'

'Yes, I'm a marble faun. Nature's body, reason's mind. The flesh is splendid, but art also has to speak of the real treasure, the splendour of the mind within.'

'Of course,' says É-M, 'the one thing we can't possibly see.'

'Exactly. Which is why as a philosopher I have a mask that must deceive any but the very greatest artist. Since my mental actions operate so quickly, my expression can never stay the same for more than one second. To be quite honest I always have the feeling I haven't even begun to exist yet, that everything is yet to come. One of these days I shall think something so splendid I shall become truly immortal.'

'When?'

'How do I know? Tomorrow, perhaps? Who knows what I'm capable of. I'm sixty and I haven't even used up a quarter of my powers yet.'

'Would you like us to portray what you're going to look like ten years in the future?'

'Why not? I mean, just look at what you've done, Falconet. You've made me look like some fat ambassador. Some big-eared general. I don't look like a philosopher at all. Maybe I should have two fingers to my ear.'

'Maybe you should,' says Falconet, wiping the dust off his hands furiously. 'Sir, you are completely impossible.'

'Impossible?'

'You always were impossible. In Paris you were impossible. In the womb you were impossible. Now you're even more impossible. You don't begin to understand art.'

'And you, sir, don't begin to understand the mystery we are now examining, the ineffable mystery of the human face.'

'No?'

'No. Art isn't simply an artificial construction.'

'How would you know? You who've never tried to construct it?'

'Because I am a philosophical observer of it.'

'A critic.'

'Yes. Art's conscience, art's consciousness, that's what I am.'

'Oh, you go to all the Paris salons and write about them, yes. You post your arrogant little opinions all over Europe. You make

painters beholden to you, so they flatter and praise you. But you
don't understand one thing about the paintings you write about.
You stand in front of them, you doff your hat, you raise your glass
of wine to them, and invite them to understand you.'

Our man looks decidedly hurt. 'Yes, I'm a critic, that's what
I am. And you may recall that in the course of those opinions I
posted all over Europe I praised you to the skies. Without my
essays you might never have come to Russia at all.'

Falconet laughs. 'Now you tell me. And don't you know, it
was the worst mistake of my life? Maybe you meant well, maybe
you didn't. But now I stew at the heart of Barbary, and you take
the credit. Everywhere you go, it's always the same. You've got to
be the little *maître*. Always some advice, some instruction to give
to everyone. You always know how to do everything so much
better. Just because you wrote an Encyclopedia.'

'Naturally. A builder may have a skill. A painter may have a
talent. But I am a philosopher. What I have is an understanding.'

'Soufflot's dome in Paris, for instance,' says Falconet, mock-
ingly. 'I'm told the latest thing is you're telling him how to build
that.'

'Of course.'

'And who will get the blame if it falls down, you or Soufflot?'

'Ah, but who will create the dream, if it stays up?'

'I thought so. That's quite enough. Very well, good day.'

And for some strange reason Falconet is on his feet and
marching furiously out of the atelier.

Our man stares after him, an innocent surprise plastered over
that strange, impenetrable and ever-moving face of his.

'Did I say something?' he asks ingenuously, turning to Marie-
Anne.

'Yes, *maître*, of course you said something. Now, sit down, put
that book away, turn your head to that wall, and don't say anything
whatever. If you really do want me to do your portrait bust.'

'But he can't go like that,' says our man. 'Étienne-Maurice,
now wait!'

In the doorway, lit by the furnace, the sculptor turns. '*Monsieur?*' he says.

'My dear fellow, now I know why it is the Tzarina keeps

telling me you're impossible to do business with. But I'm sure you'll be delighted to know our good friend Grimm has made you the most splendid offer.'

Falconet looks at him: 'Yes, what's that?'

'He's been amazingly generous. He's offered to buy one or the other of these two busts you're each doing of me.'

'Which?'

'Why, whichever I decide is the better, of course.'

Falconet turns, and walks back across the red glowing atelier. He comes back to his work-table. He takes up his sculpting hammer; he raises it high. It hovers above the philosopher's head for a moment; then it smashes down. Our man – the plaster version, his other little self – shatters into a cloud of whirling pieces. The hairpiece, a version of the expensive new wig he bought on Nevsky Prospekt, pulverizes. Dust flies. Large lumps of thinker drop onto the floor . . .

'Good God,' says Melchior Grimm, when, a couple of days later, our man tells him the story, 'what had you done?'

'I'd done nothing.'

'I really think you must have annoyed him in some way.'

'Not at all. The truth is, it was a truly brave and amazing thing Étienne Falconet did. Choosing to smash his imperfect work, right there in front of his fellow student and his old master.'

'You must have goaded him into it, surely.'

'I didn't goad him into it. His guilty artistic conscience goaded him into it. It was no loss, believe me.'

'It wasn't a good statue?'

'A very bad one, I assure you. He has a problem with faces. Pottery would suit him better. But I still don't know how a man of his talents could possibly miss some of the most remarkable features of his sitter.'

'Perhaps he saw some remarkable features you didn't know about.'

'It's possible. But I can't tell you how glad I was to be rid of it. Even if it did mean I had to stand there and witness the pulverization of my own head.'

'There's nothing left of it?'

'Well, yes, there is. The ears. They must have survived because he sculpted the wig separately and then stuck it on the top. That's what bore the brunt – the absurd Russian peruke you had me go out and buy on Nevsky Prospekt.'

Grimm looks excited. 'The ears of Doctor Diderot? Did you happen to keep them?'

'They're here, in my pocket,' our man says, and takes them out.

Two splendid stone ears, preserved whole and still joined together by a strip of stone skull, sit on the table. Grimm picks them up, and twists them in his hands. They're two little white birds. Two intricate and twisted orifices, two strange passages of ingress spiralling inward into the deepest chambers of the mind, the reason, the senses.

'I shall buy them from him,' Grimm says.

'What, my ears? I thought you'd buy Marie-Anne's bust.'

'A good bust, is it?'

'Excellent. The girl, you see, has no illusions, no pretensions, no false pride. She listens to her masters. Her bust is just as good as his was bad. The charmer truly understands me.'

'You mean she flatters you?'

'No, I mean she understands me exactly as I would wish to be understood.'

'Very well,' says Grimm benignly, 'I may very well buy that too. And perhaps even present it to the Empress. Oh, by the way, old fellow, your days of peace are over. She and the court are returning to the Hermitage tomorrow—'

And it's quite true. Next day the streets that for two weeks have been so empty have grown full, and they are all back again. Horses are trotting, guardsmen are drilling. The countesses and the governesses are back again on Nevsky Prospekt. Outside the Winter Palace, court servants and coachmen are unloading the same massive burdens they so dutifully loaded up only a couple of weeks ago. Purveyors of silks and shippers of wine, the makers of snuff boxes and clocks, are back in the Hermitage corridors.

The butchers and poulterers are once more doing thriving business in the palace kitchens. Gilded invitations to evening receptions, large and small, pass round the city, promoting the usual bursts of envy and weeping. Women in their best dresses reappear in the sledge-carriages. Garlands and icons fill the streets and deck the palaces, for now the Empress has returned Christmas and New Year are coming after all. The churches and cathedrals are full again. The bells ring hourly, the monks intone. It's time to return to the palace . . .

Only to find that things have changed. When he enters the small stateroom, it is the Princess Dashkova who stands there. With her is Doctor Rogerson, cracking his fingers.

'She's not exactly herself,' says Dashkova.

'My belief is it's this Orenburg rebellion that's upsetting her so much,' murmurs Rogerson.

It seems that with the Empress away or in flights of philosophical speculation trouble has chosen to break out in the provinces.

'It's serious?' our man asks.

'*Verra*,' observes Rogerson, for whom everything is always serious.

'The Don cossacks always revolt whenever we go to war with the Turks,' Dashkova explains.

'Do they? I've seen so little of Russia.'

'Nothing at all,' says Dashkova, 'or you wouldn't believe what people tell you, when they say Russia is just like Paris. Orenburg's a long way from here, in a region of total barbarians. It's peopled by kaftaned fools and roaring ne'er-do-wells we've been trying to get rid of for at least half a century.'

'Meantime retaining all their lands and possessions, of course,' murmurs Rogerson. 'Now there's terrible bloodshed, the most shameless atrocities.'

'Is it Pugachov, the imperial impostor?' our man enquires.

'Yes, of course. He goes everywhere with his raging cossacks, slicing and slaughtering whom he pleases. His followers are drunk, and some of them are mad.'

'Happily it's a good long way away,' says Rogerson.

'And every day getting nearer,' says Dashkova. 'You can understand why she fears for her throne.'

'She's coming,' says Rogerson.

'I'm going,' says Dashkova.

And there she comes, in a general's surcoat, two whippets at her heels. She nods first to the left, then to the right, then straight in front, in the Russian court fashion.

'Come in, Mr Librarian,' she says. 'Perhaps you know we have some problems.'

'Not a time for philosophy?' he murmurs.

'Oh, I hope so, I hope so,' she says . . .

DAY FORTY-FIVE

SHE sits down, surrounded by her English whippets. HE crosses solicitously to her side. In the different corners of the courtroom the various cliques are gathering again.

HE
How was your visit to Tzarskoye Selo?

SHE
Wonderful. Very peaceful. I tobogganed every day. I only wish you had come. Have you spent these last days well?

HE
As well as permitted, by the Neva colic. How can it be that what's so agreeable when it enters us at one end grows so discomforting when it departs at the other?

SHE
But apart from that, what else did you do?

HE
I had my bust done, twice. Had my portrait painted. I'm learning Russian. And I wrote, Your Majesty, quite prodigiously. A refutation of Helvétius. An amusing tale about a servant and a master—

SHE
And who is wiser, the master or the servant? Let me guess. The servant. I'm sure you're a pupil of Beaumarchais.

378

HE
It's exactly the reverse, Your Majesty.

SHE looks at him gravely.

SHE
Do you know, while I was at Tsarskoye Selo, two little
Germans came from Prussia to see me? They told me all about
you. They say all your work is plagiarized from wiser men.
That none of your ideas is complete. That you wrote a most
indecent novel you are now heartily ashamed of, about a
woman who could speak from her most private and improper
place—

HE
Not ashamed at all, Your Majesty. I should be quite happy for
the Empress to read it.

SHE
They said you were a dreadful bore, a foolish pedant, a
philosopher who knows no mathematics and cannot make a
proof of anything. They say you don't know if God exists or
not and therefore confuse everyone—

HE
God in particular, I should think.

SHE
They say you are a natural tyrant who pretends to love liberty,
and a man who prefers delusion to evidence. Anyone who
listened to your ideas, they said, would surely rot in hell—

HE
These two Germans. Did they say if they were friends of
mine?

SHE
They certainly seemed to know you very well.

HE
You know who they were, of course. Agents of King
Frederick of Prussia.

SHE
Evidently my German cousin doesn't like you.

HE
He spreads calumnies about me everywhere I go. My offence
being simple. Instead of going to his court, I came to yours.
Instead of expressing my adoration to him, I chose to proclaim
it to you. So he has decided to hate me, and I repay the
sentiment in kind.

SHE
Don't you know it's a capital offence to hate a monarch?

HE
Well, most subject peoples in the world are apt to commit it.

SHE
And then what happens? They fall under the sway of monsters
like this man Pugachov, who is now killing my subjects by the
thousand.

HE
An irrational impostor.

SHE
Believe me, they are not a bit rare. Now another one has
appeared. At Livorno in Italy.

HE
And does he also think he's Peter the Third?

SHE
No, she thinks she's the daughter of the Tzarina Elizabeth,
my predecessor, and so the rightful heir to the throne.

HE
Is it true?

SHE
She calls herself the Princess Tarakanova, also the Countesss
Pimberg. She says she carries her mother's will everywhere
with her in a box. Proving that she has title to the Russian

crown, and I'm the impostor. You've seen inside these royal bedrooms. You know anything is possible. Imagine what little Didros might be waiting somewhere in the wings?

HE
Indeed, Your Majesty.

SHE
But no, it isn't true. Her story's absurd. She says she was smuggled out of Russia and brought up by the Shah of Persia, who has never heard of her. Sometimes it was by Mustapha, or the Kublai Khan.

HE
A clever little mystification.

SHE
The girl's an adventuress, a cute little crookerina. Now she's dangerous, because the Poles are supporting her. And she's made things worse by claiming Pugachov is her brother, and he really is Peter the Third—

HE
One usurper supports the claims of another? It hardly seems logical.

SHE
Realpolitik. If it's logic you're seeking, I suggest you avoid royal courts in the future.

HE
What has happened to her?

SHE
I took a leaf from your own book, Monsieur Didro.

HE
From mine?

SHE
Indeed. I arranged a . . . what did you call it? . . . a clever little mystification. With the aid of my old friend Alexei Orlov.

HE
Who also settled the affairs of Tzar Peter, I think?

SHE
That's not a matter on which I recommend you to think. Call
him a very loyal subject who has been my true friend and now
commands my fleet in the Mediterranean. He found the lady
quite easily. She'd been sleeping with Sir William Hamilton,
as who does not.

HE
The mystification?

SHE
Count Alexei paid his own court to her and asked her to
come and visit him at his palazzo in Pisa. He'd rented one,
of course. Soon their heads were lying together on the same
pillow, and they agreed theirs was the perfect relationship. She
had divine right to the throne of Russia, he had the navy. He
told her he despised me for not rewarding him properly after
my accession, and preferring his brother Grigor as my lover.

HE
A perfect couple, I quite agree. But they would have to get
you out of the way—

SHE
Exactly. He assured her the army and navy would be behind
him. She asked for proof. He offered to arrange the perfect
nuptial ceremony. They would marry on the deck of his
flagship, as the Russian fleet engaged in a mock naval battle.
The events took place, and the sailors rallied round her,
shouting 'Long live Elizabeth, Empress of Russia.'

HE
And?

SHE
And then she descended to the admiral's cabin, to begin the
honeymoon, and was at once arrested. The ship sailed at once
for Kronstadt, and there we are—

HE
Where is she now?

SHE
Chained in a dungeon in the Peter and Paul over there. The
governor – he's brother to your old friend Dmitry Golitsyn,
by the way – is interrogating her fiercely at this very minute.
It appears she's even more of an impostor than we imagined.
She can't speak a word of Russian. It seems she was born in
Baghdad and grew up on marvellous stories.

HE
It's true the Arabians are good at stories.

SHE
Alas, she has told one too many. So what do you think of my
little mystification?

HE looks at her.

HE
She's an innocent, surely. You couldn't harm her.

SHE
Of course not, if it were left to me. But if I did everything
myself, there'd be little point in keeping a Secret Office
to search out my enemies. She'll be held in a dark cell,
interrogated further, and I've no doubt she'll confess to
everything, if not more. Then she'll write me wild letters,
beg me for mercy—

HE
Which in the name of reason I hope you will accept.

SHE
Which in the name of realism I shall certainly refuse. In my
life in this world, I have always been as kind as I can be. But,
my dear friend, believe me, I have learned my lesson. I rule
in a country of legends and fantasies. In Russia any lie is
believed, and any act of reason is seen as folly.

HE
How old is she?

SHE
Twenty-three. But I doubt if she'll see twenty-four.

HE
In the name of friendship, I ask you to spare her. She's killed
no one. She's just made up a few fantastic stories.

SHE
She tried her game, and she lost it. Now she stays where she is
until she's entirely forgotten.

HE
Please. I beg you to let her go. Your Most Serene and
Imperial Majesty—

A sudden silence runs right through the court.

SHE
Sir. Whatever you write, whatever has happened between us,
a servant is still a servant.

HE
I merely ask you to show mercy.

SHE looks at him. The COURTIERS wait.

SHE
Of course, my dear Didro. You shall see my mercy. It's
Advent now. Till the new year comes, there's no need for you
to write me any more papers—

SHE goes.

END OF DAY FORTY-FIVE

TWENTY-NINE (NOW)

EVERYWHERE I LOOK AROUND ME there are books. They surround me on all sides, racked and stacked in extended rows of makeshift wooden shelves, scattered randomly over the ancient desks and reading tables, heaped up high on the floor, and piled in wild disorder beside the walls. The books are old, and seem to be more or less of one age. They're library-bound, in hard brown leather, white calf, red morocco, their titles stamped out in gilt or heavy type. They are there in all the classic sizes: octavos, folios, quartos, duodecimos. Some have survived a couple of centuries of existence in fine shape, but a good many show the damage of time or other kinds of rough treatment, cracking out of their bindings and stitchings and reverting to printed loose leaf. The place I'm standing in is a back area tucked away among the reading rooms and stack-rooms of the enormous vaulted public library. It smells of print, paper, sweating rags. Though it's ill-lit and dusty, it also manages to be damp. The floors are wet with the heavily imprinted footsteps of the many people who have recently been walking in and out of here, seemingly without any real purpose or reason. Water drips from cracks in the ceiling, and falls slowly onto a stack of books in the corner which is gradually changing from brown to black in colour.

'I think I can leave you here for a few minutes? I'll just go and bring us back some hot tea from the samovar,' Galina has said to me a few minutes back, after first bringing me into the great library, showing me into this quiet, odd, deeply untidy back room, sitting me down.

'But what is this, Galina, where are we?' I've asked her.

'What do you think?'

'Surely this can't be the library, the Voltaire and Diderot library?'

'What is a library, do you know? A pile of books? A big room? A great building? I won't be a moment, *mon ami*. Have a look round and tell me what it is you think you can see.'

Left, I'm now walking slowly round the room, wandering from shelf to shelf, desk to desk, and pile to pile. The room has one dusty window, with a large desk placed in front of it. On the desk are more of the books, these left open, as if someone has been reading or processing them. On it too is a plaster statue, a flighty spritely head, which is placed so that it seems to look out of the window at the busy public square outside. The head is surely Diderot's – the one done, I rather think, by Marie-Anne Collot, though I have no means of being sure. To one end of the square outside lies the busy Nevsky Prospekt, filled with its rushing traffic and its whirring trolley buses; to the other is a grand classical façade, the front of the Pushkin Drama Theatre; everything in this city is named after one writer or another. In the central garden is another statue, seemingly the chief focus of our bust's attention. High, coroneted, upright, imperial, it's Mikeshin's pompous late-nineteenth-century grand view of Catherine Veliki, otherwise Catherine the Great.

But my own interest is really with the books on the shelves. They mostly run in sets, special editions, sequences, collecteds. In fact they have the look of being someone's private library, back in the days when cultivated men and women kept a genuine store-house, a sequence of grand leatherbound monuments to their own true seriousness. Here are many of the great works they would have needed: the speculations of Descartes and Leibniz, Hume and Shaftesbury, Montucla and Beccarria. The bound pages of the great dramatists – Racine and Molière, Shakespeare and Marivaux. The verses of the noted poets, from La Fontaine to Colly Cibber. The essays of the great thinkers, from Montaigne to Montesquieu. Works of political economy, medicine and science: Haller and his physiology, Newton and his mathematics. Alphabets and hymnals, sermons and speculations. Prayerbooks and opuscules, lexicons and encyclopedias. Many works of travels: Bougainville's voyages, Voltaire's letters from the English. Works that seem like travels:

Swift's Gulliver, Galland's version of the *Thousand and One Nights*. And those yet stranger books that came from an age of travel and invention, the fictions called novels: the adventures of Don Quixote and his servant, of Gargantua and Pantagruel, of Roderick Random, Clarissa, Tristram Shandy.

Whose books? Most afford no clue at all to their owners, but some do. A number have been printed on their owner's private press, and more are stamped with the coat-of-arms of their prince-like owner: the great Monsieur Voltaire. Others bear a familiar signature in a spikey, jagged hand: Diderot. Voltaire's books have the finer bindings, Diderot's show evidence of the more impassioned use. In the fashion of the times, the books have been used by both to make more books. Voltaire has filled his own with underlinings, great emphases, judgements, annotations, some of these written in the end-papers in a miniature version of his round wide hand. Denis has used the rag pages even more freely, and filled up every spare page with instant reactions, fresh speculations and stories, and written not just round the text and down the margins but across the printed type itself. His reactions are clear. The sentimentally feminized stories of Samuel Richardson – tales of the hunted maidens Pamela and Clarissa – have driven him to passion, and possibly something more: maybe here are the first glimpses of his own literary jewels of indiscretion. The writings of Helvétius have annoyed him. Those of Sterne seem to have provoked him to something resembling mania.

So books breed books, writing breeds writing. The writer starts out as reader in order to become the new writer. In this fashion one book can actually become the author of a new one. And the new books, the books these two authors have then written in such numbers, lie in this odd room as well. Voltaire's huge narrative of the struggles of Charles of Sweden and Peter the Great (eleven years in the writing); his history of the Reign of Louis XIV, which so troubled the reigns of his two successors; all those secret books he wrote that everyone knew about, the books that, printed under mysterious pseudonym or perhaps under no name at all, still managed to get themselves celebrated or burned right the way across Europe. Here's the philosophical encyclopedia he wrote to provide his critical supplement to the greater *Encyclopedia*; the poems and squibs and flatterings; the plays. Here are the bitter little texts that ruined entire reputations and were known to be by Voltaire simply because he'd already gone to such trouble to deny authorship before the books were even published. Here's the incomplete *Thérèse*; the tale of the wise Zadig; the even greater tale of his innocent optimist, Candide.

As Voltaire, so Diderot. Here's the famous and shameless tale of the indiscreet talking jewels, Diderot's vagina monologues, which solemnly sits on the shelf next to his reflections on the mysterious worlds of deafness and dumbness. Here's the libidinous romp through the nunneries, next to his thoughts on embryology. His books are many, but what shouts them down or crowds them out is the famous *Encyclopedia*: that amazing book of books that brought the first philosophes together, adding Voltaire to Rousseau, d'Alembert to d'Holbach; then took them through danger, turned strangers into friends and friends into the most implacable enemies, made their fame and shaped their influence, that defined their futures and posterities, spread light and learning, confusion and infection; that started out with dangerous intellectual adventure and ended in commercial competition, moved from being outrage to commonplace, from danger to safety, had all the publishers fighting each other and the readers competing, and in the end made learning some of the biggest business in the world.

It was, I'm now starting to remember, a very strange book indeed. For one thing its most explosive criticisms of the church and the state were oddly hidden away amongst the 70,000 articles, cross-referenced away in the weirdest of subjects, meaning that you had to explore the most innocent of topics in order to discover the most dangerous of thoughts. Then the volumes were surrounded by every kind of deception and concealment, passed on from publisher to publisher and printer to printer, in France and elsewhere. Going through edition after deceptive edition, it became the great bestseller, the big book of the age. Publishers fought to have the rights to it, pirates multiplied. Texts and formats kept changing, the printing was rushed from place to place.

And here on these shelves are a good number of those editions: the folios, quartos, octavos. This is a pirate edition from Geneva that's come out in thirty-nine volumes, and another from Lucca, and yet another from nearby Livorno, that has come out in thirty-three. Le Breton published the true first edition in Paris, which started in 1751 and reached twenty-eight volumes by 1772, one year before Diderot came here to Petersburg. The set is here, with an editorial slip inside the first explaining that somewhere there exists an extra volume, containing all the entries or sections Le Breton removed from the project without Diderot's knowledge to avoid trouble with the censor. There's a Russian edition (so one did come out after all), and over here there's a handy abridgement, which brings the total set down to twelve volumes.

And then there was its natural opposite, the *très grand projet* of the media magnate Panckoucke, the man who loved the product so much he bought the company, buying all the rights and permissions and then everything else to do with it he could think of: Voltaire's papers, Buffon's papers, all the world of fresh new learning. The dream in his mind was an ever greater encyclopedia, a vast revision, the *Encyclopédie méthodique*, that would dwarf the original and then perpetuate itself into all the ages to come. It would be ultimate, absolute, not just containing all knowledge but codifying it according to the most complex of systems, turning old words into a new window on the world. The alphabet was far too simple; what was needed was a new system of interlocks and interfaces. The work would be divided, sub-divided, each new segment turning into a distinct yet interdependent encyclopedia of its own. It was like building a great new capital city. Every street and pathway would be part of the web, linked into every other in an unbroken yet endless chain of universal knowledge which was supplemented every day.

To make Panckoucke's wide-open book, no expense was spared, no talent and no sphere of knowledge was neglected. Great men were summoned; so were big teams of plodding hacks. Flowcharts were plotted, along with formats and concepts and timelines. All forms of organization were employed. Scissors and paste were put to work; textbooks and lexicons, dictionaries and medical works, prayerbooks and opuscules, law-books and primers of botany were gutted, torn up, mixed and matched. As in some great intellectual forest, many different trees of learning were planted together, side by side, and most of them grew fast. In no time at all the project was running at 125 volumes and showed no signs of stopping there. Volumes had come out to satisfy the first subscribers, who had to be warned that they were in for a long prospect, for work after work would follow as the travel through learning enlarged. The plan spread and spread; and so did the problems. Text didn't arrive (it never does), so volumes were delayed, one delay then spawning many others. Costs multiplied, subscribers fell away, and profits plummeted. Contributors began to tire, take other work, or die, for dying was just coming into fashion.

For it really didn't help that in 1789 – just as things seemed to improve and profits suddenly began rising – France chose to erupt in revolution. Now contributors became quite seriously unreliable, and many of them began to disappear at speed. Some fled the country, some fell silent. More than usual departed the human scene, thanks to the achievements of Dr Guillotine, who duly earned himself an entry. The faithful subscribers stayed faithful no longer. Printers were constantly hanged or butchered, and book-sellers turned cautious. The volumes altered in appearance; they were stripped clean of their royal dedications, and appeared with a tricolour in their stead. As for the Age of Philosophy itself, that too was changing, and probably dying: militarism and melancholy were the flavours of the day. No longer were wise men called on to advise monarchs and princes, or test their wits against the unreason of the church. Thinkers became rebels, rebels became revolutionaries, revolutionaries became soldiers. Sense gave way to sensibility, reason to romanticism, and a gloomy strutting Napo-leonism became the look of a man. It was the day of the career open to talents, so scholars turned both *normale* and *supérieure*. The calendar stopped, and time itself was begun again. Yet, despite all the trials and testings, the *Encyclopédie méthodique* managed, like the endless chain of Napoleons, to survive. By the time it was done it was one of the great projects of the Empire, running to 201 volumes, by now so out of date they went totally unread. A set of unbelievable dustiness runs across several shelvings close above my head.

Galina still hasn't come back, so I take down a stack of books from the shelves and carry them over to the desk by the window. I've gathered up a pile of the original *Encyclopedia*, the first Le Breton edition, because I want to play Diderot's own encyclopedia game. This involves following out the teasing sequences that lie hidden among the alphabetical entries. Thus '*Droit naturel*' easily leads us on to '*Pouvoir*', which steers us to '*Souverain*' and then to '*Tyran*', and all this, if I remember rightly, is part of the sequence of over a hundred entries written by Diderot himself. But, playing the game, I soon hit a problem. The first six volumes I start from are fine, taking me through the alphabet from A to FNE. But something has happened to the next step: the volume FOANG-GYTHIUM is missing, not to be found in the room. And where's volume XI, and volume XIV? The problem gets me looking at some of the other sets on the shelves. They too are in similar condition. Part of Richardson's *Clarissa* is absent too; the set has no Volume II. Something odd has happened to Lemuel Gulliver's travels. In this library the unlucky and sombre ship's doctor seems to make only two voyages; in all the other versions he goes off on four.

Next I notice a set of books I've already been thinking about, Sterne's *Life and Opinions of Tristram Shandy*. I've not forgotten the day of his modern funeral, and his little library in Yorkshire. If these are Diderot's books, then the six-volume set Sterne shipped out to Diderot in advance of his visit to Paris could very well be here. I take down the set on the shelf, and look inside; on the title pages an inscription is written (though Sterne, like a modern novelist on a book-tour, did sign a great many copies). But something is wrong here too: the six-volume set lacks volumes 5 and 6. And so it goes on, from shelf to shelf all the way round the room. The entire library is riddled with these odd gaps: blanks, apertures, elisions, or (as the theoreticians now like to say) aporias. Everything's in this same odd condition of incompleteness, of 'almost'. When is a library not a library? When all the sets and sequences are fractured, as they are here. The alphabetical runs of the dictionaries are short of a few letters. Periodical works have broken calendars, with whole seasons, years, or decades gone astray.

High heels are sounding on the stone flooring; Galina is coming back. She comes and sits down at the desk by the window, and puts down two glasses of tea.

'Did you find anything interesting?' she asks me innocently.

'I'm not sure what to say,' I answer. 'I presume these are the books of Voltaire and Diderot.'

'Some of them.'

'But I don't understand what's happened. Why is nothing complete?'

'Not complete?'

'Yes, all the gaps, the omissions—'

From across the desk Galina looks at me oddly, as if wondering whether she can trust me with some intimate truth or other. 'I am sure you truly love books, *mon ami*.'

'I do, I always have.'

'You see, I told Bo it was not a good idea to bring any of you here at all. That he should arrange something different.'

'It looks as if he has.'

'It's true, I thought he had told you all not to come here. I didn't expect anyone at all. When I came to the boat this morning I thought he'd arranged a different tour. He didn't say so?'

'Not to me. That's why I expected to see the Diderot Library. But what have I seen?'

For an answer, Galina goes over to the wall and takes down a nineteenth-century engraving, which she sets in front of me. The drawing depicts a large handsome room, furnished with desks, classical pillars, glass bookcases, obelisks, a statue. The inscription is in Cyrillic, but it's evident enough what this must be: 'The library of the Hermitage?'

'Yes,' says Galina. 'A wonderful room. The Tzarina wanted to make it very beautiful. Remember, she thought she had brought Russia from nothing to something. Scythian barbarity to Athenian grandeur. So her library of reason had to be one of the finest libraries of the age.'

'And what the Tzarina wanted she always got.'

'Of course. It must have been perfect, you know. The seven thousand books that came from Ferney, the library of the world's greatest philosopher. Then the almost three thousand more volumes that came from Didro, the library of the *Encyclopedia*. Ten thousand volumes altogether, a collection of books just as important as any of the great pictures she hung on the Hermitage walls.'

'It must have been.'

'I already told you what happened next. There was the revolution in France. And then at the end of her life the Empress herself changed greatly. It's said her whole life disappointed her. She got old, fat, fearful. Also she became gross, decadent, superstitious.'

'And her lovers got younger and younger.'

'*Oui*. When King Louis was executed, she put on a black dress. I think it destroyed every hope she'd had in these things. Philosophy, learning, science, enlightenment.'

'So she sent Voltaire up to the attic and locked the library doors?'

'Yes. And from this time strange things started to happen in the Hermitage.'

'Strange things?'

'A locked library is a great temptation. And the place was filled with treasures. Didro's papers. The police file Sartine kept on Voltaire. Many important things. So of course all the little Chichikovs came. The doors were locked but they were easily opened. Treasure is treasure, it is always plundered, officially, unofficially. When Stalin needed some more foreign currency, he just sold pictures from the Hermitage. When the Germans came, they looted everything they could.'

'You mean they took the books from the library?'

'Of course.'

'But I don't understand. No intelligent thief steals just part of a set. A couple of volumes from a collected edition? And who'd steal just three volumes of an entire encyclopedia?'

'It depends who steals, for what. Some people like to possess, others to destroy.'

'It just doesn't seem right.'

'Besides, if you want to lose a book, where do you put it?'

'I don't know. In a library?'

'Of course. In a library books are found, but also they are lost. Sometimes they are taken away, sometimes brought back and put in the wrong place. We try to keep a catalogue, but even the best catalogues are wrong. And this library has been moved many times. When it came from the Hermitage, no proper list was kept. There was the Revolution, the Siege, when books were moved to the basements. When the time came to put them back, no one was sure where. Only one person really thought about the old library in the Hermitage. Only one person tried to restore it as it was.'

I look at her: an elegant grey-haired lady, in a fine flimsy French dress, fingering the brooch at her breast.

'You mean you, Galina.'

'*Oui, d'accord*. But imagine, here you are in one of the world's greatest libraries, like the Berg, or the Bibliothèque Nationale. But it's still a library with nothing: no complete catalogue, no full record on computers. We don't have these clever shelvings they have in London or Paris, or teams of scholars to classify everything. Maybe there are five million books here, and maybe ten miles of shelves. Somewhere in all that there were once ten thousand special books, the library of Voltaire–Didro. It's not hard to find some, the ones with Voltaire's mark on. Some you can identify only by the annotations: Voltaire's hand, Didro's. For forty-five years I tried to go to every shelf and look at every eighteenth-century book. If I thought it belonged once to the Library of Reason, I bring it here. Every book in this room comes here for a purpose. Maybe it was once in the library, or maybe in some way it will lead me to the others.'

The room suddenly seems sad. I look around it, at the rough shelves, the incomplete sequences, the damaged spines, the volumes soaking with a leak of rain.

'How many do you think you've identified by now?'

'Five thousand, perhaps.'

'What about the rest? Do you think they're still there, somewhere in the library.'

'How can I know that?'

'Surely there's a better way than checking every single book.'

'Of course, if I could find Didro's *Book of Books*. It's said he kept a list of all his books.'

'Is it here?'

'Maybe. Maybe in his papers.'

'His papers? So you don't know everything that's in his papers?'

'The papers were confused too.'

'There are still manuscripts that haven't been published.'

'I expect so. Yes, of course.'

'But haven't the scholars been through everything?'

'Almost. Everything we have found so far.'

'Have you read his papers?'

'Not all. First I want to put back the library of the *Encyclopedia*. Restore it as it was before.'

'You will, Galina. I feel sure.'

'I am glad you are sure, *mon ami*. I tried already for forty-five years. I am not so sure any more.'

I get up, and look out through the dirty glass of the window. The square is filled with cold drab people, walking briskly through the hard-blowing wind; they all seem much more than a world away.

'Surely you can get someone to help you? A foreign scholar?'

'You can see how Russia is now. Now the bad times are over, the worse times come. Who knows what will happen, if we will go forward or back? We always call ourselves civilized, cultured. But our sufferings make us brutal and our poverty makes us weak and degraded. People still starve here like they did in wartime, and wages don't get paid. There's no true state, no real order. The people who survive are those who have learned to be cunning or how to commit crimes. In times like that, why would anyone care?'

'You care.'

'*Moi?* But I am nobody. No, it's not true. I am a ridiculous old woman, who for years has tried to be elegant and Parisian, be the way Petersburg was. I wanted a life among pictures and books. In other words, I am a silly woman who ignored the truth, and does not understand the world.'

'I don't think so.'

'Please. You see with your own eyes what is happening. Each day I dress and I walk through the city to come here. Each day I try to build my Library of Reason. Each day someone, some little Chichikov, walks in off the street. We don't have proper guards, he can go anywhere, do anything. If a door is locked, it only takes five roubles to get someone to turn a key. Those people come and they know exactly what to look for. They get their commissions from collectors, in Italy, America. He finds the book or the manuscript, and ships it abroad for a profit. Now it gets worse. Young children walk in off the Nevsky Prospekt, and pick up books to sell to the foreigners on the streets. As I put things together, someone takes them away. If I find a new book for the library, someone walks in and takes ten. One day, there will be nothing left. There will never be a library of reason. So you see I truly am a fool.'

'No, truly, you're not a fool.' And then, to my surprise, I'm holding in my arms a handsome white-haired woman, scented by Chanel, dressed by Poiret, at least seventy years old. And I'm holding her tight and embracing her fondly, trying to kiss away the bright tears that suddenly fill her eyes . . .

THIRTY (THEN)

THEN, SUDDENLY, it's a time of endings. Christmas has been and gone, in a great and Byzantine display of festivities, a New Year has dawned in the northern darkness, and everything changes. It's as if the ornate celebrations that have lit the sky for a fleeting moment are the bringers of a greater darkness that descends, like night and snow, over everything. The last pages of the calendar, which turn differently here, have finally turned, and strange new creatures seem to appear over the horizon as the new book of pages dawns. Over the season, the snow has fallen steadily and thickly: turning streets into great white pads, creating the most incredible night spectacles as a million huge flakes sail down slowly past the thousand candle-lit windows of the Winter Hermitage. The Advent season has filled it with great festivities, crowds that are nearly mobs, drunken nobles, arrogant princelings, stumbling generals who have attended the spectacles, watched the sweet plays and operas, even danced in the public staterooms with a newly visible empress.

But here too things are changing, and now the new year darkness has begun to fall too. Plainly not all is well. The snow that began by cleansing the city has now captured it, blanketing all. Horses trot through the streets with frozen beards hanging from their mouths. The urine turns to yellow bricks on the ground beneath their feet. Carriages slide along on huge runners. Long toboggans dragged bodily across the ice of Lake Ladoga keep the city fed. The Baltic is solid-frozen, so nothing from the real Europe which the city mocks comes in. His error in not going deeper into Russia when the weather let him only becomes more apparent. For the snow blanket is so deep that no journey is made now unless entirely necessary; for a soft elderly fellow like himself

397

it's quite impossible. Only if he resolves to remain in Russia through another summer season will he see in detail the place he has described, his imagined Utopia.

Otherwise it will remain almost as it was before he came, a dream-like scene lit by the (as he now suspects) highly unreliable information that, in answer to his endless questions, has been so sedulously fed to him, by empress, courtiers, scholars and academicians, and which is now supposed to be the stuff of his next great project, so warmly promoted by dear old chancellor Betskoi: his Russian encyclopedia. But is it really true that all over Russia the serfs eat turkey daily, in the same way the unlucky peasants of poorer countries eat gruel or stale bread? Is it really the case that in this fine and decent land no one is ever tortured without excellent reason, ever detained without good cause? Is it really true that its gold reserves are the world's greatest, and its emerald mines are beyond compare? Is it unquestionably so that the cossacks are all loyal and consenting subjects, or that the Tartars far to the east all read Voltaire and Bossuet and speak the most perfect French?

Yet if it now seems unlikely (for he truly does not want to stay another year) that he will ever move closer to deep Russia, something out there, something stirring in the deep vast nation, seems to be moving ever closer to him. The remarkable rebellion that began when a witless impostor emerged in the Cossack lands out beyond the Volga has turned into something different: something so serious, so strangely menacing, it affects every single thing that happens in the court. Pugachov is a strange impostor, but he matters. Now known through the nation as Emperor Peter Federovich, the wonderfully revived Peter the Third, true husband of she who has become the false usurper, he marches like some operatic hero through the southern towns and villages. He dresses in the grandest robes, goes everywhere bearing his sceptre and axe. His retinue is huge, dressed up as courtiers and priests. His wife has assumed the role of the true tzarina, a stout mockery of the Empress herself. His courtiers have adopted names like Orlov and Potemkin. All point to the marks of the scrofula that prove him to be the one true tzar.

Over the winter his army has grown vast. He attracts rabid Old Believers, wild nationalists, resentful military conscripts, disappointed generals, frontier cossacks, mounted and wandering tribesmen, defiant fleeing serfs. They have become an army like Kublai Khan's, another eastern invasion. Everywhere the Old Faithful are turning against the false atheists, and the servants against their masters. The upstart tzar offers bounties for slaughter, prizes for genocide: landowners are slaughtered by the hundred, their wives raped, their children stolen and impressed into fighting service, their serfs released, their cattle killed, their houses and mansions torched. Captured officers are publicly tortured and mutilated, in barbarian atrocities answered by the loyal troops, who have set up torture-wheels in all the village squares. Ten thousand Yaik cossacks have set winter siege to Orienburg, and it now looks likely to fall, while another huge revolutionary army encircles Kazan, so well armed their artillery pieces are blasting down the walls.

But worst of all the impostor's emissaries are infecting the other capital, Moscow, stirring up mass demonstrations and protests, riots and cruelties, and making the city impossible for its own court to visit. Pugachov has unlocked the grandest of old Muscovite dreams: dreams of a Grand Tzar of the Old Believers, who will cleanse all the lands of European influences, bring the court home to the true mid-Russian capital, return everyone to the old, mystical, brutal, honest Scythian ways. Disorder slips everywhere now, infecting everything, spreading through all things just like the malady of the Neva. Fear and anxiety unsettle the entire court. The Turkish war where Potemkin wins victories and the Cossack rebellion where the generals yield ground run dangerously side by side. It occupies all the chanceries, it calls forth all the regiments. Our man has come to Russia in a time of revolution, where everyone is preoccupied with their own fates and their best loyalties, should unreliable Moscow fall before the summer comes, the Tzarina topple, the great rebellion succeed.

It's no time to be a philosopher. He still goes to court from time to time, dressed in his black philosopher's suit. But he knows he's not needed, and he senses a great suspicion, not at all helped by the campaign that Frederick's emissaries have been so busily waging against him. Her Serene Majesty is no longer serene. Revolution and war have worried her, darkened her, robbed her not only of delight and amusement but any joy she had in the cunning of reason. Her place is no longer secure, the risks of the past have begun to haunt. Perhaps nature – she is forty-five now, after all – and the need for help have made her feel she needs some new attentions. At any rate secret letters have been sent out to the Turkish battlefront, and now shaggy, one-eyed Grigor Potemkin, the hero of the Tauride, has been summoned back right across Russia to take his place at court.

Our man sees her still. He still writes his papers; still takes his snowy walk to the Hermitage; still sits on the great sofa amid the whippets; still touches her hand and slaps her knees; still expresses his fondness and pays his respects. But she's not looking, and she's not listening. The sessions have grown shorter and shorter, rarer and rarer. The papers he writes lay on the table unread. And disorder within matches the disorder without. The colic bites harder than ever, the cold hurts even more. The world beyond, the world he calls the real world, seems ever more distant, terribly so, to the point where he can hardly summon it or the feelings he once felt. He has almost entirely ceased to write letters now, unable to believe his words can possibly reach beyond the great veil – of fog, snow, confused history. The days grow ever darker. The worms seem to wait for him under the arctic snowcap.

All he wants, if only he could summon the courage and find the moment to say so, is to find a carriage, acquire a guide, leave the country, risk the long white wintry journey home. But how to tell her? It's even harder to leave than to come.

DAY FIFTY-FIVE

Thick snow outside. SHE sits on her imperial sofa, reading a book. It's her favourite English novel, Tristram Shandy. *HE comes in and sits down. SHE raises her head, as if really pleased to see him.*

SHE
Why don't you tell me a story?

HE
A story?

SHE

I've had enough of philosophy. And you are not really a true philosopher, are you?

HE

I hope I am, whatever Frederick says. At least, I trust I'm a man of reason.

SHE

But it's monarchs who appoint philosophers. And today I prefer to appoint you a storyteller.

HE

Very well. This is a story about two famous travellers, two great men you may very well have heard of. One was the French observer Montesquieu. The other was an Englishman and a friend of his, the Earl of Chesterfield.

SHE

Yes, I know of both of them. Well?

HE

Tell me, do you know Venice? Marco Polo's city.

SHE

No, I've never been there. I know it's a great republic. A strange water-city of masques and carnivals—

HE

The mountebanks, the magicians, the fortune tellers, the rope-dancers. The Doge in his horn-shaped hat, the ladies with their breasts wide open. The crowds, the operas. The fireworks, the huge public feasts. The nationalities – the Arabs, the Orientals, the Turks, the Armenians. The babel of languages. A city of strong moods, strange adventures, deep secrets, dark waters. Do you know they say even the priests and monks go around most of the time in obscene masks and strange disguises?

SHE

A wondrous place, I hear.

HE

A wondrous place, and perhaps this is why men of rank and power from all over Europe have long loved to go there. For the deceptions, the dissipations, the secrets, the islands, the churches, the rotting palaces, the long canals just like those in Petersburg.

SHE

The paintings. The glassware. The glorious silver—

HE

Also the remarkable variety of women. The whores, twenty thousand of them. The brothels, the procuresses.

SHE

Casanova told me the nuns of Venice had given him more delicious excitement than any women in the world.

HE

At any rate, as you know, Venice is a city state, a republic that has never risked itself with kings or emperors. Even the pope has said he seems not to rule there. Instead it's governed by the Doge and a council, chosen from the leading families, and elected by the strangest of ceremonies—

SHE

I was expecting to hear you celebrate its republican spirit. Though the other day you were telling me Venice showed how a republic could be as repressive as a tyranny—

HE

It's true, Your Majesty. Venetian laws are famously strict, and administered by a cruel Inquisition. As Casanova may also have told you. The council itself is large but shrouded in laws of such strict secrecy its members are forbidden on pain of death from conversing with foreigners.

SHE

I've heard of such laws. But naturally in any state there are times when such restriction is entirely necessary—

HE

And that was the opinion in Venice. But of course that meant there were spies everywhere, reporting to a secret office. And this often resulted in great misery. For instance, one leading senator had an illicit love affair that excited him so greatly he could scarcely wait for the meetings in the Doge's Palace to finish before he threw himself into his mistress's embraces.

SHE

I recognize the sentiment.

HE

Unfortunately the quickest path to her Palazzo passed through the French Embassy. Love is blind, you know, but the Secret Office is all-seeing. Soon he was spotted, thrown into the Doge's prison, and interrogated by the Council of Ten. He could have saved himself by naming his mistress. But, as a man of honour, he chose not to. He was beheaded, and his head displayed on a pike.

SHE

The lady should have spoken.

HE

Her husband was one of the Council of Ten, the Inquisition.

SHE

Forgive me for complaining, my dear Didro. But I did appoint you to tell me a story. Are you sure you know how to tell one? You began by talking of Montesquieu and Chesterfield—

HE

Indeed I did. I'm grateful you've spoken. A writer always needs a reader, a tale-teller, a true listener. Well, it so happened these two great travellers met once in Venice. And they fell into a small quarrel, about their two nations, which have never quite got on—

SHE

It's so. Often to our advantage.

HE
Milord expressed the view that the French had more wit than the English but less common sense. And Monsieur said in that case he was delighted to be French, because it was better to have true wit than brute common sense.

SHE
Very true—

HE
Now, Montesquieu was always a very shrewd observer of foreign customs, always asking questions and making notes on what he'd learned.

SHE (*amused*)
I've met such people.

HE
And one night he was writing his notes when a stranger, French but very ill-dressed, was shown in. 'Sir,' he said, 'I have lived in Venice for twenty years, but remain your compatriot. That's why I've come to warn you. In Venice you can do almost anything you care to, except one thing. Never meddle in affairs of state.'

SHE
Quite so, Monsieur Didro.

HE
'One misplaced word, one indiscreet document, could cost you your head. And it's come to my notice the Secret Office is watching you. The spies – they have battalions of them – are tracking your every movement, watching your every mood, and reporting on you.'

SHE
Naturally. Such investigations happen in a well-run state.

HE
'Indeed I know for a fact you'll be getting a visit shortly. Probably in the darkest hours of the night.'

SHE

In fact four in the morning is the very best time.

HE

'So, if you've been making notes, consider. It could just cost you your life.'

SHE

I have always said so. I presume the man wanted a large reward.

HE

No. Montsquieu offered him money, but he firmly refused. 'No, president, the only reward I ask is this,' said the fellow. 'If I've come one day too late, please don't denounce me and lose me my head.'

SHE

The usual request.

HE

So the moment the man had gone Montesquieu gathered up everything he'd written about Venice and threw it in the fire. He called his servants and ordered his chaise to be ready for three in the morning, to save his life. He was just about to leave when a knock came on the door.

SHE

Oh dear.

HE

It was the Earl of Chesterfield. Naturally Montesquieu told his friend exactly what had happened. Chesterfield thought a moment and then said: 'Wait a moment. This man? You'd never seen him before?' 'Never in my life.' 'Badly dressed, you say? He was after money then?' 'No, I offered him a large sum, but he refused.' 'Odder and odder,' said Chesterfield. 'The fact you were being investigated, where did he get it from?' 'I don't know. I suppose the Council of Ten or the Secret Office.' 'But why would they tell someone like that?'

SHE
Perhaps he worked for them himself?

HE
Exactly so. 'Except,' said Chesterfield, 'why risk his job and his life too for the sake of warning you? It makes no sense.'

SHE
I must say your Chesterfield speaks excellent sense himself.

HE
'So what is going on?' asked Montesquieu. 'Who could the fellow possibly be?' Chesterfield thought some more, then he struck his brow. 'One thought. Just suppose this fellow who came was—'. 'What? An agent provocateur?' 'Perhaps. Or possibly?' 'Go on, do you think you know who sent him?'

SHE
Surely the Doge or the Secret Office.

HE
'Surely the Doge or the Secret Office,' said Montesquieu. 'No, I'd say someone even cleverer and more calculating,' Chesterfield said. 'His name is Chesterfield, and he just wanted to show an ounce of English sense is worth a ton of French wit. Because if you'd had one ounce of sense you'd have worked it out for yourself and kept hold of your manuscripts.'

SHE laughs loudly. COURTIERS look in.

SHE
I hope Monsieur took it in good grace.

HE
What would you have said, then?

SHE
I? 'My good fellow, you've shown me there are witty men in England. One day let me show you there are sensible men in France.'

406

HE
And if only he had—

SHE
What did he say?

HE
He shouted, 'You vile scoundrel, you British rogue, you've made me burn my entire book. I shall never forgive you.' Then he rushed downstairs, jumped into the post chaise, and didn't stop till he reached the Papal state of Rome. He contemplated the ruins, and began yet another of his books—

SHE
So that's what really happened.

HE
No, Your Highness. None of it happened. You asked for a story. I made one up to please you.

SHE
It's a false story?

HE
It's a story.

SHE
Wait, you're confusing me. In that case my ending could be just as true as yours.

HE
Certainly. An excellent ending. Perhaps if the tale is printed in the future, that's the ending it should have.

SHE
But which one is right?

HE
None is right. And the listener makes the story as much as the teller.

SHE
Well, which is better?

HE
Neither is better. Both are possible. Perhaps I prefer my own because it seems closer to what is written in the great Book of Destiny above.

SHE
You don't believe that? That fortunes are made and fates are plotted before we even start? Surely, if everything were predestined, we would have no freedom and therefore no achievement. We should simply be victims of life's tyranny. There would be no greatness. We might as well do nothing at all.

HE
You say we need freedom. Well I too should like to—

SHE
You should like to what?

HE
I should like to change the fate that seems written down for me in the great Book of Destiny above—

SHE
Oh dear, Mr Librarian. Why do I suddenly fear you want to go?

END OF DAY FIFTY-FIVE

THIRTY-ONE (NOW)

GALINA'S APARTMENT is somewhere in a muddle of smaller
streets that lie just off the Fontanka Canal. We go down a wide
dirty roadway and enter by a great street-gate into a courtyard
filled with logs of wood for the stoves. Children play, women sit
talking, washing flaps, the walls are chipped and cracked, the windows
unpainted. Inside the inner doorway is a wide neglected staircase
of broken stone. Once this must have been some noble's palace,
but it's gaunt now: its neo-classical grandeurs roughly partitioned
off and shaped into people's flats. Now it's a building of murky
interiors, wandering residents, open doors, disturbing smells. Two
floors up Galina stops on a dark landing, takes out a key, and
unlocks a black door. She is lucky, she tells me, she is always
lucky; she is the one who has an apartment with a door that can
be locked. We go inside to a survivor's space: a narrow hall hung
with clothes, a tiny kitchen with a sink and a portable stove, a
living room with a daybed sofa, a drab and clanking bathroom.

Yet the fine-plastered walls created for the old building are
high and grand, the cornices splendid, a chandelier still hangs from
the living-room ceiling. Galina has filled up the flat, covering the
walls with shelves, wardrobes, cupboards, between which hang
icons and paintings. Everywhere there are books, everywhere
bindings and bibelots, snuffboxes and pomanders, vases and photographs, a mass of small things grandly displayed. A sewing machine
sits on the table, a vast row of dresses in the wardrobe, and rich
French perfumes scent and savour the flat. There are posters of
Paris on the walls, and Delaunay drawings of the Eiffel Tower.
There are bottles of French brandy, one or two of wine. Galina
sits me down in comfort. She lays out bread and olives; she pours
me a glass of brandy; we begin to talk.

I'm not sure why I'm here, but we've certainly done our proper literary duties: been to the Pushkin House, the Nevsky monastery-graveyard, the huge marble tomb of Dostoyevsky, laying a flower on the grave of the writer who best caught this city in its misery. We've then walked the streets in this neighbourhood, the area where he lived once and where he set the urban miseries of *Crime and Punishment*. A persistent sombreness of the kind he depicts still lies over everything in this city, and even seeps into this flat. Galina talks at first about the library, the past, the city's writers: Pushkin and Lermontov and Bakhtin and Bitov. I look at the photographs, ask her questions, but it's a long time before I can get her to talk about herself. Then slowly she admits to the life I can't see: a husband, a painter, who was arrested in the 1950s in the time of Stalin and disappeared in the Siberian camps. There are two children who grew up and went to Moscow. They were turned against her, and don't come back any more. She's always been different, always under suspicion. But she's been lucky; she's always managed to survive.

We go round the corner, to a tiny Russian restaurant, and at a small table eat a cabbagy Petersburg meal, drinking a bitter bad wine. I ask her about Paris, and now it turns out, though she loves it so much, she's never been there. She wanted to travel, but was never allowed to; her interests were far too western to permit her to go to the west. She still longs to go to Paris, knows all there is to know about it, can imagine everything of it in her mind. But she's lucky, so lucky, because these days all such things are permitted, and in any case so many westerners come to see her. It's amazing how many are interested, how many care about Voltaire–Didro, how their books are still read. The French scholars come often, hoping for new treasures. But it's really surprising, how little they understand Russia, and how very Russian Didro really is. And as for what Russia needs, Catherine herself would have understood it: not more hard labour, more brutality, more cruel or stupid tyrants, whom the land breeds like cabbages, but more bright light and civilization.

We walk back to the apartment, go inside again. Galina insists on lighting coloured candles all around her room. And soon she's opening cupboards and boxes, showing me papers, letters, photographs, old documents. There are prints of eighteenth-century Petersburg, cautious letters from French academics who wrote to her back in the fifties. There are photographs of picnics, people she's worked with at the library, programmes of the many operas she has been to, poems she has written. Mementos like this always remind me of how fragile a life is, how we try to hold on to a shape and meaning for it, and yet always finding it's drifted away. We feel real and whole, but nothing else about life does, not even the buildings or monuments we set up to spare us this sense of exile, the pain inside modernity. She opens books, showing me plates and engravings: Russian cities, great festivals, river picnics, processions, parades. She produces fine fashion magazines: ancient copies of Paris *Vogue*, where turning the folded down pages I can see the dresses she has so painstakingly copied on the sewing machine in the corner.

The night is passing away, and we keep on talking. Only when there's a touch of morning light in the sky out beyond the half-draped windows does it seem time to go. On the cold empty street beyond the gates of her apartment, she stands in her red dress, holds me tight, and kisses me very hard. The world seems sombre and very menacing at this hour. Cats and dogs prowl through the rubbish, walkers clatter in a nearby street, the black canals are sucking noisily at their own banks. Perhaps there's a curfew; she doesn't know. But somehow she finds me a night taxi, stopping me just as I'm about to get inside.

'Remember, now those Reds are gone, Russia will only get better. It's true, *mon cher*, believe me.'

'Yes, Galina, of course I believe you.'

'And why do you believe me?'

'Because I hardly know Russia, and I want to believe you, that's all.'

'I wish I could believe myself. I'll call you when I get to Paris, *oui*?'

'I very much hope you do. I'd like to see you again.'

'You don't think I will go? Of course I will. Nice people invite me there all the time. Your friend Bo has promised to help me.'

'I'm sure he will.'

'I just cannot tell you, I have so many beautiful friends who never forget me. I don't go far, but all over the world people know me.'

'Of course. You're wonderful. Goodbye then, my dear Galina.'

'Goodbye, *mon cher ami*,' she says, holding me tight. 'Listen, I'm glad. I'm glad you like books.'

'Of course I do.'

'And to make you remember me, a little present. Don't look yet. Perhaps it will make you come back to Russia.'

'I hope so.'

She kisses me again, sweetly, and slips something into my overcoat pocket: a packet of some kind, thin and hard, and wrapped in a light tissue paper. The taxi drives me away. I can still see her back there through the rear window: in the middle of the cobbled street, standing by an arched bridge over a black canal, her fine grey hair blowing, and the wind swinging and swaying through the silk of her red dress.

We're sailing at noon tomorrow; I shall not get out into Petersburg again. I look through the window at the grim gloomy quarter, the area of struggling cobblers, pawnbrokers and saddened clockmakers Dostoyevsky wrote about. We cross the black Neva, riding by the dark Hermitage. A blue dawn is just beginning to rise coldly out of the darkness from the harbour waters of Vasilyev-sky Island as the taxi deposits me by the dockyard, not far from the ship. Arc-lights illuminate the metal rails and show the lapping tidal water; everything creaks silently, all the cranes are still. Faint decklights illuminate the floating hotels, and the *Vladimir Ilich* at its moorings. The terminal building is locked and nearly dark, but somewhere in there a few conscript soldiers are talking and smoking. They unlock the doors, take the handful of roubles I offer them, accept a packet of cigarettes. I walk through the gaunt strange reception hall, with its shattered windows, its empty passport booths, bare customs benches.

Beyond it, on the waterfront, a sailor with an automatic in his waistband stands at the foot of the gangplank. He's seen me before; he quickly checks my boat-pass and waves me aboard. I walk aboard the big silent hulk, and through the sleeping, creaking slip to my small metal cabin. The packet Galina gave me still sits in my pocket. So far I've really not cared to inspect it. Now, before I go to sleep, I take it out and strip off the wrappings. What emerges is an old leather-bound book, faintly scented with Galina's Chanel. Its spine is damaged and cracked, but it's two double volumes of a work by my favourite writer: *Tristram Shandy, Volumes 5 and 6.* This is the end of the book's first part, the part Sterne completed and published before he went to Paris and met Diderot. I look inside: Sterne's signature is on the title-page, and someone's spiky handwriting decorates the margins.

This is the volume that does come to a famous ending. It concludes, more or less, with Sterne's famous squiggles, his way of explaining to us what a story is and how a good plot works, by going in a straight line from here to there, the way you plant a row of cabbages. Then he gives a little chart of the hopeless baroque mess he has made of his own plot, his story turning off course, turning back on itself, tripping up, missing a fragment, starting up again. He's left a blank page for the reader to put things right, but surely things are getting better. Soon he'll be writing in a straight line: the line of rectitude, as the Christians say; the best line, say the cabbage planters; the line that's often confused with the line of gravitation; the line that, when the next volume starts in the future, will have taken him over the sea to France.

The text ends, and then the spiky handwriting picks up, scribbling furiously on the rest of the leaf: 'How did they meet? By chance, like everyone else. What were their names? What's that got to do with you? . . .' I turn the remaining pages and there, in the end-papers, is a slip of old paper, yellowed, foxed and faded. I take it out and carefully open it up:

JACQUES [I read]
Oh, come on now, master, just admit it.

MASTER
Admit what, you little rat, you dirty dog, you utter scoundrel? That you're the most wicked of servants, and I'm the most unlucky of masters?

JACQUES
Admit I've proved my point. That for most of the time we act and do things without meaning it—

MASTER
Nonsense.

I know what this is, of course. Books breed books. The end of one is often the beginning of another. Which then ends itself, no doubt then to become the start of yet another. But, perhaps because nothing ever ends in the way it was originally meant to, the author sometimes goes back into it again, begins to rewrite it, starts to revise the story, or even begins to tell the whole thing over again . . .

I refold the paper, and shut it back up in the book. Then I open up my suitcase and, lifting my shirts, I push the book down as far as I can into my luggage, thinking that perhaps I now know what has been happening to the great Library of Reason.

THIRTY-TWO (THEN)

DAY SIXTY

A bright sun is shining through the windows of the Hermitage, casting a liquid light over the waters of the Neva below. The birds in the arbours outside the state rooms are full of song. SHE sits on the sofa, beneath the big portrait of an earlier self. Her English whippets are beside her. The COURTIERS are quiet, the room almost empty apart from DASHKOVA. HE comes in. His hands are behind his back.

HE
My dear lady. The last time. The very last time.

SHE
The last time, my dear dear Didro. So today there is no paper.

HE
But there is. I've just finished writing it.

HE takes his hands from behind his back and presents her with a paper. SHE looks.

SHE
'Peace Treaty of Sankt Peterburg, between a Great Sovereign and a Poor Philosopher.' And just why do we need a peace, when we never were at war?

HE
It's true, we never were, dear lady. I don't think two people of opposite parties ever got on better. But there are my demands.

SHE
Your demands? Who allowed you to have demands?

HE
I allowed myself. I must tell you they're exceedingly small demands.

SHE
Yes. Tell me what I can do for you?

HE
Nothing. You've done everything already.

SHE
Then I shall sign it at once, without even reading it.

HE
No, that won't do at all. Even though I now understand very well how your fellow-monarchs managed to sign and then break treaties without ever reading them. You read my other papers, please read this—

SHE
What does it say, Didro?

HE
First, it explains I have no wish for gold. I should hate it if all the eulogies and flatteries I intend to press on the Empress when I return to Paris should appear to be paid for. I prefer to be believed.

SHE laughs.

SHE
Very well, dear friend. But are you rich?

HE
No, madame. Content, which is better. But I have made certain requests. Your Majesty will surely remember how I struggled to arrive here, and how hard I worked when I came.

SHE
Sir, you were quite extraordinary. There is no one in the world quite like you. You will never be forgotten.

HE

So I am sure Your Majesty would not wish me to go
home with nothing. I simply ask you pay me the costs of
my journey, coming and return. They are not extensive,
a philosopher shouldn't travel like a lord.

SHE

Can you tell me how much?

HE

Fifteen thousand roubles would cover it, I believe.

SHE

Then you shall have double. Dashkova, get it from the
exchequer.

DASHKOVA takes a key and goes.

HE

Second, I request no expensive personal gift, but there is one
small thing I would welcome. A tiny thing, something that's
yours and I would value because I know you have used it
every day—

SHE looks at him with amusement.

SHE

What is that, sir?

HE

Your breakfast cup and saucer, that is all.

SHE

Nonsense, it would smash on the journey—

HE

You will see it is already in the treaty, if you read—

SHE

I have something better for you. Something I have already
selected for you, my dear librarian—

*SHE opens her bag and takes out an agate cameo ring. Her own
portrait has been engraved onto it. SHE hands it to him.*

HE

It's beautiful, extraordinary, Your Highness. Third, I hope you would help me with my journey—

SHE

Where do you go now? Samarkand, the Great Wall of China, somewhere over the steppes?

HE

No, dear lady, home. By the fastest way possible.

SHE

Frederick of Prussia has sent for you again. So has the King of Sweden. And Voltaire wants to see you at Ferney, remember.

HE

They can't have me, I'm sorry. I can't tell you how sad I shall be to leave you. But I shall be even more happy to see my dear ones again.

SHE

Your wife, you mean?

HE

My dear dancing daughter. My sweet indifferent mistress. My friends, my talking circle. And yes, even my quarrelsome wife.

SHE

Very well. You shall have a coach, a splendid new English travelling coach I purchased only this week. And I shall provide you with a chamberlain to guide you on the journey and take you back to Prince Golitsyn there in the Hague. Anything more?

HE

Yes, Your Highness. If it should be when I return to Paris I must suffer for what I've done – a spell in the Bastille, for instance – I hope you'll protect me. Look after my wife, who could starve without noticing. Protect my dear darling daughter, who has only just given birth—

SHE
It's done, it's all done. You have all of your treaty. So was it all really worth it? All those great *versts*? All that Neva colic?

HE
That's not a question for the philosopher. That's for the monarch to say.

SHE takes his hands.

SHE
Then of course it was worth it, dear Didro. Don't you see how I've sat entranced by all your thoughts, the strange things that spring from your genius—

HE
Entranced by some things, enraged by others—

SHE
Yes, but, my dear man, you've done wonders. You've taught me everything. How to run a just society. How to create education, develop manners, encourage the great arts and crafts—

HE
How to run a police force. How to construct lighter cities. How to found banks and create improvement.

SHE
You've taught me about usury and luxury. God and the devil. Gambling and divorce. Life and liberty—

HE
The pursuit of happiness—

SHE
Mulberry trees and pig farms—

HE
And you have shown me what I never expected to see. The martial power of a Brutus, arrayed in all the charms of a Cleopatra—

SHE

You've written me those splendid papers, told me those wonderful stories—

HE

I shall never forget how Your Majesty chose to ignore the distance between us and brought herself to my level just so I might raise myself to hers—

SHE

No, I have been your pupil, you have been my master.

HE

I have been your servant, you have been my mistress— Such was the daydream of Denis the Philosopher.

SHE

You left your papers? My new Russia?

HE

In your state papers. I know they contain foolishness and folly—

SHE

Yes, my dear dreamer. You know, there is just one difference between us. You're a philosopher, and work on paper, which is supple, obedient, does just what it's told. Where I, a poor empress, must work on human skin. Which is itchy, irritable, and grows raw to the touch.

HE

Yet, if you'd followed me, you would surely have created a great society, and made your nation the envy of all humankind.

SHE

Yes, and if I had listened to you thoughtlessly, every single institution in my empire would have been upturned. Monarchy, law, the church, the budget. The nation would have disintegrated, the borders would collapse. Perhaps if only your visit had come at some other time. When I wasn't at war with the Turks, when I wasn't resisting Pugachov—

HE
Yes, Pugachov. Well, now you have captured him, what will happen?

SHE
He sits in the middle of Moscow in an iron cage, so the people can see he's really not the anointed of God. Just Emelyn Pugachov, a stupid farmer, who thought his fortune had been rewritten in the great Book of Destiny above. Of course, if I were the only one he had harmed, I should seek to forgive him. But no brute invader since Tamburlaine has killed so many of my people. He's lived like a scoundrel. Let him die like a coward—

HE
What will happen, then?

SHE
He'll be beheaded in front of the people. All his people will be exiled to the frontiers, and his village burned.

HE
And Countess Pimburg? Princess Tarakanova?

SHE
Dead, alas. It seems the poor creature all the time had tuberculosis. That is what killed her—

HE
But an underground cell in the Peter and Paul wouldn't have helped. So, the truth is, I made no difference.

SHE looks at him.

SHE
But you made every difference, my dear Didro. You and Monsieur Voltaire can tell the world now that my ideals always reached higher than my deeds. I sometimes think we dreamed each other. I dreamt you, and you say you dreamt me. Take off your jacket!

HE
What?

SHE
That black coat. Everyone's sick of it. We have a new one for you. Put it on.

SHE holds up a bright-red jacket, heavily frogged, and helps him put it on.

HE
I really never cared for new clothes.

SHE
What do you say, Dashkova?

DASHKOVA looks him up and down.

DASHKOVA
A dashing man. A true philosopher-king.

SHE
And with that goes a bearskin jacket. To keep you warm on the homeward journey.

SHE holds his hands. They embrace each other.

HE
You remember Voltaire once wrote history was a trick the living play on the dead? Well, I have come to think Russian history is probably a trick a clever empress played upon Voltaire and me—

SHE
Nonsense. No, don't go. Send for your wife and family. Build yourself a great palace here.

HE weeps. SHE looks at him.

HE
No, my dear. My wife's an old woman with sciatica. My sister-in-law is eighty. My mistress has probably forgotten me. My daughter has a baby at the breast. My son-in-law has high pretensions in the textiles trade. And where I used to count up

the future in decades or years, now I count it in months and days——

SHE
Nonsense, Didro, you'll live for ever.

HE
You'll guarantee it? Is it in the treaty?

SHE
Yes, it's in the treaty.

A huge shaggy BEAR-LIKE MAN, having only one eye, and wearing a loose Turkish kaftan, has entered the room, eating something. SHE looks, hurries over, embraces him.

SHE
Oh my darling. My dear Potemkin——

HE goes, unobserved.

END OF DAY SIXTY

THIRTY-THREE (NOW)

SO AT LAST HE'S GOING, leaving Russia after all. And so, it seems, are we. The *Vladimir Ilich* might just as well never even have disembarked its swarm of passengers three days back. For here they all are again, or their kin: a swarming confused crowd just as noisy and pushing, just as hard to get on and convey in the other direction as the surging mob that, only a week back, crossed the Baltic in reverse, sailing from Swedish bourgeois civility to Scythian fantasy and confusion. The last passengers disappeared into the vast and evidently unconquerable world of Russia; these have emerged out of it to swarm the other way. Once again the dockyard below is full of business. Dirty buses decant lines of would-be voyagers; taxis deposit travellers for the better cabins. Cars in rows, cars of every kind from the smartest to the most futile, cars that are escaping Russia or returning west for service, are lining up to enter the ferry doors. Containers, pallets, packages of all kinds are swinging on the crane hooks and entering the vessel somewhere below. The traders and negotiators, touts and market people have reappeared in even vaster numbers. There on the dockyard concrete, or in sudden new kiosks that have appeared at will in the terminal building, they are selling everything, old and new, useful and useless, antique and bric-a-brac, licit and illicit, in a frenzy of transaction.

And even more unusual transactions are taking place in the gaunt concrete customs hall and at the wooden passport booths, where the oddest kinds of person are lining up in rows. Back from a quick visit to the city to buy some last books and final CDs, I wait. Around me are Tartars who, strangely enough, are equipped with Swiss identities; Albanians who proudly sport brand-new Hong Kong British passports; Vietnamese who in all conviction

424

claim to be of Norwegian stock. Here are remarkable families: parents have children who are far older than they are, brothers have sisters of completely different shades and nationalities. But that's how it is now: we live in multicultural times. The world is a melting pot, the self is a transactable item; and if you have a wad of creased roubles that can stick up out of the top of your papers, then whatever your story it will be not so much believed (who believes stories?) but permitted, because nowadays every kind of story can go.

So, with their stories accepted, their excuses allowed, our newest travellers swarm up the gangplanks, pushing and shouting, heaving and screaming. On their shoulders they carry some or all of the following: icons and gilt-framed paintings, altar rails, gilded Russian crosses, silver samovars, old cameras, car exhausts and other motor parts, opulent silvery pelts and other animal skins, whole fish wrapped in reeds, crates of glassware and pottery, clothing, jewels, cases of caviar, sacks of dresses, boxes filled with books. From the bridge deck Lenin watches, with an increasingly confused gaze. So do we, the regulars, the habitual travellers, those for whom this vessel has come to be a home and a way of life. We're the ones who know the best deckchairs, the ones who have a favourite waiter, the ones who know the finest brands of vodka and which are the sweetest cakes. Now our several days of hotel quiet are over. The crew's returned and they're back in action. Once more they play their balalaikas in the lobby, do their Caucasian dances and their boyar leaps. Once more the samovars bubble and the seedcakes sizzle. It's this way to the casino, that way to the duty free—

Whatever may have been happening in Russia over the last few days – and if you are there you can never really quite see it – and however this might have been an autumn of tragedy, crisis or just brute misery, not that much seems to have truly changed. It's as if in a restive struggle between apathy and Utopia, apathy has won again. Conflicting flags still fly round the harbour: the hammer and sickle here, the old–new tricolour there. Commerce and barter are thriving, not least among the traders down on the dock, who are just now grabbing the last dollars and krona, marks and roubles, and packing their cases to go home. Misery is thriving too: women wail in the streets, drunks lie in the courtyards. Opera plays, ballet prances. Crime prospers mightily, drunkenness is universal, poverty spreads, the beggars multiply in the streets. It's an extraordinary world with extraordinary problems, and it would take many, many notebooks just to explain them all.

The ship's cutting loose. The band is playing again – with just as much confusion, but this time with a little less enthusiasm, perhaps because we are all not coming but going, not landing with full pockets but departing with half-empty ones – though, true, a few last grateful coins go flying over the rails, no doubt for a little good luck. We're leaving with a sense of awe but perhaps too with that famous sudden surge of relief that many have felt on departing Russia. For the truth is that, though the self may be an anxious item, and we are all no more than a face drawn in the sand on the very edge of the waves in a collapsing cosmos, the self as we've invented and pampered it, the private self, the personal self, is a being worthy of treasure. We watch the shore's embrace relax, the hawsers drop off into the harbour's oily waters, the dockside pull suddenly backwards, so that the ferry terminal, disappearing into the fog of Baltic mist and urban pollution, at once begins to lose all its familiar flaws and imperfections, and looks whole, wonderful, gleamingly modernist again.

Beyond there is a long view of the city skyline: the golden flèches of the Peter and Paul and the Admiralty, the golden dome of Saint Isaac's Cathedral, from which, looking down, I have seen this same Baltic seaway shading off into the fog. Into that fog we sail. Now from the chilly bridge deck we can see the fortress of Kronstadt taking on shape in the seaway, and somewhere over there, on the southern shores of the wide estuary, we seem to see a huge hammer and sickle statue rising up. But then there are other things: apartment blocks, perhaps the great roofs of palaces, and then the sea is all. Tankers and mother ships plough through cold October water. Below our own ship is growing noisy, with that general sense of release, hope, expectation that passes through a vessel when it breaks loose from the landmass, and heads out for the open sea.

'Really, did you?' I'm saying to Birgitta Lindhorst, for the red-haired nightingale has kindly chosen to join me by the rail. 'You mean, right there on the stage of the Maryinsky Theatre?'

'Of course,' she says. 'And I am so sorry, because I expected you would come along there to watch me.'

'Which I certainly would have, if anyone had bothered to tell me about it.'

'Bo says he told everyone about it. A special performance, my wicked little darling, and entirely in my honour.'

'Of course.'

'I looked exactly like a queen, they all told me,' Birgitta says.

'I'm sure. A true apotheosis.'

'Well, a gala, and of course finally they asked me to sing again from Onegin.'

'I thought so. Tatyana's letter?'

'Of course. "Oh, was it you who seemed to hover / Over my bed, my gentle lover?" It was so sweet.'

'I'm sure it brought down the house.'

'A standing ovation, ten minutes.'

'Wonderful.'

'And guess how many bouquets?'

'I can't imagine.'

'Forty, my darling. Really, it's true. Twenty bottles of pink shampanksi. Crate after crate of caviar.'

'I knew you were the greatest.'

'But you didn't come.'

'I'm sure all the others did.'

'All the others, and not you. Come to my cabin tonight. After dinner.'

'I'll think about it.'

'Twenty bottles of shampanski, my darling. Crate after crate of caviar.'

'I know. But the Russians do know and love their great singers.'

'It's true. That's what I tell my husband.'

'Your husband? I thought he was singing Scarpia in Bari, or something? And you wanted to kill him.'

'You didn't see my husband? He came for me with a Zil.'

'Well, you were going to go for him with arsenic.'

'He's singing there in the Verdi season. Why did you think I came to Petersburg?'

'Well, long ago, I thought it all had something to do with Diderot.'

'So, here you are again,' says Alma the Snow Queen, suddenly appearing behind us as Kronstadt slips from sight. 'Always at it. Don't you realize we are all down there waiting? Don't you realize the project is beginning again?'

'It's not over?' asks my red-haired nightingale.

'Of course not,' says Alma. 'It's never over. The Diderot project is everything . . .'

Once again we follow our Snow Queen down below. Tatyana from Novgorod once more stands red-cheeked behind the till in the Blini Bar. Tatyana from Smolensk is frantically dusting off the bottles in the busy Duty Free. But when we get to the conference rooms the girl holding the tray of pink shampanksi out to us is someone quite different: not our dear, familiar Tatyana from Pushkin, but, as the young lady tells us, Irini from Omsk. The Enlightenment Pilgrims are slowly gathering. Sven Sonnenberg has evidently acquired a big fur hat on his travels, which he wears like a pom-pom, and Agnes Falkman has found herself a bedraggled peasant dirndl. I ask them how their country journey has gone. Sven has evidently found the Russian countryside less neat and orderly than he expected, and the union officials Agnes was hoping to meet seem no longer to exist. Others arrive: Manders comes in, smiling politely, and Lars Person appears, giving us his dark and saturnine nod. The one person I don't seem to see is Jack-Paul Verso. Then Bo steps into the middle of the room, claps his hand and raises his glass.

'*Skal!* my friends!' he says. 'May I make a little toast. To our wonderful Diderot!'

OMNES
Skal! To Diderot! Denis! etc.

BO
May I welcome you all back to the ship. And I hope you all had a very excellent time in the glorious Venice of the North?

OMNES
Yes . . . We did . . . *Jo, jo* . . . It was wonderful, Bo . . . You did it marvellously. Galina too. Etc., etc.

MOI
Yes, Bo, we did, we had a really excellent time—

BO
Thank you, my friend.

MOI
. . . but you don't mind if I ask you something?

BO
Not at all. Here we are all enquirers. Please.

MOI
I did really love your Diderot Project. But I just wondered if
you knew what it was?

Smiles and laughter appear all round at my innocence.

BO
You mean, you don't know?

MOI
I've no idea. All I know is I came under the impression we
were going to look at the Diderot archive in the public
library.

BO
And what happened to you?

MOI
Well . . . I went to look at the Diderot archive in the public
library.

BO
Exactly.

MOI
I see. You arranged all this so I could go and look at the
Diderot papers—

SVEN
Nej, nej. I understood the purpose. We all came to Petersburg
to look at tables.

MOI
Why at tables?

SVEN
This is what Bo told me. He said Diderot was the teacher of
all craftsmen. It was thanks to his lessons that all the carpenters
of Russia learned to create perfect templates, ideal designs,
construct the best lathes, construct great monuments and
palaces, and build very excellent tables.

BO
And wasn't I right?

SVEN
Yes, of course you were right, Bo. They make the most
excellent tables. I have brought one of them back with me—

AGNES
But it wasn't only tables.

MOI
Ah. No?

AGNES
As Bo explained to us when he visited our union, it was
Diderot who devised all the principles of *techne*, the plan of
human work. How we relate skill to person, craft to idea.
How workers acquire apprenticeship and dignity. It is in his
notebooks. That is why he thought I would like to see
farming co-operatives.

BO
You did, I hope.

AGNES
Well, not quite, they have all disappeared, but this is not the
fault of Bo.

MOI
But you, Mr Manders? You didn't come here to look at
farming co-operatives, did you?

ANDERS
No. I came to meet the excellent mayor of Petersburg.

MOI
To talk about tables?

ANDERS
No, to talk round or over them. Bo arranged for us to
get together on several matters of Baltic-wide cultural
co-operation. Naturally at this stage I cannot divulge the
results. But I can say that, assuming events in Russia ever
become what most of us would call normal, there will be
some very excellent consequences—

MOI
I'm delighted. And is that why you came too, Bo?

ALMA
Nej, nej. Bo was invited to attend an important congress at
Petersburg University, where they awarded him an honorary
degree—

BO
Merely to celebrate my recent work on A.I.

MOI
Well, I really am delighted, Bo. What a splendid honour. But
who or what exactly is A.I.?

BO
You don't know? Artificial intelligence, it's what we all live
by. The thinking machine. The computer. The simulation
of cognition and the workings of the brain. Maybe you
remember, it was Diderot who invented the first thinking
machine. It was actually a kind of encoding and decoding
device that was meant to keep the secrets of diplomats and
politicians.

ANDERS
To save them the trouble of thinking.

MOI
What did it look like?

BO
We don't know. It was probably a concept, entirely imaginary. Just like the Turing Machine.

MOI
But the Turing Machine wasn't imaginary, was it? I thought Turing devised it to crack the Enigma code, and it became the first computer.

BO
Yes, but Turing wanted to keep it imaginary.

MOI
I don't understand, why?

BO
So that it would remain like one of Einstein's thought experiments, he said. It would be an elegant system in our heads.

MOI
Turing wanted to invent the imaginary computer?

BO
Jo, he wanted to show we could create a machine with a set of functions that could reproduce all the processes of reason. But the machine would be an artificial intelligence that would always remain inferior to the real one.

MOI
But you, Lars—

LARS
Who, me?

MOI
Yes, you didn't come to Petersburg to consider artificial and real intelligence, did you?

LARS
Yes, in a sense. You see, Bo arranged for me to give a master
class at the Pushkin Drama Theatre. I was trying to explain
the Diderot Paradox — the paradox of the actor, the paradox
of the comedian. The peculiar fact that the actor must have
another self to create the self he or she plays. It's the problem
of the face and the mask. How many masks do we take off till
we come to a real face? And of course it's not just the problem
of the actor, it's the problem of every human being. Are we a
man or a mask?

MOI
But what's the answer?

LARS
The answer is too difficult. But not for the actor. Because the
actor is the person who always truly understands that every
individual must acquire the power to become his own double.

BIRGITTA
And that life is a performance.

LARS
Sometimes a gala performance.

BIRGITTA
Yes, what an evening that was, Bo, my darling! A *grande
hommage*. And it seems our darling Bo arranged it with the
Maryinsky some time ago.

LARS
A truly glittering evening, diva.

ANDERS
And so wonderful to watch it from the royal box.

MOI
Ah, you were there too?

SVEN
We were all there.

MOI
I wasn't.

ALMA
Nej, nej. Your seat was empty. When we tried to find you,
you had occupied yourself with something or someone else.
Is it possible?

MOI
Yes, it's possible. But apart from the gala at the Maryinsky,
each one of us was doing something different? So how was
this a project?

BO
My dear professor, surely the answer is obvious. Put
everything together and we were doing almost everything of
interest there is to do. Within reason.

MOI
And getting a grant for it too. Which reminds me. What
happened to Professor Verso?

OMNES turn and start looking all round the room.

BO
For once this is a very excellent question. Does anyone know
what happened to Professor Verso? I presume he returned to
the ship—

ALMA
Bo, you were not listening, as usual. I told you he didn't come
back to the ship. His cabin has not been slept in for three
nights.

ANDERS
So what was he meaning to do in Petersburg?

LARS
He was supposed to be interested in the state of post-Marxist
philosophy—

MOI
He was also very keen to visit Tzarskoye Selo.

ANDERS
I understood he really wanted to go to Moscow.

MOI
Does anyone know what happened to Tatyana from Pushkin?

ANDERS
Another good question. Perhaps Irini knows.

*ANDERS and IRINI converse in Russian for some minutes.
OMNES sip a little anxiously at their pink shampanksi.*

ANDERS
Well. It seems Tatyana Tatyanovitch is not on the ship either.
Nobody ever went to Tzarskoye Selo. Verso and Tatyana
were taken to the Moscow station and they were last seen
buying tickets for a train. Perhaps the train went to Moscow,
or Novogorod, or Smolensk, or Vladivostok. These are
various ideas that have been put by Irini. But apparently our
friend had it in his mind to make a long journey somewhere,
nobody is very sure where—

BO
Well . . . I always had the small impression our Professor
Verso was not so reliable.

ALMA
I am not even sure he understood the true purpose of our
grant.

BO
His paper, I mean. I'm sure I had seen it before. I'm not even
sure it was his own paper. When I looked at the photocopy
more carefully, I found it had on it a quite different name and
a quite different date.

AGNES
Maybe we would not be all that wise to publish it.

ALMA
Professor Verso is a grown man, of course. I suppose he can
do what he likes.

435

BO

Only within reason. Now he has disappeared totally. He might just as well have never joined us.

MOI

Like a face drawn in the sand on the edge of the waves.

BO

Yes, I suppose so. But apart from this one small matter, I hope you agree this journey has been very useful for all involved. What about you, for instance?

MOI

Moi?

BO

Indeed, my old friend. You went to Russia. You looked at historical papers. You made various friendships, I believe. You are a writer. Surely there is some kind of story in it?

MOI

I'm not sure. I hope so.

BO

Believe me, you will find something. And I hope you found something you wanted in the library?

MOI

Well, yes, I did. It seems there are still stories by Diderot that remain unpublished—

BO

So there we are then. We seem to have satisfied almost everyone. *Skal!* The Diderot Project!

OMNES

Skal!

BO

And now who is going to give the first paper tomorrow morning? Perhaps we should have a vote on it.

ALMA
No, Bo, a vote is not necessary when we all agree.

BO
Well? What do you all think . . .?

THIRTY-FOUR (THEN)

THE SLOW JOURNEY HOMEWARD is going to prove just as terrible as he's already started to fear. In fact well before it's over it will turn out to be one of the worst adventures of his life. Illness — that eternal Neva colic — and the locked-in winter weather have kept delaying his departure. Every day Grimm has called, seeking to change his mind and travel with him to the King's court at Potsdam, where all is forgiveness, and the banquet has already been laid. Every day he's refused. By the time he leaves the city it's early March. A disappointed Grimm, a sweet Marie-Anne Collot, a dear foolish Narishkin — his perfect Lui, the eternally generous host whose debts, in a last act of thank you, he has managed to get the Empress to say she will repay (and maybe she will) — are all there in Saint Isaac's Square to wave him on his way. Only Étienne-Maurice Falconet is missing: the man he once had the kindness to invent remains, for some unknown reason, grudging to the end. And then, to his great surprise, Monsieur Distroff de Durand, shortly to be leaving Russia himself, turns up outside the Narishkin Palace to wish his journey well.

'Just a little something to fill up your luggage,' he's said with a friendly wink, handing a package into the carriage. 'It might just prove useful to you when you get back to Paris.'

'Tell me then, what?'

'It's a map of some new Russian fortresses they're building against us along the Black Sea,' says Distroff. 'Simply pass it to the Foreign Ministry when you get there. And maybe they won't hang you after all.'

It's four o'clock on a cold afternoon when, at last, he rides out of the city where all the dreams of his lifetime have been so very fiercely tested. Behind him he can see its high onion domes and golden flèches, disappearing into a gelid green fog beyond the still deep blanket of snow. Winter has certainly not departed yet, but the earth is warming now, and the snowcap is shrinking. The ice in the Baltic has begun to crack open, the rivers of Livonia and Courland are all running fast and deep. He's riding high in that gleaming and brand-new English carriage which the Empress has newly purchased and, in all generosity, then put at his service. It's delicately made, plushy, varnished, huge-windowed, vast enough to carry a comfortable bed inside. Truth to tell, it would probably be far happier rolling genteelly down London's Piccadilly. For these northern routes are hard still, ice-packed, deep-rutted. And the grand shining English coach – which everyone confusingly calls a Berliner – is soon making very heavy weather of the very heavy weather.

So in his own way is he. On one finger he wears the splendid agate ring into which is carved, with her own knife, the Empress's portrait. He knows very well he's not really left her service, and he probably never will now: all he's doing is carrying off his duties somewhere else. As, in the great warm bearskin coat she has given him as another parting gift, he rides away from his life's most remarkable experience, he knows something has happened. Everything has altered, and he's not a bit the man he was when he came. The difficult journey, the hard and imprisoning winter, the jealous court, the amazing dreams, the Neva fevers, and the unreal and remarkable pleasures that have been so strangely granted to him by the most formidable and powerful woman in the world, the Cleopatra of the age: every one of these things has deeply changed him, aged him, somehow brought him several steps closer to the dark silence in the eternal nowhere and nothing that lies just beyond life's short burst of light. He thinks of the great château where, in writing, he's had Jacques and his master spend a night. He recalls the fictional sign he's set over its portal: 'I belong to nobody, and yet I belong to everyone. You were here before you entered, and you will still be here even after you've left.' But is any person ever still here after they've left?

It isn't that any of his ideas have changed; not really, not exactly. But they've grown more contradictory, volatile, unreliable, inconsistent, passionate: quite unpredictable, even to him. And still more has happened to his vital emotions, which seem to have become strangely frosted in this hard arctic weather. Wife, darling dancing daughter, Sophie Volland; they all feel infinitely distant, like figures seen on the other side of glass, waving ghosts who can never be fully regained. The huge English coach, dragged in the Russian fashion by three shaggy post-horses, shakes, rattles, bounces, slips. The bedded carriage seems to have become his house for ever; he even refuses to stop and eat. The colic is with him again, made more stabbing than ever by the rough passage, the bad water, the even worse hotels and inns that appear on the way.

Happily the chancery companion the Empress has provided, Athanasius Bala, is a pleasant and honest young fellow. In fact he's a bright likely lad who's been given a shaggy old patriarch to look after, and tries to do his best. He's been solicitous beyond belief, encouraging our man to lie down on his journey (and the carriage bed is rather wonderful), to read and snack and talk and drink. Now, as the trip grows more tiring, Bala spends much time sitting anxiously and thoughtfully beside him, occasionally shifting the fur coat that lies across him, wiping his brow, or handing him his volume of Horace. Of course it's completely unnatural for our man to stay silent for any length of time; and of course he doesn't. In the feverish spaces of his mind, the most urgent and torrential ideas are seeking to flow – as fierce and fast as the spring torrents clearing away the ice and rushing down the rivers they kept crossing as they slip and splash their way down the Livonian coast.

'The dome of Saint Peter's in Rome . . .' he begins.

'Domo?' asks Bala. 'I don't know domo. Duomo?'

'Like. But that means cathedral. So what rises up high above a cathedral?'

'Angels? Spirits?'

'No, the drum.'

'Drum, pipe and drum?'

'The dome.'

'I don't know dome or drum, I come from Greekland.'

'Greek? You're a compatriot of Plato?'

'Domo? Plato?'

'Where from in Greece?'

'Him, Plato?'

'No, you.'

'Athena, you know Athena?'

'Yes, I know it very well.'

'You have been there?'

'No, I haven't been anywhere. Except Sankt Peterburg. Do you know where we're going? The Hague?'

'I don't know Hague.'

'It's a place in Holland. You're supposed to be taking me there.'

'Holland?'

'A free republic, like the cities of ancient Greece.'

'We go in Greece?'

'No, we don't go in Greece. We're going the other way.'

'In Germany?'

'No no, don't go to Germany.'

'We have to go to Germany.'

'Then don't go to Berlin. Anywhere but Berlin.'

'Where, please?'

'Go to the free city of Hamburg.'

'Where is Hamburg?'

'Never mind. What are you interested in?'

'Everything. Politic. Historia. Government. Law. Poesy. Love. Mostly love.'

'All right, Bala. Just sit there, and read your book.'

'I don't read.'

Oh, young Bala is charming, helpful, open, delightful. But where, oh where, is Lui?

On the third day he appears in the carriage. 'You know me perfectly well,' he says, bouncing up and down on the seat opposite. 'A real old cuss, as the Burgundians say. How did you like your empress?'

'A most formidable woman. Impulsive and impassioned, yet extremely open to reason.'

'Women like that exist to claim that one day they will be quite as important as men. I had heard she has the most amazing powers. I hope you tried them.'

'Perhaps I did. But why would I tell you?'

441

'I tell you everything, don't I? Did you make your peace with Falconet?'

'No, I didn't. I shall never speak to him again. I invented Falconet.'

'That must have annoyed him.'

'I praised his work to the skies, I sent him to Catherine. All his conceptions were mine.'

'Except he doesn't think so.'

'He should.'

'Sons must always struggle with fathers.'

'And nephews with uncles?'

'Precisely. Didn't you hate your father?'

'No. Well, a little. When I was young and stupid. And he was old and stupid.'

'Why?'

'He resented my marriage.'

'There you are then. One generation never understands another.'

'No, he was right. In the end so did I.'

'Didn't you once try to commit him to prison?'

'Only when he tried to commit me to a monastery.'

'There you are. There are always some of the dead who plague the living. Can't be helped. Goodbye, Mr Philosopher. Time for the opera.'

So onward they go, by Narva and Revel, through this province and that one, curving round the shores of the Baltic. Then they are at the border, at Riga, the place where long ago she offered to print a fresh version of the *Encyclopedia*, French, free and uncensored. He's a step nearer Europe, the fever has diminished a little, though the weather has not improved. Indeed here the winter seems deeper, the wind seems to bite harder, and they nearly come to grief. Thick ice still covers the waters of the River Dwina, the border that marks the end of this imperial nation and the start of the next one. But when the weighty English carriage rides out on to the ice, the wheels break through, the horses struggle in the water, and flood and ice-flow rush into the cab where he lies. His volume of Horace goes floating away under the ice. Only a quick-thinking Bala proves his worth, and manages to save the day. He summons men with hooks to help them; then, standing in the freezing water up to his waist, he tugs, heaves, gets the whole endangered enterprise and a shaking and shivering philosopher back on to the hard shore.

Our man responds to the great misfortune in the best way he can. He writes a poem celebrating the rescue of philosophers, verses that he's improvised, or so he claims, at the very moment of disaster ('Muse of immortal glory / If for laurels you grow keener / Come quick, and tell the story / Of the crossing of the Dwina'), and sends it back to his dear empress. This mishap on the ice is only the beginning. For the grand English coach – which has manifestly not been made for the rough Baltic winter – is steadily failing as it drags on and on its way. On the bridge at Mittau it finally comes to grief: shaken to bits, it sags into a shapeless plywood pile, collapsing down on to its broken wheel-hubs for all eternity. Our man falls down in the escape, then nearly kills himself a second time by dropping in the river. Bala helps again. He's survived once more, though this time there's a very expensive coach to explain away. He writes a letter of apology back to Sankt Peterburg ('It's this adventure on the Mittau bridge that makes me appreciate the kind admiration of Monsieur Bala. He has promised to explain himself to Your Imperial Majesty the heroism I displayed at the unhappy moment of the strange rupture of the most beautiful and commodious coach you issued me with . . .'). By the time they've reached Hamburg – steering by Konigsberg, Danzig, Stettin to avoid the fearsome Junkers of Brandenburg-Prussia, and any possible claims on his duties from the Philosopher Tyrant – they've already smashed their third carriage.

Not till they get to Hamburg does he start to feel safe. Here big Protestant churches rise high on the skyline; fine Hanseatic ships and tarry merchant barges rock back and forth in the inland harbour, spars clicking and chains rattling in a glorious water-music. There's the jollity of sea-captains, the proud sturdy spirit of a free and independent state. With churches like this, here's a city of fine and high-sounding music. Its kappelmeister is Hamburg Bach: Karl Philip Emmanuel, the great organist (though probably yet another protégé of the flute-playing Prussian king). But where geniuses gather it is only polite for the one to announce his arrival to the other. 'I am French, my name is Diderot,' he says in the little note he sends off to the great organist. 'I've arrived in a chaise from Sankt Peterburg, with no more than a dressing gown under my topcoat, and no decent change of clothing. I would love to acquire a sonata from you, but I'm really not fit to be received.' The sonata, in the great musician's own autograph, duly comes.

So at last, four carriages, 635 *versts*, 31 days onward, he reaches his intended destination: the Hague. Now it's the very start of April: spring. The charming fields, so amazingly flat that every little sand heap becomes a Dutch mountain, are already full of blooming daffodils and those egregious modern tulips. There at their residence on the windy Kneuterdijk, Dmitry Golitsyn and his German princess – who has already fattened and grown much more pious, as people seem to as a result of a Dutch winter – are hospitably ready and waiting. Much of his heavy luggage has come already, coached on down from Hamburg. Dear Bala is thanked, rewarded handsomely, and sent off on his return journey – though, since he appears to think he's somewhere in Hungary, our man is left worrying a little about where he will finally end up. But he's tired now. At his age it's all been far too much. With Dmitry's permission he retires to bed and sleeps for several days.

Then, after a day or three, he's up again. He's chosen to live here for a short while, rather than to return to Paris, because he's quite sure it's not all done yet; his mission as imperial philosopher is by no means over. Now the siren call of the Empress is with him again. Their arguments, their banterings, their tiffs, their makings-up, the shuttlecock and battledore of daily conversation: they're all still vivid in everything he writes. He no longer yearns for entertainment. The learned Dutch professors now bore him, and even those stout and big-bosomed burgher women don't seem to lure him any more. Another woman is on his mind: a lover, or the ghost of one. She's reminding him he's nowhere near finished his enquiring vital life; in fact he's hardly started. He gets up early every morning. He writes, he writes, he writes . . .

Yes, the frenzy's back, and he knows he can do it all again: begin, all for the benefit of Russia, a whole new and fresh encyclopedia. He'll use the arctic wisdom culled from all his notebooks. It'll be even bigger, better and wiser than the biggest and best book in the world. As already arranged with a helpful Chancellor Betskoi, it will all be paid for, printed, distributed in Sankt Peterburg. And of course it will have a fresh royal dedicatee: this time not some over-dressed waster of a French monarch who, soaked in pleasures and amusements, has managed to lose half his empire and spend all his treasury, but a true modern Minerva.

'To the honour of the Russians and their empress – and the eternal shame of all those who have rejected wisdom and learning'; that's what its dedication will say. And by virtue of this task, he now announces to his dear and favourite sovereign, I shall not die without having imprinted on the earth such traces as time cannot efface.

With the great book goes the great plan: the Russian university. He conjures it into existence every night, imagines its grand halls and corridors, always thinking of her serene majesty, who has been so kind to him and who still fills his dreams every night. The Russian university will be built, of course, in the great strange city he has already half imagined. It lies by the water, staring into the Neva. It has high façades, great *Aula*s and windows. Everyone can attend it – without exception, whether from cottage or palace. It will be a living, moving encyclopedia, and all the fruits that hang on the living branches of the tree of knowledge will be its province. Except there will be no departments of theology to turn its enquiring students into demons of fanaticism, preachers of only one truth. There will be no departments of medicine, which are otherwise known as departments of murder. No departments of pure philosophy, for they produce ignorant lightweights who become actors, soldiers, tricksters and tramps. There will be no first-year courses in the wisdom of the ancients: who wants to learn how to be a Roman citizen when the age of Rome is done? No one will be compelled to study Greek or Latin, when there are so many new languages to learn. None of the professors will be priests or Jesuits, and no robes or tonsures will be required.

No, this new university's bright and beautiful students will live in fine buildings and chatter in every tongue, nourish every decent and civilized opinion that is of service to humankind, freely, frankly and liberally discuss all the ideas. All the subjects will be practical, useful, contemporary. There will be instruction in the

445

making of chairs, the building of perfect domes. There should be lessons in machinery, and how to grow mulberry trees, as they do all over Russia. The best students – but only the very best, the students of genius – will be allowed to study verse and tale-telling and become philosophers or poets. A university should, he pronounces, have only one goal: it exists to make people virtuous, civil and enlightened, so advancing human progress. For the problem of our world is this: too many of its minds are dull, vacant and empty. Even the poets and philosophers of the new age are witless, and bray their noise and cackle through the nightwaves without thought. Yet such too is the age that on every street-corner the young people are crowding, shouting, 'Education! We know nothing! Teach us! Education, education, education!' He has the perfect solution: a democracy of general education, topped off with an elite of thought and art.

No sooner has he worked out this beautiful, fantastic, splendidly unworkable plan (the Empress files it away in a locked drawer, in the hope it will be forgotten for ever; in fact one day two centuries on it will become the commonplace lore of every drab weary western polytechnic) than he sits down to a second task he has assigned himself: a deep critique of the Empress's 'Grand Nakaz' – 'The Great Instruction'. He studies with his usual care, pronounces it to be one of the greatest and most important documents of the age. It's such a pity just a few small things are missing: 'The Empress has somehow said nothing at all about the emancipation of the serfs. Yet this is a most important point.' He adds a proposal or two for the abolition of tyranny: 'A society should first of all be happy. It is impossible to love a country that does not love us.' Rounding off his notes, he draws the frank, instructive, very bold conclusion: 'If in reading what I have written she finds that her conscience stirs and her heart jumps for joy, then she will know she no longer needs serfs and slaves. But if she trembles, feels weak, grows pale, then she has surely taken herself for a far better person than she is.'

Meantime, as he waits for the Empress to gather up her response and declare her gratitude, he wanders round Holland, making notes for yet another book. Sometimes he goes to gaze on the great lonely windmills that grind at all hours round about

Zaandam, or stands and considers the geometry of the flat grids of fields, which neither the usual rise and declivity nor the history of settlement and ownership seem to interrupt. Sometimes he goes to Scheveningen to stare at the imperious North Sea, where the wooden warships moor (he goes aboard one), the fishing boats swing their booms, and the herring are rushing. Sometimes he visits the synagogues of Amsterdam, sometimes he calls on the publishers, who have published or plagiarized so many of his books. He pronounces that Holland is the land of liberty, the Hague the most pleasant village in the world.

People now find him strangely gloomy and detached. Surely this isn't the same Monsieur Diderot who came to them bubbling with so much scandalous atheism just the summer before? Perhaps this is because no news at all comes back from Russia. The messages he's awaiting, the funds he's needing so he can set properly to work on the new Russian encyclopedia – a couple of hundred thousand livres for editorial expenses, the price of an apartment in Paris to house its demanding activities, fees for the editorial assistants he's already set out to hire – simply do not arrive. Instead what comes are whispers and murmurs that, much as she admires and loves him, the Empress has begun to have doubts. She's no longer sure about her new encyclopedia. She's put his proposals for a Russian university firmly away. As for his considered comments on the Great Instruction, they have been disposed of yet deeper, forbidden from sight and locked up under quadruple lock and key.

'Genuine twaddle': this is how she's described his splendidly liberal opinions in one of her fond frank letters to Grimm. Who, like any good old friend, hasn't wasted a minute in passing on her adverse reaction to the place where it will hurt most. His letter enclosing her views passes on some further information. It seems afternoons in the Small Hermitage have not been the same since he left. Nowadays it's big Grigor Potemkin who is granted the full attention of the Empress in those pleasant quiet hours between three and six. Victorious over the Turks, the man wanders the corridors in his oriental kaftans and turbans, if not totally naked; and now he's taken possession of the apartment-bedroom next door to the Empress. The entire court has responded by growing extremely louche and eastern since his arrival. Oh, one other thing about him: he doesn't like the French.

Little wonder our man feels increasingly bewildered and adrift. At home his mystified wife and daughter are asking about him, sending their messages. One day very strange news arrives from Paris: the king, that wastrel old monarch, is dead of the smallpox against which he'd refused to inoculate himself (unlike the Northern Minerva, who put herself first in the firing line), and has been quietly buried at dead of night. An inglorious reign, elegant, clever, lush, sophisticated, marked by display, misery and historical woe, the loss of the two French Indies in America and the East, is over at last. An heir has succeeded, new ministers have been appointed. Yet, writing, our man hardly notices. Until one day a chaise halts outside the Embassy. From it, in the company of a couple of rich young Russians, steps a very, a very very old friend. It's Melchior Grimm, looking rich, conceited, perhaps even a mite concerned.

'My dear dear fellow. You've dashed here with some good news from Petersburg?' our man cries in delight, embracing him in his usual hearty way. 'I've come from there, yes. By way of Warsaw and Potsdam. Oh, Stanislaw of Poland and Frederick of Prussia both asked after you.' 'Name-dropper.' 'And I've been appointed as a courtier to the court of Hesse-Darmstadt.' 'Wonderful. Take a bow.' 'I turned it down.' 'I'm glad to hear it.' 'I got an even better offer from the court of Saxe-Gotha. Also the court of Saxe-Weimar.' 'Take two bows, then. Why not? You must spend all your time bowing and scraping at one court or another.' 'People do find me useful.' 'I'm sure. But do remember, you used to be a philosopher.' 'So did you.' 'I remember you when you were an honest man. Before you started all this dining with royalty. Why is it when we two travel we always swing about like the arms of a compass, one going in the opposite direction from the other?' 'Because I like to visit San Souci, and you always try to avoid it.' 'Yes. Well, did you bring me a message from the Empress? I'm still waiting news of my Russian *Encyclopedia*.' 'It so happens I have business in Antwerp, then Brussels, then back in Paris. That's why, my old friend, I thought I'd come and take you home.'

Our man stares. 'To Paris? How can I go there? After what happened in Russia they'd throw me straight into the Bastille. Surely you know that?'

'Nonsense,' says Grimm, 'the old king's dead. The new one's young, fat and innocent. Paris is wonderful. Turgot has taken charge, and turned it into a city of philosophers. It's electricity everywhere, bright light all around. Everywhere there are little philosophers, strutting about, pronouncing their atheism, preaching new parliaments and great reforms. Science prospers. Music soars. Mozart plays. D'Alembert's been made secretary of the Academy. Intellect flourishes. Everyone reads. Everyone's buying your encyclopedia. The Age of Reason has come to the Palais Royal at last.'

'No. It just can't be.'

'I assure you,' says Grimm. 'And now the Americans are coming, so anything's possible. And you remember Beaumarchais, the man you said you taught to write plays?'

'And so I did. Did he write any?'

'Indeed he did. But now he's the close favourite of the new king. He's sending him everywhere as spy and emissary.'

'Beaumarchais here, Beaumarchais there.'

'Yes. I tell you, it's time to come home.'

'No,' says our man, 'I must stay here and await the bidding of the Empress.'

Grimm takes him quietly by the arm. 'My dear old friend, this *is* the bidding of the Empress. Travel's over. Go home.'

'Ah. How is she, then?'

'She writes to me almost daily,' says Grimm. 'Sends me her epistles to the Grimmalians. Tells me what she means to do with Poland. I truly think I'm her closest confidant.'

'What does she confide?'

'I should say she's feeling very happy.'

'Does that mean Pugachov's out of the way?'

'Tortured and beheaded. But it's all a bit more personal.'

'You mean she's in love with that bear Potemkin?'

'Head over heels in it,' says Grimm. 'Just listen to what she writes in her latest letter to me: "This is quite extraordinary. The alphabet is just too short, its stock of letters really not enough, to say just what I feel."'

449

'It was big enough for the *Encyclopedia*,' says our man. 'Very well then, I see she has other things now. All right, I'll come to Paris.'

But, before he takes the high road, ventures the last lap, the long way round through Antwerp and Brussels, he sits down and writes a thoughtful letter. He addresses it first to Sophie Volland, but then adds in the names of her sisters. And he says:

My dear ladies

Perhaps you are trying to drive me to utter despair, since I haven't heard from you for at least a century. Perhaps you have forgotten me. Or perhaps you imagined – I confess I did myself – I had gone away and would never come home. It's true if anyone had said when I left Paris I was risking a journey so hard, so long, so strange and so absurd, I would have flatly called them a liar. I remember what I told myself: 'You will travel to the court and be introduced to the Empress. You will thank her for her patronage. Perhaps a month later she'll request to meet you, and ask you a few questions about a few intellectual things. Then you will bow, take leave of her, and come home.'

Dear friends: Isn't that just what would have happened at any other court beside Petersburg? Yet there I had access to the Empress's quarters every day, from three in the afternoon to five, even six. I entered, I was shown a chair. I had prepared many ideas in Paris, but they fled from me on the very first day. I began to talk, in that frank way you know of, which some call wisdom and others think total folly. For five months I lasted at court, without, as far as I know it, raising any ill-will, or from her at least, and without in any way having the bit set on my tongue.

So, as for this journey, which you warned me was so foolish (and I was glad to agree), I really would not have missed it for anything. I'm left with the satisfaction of repaying a great obligation (to become the librarian of my own library!), and making a new friend, and a most powerful protector, for the rest of my life. When I left, she truly overwhelmed me with favours. I return, let me tell you, laden with honours. I really believe that had I wished it I could have stripped the Russian treasury bare on my departure. But with her I acquired something far more precious than money: my freedom and my frankness of speech.

I confess to you, then, that this has been quite the most remarkable experience of my whole life, and that when I return to join you you will have to put up with everything I have to say about the world's most remarkable woman. For that is what she is. But now, dear ladies, I am returning home, for good. There will be no more journeys. I suppose I might have . . . well, let us say ten more years left in my bag. Two or three of them will be wasted on colds, colics, dropsies and rheumatics, and other annoyances of body and age. Two will go on food, drink and society, and two more on mistaken projects or foolish thoughts and ideas. The rest I must try and preserve for wisdom, and whatever other few pleasures a man past sixty might expect.

Oh, the horror and the misery of age! Once I imagined that with the years the head grew harder and the heart grew tougher. It's not a bit true, I find. All things in the world continue to touch me, move me, thrill me, seduce me, upset me, terrify me. And when you see me again I shall be the biggest and most sentimental little cry-baby you ever saw—

If you were to ask me, I really can't tell you whether I liked Russia or not. Perhaps I went there in search of some strange but important illusion, a splendid yet truly absurd human dream. Certainly, like a dream, it has lost me, bewildered me, baffled me with fresh new ideas of sense and nonsense, justice and order, virtue and vice. Russia is the strangest and most unreal of countries. Its people are mystics, obsessed by the promise of the future and the wonder of their vast land. Yet they cannot let go of old history, which haunts them like ghosts, and in the end they must always look more into the past than the future, and more into the darkness than the bright light. I fear they have been encouraged in too many fantasies, have had too many leaders, followed too many impostors, suffered under too many despots, known too many revolutions, been told too many lies. It's as if they have only lived in a time of floods and earthquakes, tremblings of the soil, and have never known how to feel the solid ground beneath their feet.

So the truth is that, for all my foolish questions, all my nosy wanderings, all my enquiring visits to the academies, libraries and studios, all my interviews with shopkeepers and traders, craftsmen and artists, bankers and sailors, all my consulting of books and papers and histories and charts and maps, all my notes and drawings, I could write you an encyclopedia about it and still not for a moment understand it. I was foolish, I confess, not to travel further, go onward to Moscow or the lands of wolves and snow, the way to the Orient; now I realize that. But there was plague in Moscow and bloody Cossack revolution in the regions, and I have never been enamoured of such things. I prefer my thoughts and books. In consequence I never once left the strange city of Petersburg, and I never strayed far from the court – in other words, that babbling, gossiping, stabbing, poisoning confusion of boyars and generals, nobles and shopkeepers, patriarchs and whores, divinities and satyrs, dreams and secrets, elegances and cruelties, grandeurs and utter debasements and decadences which is the Russian court.

Maybe that's how it always has to be with philosophers. We who think we understand truth, wisdom, utility, freedom, liberty, happiness and the cosmos really know nothing at all about life as it is. Those of us who think we really understand power – state, monarchs, tyrannies, despotisms – have seen those things only as we enjoy wine by looking down the neck of a bottle. For what a difference there is when we see a painting of a tiger painted by Oudry at the summer exhibition, and when we meet a real tiger in the forest.

Well, I have seen the real tiger in the forest.

In a short time we shall meet again, dear ladies. I'm bringing you treasure from Siberia, I have collected some of the very finest shards of marble and precious mineral for your cabinets of curiosities, and every single one of them worth a kiss. In fact I can't imagine how our kissing will ever stop, since Siberia is, as you know, one of the vastest places in the world.

Goodbye, ladies. Soon I shall reappear on your stage and never leave it . . .

Je suis, etc.

Even the final stretch of the journey to his home is strange. The night before he leaves the Hague, he observes by the light of a candle his dear old friend Prince Dmitry Golitsyn on his knees in his guest's bedroom, carefully forcing, opening up and going through every single one of his trunks. When he inspects the outcome in the morning, checking through all his hoard of papers, the packed ranks of his notebooks and drafts, he discovers that his much annotated copy of the 'Nakaz' – the Empress's 'Grand Instruction' – has been removed; so have all the notes he's written about it. Before he has time to consider what to do (surely these can only be his empress's orders?), Grimm's carriage arrives. Farewells are warmly said; nothing is mentioned on either side. He and Grimm ride off through the wind-milled landscape, across the Austrian Low Countries, to Antwerp, Ghent and Brussels. But here, strangely and suddenly, Melchior announces he has important business, and places our man on the Paris diligence. On this, the last leg, an English lady resident in Paris rides with him. Taking out his notebook, he asks her questions. Which of the two languages she's used is the purer?

'I like English for my mouth, French for my ears,' she says.

He thanks her, writes it down.

'Monsieur, sir, my good dear sir,' she says, in extremely good English and French, 'forgive me for mentioning it, but that is your hand upon my knee.'

And then here they are: the new black walls and great new toll-gates that mark the ever extending borders of the modern Paris. For they're building here too: a great new Place down by the river, a finely restored Palais Royal, a splendid new Pont de Neuilly. In Montparnasse Soufflot's new church, his Roman Pantheon, rises high; in fact they are just beginning to work on the raising of its glorious and millennial dome. It's eighteen months since he last saw Paris, and almost exactly twelve since he entered the gates of Sankt Peterburg. Now it's October once again, and here in the finest of all great cities the weather is autumnally mild. Leaves hanging yellow on the plane trees, light evening shawls for all the gaily painted ladies strolling through the shameless new Palais Royal to the Opera. At last he unloads himself out of the carriage, right there outside the apartment in the rue Taranne. Frankly he's now a far older, a far greyer, a far stranger man than he was when he started. The postilions put down all his luggage, heavy with books and papers, and look around.

The Great Particularist, mob-cap over her dense grey hair, is there, standing waiting with her arms folded in the doorway of the building.

'Monsieur,' she says.

'All right,' he says, 'go on then, look in my luggage. Please. Count my handkerchiefs, check my socks. See if I've lost a single one of them.'

'I certainly will,' she says. 'So, you've come home.'

Yes, he's come home. While a stew boils on the stove, he goes up the stairs and unpacks it all: the great jewelled Russian Bible the Metropolitan has given him, worth a fortune; the Siberian minerals, the bearskin coat, the imperial cup and saucer her lips have smacked on. And the sixty-six fat notebooks where he has written down everything: the plan of the perfect Russia. When he goes to the Ministry, nobody there seems in the least interested in the secret plans of Caucasian fortresses he's carried right across Europe at such risk.

Soon winter arrives: yes, I promise you, even here in Paris. Back in his familiar study, amid the rich leathery friendship of his rare and wonderful books, gladly wearing his dirty old dressing gown, he waits. But nothing, or nothing of what he's expecting, comes down the way from imperial Petersburg. People are saying he seems much older now. They think the journey has tired him, destroyed him, made him feeble, made him vain. He wonders about these things himself, writing a letter to Grimm:

As for me, I'm already sending my weightiest luggage off in advance. My teeth wiggle, my eyes fail after nightfall, my legs get very lazy and beg for the aid of two sticks. I still can't tell the time, and constantly confuse hours, days, weeks, months and years. I still talk all the time, still maintain my innocent faith in the external world. And though my legs stagger, my eyes blur, and my back makes me look like a turtle, my wizard's wand still rises. My dear friend, all is well.

THIRTY-FIVE (NOW)

HERE THEY COME, sailing grandly through the islands of the archipelago: the great white or blue ferries, the huge steel-jawed and car-consuming monsters, the squared-off office blocks, the floating coffins are sweeping down the inland seaway once more, heading out to the Baltic. There they are, riding athwart us, their loud sirens blasting out imperiously over the little hump-backed granite islands: the *Sibelius* and the *Kalevala*, the *Baltic Clipper* and the great *Estonia*. They pass us close, so that we can easily see that their saloon bars are already open and active, their duty-free shops getting busy, their passengers now emerging blinking on to the stern and the green-swarded sun-decks and looking out curiously over the vast shoal of islands. We, of course, are running the other way, inland from the Baltic, not leaving port but coming into it, navigating the difficult awkward passages of the archipelago, where some of these rocks lie so close they almost clip our sides, and bearing toward the inland city of Stockholm, on its web of islands; its tall smoke plume lies faintly on the horizon way up ahead.

The red sun's sliding. And here on the *Vladimir Ilich* they're already shutting everything down. Up on the bridge deck, sailors are stacking up the cushions from the deckchairs and swilling down the boards. Below our last drinkers are drinking their final drinks, our last fixers are making their final fix, our last gamblers having a last encounter with chance in the casino. The last mud-packs are coming off in the beauty salon. The last purchases are being made in the duty-free shop, where poor Tatyana from Novgorod works without any attention at all from her funky professor, whose face was once so visible to all the crew till it dissolved into the sand on the edge of the waves. As for our Enlightenment conference room, that was long ago closed and locked. As far as the Diderot Project is concerned, reason has run its entire course. There were a few last papers: Manders considering Diderot's Baltic cultural policy, Agnes examining his likely opinions on union recognition, Bo on Diderot and artificial intelligence and, the final speaker, Lars Person, who tried to explain to us the Diderot Paradox. Hard solid stuff it all was too, not a story to be heard. Yes, the book will be fine. The grant will be paid. Everyone will be happy. We've made the farewell speeches, had the farewell dinner, drunk the farewell toasts. For this year if not eternity, the Diderot Project is over and done.

And everyone is happy. Up here on the bridge deck with me is Agnes Falkman. To tell the entire and honest truth, as I know you always like me to do, we two have become pretty good friends on these past few days of our Baltic adventure: in fact ever since we left Petersburg and our Swedish nightingale summoned Sven Sonnenberg to her splendid suite of a cabin, evidently preferring silence to noise. Not a sound or murmur has been heard from either of them for three days, apart from a few staff instructions about food they would like to have taken to the cabin. So Agnes and I have had the chance to spend a few days together, talking, reflecting, even considering the few strange pages of manuscript that someone has tucked into my little leatherbound volume of *Tristram Shandy*, which I look at every day. What is it? The end, perhaps, of Diderot's novel? Some other novel, or play, some tale for the future? The end, perhaps, of a story that has been written somewhere, but so far only up in the Great Book of Destiny above? At any rate, these unpublished sheets seem to me like the seed of many new stories. I hide them back in my case.

Now, standing side by side under the untiring gaze of Lenin, Agnes and I have emerged to look out for the first glimpses of her home city, splendid bourgeois Stockholm, where all is not confusion, crime and anarchy but civic sweetness and light. Even in the couple of weeks it has taken to make our Baltic journey, the entire season has changed. The close of summer has turned into the gloom of autumn and is beginning to become the sharpness of winter. The yachts and cruisers moored to the piers at the cottages of the archipelago are now out of the water or moored in their sheds. The summer cottages are blocked off with their winter shutters. Cold winds flap the flagpoles at the end of the piers, where the flags themselves have been struck. The landscape gets busier: more houses and church spires, more roads and roaring cars. And ahead a fine urban skyline emerges. There in profile is the modernist brick block of the City Hall, where they award the Nobel Prizes, the green copper roofings of the parliament and the great Royal Palace, looking just as cold today as it must have done when poor Descartes stumbled into it every morning, the plain straight Protestant spire of the Storkyran Cathedral.

'Stockholm, my lovely city,' says Agnes, pulling her scarf tight round her neck. 'Really, you ought to try and stay here for a few more days.'

'That's very hospitable, Agnes. But I can't, not really. The diary's full. All kinds of things I have to do.'

'Of course it's too cold for sailing. But we could still take the ferries and go round the islands.'

'If only . . .'

'Soon our people will be getting ready for winter. In Sweden we so very much love the winter. We are really winter people. The winter makes us very happy. You would love it. Try to stay.'

'I thought people in Sweden got depressed in the winter.'

'No, please don't believe it. It is not fair. This is our Swedish problem, everyone has the wrong image. In Sweden we're not the least bit as gloomy as you think.'

'No, I'm sure.'

'The problem is really yours. You are simply not serious. There is not enough gravity.'

'I'm afraid that's perfectly true.'

'If you stayed a few days I could help you.'

'Really?'

'I have a degree in counselling, another in bereavement therapy.'

'I thought you were a workers' union organizer?'

'Yes, of course. But remember, in Sweden we are all workers. Those in bereavement and counselling are workers too.'

'Ah, the bourgeois proletariat?'

'Exactly. After all, we are mostly women.'

'The new victors, then.'

'*Nej, nej,* the eternal victims, you know that. Anyway, if you really can't stay here, we had better say goodbye.'

'You've really been very kind, Agnes, and it's been wonderful to meet you.'

'Yes, but—'

'But nothing. Except I'm a writer and I have to go home and write something.'

'Your paper for our project, I really hope.'

'Well, no, I doubt it.'

'But we will need it for our book.'

'What is this book?'

'Very important, a book about new knowledge-based systems.'

'I don't see how a paper by me could help anyone with that. In any case that's the last sort of thing I'm going to write.'

'As long as it is not another story that isn't a story.'

'Why not?'

'Because it is very annoying.'

'Well, I'm not sure at all what kind of thing it is yet. Just something.'

'Maybe you'll let me see it some time.'

'I might. I should have to come back to Sweden.'

'Of course you will come back. I can get you a grant for it. Oh, look, there is the Vasa Museum, did you go there? What did you think?'

'Rather chilling, I thought.'

'The tomb of a ship, the tomb of an empire,' says Agnes. 'All too old, all too colonialist. These things are gone. Sweden does not need a history, it is quite different now. Now we are in the modern age, when all people should feel equal to each other and everyone should be happy.'

'How very true.'

I look out on Central Stockholm, lying in front of us, on its hillsides over the water. Great public buildings, high urban motorways, pleasant cafés, comfortable parks. A civilized city, a civic city, a city where things are not all defunct or defective, where tomorrow is not sliding away into a grim and suffering yesterday, where social attention is paid and money is well spent. On board we're going into docking mode: chains are running, hawsers

459

swinging, gangplanks hanging loose over the side. From the tannoys the whole ship is booming with Russian instructions. The fur-hatted boyar stewards, the red-cheeked cabin maids, are busy carrying luggage up from below. I can see my own battered suitcase, heavy with books, papers, notebooks, lying next to the fine Vuitton splendours of our great diva. Pushing crowds of passengers are filling the public rooms, shoving their way toward disembarkation: the Tartar Norwegians, the Albanian Scots, the Siberian Japanese.

And there in the lobby Bo and Alma have once more raised their now tattered banner to reason. DIDEROT PROJECT, it says for the very last time. But now it's a matter of the final farewells. The pilgrims gather round; then, in a sudden flurry of fond emotion, they have all begun hugging, embracing, squeezing hands. And who's with whom? Birgitta Lindhorst has reappeared in all her grandeur, but the person who is carrying her coat today is Anders Manders. Sven Sonnenberg is somewhere over there in duty-free, having a very serious conversation with Irini from Omsk; he's holding a table. Agnes Falkman, evidently disappointed in our farewells, has gone over to Lars Person and they seem to be talking of sharing a taxi home.

So: where are they going? Well . . . how does anyone ever really know where they're going? Where have they come from? Simply the last place over the sea. What are they all saying? I just can't be sure what they're saying, since the end of a trip is always so noisy and confusing, no one remembers what ought to be said to anyone else, and everything – ideas, values, relationships – that has been important to so many for so many days dissolves like a face drawn in the sand as the tide comes in. In fact at the moment of departure it's somehow as if everyone begins to shrink, and all common experiences immediately start to shrivel, become history, or memory, which is our own personal form of history and which, memory being so imperfect an instrument, is also the beginning of forgetting.

Then Alma the great Snow Queen comes over and seizes me hard by the arm.

'What now?' she says.

'What now? I'm going home.'

'No, don't leave us, don't go.'

'I have to.'

'Stay in Stockholm tonight. Now I know you a bit better I can take you somewhere really bohemian. Not that awful place we went the first night. And you still didn't try our crayfish—'

'I'd really love to, Alma. But I've already confirmed my plane flight and called home.'

'If you must. But remember, when you take your taxi out to Arlanda, don't let them charge you too much money. In Sweden our taxi drivers are very honest, but they often go round by the long way.'

In his fine Burberry sports jacket Bo comes over. He wipes his glasses and shakes my hand earnestly.

'My dear fellow, what a really excellent paper it was you gave us,' he says.

'Was it? I thought you really didn't like it.'

'Of course I liked it. I gave you that impression? How did I do that?'

'You said you didn't like it.'

'*Nej, nej*, your paper was perfect. If you just leave me the text I will publish it in the proceedings.'

'No, the whole point was it never had a text. I didn't write it down.'

'But I know you. You will.'

'If I can remember it.'

'How could you forget it? It was one of your stories. Don't fail us, please. It was so much in the spirit of Diderot.'

'The perfect spirit of Diderot,' says Alma, looking me in the eye. There's something about her look that makes me think I just might have been wrong, and this lady isn't quite such a Snow Queen after all. Meantime Bo is writing something on a slip of paper, which he then slides into my jacket pocket.

'Your invitation to next year's conference,' he says warmly.

'You've planned next year already?'

'Of course, one must always think ahead. It's on the top of a mountain in Norway. Very beautiful.'

'Exceedingly beautiful,' says Alma meaningfully.

'So why discuss Diderot on top of a mountain?'

'*Nej, nej,*' says Bo. 'Next year the conference is on Ludwig Wittgenstein.'

'The Wittgenstein Project?'

'*Jo, jo,*' says Bo.

'I'm afraid I don't know too much about Wittgenstein,' I say. 'Except he had a nephew.'

'All in the aid of reason,' says Bo.

'No, I don't think so,' I say.

'Oh, tell us you will come!' cries Alma. 'How can we possibly have a conference without you?'

'But I really don't think I could manage a paper on the subject of Wittgenstein,' I murmur.

'Good, do you hear that, he is saying yes,' says Bo. 'Whenever he says no he always really means yes. Isn't it true?'

'Of course.'

And Alma grabs me and gives me an extremely splendid kiss. No, I've been wrong about the lady. She's not a Snow Queen after all.

So, as the critical bronze gaze of Vladimir Ilich surveys me to the last, I walk down the gangplank, and into the drab wooden customs hall on Strandsgardeskajan. A neatly dressed customs officer eyes me thoughtfully, and begins a polite but efficient search through my luggage. From beneath my shirts he draws an old leatherbound book.

'It's valuable?' he asks.

'Not really,' I say cunningly. 'It's not usually the books that are valuable, it's the words that are written inside them. And we can hardly charge a duty on those.'

Faced with this stirringly liberal thought, he gives me another glance and begins to scour through the pages. Finally he comes across the wad of ancient paper stuck into the end-papers. He looks at the faded handwritten sheets, the words in French that seem to tell some tale or other about a servant and a master.

'Papers?' he says.

'Yes, but they're not important. Just someone's notes on the story.'

'No, your papers,' he says.

I show him.

'*Tack, tack,*' he says.

'No duty?'

'*Nej, nej,*' he says, smiling at me.

All is well: I have papers, therefore I exist. I repack my shirts and strap up my case.

Feeling richer by the instant, as travellers sometimes (but not often) do, I walk out to the terminal exit. I stop a moment, turn and look back. Behind me, in the long rows that are still waiting for passport control, I can see them all – my fellow Enlightenment Pilgrims, standing in the dark but waiting to get into the light. There's red-haired Birgitta the nightingale, and dapper Anders Manders; there's saturnine Lars and bright folkish Agnes, serious Bo and unfrozen Alma. Except somehow, subtly, they seem to have changed around. For isn't that Bo with Birgitta, Agnes with Lars, Alma with Lars Person? Never mind. Such are the mysteries of conferences. I walk outside and into the light. Over there is the taxi rank. A long line of Volvos stands waiting; I head for the first, and the big blonde driver helps me to put my luggage inside.

'Arlanda,' I say.

'*Tack, tack,*' says the driver, full of gratitude, and switches on his most enormous meter. Slowly, considerately, with the greatest respect toward all pedestrians, we drive away from the great white vessel and the Man of History, away through the container port, out into the pleasant, decent civic streets of Stockholm . . .

Now it just so happens that – according to what, as it will all so clearly turn out, has already been written in the great Book of Destiny up above – in just two years on from this time I shall visit Saint Petersburg once again. On that occasion that still sits waiting for me in the future it will be slightly later in the year: in fact in the last days of November, when the final crisp sunshine has gone, the days have grown short, the statues in the Summer Garden have all been shuttered, and the snow, bitter and hard, has already begun to fall. The skies at that time will be as dark as lead. The streets will be an ice-rink or a skid-pan, and on the Nevsky Prospekt, outside my guard-protected hotel, it will be almost too dangerous to walk out. Times will be no better and probably quite a good deal worse. Women will still stand on squares of cardboard in the street, selling their old dresses or a household pet. Beggars will lie drunk and dying in the subways, wrapped passive bundles will sit outside on doorsteps, more armed men will guard even more shuttered banks.

This time I shall be not sailing but flying, and I shall be travelling with a small group of British writers, who have come to open a library in a charming room of old books that doesn't exist yet. The library is a writers' library, a library with a purpose, a library with a strong literary idea: it's the Mayakovsky Library, housed in the centre of Petersburg, in a charming old Golitsyn Palace which overlooks the black Fontanka. In its charming rooms private and public collections will come together, helped by the British Council, which also resides in this building, and the Petersburg Public Library, which I shall recall as the Saltykov-Shcherdrin, but which by then will be called the Russian National Library. I will come because, as you now know quite well, I love travel and libraries; but also because I hope to see, again, Galina. When I arrive, my very first question will be about her. And I shall be told at once that Galina is dead: that she died, in fact, just after our Diderot pilgrimage which right now is ending; that she never managed to do the thing she most wished to do, make a trip to Paris; that the Voltaire collection is still being re-assembled, but perhaps not in the old wonderful way . . .

But all this is a matter for the future, and who now can possibly know any of these things? In any case the present is all too present, and busy and demanding enough. I'm checking my flight time, and riding in a taxi through the heart of Stockholm, most pleasant and decent of cities. 'No smoking, no drinking, no eating. Airbag provided, side-impact protected, air-conditioned, safety locks. Fasten seat belt, do not speak to the driver. Special supplement to the airport,' it tells me on the dash. Inside this safe and highly informative cage I sit, surrounded on each side by slow-floating Saabs and considerate Volvos, all of them with their lights warningly on. We're navigating the great motorway web that links the city and ties together some of its many islands. Now we're passing the gardening centres, the furniture warehouses, the automobile franchises, the fast food palaces, the Ikea superstores and all those smart-looking out-of-town sheds that mobile phone and personal computer companies need these days to keep us in touch with the global traffic in signals and signs. All around me there's the triumph of the bourgeois, the reign of the decent, the tedium of the commonplace, the lure of the expensively commercial, the grand if faded wonder of social democracy, the waste and redundancy of the age of shopping, overload and far too much. Then we pass on into pleasant lakeland, pine–and–birch forest. And now, suddenly, all the motorway signs up there are pointing the right way: Arlanda, Arlanda. I'm riding home . . .

But why, oh why, do I have the feeling this trip is going to cost me a bomb?

THIRTY-SIX (THEN)

NATURALLY, for all his years and for all his weariness, our man is quite incapable of staying idle very long. Soon he's again taking his five o'clock walks through the streets of Paris, wandering through the elegant and erotic refurbishments that have been done to the fine Palais Royal, where everything is on offer. Here the newspapers and periodicals are sold, the banned books are eagerly distributed and taken home, the city's finest whores in their most elegant and teasing costumes flit through the arcades in front of the shouting merchants and the wandering beaux. In the old way he discusses with himself questions of politics and love, taste and philosophy, letting his mind rove wantonly. By night he dines as he always used to with the city's great men of learning, who are also beginning to show their years: d'Alembert, d'Holbach, Helvétius. He hears of the strange solitary doings of Rousseau, the sharpest new barbs of Voltaire. He returns to the salons of the great married ladies – so many of them now, all offering their services as players of music, writers of books, grand Semiramises, mistresses to philosophers and men of true wit. But the grand ladies are younger now; so are the men of true wit. When the weather is wet, he strolls to the cafés, sitting down, as ever at the tables of the Café Procope, or wandering into the Café de la Régence, watching the clever men shift the pieces across the chequerboards while he digests the latest scandals, reads the latest broadsheets, scans the latest fops.

And as usual Grimm's political instincts have proved entirely right. Paris has changed. It's changed completely, entirely, epochally, epistemically. For the moment at least there's a quite new spirit to this relaxed, youthful, louche new reign, with its pastoral dreams and its panderous court at the Hermitage. Everything feels just a bit more tolerant, a bit more permitted, though somehow also more anxious, more volatile, for this is a world where freedom is taken almost too freely, to the point where it dissolves in all directions. Decadences multiply, sex is grosser. Women tease men in a great claim of power. It's grown more difficult to enrage the censor, though his Jesuitical friend the Abbé Raynal has already done it, and his own turn will surely come (as indeed it does, for it's already written there will be one more grand brush with the book-burners before his days on earth are done). At his age it gets harder, ever harder, to sound like a fiery torch or a radical young man – especially when there are so many much younger men doing just the same kind of thing.

In fact a whole grand gallery of young philosophers is now beginning to fill the clubs and cafés, as if these days there were simply no occupation other than thought. There they sit, drinking their wines, supping their rich Arabian coffees, dressed up in their fashionable silks and brocades and their large Voltairean turbans: having their shoes cleaned, flaunting their wit, pronouncing their atheism, confessing their humour, dissecting the universe, chattering like monkeys about whatever it is – life, or liberty, or the pursuit of happiness – that happens to be the vogue of the week. When do they think? When do they find time to write?

Certainly there's no shortage of their scribblings, and our man knows exactly whom to blame. It's Panckoucke, of course, the great media mogul, who has been buying up everything: grabbing newspapers, book-titles, imprints, novelists, thinkers and journalists by the score. Now he's publicly rebuked our man for failing to update his own encyclopedia, and is announcing the need for a mega new one, the biggest and grandest multimedia project the world has ever seen. Where our man has invested wisdom, intelligence, risk and exile, he simply invests money; for in the new Paris everything is for purchase. And yet the whole greedy thing has the King's blessing, it seems: as long as the game is commerce and not criticism, nobody minds at all. Now Panckoucke and his agents are running round all the cafés and clubs, tempting the philosophers, hiring the researchers and the copyists, hunting down hacks. Money is no object; he's paying absurd fees for absurd thoughts, and inveigling the investments of any kind of subscriber, not simply the wise and learned readers his own grand volumes were meant for. Critique has become commodity, light has become power. As for our man: truth is he's famous, he's fashionable, he's failing, and he's finished.

Yes, Paris now is exactly as young Beaumarchais – another of the many men he's invented and set off on his profitable way – describes it in his newest play at the Comédie-Française, the one about the barber-factotum, another tale of a servant and a master: 'Such a barbaric age we live in. I can't see it's produced a single thing we should be grateful for. Only every kind of stupidity and trash: atheism, magnetism, electricity, religious freedom, inoculation, quinine, terrible plays and modern rubbish, Diderot's *Encyclopedia* . . .' Yes, times have certainly changed – but it all goes so far and no further. There are political reforms and new freedoms. Sex is coarser, passions are cruder, appearances are crasser, violent actions win more approval. Science prospers, invention flourishes. Thought has grown far more instrumental, far less abstract. There's a great flurry of discovery: inoculation, the flowings of the blood, the marine chronometer, the wily ways of mad Dr Mesmer who stares into everyone's eyes, magnetism, electricity. Distant islands are set foot on. People are trying to travel on rivers by the aid of paddles and steam. In the parks outside Paris, in front of the most enormous crowds, others are tying themselves or their animals to huge floating bladders and trying to ascend high in the sky.

Still waiting news from his northern patron, he attempts a number of topical inventions of his own. He devises a household printing machine that allows a man a simple means to make his own books; if pressed, he thinks he'll call it a type-writer. He creates another machine for the encoding and decoding of messages, modelled on the lively brain of d'Alembert, and designed to help politicians transmit their secrets. In his spare time he tries to square the circle. A fresh spring comes, and still nothing arrives from Russia. By now it's not too hard to grasp the point. There will never be a Russian encyclopedia. No one will ever build his glorious Russian university. His daily papers for Catherine must be mouldering away somewhere in the back rooms of the Hermitage; as for the sixty-six notebooks he created them from, he shoves those away under lock and key. Now he goes round the galleries and starts to sell off his Russian treasures and trophies, which would have served for his new encyclopedia: the cabinets of Siberian minerals, the glorious Orthodox bible in Cyrillic presented to him over the Christmas ceremonials by the glittering and dome-hatted archimandrite.

Time to think again about what it means to be a modern Seneca. Perhaps the whole great question of the good society, of the thinker's proper service to morals and society, needs a totally different solution. But what? He goes to see his old friend, the fat Abbé Guillaume-Thomas-François Raynal. Big, burly, a loud laughing noise at all the finest dinner tables, he too has created one of the greatest books of the age: *The History of the Two Indies*, the most wonderful and vexing book of the day. Some have called it the other *Encyclopedia*; and, banned in France for its liberalism, it's published in Holland and Geneva, and read almost everywhere. Our man has contributed to it before in its earlier days. What is it? Well, a sort of a history, a kind of philosophy, a handy compendium of the promises of international commerce and industry. It's a work of reform, a work of anthropology, a work of true human feeling. But in truth it's really a grand lamentation: a dark cry over the lost of the two great French empires, one by the Himalayas, the other reaching in a great arc from the icecaps of the Arctic to the tropical richness of the Bay of Mexico, the Indian lands so sweetly called Louisiana – two French imperial lands which, thanks to an accident of history and the incompetence of a now-dead monarch, have been lost by the French to the British just a little more than a decade before.

Lovely Louisiana, from the icecaps and codbanks of the Arctic to the tropic plantations of the Mexique Bay, from the wonderful downpour of Niagara to the turtled lands of the Floridians: what Frenchmen could resist it? The British have been there and now they have won it; but it's the French who have explored and toured it, asked its great questions, mapped it, found the way down the four great rivers – Mississippi, Ohio, Saint Lawrence, and Oregon – which have carried the pelts, floated the Indian canoes, opened the bluffs and the prairies, and spoken of the soul of nature and natural man himself. While the British sat on the coastlines and saw trade, the French – the great explorers and

469

missionaries like Champlain and Hennepin – found wonders, mapped landscapes, named the continent in French. America is a French fiction into which the British have blundered, and now they are blundering still. Clearly Raynal's book calls for yet another revision. Our man is happy to offer his services. The Abbé sets him on.

Soon he's writing frenziedly, 'doing a Raynal', as he tells his friends, working on it night and day. He lets Raynal record the economic data, the prospects of trade, the dry statistics, the historical evidence, the facts of geography and the dreary details of noontime temperature – while he adds the great decorations and deconstructions of philosophy, speculations on the spirit of society, the sins of despotism, the dangers of arrogant monarchy, the wrongs of slavery, the rhythmic vision of the rise and fall of empire that only he (and Edmund Gibbon) could give. Thoughts that served well in Petersburg strangely fit the Americas too.

'God hates tyrants,' he writes, 'and has printed on men's hearts a love of freedom. Under the supreme will of despotism there is only terror, servility, flattery, stupidity and superstition. That intolerable situation ends either with the assassination of the tyrant, or the dissolution of the empire.' Little wonder his writings are once more fated to be burned in Paris by the public hangman.

'Democracy arises on this corpse,' he adds, 'and the annals are filled with heroic deeds. Laws reign, genius flowers, sciences flourish, the useful trades are no longer held in poor esteem. So, Kings and Ministers, love the people, and you will be happy.'

Then, remembering a great empress and the difficult problems of writing on human skin, he adds a coda: 'Unfortunately this state of happiness is only momentary. Everywhere revolutions succeed one another, at a speed one can hardly follow. But the laws of nature tell us that all empires are born and then die.'

And our man isn't the only one to think these matters important. 'The discovery of America, and that of a passage to the East Indies by the Cape of Good Hope, are two of the greatest and most important events recorded in the history of mankind,' writes, at just this time, a certain dry Scots professor, Adam Smith, in a grand account of *The Wealth of Nations*. 'Two new worlds have been opened to industry, each of them greater and more extensive than the old one.' Smith may think he is writing of a British empire possessed, a project that can be realized. But he seems already to have sensed the illusion: 'The rulers of Great Britain have, for more than a century past, amused the people with the imagination that they possessed a great empire on the west side of the Atlantic. This empire, however, has hitherto existed in imagination only. It has hitherto been, not an empire, but the project of an empire; not a gold-mine, but the project of a gold-mine.'

But Smith writes as a Briton, from the land not of wit but common sense. For a Frenchman things are different; all there is to see is a lost world, a fading paradise, a land of dying wonders, of tumbling ruins, mournful landscapes, vacant spaces, fallen dreams. Yet soon that will be true for the British too. For, in the lovely lost lands of Louisiana they too have chosen to display power and monarchy in a grand act of political folly. Even while the dreams of their colonists on the Eastern seaboard begin to spread ever westward, they are stirring them to fury, arms, and rebellion. And in that hasn't philosophy – true philosophy, French philosophy – played its crucial part? When, in the year Smith publishes his book, a congress of these British American colonials gathers to declare its Independence ('We hold these truths to be self-evident'), the self-evident truths they choose to commit to paper ('all men created equal . . . endowed by their Creator with certain inalienable rights . . . Life, Liberty, and the Pursuit of Happiness . . .') all seem curiously familiar to our man. It's just as if he has written them himself; in fact he thinks he very probably has.

Well, the transatlantic insurrection is naturally more than enough to delight any Frenchman. Soon all of Paris is filling with heroic American dreams. An entire generation of young nobles, longing to give the British a pasting, exhausted to boredom by a whole dull decade of peace, still smarting to the quick from the old American losses, is ready to be up in arms. Seeking to be a national hero, the youthful Marquis de Lafayette is already fitting out a ship, the *Victoire*, and filling it up with troops and weapons to go filibuster for the great transatlantic cause of liberty and Anglophobia. Even our man's own theatrical creation, the rogue-clockmaker Caron, now come to fame as Beaumarchais, is devoting the profits of his barber-drama to the cause, and trying to rouse the King, in whose ear he is known to whisper, to action: 'It is Britain, sir, whom you must humiliate and weaken, if you do not wish her to humiliate and weaken you at every turn.' Now he's devised his own distinctive mystification. He's invented a fake import-export firm to smuggle arms to the insurgents, and charted a vast freebooting fleet of forty ships, aided by money from France and Spain, but mostly at his own expense. The truth is it's Figaro the barber-valet who will devise and finance the American Revolution. And his money will never come back.

One evening, with the Great Particularist riding at his side, our man goes out for dinner chez Beaumarchais. Clockmaker Caron now lives very grandly, entertaining like a gentlemen and keeping several mistresses on the side. Indeed the man is everywhere these days, one minute engaged in some elaborate sexual shenanigans in Seville, the next just back from London where he's been engaged in high level spying and revolutionary conspiracy. But tonight he's entertaining a rather special and unexpected guest: a guest who has come over in considerable secrecy from the Americas. He's a truly noble savage, a man who has all the skills and wisdoms of the greatest Parisian scientists, yet combined with all the innocent sagacity and the instinctive political virtue of one of nature's own self-constructed philosophers. Ages have not withered him, nor history shaped his infinite variety. Now he's crossed the Atlantic on a thirty-day voyage much-menaced by the British – which has not deterred him from making a whole new set of scientific discoveries on the matter of flying fishes and the flow of the Gulf Stream.

He's been landed exhausted at Nantes, but promptly whisked in secret to Paris. Now he resides in grandeur at a safe house presented to him in Passy, where his covert presence has soon become a matter of general knowledge. For good homely things can't be kept secret for long, and genius merits its homage. In fact he's already in the process of becoming perhaps the most famous man in France. They're making teapots with his shaggy, folksy, sexy head on. He's already much better known than Marie-

Antoinette, and a good deal more popular. Half the most elegant and beautiful ladies of Paris have been tempted by his wit, his wisdom, his lumbering gallantries and his naked indiscretion. Madame Brillon is known to be besotted with him. Madame Helvétius is publicly considering his recent generous proposal of marriage. And even for the husbands, who have all of course read Rousseau, he is none other than Poor Richard: one of nature's heroes.

Such great things he's done, and all that without even leaving the American swamps and forests (give or take a visit or two to the Royal Society in London). He looks like a trapper or a logger, but he's revolutionized the radical art of printing, and transfigured the household stove. With a Bostonian's self-reliance coupled with a Philadelphia Quaker's simplicity he's reached his hands into the heights of the sky and plucked down lightning. In short, he's the Electrical Ambassador, wired to the universe. Now he arrives, wearing that famous, original Canadian beaver pelt on the top of his head (oddly enough, Rousseau used to wear one exactly like it). His suit is plain, his hair shaggy and undressed. His expressions benign, he beams at the world over a pair of bifocal spectacles he's believed to have invented and ground himself.

'*Mon cher* Monsieur Frankling!' our man cries out, embracing the grainy, tweedy, eye-glassed figure warmly.

'And who have we here now? Not the great Doctor Dee Diderot?'

'Yes, this is Diderot, or whatever's left of him. A wearing-out sort of fellow, a little halt and lame now.'

'You're but a child, sir, I'm older. Listen, that was one of the best books I ever read, your encyclopedia.'

'You actually read the *Encyclopedia*?'

'Sure I did, all of it. You know the entry I remember best? The one on 'Encyclopedia'. Who wrote that?'

'That's mine, I wrote that.'

'I recall you made some observations on the enormity of our revolution in modern thought. Imagine, you said, the dictionaries of just one hundred years ago. And you added: "You won't find under 'aberration' any notion of what astronomers now mean by the term. As for electricity, you added, you will find only false notions and ancient prejudices.'

'Of course you were the great transformer I had in mind.'

'Well, you see, sir, I always remembered the lesson I put into the mouth of Poor Richard. "If you don't want to be forgotten, / As soon as you are dead and rotten, / Either write things worth the reading, / Or do things worth the writing." I hope I've done both.'

'You have, sir, and now you are giving us the hope of freedom.'

'True. What we may shortly have – if the Great Creator allows it, your King supports it, and dear Beaumarchais here will pay for it – is a brand-new nation.'

'A nation, I'll pay, of course I'll pay,' says Caron, otherwise Beaumarchais. 'But that's simply the beginning, my dear man. After freedom we're going to need a society, I mean an entire social system, a right and equal way of doing things. Now there's the problem for us philosophers. Tell me this, have you ever been in America, Louisiana, Monsieur Diderot?'

'Only in my mind. And my writings. *Les Deux Indes.*'

'I know. I send Raynal his statistics. That's why it's so boring.'

'Hardly boring. I believe we have a better America on paper than you yet do in life.'

'But that's what I mean, sir. You must go there. I really wish I could put you on a ship there right now.'

'My legs, sir.'

'You'd see wonders. A glorious land or continent that represents nature in its perfection, its mystery, let me say its grossness. A world that still has to cross the bridge from nature to society.'

'Monsieur Diderot too has seen wonders,' says Caron.

'Yes, sir, I think you went to Russia?'

'I did. Another society at its own beginnings.'

'No, sir, Russia isn't new, it's just pretending. You went for the right reason to the wrong place. North America is the first time civilized human beings have ever been in a position to devise an entirely new society without suffering the weight of an old history.'

'Then you do need philosophers. After Eden there has to come civilization.'

'And after civilization?'

'Decay and ruin, such is the course of empire.'

'See for yourself. Come, sir, I shall arrange it. Promise me.'

'But my legs, sir, truly, my legs.'

'And what do you do next in Paris, Monsieur Frankling?'

'What do I do? What can you possibly do after meeting Diderot? You go and meet Voltaire.'

'He's in Ferney.'

'But is he, sir, is he? Ask again.'

'You mean he's here? Then I have to meet him.'

When our man returns to the rue Taranne that night, he finds himself staring again at the manuscript he has left lying open on his desk. He thinks again of the big man in the half-glasses and the beaver hat. He thinks of the Indian wonderlands, the great swamps and forests and tree-frogs of Louisiana, the great downpour of falls at Niagara, the Indian peoples, the smell of the skunk, the caribou splashing in the lakes, the noise of the whippoorwills in the woods. He writes a little blessing to those dear Louisiana lands, the old transatlantic provinces, now to have a different future: 'May there never be born in any one of them, or if so may he die at once, by the stroke of the hangman or the dagger of a Brutus, a citizen who is so powerful, and so much the enemy of human happiness, to devise for himself the project of becoming its master.'

He thinks a moment, and then adds a benign coda: perhaps if so the world might create just one republic that is able to defeat the law otherwise written in the great Book of Destiny: 'The decree pronounced against all the things, all the societies, all the people of this world; that all have a birth, a flowering, a tiresome old age, and then a death.'

And so, thanks to Franklin, it finally happens. The two men who really do have to meet sometime during their lifetimes manage to meet at last. There, in the bare darkened drawing room of someone's Paris hotel particulaire, he sits, clad in a dressing gown, the most famous man of the age. He's been carefully arranged in a big armchair. His bony feet are naked, a turban is wound round his head. He's eighty-four years old now, visibly tired, coughing heavily. Over that long lifetime that reaches across reign after reign he's written more words than almost any other wordsmith could manage: more even, when our man honestly thinks about it, than he has himself. His collected works will run to over a hundred volumes, constructing yet another financial disaster for poor Caron, Beaumarchais, who when he turns his eyes from sponsoring American insurgency will decide to buy up all his posthumous papers and rights. Then his papers themselves will scatter themselves like parachuting seeds through all the libraries, private and public, of the world. His letters already cover the world in hopeless variety: so many, to so many people, on so many different things. He's performed in all the familiar genres: poetry and prose, comedy and tragedy, fiction and history, satire and squib. He's assumed many identities, taken over a hundred pseudonyms; even the name by which all know him, Voltaire, is not his true name. Just finding the man again – tracing his signatures, discovering his different roles in life, finding his books and records – will provide many with their own life-work.

Now, in this April of 1778, he's come back to Paris. Posterity stalks him everywhere he goes. Even his old enemies have become his friends. 'Author! Author!' they shouted out two nights ago at the Théâtre Français, where his latest creation, the tragedy *Irene* (neither age nor travel stop him writing) is now playing. Court and censor have always denied him; yet court and censor were there in the audience to hail him – with the one conspicuous exception of His Serene Majesty himself. Mozart is playing in Paris, but this particular auditorium is on this night where everyone wishes to be. The dark classical tale has unfolded, but that is nothing compared with the second and greater drama. The author's bust by the excellent Caffieri is set centre-stage. The comedians and tragedians reappear to place laurels on his head, in the supreme apotheosis. Then, as rumour buzzes through the theatre, the shout begins to rise. 'Author! Author!' Soon the plaster cast is replaced by the living author, fetched down from his box, the laurels on the bust removed and placed on the living head. 'Author! Author!' The standing ovation lasts for more than five minutes. 'Author! Author!' shout the vast street-crowds of Paris the moment he sets foot outside. 'I may suffocate, but it will be under a shower of roses!' he cries with his usual grace and felicity, as he struggles through the mêléc to make it to his carriage. Apotheosis!

'Monsieur Talleyrand was here, and also Monsieur Frankling,' says Madame Denis, stout and ever self-interested, as she leads our man up the stairs of the private hotel.

'How was Monsieur Frankling?'

'Oh, the American insisted in speaking in French, and he insisted in speaking in English, so nobody understood anything. But it was very important. If only Rousseau had been there as well.'

'Oh yes,' murmurs our man. There are vast paintings on the staircase, torches on the walls. In a room where the shutters are almost closed, he's sitting there shaded in half light. It all feels so familiar, as if it has happened once before. There are the monkey features, there is the wicked grin, perhaps just a bit sunk back into itself these days. There he is, witty and snappy and spiteful at an age when most men would be bent and bitter and glum: the brigand of Lake Geneva, jack of all trades and master of most of them too. His spiky tongue licks his large red lips as he sits there shoeless in the armchair: exactly as he sat in the statue that haunts the Empress's court.

Madame Denis moves the rugs and cushions and sits down to eavesdrop on the talk. But what can be said to him? He's often been bitter and spiteful, yet no one has done more for humankind: defended liberty, supported freedom, brought the wisdoms of Locke and Newton into the Popish thought-world of France. He's known exile, beating, disgrace, prison and excommunication. He's lived with the great powers of the age, and played his part in raising them high or bringing them low. He's paid plenty of homage to princes and popes and potentates, but with cleverness and cunning enough they now pay homage to him. These days it's Frederick of Prussia who flatters the philosopher, rather than the other way round, and who plans monuments in his honour, even sending him his bust from Potsdam with inscribed on the base not his name, Voltaire, but one simple word: 'Immortal.' So he is.

Now he's a crown prince of Philosophy: grand, glorious, very rich. His wealth sometimes seems a mystery, given his claims to persecution. Yet however he won it he's put it to use: acquired his own hectares and territories, founded his own city, created his own Hermitage. Once Ferney was said to be on the edge of Geneva; now it's Geneva that sits on the edge of Ferney. He's cultivated his gardens, grown his pomegranates, tended his vineyards, reared his fat sheep, thousands of them grazing once uncultivated fields. He's set up studios, workshops, lofts, factories; eighty watchmakers depend on his employment. He's entertained everyone, either at his huge table at Ferney or through the more abstract means of print and book. Ferney itself has become his private city, empire, court, a principality where princes come to attend on thinkers. His plates are of silver, his coat of arms decorates every door. He wished to be honest, and he wished to be famous; he wished to be virtuous, wished to be noble; wished to be Olympian and indifferent, wished to be very rich. In his eighty-four years he's succeeded, made his grand deal with Posterity. He's written and performed in all of his own plays; and for an eighty-year lifetime he's played in the biggest play of all, the one with the noble hero whose name was Arouet but is now called Voltaire.

He's coughing, spitting, and probably dying, wearing himself out in Paris in one vast final moment of fame. Yet as Frederick has admitted at last, he truly is immortal. He's become his own statue, transfigured himself into his own waxwork, grown into his own bust. He's sitting there Houdon-like, the same grinning monkey, but lit up with sparky animation; the stout niece sits protectively beside him, eyeing his visitor distrustfully, handing him protective cups of chocolate. He's the talk of all Paris now, everyone chattering about his safe return.

'Cher maître,' our man says, going forward, kneeling, putting out his hands. 'Embrace me, as one honest man to another. I am Diderot. I think I'm not entirely unknown to you.'

'My dear Diderot, my fellow Socrates, my honest and able brother in thought. We've known each other for ever, but we've left this meeting remarkably late.'

'I hoped one day I would come to Ferney.'

'But you didn't.'

'So it was written, or not written.'

'Was it? Well, what should we say to each other now?'

Madame Denis sits watching, listening carefully, no doubt knowing every wise and witty word is worth at least a livre.

'Shakespeare,' says our man, trying a fast opening serve.

'Don't mention it,' says the grinning monkey.

'I love him,' says our man.

'Amazing. And I do not.'

'Nothing in the world would please me better than to be able to stand beneath his enormous statue and reach up to touch his fine testicles,' our man ventures.

'Indeed?'

'If by that means I could inherit by proxy what is surely the world's greatest act of generation.'

'I fear you're as vulgar as he is. And I had you for a man of reason.'

'So, as I admire him, you condemn him?'

'I condemn him, my dear sir, for his grossness of imagination. I denounce him before the seats of judgement for his want of philosophy. I dismiss him for his grotesque naïveté, his confusion of artistic purpose, his unwavering want of taste.'

'In that case you hate him for his greatness, surely? For not writing like yourself?'

'It's a good standard.'

'You are condemning a man who was cleverer, wiser, more capacious even than you.'

'Now, sir, you'd better go,' cries Madame Denis, rising.

'No, Marie-Louise, I have to answer this,' says the Immortal. 'I am over eighty, older by decades than you, old enough to be truly proud.'

'You are also old enough to be dead,' says our man. 'No one could ever wish it, but before it happens tell me what I always wanted to know. You've written more than any of us, *cher maître*. Written more wisely, more fluently, more wonderfully. But did you never perhaps . . . tire of it?'

'Tire of it?'

'Tire of writing, I mean.'

'No, I never tired of writing. That would be like tiring of existing. Writing is everything. What about you? Did you? Surely not?'

'I'm here to confess at your knees, as I would never confess to any other soul in the world,' says our man.

'Tell me, my son.'

'I know my sins,' he says, getting onto the floor. 'I have talked too much. I was born to chatter foolishly and tell the truth. To anyone: friends, enemies, total strangers. It was rarely in my best interest.'

'Get up, sir.'

'I was never wise. I fell into the delight of ideas, the joy of imaginings, the wonder of fictions. I loved dialogues and dramas. I watched truth come and go. I dwelt among plots and mystifications. You know I made the *Encyclopedia*.'

'You know I know,' says the Immortal, 'I wrote for it too, at your request. Along with so many other honest men.'

'Yes, everyone wrote, everyone with a decent mind and enough honour. But I'm not proud even of that. I'm much prouder of the things I never finished, the work I left undone.'

'Why do you want to tell me this?'

'I'm already well past my sixtieth year . . .'

'Your sixtieth? I'm way past my eightieth.'

'I'm weary of strife and harassment. The world's turned foolish and gone way past me. I seem to long only for obscurity and a nice quiet death.'

'There's nothing quiet about death.'

'But, sir, when the day comes to us, what will it all have meant? For you to have been Voltaire? For me to have been Diderot? Though I realize your two syllables are destined to survive far longer than my three.'

'Of course we'll survive. All of us. Ours is the age that made the difference. And not just in France, my dear sir, in the world as it rolls.'

'In Petersburg, I saw your bust by Houdon.'

'There are several, you know. There's another in Paris. It made his name. Now they are asking him to do a plaster George Washington.'

'And Pigalle is doing one of you? To tell you the truth, he's done me too.'

'Yes, Frederick of Prussia is paying. And Rousseau is going mad with jealousy.'

'Good. It's wonderful.'

'Listen to the poem I wrote about it: "Poor Jean-Jacques, with hostile stare, / Cries: 'Not a statue to Voltaire? / Please, I'm the one your chisel should / Honour for the greater good / I must protest, it isn't fair, / Not one more statue to Voltaire.'"'

'It's perfect,' cries our man, chuckling. 'How Jean-Jacques despises us.'

'Of course. He's made an altar to himself alone.'

'Perhaps we all have.'

'And they will remember us all, sir, but in very different ways. They will remember Rousseau's empty weeping foolish heart. Your spinning chatter. My infinite wisdom. Each of us has his own metamorphosis.'

The Immortal coughs.

'I think he's tiring,' says Madame Denis. 'He got quite exhausted after his apotheosis.'

'Of course,' says our man rising.

'No no, my friend, don't go. You must tell me. What was she like, in the fair flesh? The Semiramis of the North?'

'The Empress?'

'Cateau.'

'Cateau?'

'That's what I called her. I loved her, of course.'

'But you never even met her, I thought.'

'There was a cosmic radiance. A fatal attraction. An electricity. A magnetism.'

'Obviously something to do with power.'

'I have never despised power. I helped her to her power. I did all I could to make her great.'

'She is.'

'But what was it like to go there in the flesh? To see her? To stand before her?'

'I'll confess everything to you again. It was truly wonderful. When I went there to her court from our land of the free, I was a slave. When I left her land of slaves, I felt a free man. I dare say I loved her too.'

'You did? And you walked right up to the altar?'

'I did indeed.'

'You kissed it?'

'Certainly.'

'You touched?'

'*Oui*, monsieur.'

'What? Touched her where it really matters? Her limbs? Her thighs?'

'*Oui*.'

'You didn't go into her bed-chamber?'

'Indeed, sir. I walked through the grand halls of Petersburg. I left letters under her pillow.'

'You touched her . . . pillow?'

'Uncle, please,' cries Madame Denis. 'You are exciting yourself far too much.'

He looks at the Sage of Ferney, who is staring bitterly at him from out of his deep armchair.

'You were her favourite?'

'One of several. But I admit, when I left at last, she truly overwhelmed me with her favours.'

'Favours, what kind of favours?'

'Many things. A cup and saucer. But I do believe I could have emptied her whole exchequer.'

'Gifts! Maybe you know she sent me delegations, all the way from Petersburg to Ferney,' says the Immortal. 'She sent me gold and gems and silver. Even a ring she'd carved by her own hand.'

'Yes? Like this one here on my finger?'

'A little. But it was exactly like the Arabian Nights. No sooner had one camel train arrived laden with treasure and riches than it was followed by another.'

'Well, you did advise her to conquer Mustapha, did you not? Poland too, if I remember rightly.'

'I think perhaps she deceived me a little there, over Poland.'

'And Turkey too?'

'Perhaps I should not have written all those things I wrote to her. But you know I was besotted with her.'

'I understand. She gave you fame, and you gave her fame. A perfect long distance love-match.'

'Well, then, you know more about it than I do. You went there. You enjoyed her full favours. I should have gone there, like you. How I envy you. It's not the pleasure, dear friend, it's the ritual. How I would have liked to practise it. Come to the altar, held out my hand to the flame . . .'

'I don't think she wanted you to.'

'She invited me constantly.'

'Yes, but she told Melchior Grimm not to let you near her, in case your fantasies collapsed. You remember the message she sent to you once? "Your Cateau is surely best seen at a distance." I think that was right.'

'The truth is she will have both of us,' says the Sage of Ferney, 'because I promise you, I intend to go and lie by her side in Russia very shortly. Just as soon as I'm dead.'

'Please, please, darling, uncle,' says Madame Denis, very alarmed now, 'just don't think of it. And you, sir, you've disturbed him terribly. I can't imagine what you were thinking of. Why talk like this? Isn't it time for you to leave?'

'Ah yes, so I notice from this fine Swiss watch Her Majesty gave me,' our man says, holding up a Ferney watch.

A month later, and the world's greatest man is dead indeed, his corpse heading not for Russia but being driven upright out of Paris in the dead of night in a coach pulled by six horses, as the priests condemn him for his faithless life, the people exult, and he seeks his proper burial wherever in the world he can find it . . .

And so the dark end-game begins. A month later still, and there's another: Rousseau (whom our man also invented) has also suddenly gone to his grave. This time it's a tomb on the Island of Poplars in the middle of the lake at Ermenonville. Since it's Jean-Jacques, who was all heart not head, there's much weeping and wailing: 'Mothers, old men, children, true hearts and feeling souls! Your friend sleeps in this tomb.' Soon Marie-Antoinette is there, handkerchief to nose; as with the death of some favourite and fancy princess, the whole nation seems to weep simultaneously.

Beyond the tomb lie Rousseau's confessions, the book where he makes his own grand self eminent and does for all his friends. Voltaire, Rousseau: it's the end of an enterprise, an era. Better admit it: the self, the grand and glorious self, the only reason for anything, including the existence of the entire cosmos, will soon be on its way to other things, which may amount to nothing at all.

Time passes. His back bends further. Across the Ocean the Americans complete their revolution. Russia takes more of Turkey; a small token or gift or two, but no more, comes from the Russian court. Meantime his eyes continue to fade on themselves, his breath seems to be growing short. His legs feel thick and dropsical, and his heart seems to tug and tussle inside him as it goes about its noble work. From Voltaire, Rousseau too, books and papers go north. One day it will be his study also that will be stripped bare: the books pulled down off the walls, the papers shoved into boxes, the produce of a whole life carted away. Then it will be the tomb and the great necrology, the verdict of Posterity. It's time now to set everything in order, time to make sure it's all written down. Writing is everything. Going round the cafés, watching the men playing chess, he finds four youthful copyists and brings them back to the apartment to work. They sit there at four separate desks in the apartment every day now, each of them leafing through thousands of pages in no clear order: notes and scripts and drafts and booklets and letters. When this scribe finishes a sheaf, he hands it on to the next one, who hands back another sheaf in return. Copies are made of copies, from this draft or that, until nobody remembers which was a first original, and nobody knows what's what.

And now comes a series of strange visitations, weird messages from the north. In a matter of months, three odd figures descend on him. The first is a great white-haired bear of a man, his features growing fleshless, his eyes looking guilty and strained. At first our man has no idea who the caller is: then, somewhere amidst the features, he recognizes Grigor Orlov – once the pride of the court, the most powerful man in Russia, the best lover of Her Highness till the pride rose too high. Ten years ago, he can clearly remember, Grigor hated him, wanted him out of Petersburg. Now he wishes to talk. They spend some perfectly pleasant evenings together, each of them, as it were, perfumed by the same woman. Orlov is bitter and seems haunted, haunted by the recent death of his wife, pursued by the accusing ghost of Tzar Peter the Third, who knows all too well what he has done, though the rest of the world seems to have a fair idea. Orlov carries odd tidings and wild and jealous rumour. With Grigor Potemkin dead, the Empress has changed in spirits. Now she only likes the youngest of Night Emperors – which is why the clever Princess Dashkova, long since exiled and very out of favour, has been travelling all round Britain and Ireland educating her young son in ideas and the arts, so that he can become Night Emperor on his return.

Leaving behind this poisoned cake of malice, Orlov sets off on his anxious way (it will eventually lead to the madhouse). He has hardly gone when the Princess Dashkova arrives herself, staying at the Hôtel de Chine in order to have her bust done, by, of course, Houdon. Her son is with her, Anglicized, soft-stubbled, not much more than a child. He delights in seeing her, relishes her news, taking her to dine. He asks her about Falconet's great statue: whether it was ever finished, whether it was yet unveiled.

'I've had the most dreadful dream about it,' he confesses. 'I dreamt the whole Horseman had fallen, broken loose from those slim back legs and toppled to the ground, crushing all the people beneath it.'

'No, Didro, it's there and it's looking splendid. It stands right there in Senate Square. All Petersburg was out for the ceremony. It was only Falconet who was lost. You see him, perhaps?'

'Not at all,' he says. 'I hear he works at the Sèvres pottery and makes no more statues at all.' He looks over at the son, young enough to be his grandchild; can this be what things have really come to at the last? He mildly mentions Orlov's wicked rumour. 'Orlov was here? But you know Orlov hates me. He goes all over Europe telling everyone the worst. The man is quite mad.'

'I'm glad to hear it. That explains it.'

'And besides, if my dear little boy wants to become very good friends with the Empress, isn't that a matter for him?'

On another day there comes yet a third visitor from the north. This one comes like a secret, and even calls himself the Comte du

Nord. His card arrives one day from a servant; its sender simply fails to appear. Then, one morning at Mass (our man does not usually attend, but he's there with his dancing daughter), a face he recognizes thrusts itself at him out of the throng.

'Not our famous atheist, going to mass?' asks the little Archduke Paul, at whose wedding he was a balcony witness just about ten years before. It seems he's in Paris, buying and buying, Sèvres pottery in profusion, furniture in the wildest quantities, gems and silver; he's the son of his mother in at least some respects.

'You can often find philosophers prostrating themselves at the foot of altars,' says our man.

'Or at the feet of whores? Like my mother, for instance?' cries this strange pug-eyed young man who before too long will be the next Russian Tzar.

'I loved your mother,' says our man.

'Of course, so did everybody,' says the little terror, cackling, 'but she will return to my father in the end.'

'She'll be remembered.'

'Not if I can help it.'

Our man stares hard at him, and then beyond him, looking for a moment into the bloody hues of a cruel and tyrannical future. Then the church bells ring up above him, the present comes flooding back.

Meantime, as these strange and disturbing ghosts from Russia restlessly come and go, he sits down to write again. This time it's a play: *Is He Good? Is He Bad?*, he calls it. It's about himself, of course, as so much human writing is. And it's about the lesson poor Voltaire found contradictory, and Rousseau has seemed to overlook: human beings are neither wholly virtuous nor wholly evil. They are this and they are that, one person often having a duplicity of self. It's exactly as Lui once said, long ago at that table on a rainy day at the Café de la Régence, when they talked as the men were playing chess, and Lui turned his life into such a performance. 'What have I been doing then? What you, me and all the rest of us always do. Good, evil, most of the time nothing. Meanwhile my beard's been growing and when it got too long I visited the barber and had it shaved off.'

'You shouldn't have done,' he, Moi, has told him. 'A splendid beard is about all you need to look like a proper philosopher.'

'Oh, yes, and I'm sure I'd look splendid in marble or bronze. That's all you men of genius ever think about, isn't it? Will they manage to play your funeral bells in tune?'

'Why not, if we deserve it?'

'When I was the household fool at Bertin's, we used to have gatherings of philosophers, mostly the failed ones. Never have I seen so many wretched, spiteful, mean and rude creatures in one place. Nobody's assumed to have any brains, everyone's as stupid as you are. If you want my honest opinion, all the trouble in the world comes from people who think they are men of genius. I'd smother the lot of them. And don't think I want to be one of them. I prefer being a common man. Of course it's all I can manage in any case.'

'Rameau, you've really got a nerve, you know.'

'I know. That's why you like to have me here.'

'A scamp.'

'I know. At least I'm always the same.'

'Unfortunately. A fool.'

'Exactly. But fools like me don't come cheap. I'm a wonderful bag of tricks, that's why people need me. Remember, Kings have always had fools. They never had wise men. It's only just lately they've turned the fools into philosophers, which means they are fools. What good did philosophy ever do you?'

What indeed? So what has he been? Good or bad? Wise or foolish? Who can tell? What's a life? A useful voyage through the universe, fulfilling the grand human plot that's written in the Book of Destiny above? Or a chaos, a mess, a scribble, a useless wandering, a discontinuity, a senseless waste of time? What's a moral existence? Who knows, and what difference does it make to a pug-nosed little tzar-to-be who is plainly unaware of any difference between virtue and bitter instinct. What's a book? What are twenty-eight volumes, including the plates and supplements: a great contribution to human wisdom and science, or a stock of random knowledge already out of date? What's a story? A discovery or a lie? And what's the good of all these unfinished, untested little stories: the tale about the one man who becomes two, quarrels with himself, never finds an answer to anything, but still can't stop asking questions; the one about the servant who thinks he deserves to be the master and the master who could not exist without his servant?

What's an author? A man who stands on the stage hung with laurels, or a simple pen that drifts over the page, never affirming, never settling anything, just begging a mate from whoever's there to read? What's death? The end of things, the eternal silence: or the beginning of Posterity, the start of the journey from the crypt to the pantheon, the standpoint of everything, the angle of vision from the other side of the tomb? He's feeling robbed now, nearly alone. Sterne gone, and then Voltaire, and then Rousseau. Mademoiselle l'Espinasse dead, and not long after that the d'Alembert she'd been deceiving, taking him off with a broken heart. Condillac's gone; so has Rameau's noisy nephew. And then Sophie, dear Sophie Volland, whom he once assured that once creatures had lived they couldn't possibly die completely, and that we always carried past death the loves of our former life. But how alone now: 'Alone on earth,' he writes, 'having no longer any father, brother, neighbour, friend or company apart from myself.'

But not quite. The Particularist washes at the tub as usual, and shouts at the maid. In the corner the copyists copy, confusedly handing sheaves of paper this way and that. But now the print of the page he's holding himself suddenly wobbles and shakes. His eyes don't focus. Then faces from above are looking down. 'What are you thinking about now, doctor?'

'I'm thinking about the ways of great men. About how a great man is put together. About how he has cleverly learned to reason, to tyrannize over his sensibility, become the intelligent centre of his own human bundle . . . Now, where's my hat? Where's my stick? I'd better be on my way. I have another patient to see in the Marais.' What can have happened? Why can he not move? He must have had an apoplexy: a stroke . . .

The Virginian is riding into Paris. A grave and ambitious man, recently widowed, he travels across France in his own splendid

488

phaeton, built on his own estate, Monticello, by his own two hundred slaves. The grand vehicle has crossed the Atlantic Ocean with him, first getting unloaded at Plymouth, then taking ship again across an unpleasantly rough and rocking English Channel before the shores of France are revealed. At his side rides his shy, anxious eleven-year-old daughter Patsy. Up on the box is his mulatto servant and house-slave, James Hemings, whose sister, the slave Sarah, will in due time come and join them in the city too. And now they pass over the Seine in Paris by the new bridge, the Pont de Neuilly. He's happy to confess it's the most beautiful bridge in the world, as far as he's ever seen.

Presently he's travelling splendidly down the wide and tree-lined avenue of the Champs-Élysées, into the heart of surely the world's most elegant city, certainly the biggest city he's ever seen. The sandy-haired American – and that is what he most certainly is, thanks to the new Treaty of Paris, signed here last year between the British and Americans, which affirms that the First New Nation truly exists – rides his coach between the great buildings, and books his party into a hotel beside the Palais Royal. Later this year he'll be all set up in his own grand residence, the Hôtel Taitbout, as befits a Minister Plenipotentiary come to court. 'Behold me at length on the vaunted scene of Europe!' he soon writes homeward. Then, fearing this might just sound a tad too enthusiastic for one who is worried over foreign ties, he goes on to qualify things: 'You are, perhaps, curious to know how this new scene has struck a savage of the mountains of America. Not advantageously, I assure you.'

But Europe still impresses. Though Paris is not America, though cities are bestial places compared with Virginian woods, though the poor are slaves here, and the rich put saddles on their backs, though the water's polluted, and the women are worryingly powerful and frank in desire, he does have to admit the place has its pleasures. He loves food and he loves wine; the French have both. He simply adores the architecture. There's the chance to wander the bookstores, inspect great classical buildings now in composition, examine the most beautiful and ancient of ruins. One can dine with philosophers, go to the elegant play, attend the opera. Sometimes it seems a man might pass his life here without a single rudeness. 'In the pleasures of the table, they are far before us, because with good taste they unite temperance. I have never yet seen a man drunk in France. Were I to proceed to tell you how much I enjoy their architecture, sculpture, painting, music, I should want words.' But now the world has turned upside down there are so many matters to attend to, so many negotiations for a clever lawyer to perform: alliances, rights, treaties, Dutch bank loans, shipping and trade deals, the import of American tobaccos, the elimination of Barbary pirates. And when old Franklin finishes his term in Paris very shortly, he'll be the next American Ambassador, staying there till the end of the 1780s, when for the second time in a lifetime he'll see the world turn upside down.

'Really, my dear friend, you must meet him,' says Melchior Grimm. 'His name is Thomas Jefferson.'

'Why should I meet him?' our man says, from his bed. 'You see how I am.'

'He wants to meet you.'

'What does he want? How did you meet him?'

They're talking together in a most handsome new apartment on the Right Bank. It's a comfort the Empress in Petersburg arranged for him since the apoplexy, insisting that Grimm moved wife, papers and entire library across from the inconvenient rue Taranne to the smart rue de Richelieu. She has sent her fond wishes, and a warning to Grimm ('Take care nothing goes astray, not even the least scrap'). She has been truly generous, and the apartment in the Hôtel de Bezons is wonderfully convenient for a man who can hardly rise from his couch now, though it would be even more convenient if he could only summon his powers again, get out into the street and go to the Palais Royal.

'We've been working together on the American negotiations. Oh, didn't I tell you the French government has appointed me to conclude a treaty over their American affairs?'

'No, you didn't. Now you'll be sporting American titles and honours.'

'The Americans are a simple and undemanding people. They don't have any titles and honours.'

'Believe me, they will one day. Fame and celebrity always insist on their reward. Everyone wants their fifteen minutes in the sun.'

'Anyway, Jefferson assures me I'm the pleasantest and most companionable fellow he's met in the entire French diplomatic corps.'

'I'm not surprised. You did tell him you were German, I hope? Just so there's no confusion.'

'He understands my international influence. We've become really excellent friends.'

'You buy his cosmetics for him?'

'I doubt if he wears any. He comes from the back-country, or so he says.'

'Well, you'll be off to America soon, then?' our man says. 'I can see you with a naked bosom and turkey feathers stuck in your hair.'

'Really, old friend, you will have to meet him. He firmly insists, and I've promised to arrange it. He says it's one of the greatest wishes of his life to meet you before you . . .'

'Before I die. Very well. Bring your noble savage here then, Melchior, if you must.'

And now the Minister Plenipotentiary sits in a chair in the corner, grand in his twenty guinea ministerial suit; no tacky beaver pelt on the head for him. He's come with a black servant, bearing a basket of sweet potatoes and another of American apricots, which the Great Particularist is now inspecting with evident disgust. 'I always care to bring some novelties from the New World with me when I visit,' the sandy-haired minister explains. 'I gave Condorcet a maple tree, some pecan nuts to Monsieur Malesherbes, and an entire moose to Monsieur Buffon.'

'Good, better him than me,' our man says, lying on the fine new bed a Scythian empress has purchased.

'I can't explain, sir, what this visit means to me,' says the visitor. 'I have one of the biggest libraries in the col . . . in North America. I mean to give it to the nation when I die.'

'I know the feeling.'

'I came to tell you, sir, that back in Virginia where I come from, I devoted months of my life to the acquisition of an *Encyclopedia*. I have a canine appetite for learning.'

'Our *Encyclopedia* truly reached to the lands of America?'

'It did indeed.'

'And how much did you have to pay?'

The Minister laughs. 'How much? A fortune. Guess what, it cost me fifteen hogshead. That's fifteen hogshead of sotweed, tobacco. In fact it was a good deal more than a poor lawyer could afford. Happily I succeeded in getting the state of Virginia to pay for it.'

'Tobacco? Maybe you don't know, but in France we use money.'

'We do too, sir. But this happened just at a time when the British were advancing. We had to ship the books to the far end of the State for their safekeeping.'

'I hope the trouble was worth it, Monsieur Jefferson.'

'Oh, it was, Monsieur Diderot. And one thing leads to another. Books often breed books, or so I find. Your great book started me writing a poorer book of my own. A book of American facts, sir, which I think will be of great interest in your country. I have it here with me in Paris, and mean to publish it while I remain. Monsieur Malesherbes is assisting me. Perhaps you know him.'

'Indeed. He censored the *Encyclopedia*. Your book, then, have you a title?'

'Yes, *Notes on the State of Virginia*.'

'Really? I can hardly wait.'

'It's an account of the wonders of American nature, the newest of the wonders of the world. I write it to explain the wonders of the New World to the eyes of the Old.'

'It's all really so different?'

'It would truly amaze you, sir. The great torrent of Niagara. The divine splendour of the Natural Bridge in Virginia, an extraordinary trick of nature I liked so much that I bought it. I mean to make it my Hermitage. The Mississippi river, sir, the longest waterway in the world. But most of what's there we still have to find out.'

'The wonderful lands of Louisiana.'

'Yes, that's right. But first we need to become a nation. Unite the thirteen states. Create a true constitution. Found a legal system. Construct a police force.'

'A common currency, perhaps?'

'True, sir, I've already proposed it. The copper cent, the silver dime and the golden dollar.'

'A supreme court?'

'Definitely, sir.'

'Manufacturers and industries?'

'Yes, sir, but only in due time. First we build a nation founded on the free farmer, and generate the spirit of an independent and republican people.'

'The emancipation of the serfs?'

'The slaves, sir. Not at once, but one day, definitely.'

'Education?'

'I believe learning is everything. That's why I have a plan for a university.'

'You have?'

'Sure. I intend to found a fine new university in Charlottes-ville.'

'I hope no parish priests for professors?'

'Certainly not. It will be a whole new democratic and practical way of universal learning.'

'In your country, do you have mulberry and hemp?'

'Do we, sir? There's no vegetable resource America is short of. I can give you a list.'

'Iron and bauxite?'

'If not yet, in the future, when we've settled the land properly.'

'Population of Virginia?'

'Look, let me bring you a copy of my book. It's full of that kind of dry detail. But remember, mine is just one state, admittedly the most beautiful, out of a whole thirteen. That's not counting the endless territories that reach out and out to the distant Pacific.'

'Louisiana.'

'Louisiana, right. Or whatever name we decide to call it. But first what we need is a true union. A just constitution. A civil plan. A relationship of the parts to the wholes. A capital city. A living nation.'

'You're building a new capital city?'

'Yes, sir. Somewhere where no one has ever built before. Every day I survey and measure the new buildings of Paris.

Soufflot's dome, and so on. Maybe that will help make our new Capitol building.'

'But do make sure your capital city isn't just a stomach stuck out on the end of a finger.'

'I'm sorry? I guess that's a little too metaphorical for me.'

Our man raises himself, points across the room. 'Go and look in that drawer, monsieur.'

'What would we look for?' asks the Minister, waving to James Hemings.

'There are sixty-six notebooks in there. The plan for the ideal and perfect republic. The description of a whole new land without pain or tyranny. Where light and happiness shine out over all. A great capital city. A new university. A police force.'

'What, over here, master?' asks Hemings, hunting round the sideboards.

'Yes, there, boy, wake up, do you see them?'

'Sah.' Hemings lifts out the notebooks, puts them on the table.

'"The Daydream of Denis the Philosopher"?' says Jefferson, picking one up. '"On Drawing Benefit From Religion and Making It Good For Something"?'

'*Oui*, monsieur.'

'But on the front of this book it's written: For SMI Catherine, Rousse.'

'Why don't you change that? Make it to Monsieur Jefferson of Louisiana.'

'You really want me to have all these?'

'If you read them carefully and use them well.'

'Yes, my dear, sir, I will, I most certainly will. Anyway, you'll excuse me now, I hope, philosopher. Only today I'm meeting a Mrs Cosway and she's taking me to have my bust done. By this well-known fellow Houdon. I've bought six of his things already. Including a really terrific Voltaire.'

That evening our man feels most wonderfully better. In fact he's never felt as well since the distant day when, heart in mouth, he walked into the throne room in the Hermitage over the Neva, and there saw the great Empress. His spirits soar. He's sure he's done it; he's invented a country. For Jefferson will go home, and the great lands of Louisiana will open. Beyond the coastal stretches where the once British colonials sit in their stockades or their cities, farming the land, inventing electricity, trading with their former home, lie the wonderful spaces of the interior: the unknown landscapes, the untravelled passes, lands wandered by migrant Indians, travelled by Jesuit missionaries, explored by French trappers and Spanish adventurers. There are great rivers, high mountains, vast prairies, great deserts, animals and birds of species not yet recorded, trees and vegetables still not properly described. He knows the wonders, the wealth of unnamed places, the muddy waters of the Mississippi, flowing down from Lake Itashka into the land of the hereafter, the precarious routes and untravelled passages that still have to be found . . .

With a country if not a continent invented, written on, written over, authored, with his imaginary Russia, the best fruit of his daydreams, not wasted after all, he feels well enough this evening to sit down at the table, between his wife and darling daughter. He's well enough to take some soup, and then even a little mutton stew. At the end he reaches for the great basket of American apricots his two visitors have left.

'I wouldn't, *mon mari*, no, I really wouldn't,' says the Great Particularist, fussing over him as usual.

'Nonsense, such fuss. American apricots, the fruit of the New World. What harm can they possibly do?' He eats. He coughs, his head drops. Good night, ladies, good night . . .

The autopsy required by modern medical science and the great spirit of reason reveals that the bile sac is dry, the liver is hard, and there's a severe problem of colic cystitis. The first cause of death is apoplexy, but the brain is still that of a man of twenty. The funeral is held not far away, in the fine city church of Saint-Roch, which is close to the Place Vendôme. Grimm and Jefferson are both present. It's the late summer of 1784. There's still fresh scent from the lime trees. Beaumarchais' *Marriage of Figaro* is playing at the Comédie-Française, and Rameau's *Gallant Indians* at the opera. Montgolfier is taking people up in his fire-propelled balloon, and d'Abbans has set an amazing paddle-steamer chugging up and down the Seine. There are still five more sunny years to go before the age of reason turns into the age of bloodletting. Inside the fine church, the incense surges up toward the dome, and fifty hired priests carrying lighted candles accompany the philosopher's coffin as it is carried toward the altar.

It's a rich and solemn church funeral. But why not? All this religion is paid for out of the atheistical *Encyclopedia*. As the priests intone, the remains are solemnly lowered beneath the stone slabs of the Chapel of the Virgin, the elegant domed chapel at the heart of this splendid church, beneath the great stuccoes by Falconet, depicting Glory and the Annunciation. But how odd, how very very odd . . . When, only a short time later, these same slabs are lifted up again, both the coffin and the body have completely disappeared. Neither the one nor the other has been seen anywhere since. 'Diderot le philosophe? Disparu,' the sacristan will tell you, if, as I do, you care to visit Saint-Roch today. But he who laughs last laughs best, or that's what they always say . . .

NOTE

Books breed books; many helped breed this one. Beside Furbank's biography I used Arthur M. Wilson's formidable and two-volume *Diderot* (New York, 1972), Lester G. Crocker's *Diderot: The Embattled Philosopher* (New York/London, 1966), John Hope Mason's *The Irresistible Diderot* (London, 1982), J. Proust's *Diderot et l'Encyclopédie* (Paris, 1962), Peter France (ed.), *Diderot's Letters to Sophie Volland: A Selection* (London, 1972), Paul Verniere (ed.), *Diderot: Memoires pour Catherine II* (Paris, 1966), and Maurice Tourneaux, *Diderot et Catherine II* (rep. Geneva, 1970). I used Simon Schama's wonderful *Citizens: A Chronicle of the French Revolution* (London, 1989), Robert Darnton's *The Business of Enlightenment: A Publishing History of the Encyclopédie* (Cambridge/London, 1979), Carl Becker's *The Heavenly City of the 18th Century Philosophers* (New Haven, 1932), and Durand Eccheveria's *Mirage in the West: A History of the French Image of American Society* (Princeton, 1956). Like everyone in the field, I drew on Theodore Besterman's *Voltaire* (London, 1969), as well as A. Lentin (ed.), *Voltaire and Catherine the Great: Selected Correspondence* (Cambridge, 1974). Among the many studies of Jefferson, I am especially grateful to William Howard Adams' *The Paris Years of Thomas Jefferson* (New Haven, 1997) and Conor Cruise O'Brien's provocative *The Long Affair: Thomas Jefferson and the French Revolution* (London, 1996).

I also used A. G. Cross's *Russia and the West in the Eighteenth Century* (Newtonville, Mass., 1983), Katherine Anthony (tr.), *Memoirs of Catherine the Great* (New York, 1927), Dominique Maroger (ed.), *The Memoirs of Catherine the Great* (London, 1955), Kyril Fitzlyon (tr.), *The Memoirs of Princess Dashkov* (London, 1958), Henri Troyat, *Catherine the Great* (London, 1981), John Alexander, *Catherine the Great: Life and Legend* (New York, 1989), Montgomery Hyde, *The Empress Catherine and Princess Dashkov* (London, 1935), Vincent

Cronin, *Catherine, Empress of All the Russias* (London, 1978), and Carolly Erickson, *Great Catherine* (London, 1998). I gained much from Boris Otmetev and John Stuart, *Saint Petersburg: Portrait of an Imperial City* (London, 1990), Solomon Volkov's delightful *St. Petersburg: A Cultural History* (London, 1996), Lawrence Kelly's *St Petersburg: A Travellers' Companion* (London, 1981), and Geraldine Norman's terrific *The Hermitage: The Biography of a Great Museum* (London, 1997).

I was greatly helped by David Remnick's two panoramic studies of Russia in the 1990s: *Lenin's Tomb: The Last Days of the Soviet Empire* (London, 1994) and *Resurrection: The Struggle for a New Russia* (London, 1999). I am very grateful for John Wells's brilliant translation of Beaumarchais' *The Figaro Plays* (London, 1977), as well as to Cynthia Cox's *The Real Figaro: The Extraordinary Career of Caron de Beaumarchais* (London, 1962) and F. Grendel's *Beaumarchais: The Man Who Was Figaro* (London, 1977). I cheated with *Eugene Onegin*; my references are not to any libretto but to James Falen's translation of the poem (Oxford World's Classics, 1995). I cheated too over the re-burial of Laurence Sterne. A more truthful version (giving the fine sermon of Canon Cant) may be found in Arthur H. Cash and John M. Stedmond (eds.), *The Winged Skull: Bicentenary Conference Papers on Lawrence Sterne* (London, 1971). I am much indebted to the late Kenneth Monkman, the restorer of Shandy Hall, and Jacques Berthoud, Tony Cross, Edward Acton, Jon Cook, Breon Mitchell, and Douglas R. Hofstadter, all of whom gave friendly help. One more debt. At Indiana University, Bloomington, in 1997, as I was working on this, I saw John Corigliano and William H. Hoffman's splendid opera bouffe *The Ghosts of Versailles*, brilliantly performed by the Music School: another great stimulus . . .